SUSPICION
OF
GUILT

Barbara Parker

SUSPICION OF GUILT

WHEELER
PUBLISHING, INC.
ROCKLAND, MA

★ AN AMERICAN COMPANY ★

Copyright © Barbara Parker, 1995

All rights reserved.

Published in Large Print by arrangement with
Dutton, a division of the Penguin Group
in the United States and Canada.

Wheeler Large Print Book Series.

Set in 16 pt. Plantin. 50501100135 207

Library of Congress Cataloging-in-Publication Data

Parker, Barbara (Barbara J.)
    Suspicion of guilt / Barbara Parker.
        p.   (large print)   cm.
    ISBN 1-56895-232-5 (hardcover).
    1. Women lawyers—Florida—Miami—Fiction.   2. Miami (Fla.)—
Fiction.   3. Large type books.   I. Title.
    [PS3566.A67475S86   1995b]
    813'.54—dc20   95-16352
                                                              CIP

For Laura

acknowledgments

This book was not created whole from my own imagination but woven from the suggestions, insights, and stories that many people have generously shared.

I am indebted to Lance R. Stelzer (criminal law), Karen H. Curtis (civil trial practice), and Eugene W. Sulzberger (probate), who filled in what I have forgotten (or never knew) about practicing law.

Many thanks to Detective Gary F. Schiaffo, Miami Beach Police Department, for the gritty details and some great lines.

And what would I have done without Helen M. Z. Cevern, World Gallery, Miami Beach, for her artful take on the Lincoln Road scene; Harry J. Coleman, Associated Forensic Services, Miami, for showing me how to detect a forgery; Oscar Delgado, for some great lines in Spanish; Trudi Gilbert, Everglades Marina, and Dan Leahy, the *New Moon* at the Bahia Mar, both in Fort Lauderdale, who taught me bow from stern; Liz Pittenger, Renaissance woman, for the highbrow stuff; freelance writer Rosalyn Resnick for sharing her style and her persona; and, as ever, Warren Lee.

prologue

The night she was murdered, Althea Tillett had hosted a party for her best girlfriends. The four of them usually played bridge on Wednesdays, but tonight was special, the last bridge game before Althie would fly off to Europe for a month. Ignoring the cards after the first round, they went through three bottles of wine and ended up singing old show tunes around the grand piano.

Jessica's driver showed up promptly at ten o'clock, as instructed, waiting patiently in the foyer while the women all shrieked with laughter, trying to aim their feet into the right shoes.

As soon as the taillights disappeared past the bougainvillaea at the gate, Althie came back in and locked up. The house seemed quiet now, strangely empty. Through the high windows she could see the black waters of Biscayne Bay and in the distance a line of streetlights twinkling through the trees on the Miami side. She glanced at the mess they had made—napkins, plates, glasses, an empty bottle on the carpet. The grandfather clock chimed the quarter hour.

Humming to herself, Althea unsteadily climbed the stairs, coming back down in her kimono and wooden Japanese sandals. She put *Madama Butterfly* on the CD player, the scene where Pinkerton marries Cho-Cho San. Hands

1

folded geisha-style at her breast, Althie sang with them in Italian. Bowing, she bumped into a plaster replica of *Winged Victory*, then grabbed its rocking pedestal just in time, laughing at her reflection in the windows. A post–middle-age broad in a red silk robe. She untied the belt and flashed the darkness. The best thing about this house, Althie noticed when her late husband, Rudolph W. Tillett, moved her into it, was the privacy. When the kids were gone, she and R.W. used to walk stark naked through the place, and turn up the stereo so loud the chandelier would rattle.

They had met at the opera. She had bought a seat for herself and by chance his was adjacent. During *La Bohême* she saw the tears on his cheeks and pressed her handkerchief into his hand. A year later, just after his invalid wife passed away, they married. His black- haired twins—a boy and a girl—were perfect little brats about it, but she didn't give a damn. Her friends warned her about R.W., said he was a selfish bastard, but she told them sweetly to shut up. He loved her. What else did she need to know?

R. W. had indulged her. He let her redecorate the house, whatever she wanted. She got rid of the French Empire furniture and the dusty velvet curtains and brought in a mix of Art Deco, modern Italian, Persian rugs, carved Chinese panels, and mementoes from their trips abroad. The landscapes were banished to the attic and replaced with abstract impressionists. In the living room Althie hung a convincing copy of a Gauguin Tahitian nude, and in the master bedroom a Picasso drawing—a real one—of a devil with dark, heavy genitals.

She hadn't expected such *passion* from this man. When the mood struck, he would put on his tuxedo and sit in an armchair, sending puffs of cigar smoke over his shoulder, his deep-set gray eyes fixed on Althie. With the Mozart buzzing on the windows, or the Bizet, or Verdi, she would slide out of the Pappagena bird outfit or flamenco dress or Egyptian wig, or whatever it was she had on. If he ever noticed that she dimmed the lights a little more as the years passed, he had the tact not to say so. Barefoot, Althie would dance over to him, loosen his bow tie, take the studs out of his pleated shirt . . .

For their fifteenth anniversary they went to a spa in Switzerland. He got a penile implant and she, a face-lift. Afterward, they spent a week in Paris. A small hotel. It had rained. Delicious, whispery rain.

Memories. They always made her eyes sting. Althie went over to the bridge table, began to stack plates, then sighed. Let Rosa tidy up in the morning. Althie unlatched the sliding door and walked out onto the terrace on the swelling crescendo of the Metropolitan Opera Chorus. The bay was dead calm, the air thick and heavy. She flapped the sides of her robe, making a little breeze. Summer goes on forever in Miami, she thought.

Three and a half years ago, in winter, the sky shimmering with stars, she and R.W. had put on a new Wagner CD, dropped their bathrobes on a chaise, and took their steins of pilsner into the hot tub. He found the ledge to sit on and held out his big hand. Laughing like a witless teenager, Althie pushed through the bubbles to settle down across his thighs. A little later, those whimpering noises he made—She could barely hear them over the *Götterdämmerung* pouring through the open doors. Clinging to his shoulders, she thought he was having a ferocious climax. But no. His implant still stiff as a piling, the rest of him went limp, and he slid off the ledge and under the steaming water.

On Monday she would fly to the Aegean one last time. Surely R.W., wherever he was, would forgive these little flings of hers. But soon she would look silly dancing in a tavern with a man half her age. One more trip to Mykonos, then come home to sink into a respectable dotage. She would never remarry. *Oh, R.W., my man, my love, my only love* . . .

Kimono fluttering, Althie abruptly crossed the dark terrace and slid the glass door shut, twisting the lock. The orchestra was leading up to "Un Bel Di Vedremo." She turned down the volume, then clopped through the arched entranceway to the kitchen in her wooden sandals. The silvery soprano followed.

" . . . *Vedi? E venuto! Io non gli scendo in contro* . . ." Do you see? He is coming.

Thirsty, Althie held a glass under the tap on the refrigerator, watched the water swirl closer to the rim.

" . . . *Che dirà? Che dirà? Chiamerà 'Butterfly' dalla lontana* . . ." He calls "Butterfly" from far away.

4

Althie sang softly to herself. And then her voice leaped into a cry of confusion and panic.

Something had grabbed her hair, violently pulling backward. The glass dropped, hit the floor. Icy water splashed her ankles. Now an arm was across her throat.

Someone had come into her house. A man who didn't belong there. This could not be. The alarm system—

She tried to cry out, could only choke. The arm tightened. She clutched at the wrist and her hands slid on leather. He lifted her off the floor and she kicked madly, connecting once with the wooden sandal. He cursed and swung her around, and for an instant Althie saw her own face, eyes gaping, in the window.

He slammed her into the counter, pinning her. His body was solid, his breath hot on her temple. Her throat was caught in the crook of his elbow. Now his other hand moved to grip the back of her head. She wheezed, gagged. Her head was forced around and back. Out of the corner of one eye she saw things on the counter— a bowl of peaches, a coffee cup, a novel she had begun. With a pang of regret, she realized she would never know how it ended.

The soprano was still singing in a voice pure as sunlight.

chapter one

Late on a Monday afternoon, Gail Connor sat in Larry Black's office waiting for him to finish a phone call. She should have packed up her briefcase and gone home to her daughter an hour ago, but she needed a favor.

One of the firm's biggest clients, a bank, was going to sue a major brokerage house. Two years ago Gail had won a federal trial for the bank, and wanted them to give her this new case. The decision wasn't up to Larry, but he would know what her chances were. He could put in a good word.

Gail had brought along another file, a case set for trial next week at the Dade County Courthouse. She and the other side had worked out a tentative settlement. Larry's approval wasn't necessary—Gail had full authority to settle—but it gave her a reason to talk to him. A way of getting to what she really wanted. The banking case would be massive, requiring her to fly out of state for meetings, organize a staff of junior associates, hire extra paralegals, supervise the drafting of dozens of lengthy documents. It would be the sort of ball-busting exercise required of those who deserved a partnership. Win a case like this, get your battle ribbons, no question.

She smiled to herself, aware of her own

nervousness and of how ridiculous it was to be nervous at all with Larry. As if she needed a pat on the back before asking for a simple favor. With thumb and forefinger she curled up the frayed corner of the file.

Gail was a serious woman of thirty-three, slender, and as tall as most of her male colleagues, with dark blond hair that brushed the collar of her tailored suits. She'd had no trouble getting hired straight out of law school, due in part to top grades but more to connections. Her family went back four generations, rare in this town. There had been a street named after them, before it was buried under I-95.

The little gold clock on Larry's credenza gave one soft ding. Six-thirty. The person on the other end of the conversation, she gathered, was the CEO for a shipping company that the firm was after. Apparently Larry had him on the hook and halfway in the boat. He chuckled, rocking back in his chair. Just shy of forty, balding at the crown, and dressed like a British banker, Larry Black created an aura of absolute trust. Unlike other attorneys she could name, it wasn't an act. His grandfather had founded the firm; Larry's position was solid as bedrock.

Leaving the file on a small table by the divan, Gail got up to wander around. Larry raised a hand to tell her he would be finished soon, don't go away. She nodded. At the windows she leaned on the sill, feeling the heat through the tinted glass.

Most big Miami law firms were like the clouds that formed over South Florida this time of year, late summer. They appeared out of nowhere, coalescing into heavy gray masses, swirling into thunderstorms, then breaking up in a rain of spite and bad PR, scattering partners and associates into other offices. Hartwell Black and Robineau, founded in 1922, had for the most part avoided such turbulence. Associates came and went; most partners stayed, happy with their stratospheric salaries. At the firm's main office on Flagler Street there were sixty-seven attorneys, seventeen of them partners. Gail had decided: After eight years with Hartwell Black she was either going to get a partnership or not. If not, she would quit. No point hanging on, getting overripe, people wondering what the problem was.

She heard the click when Larry hung up the telephone. He was putting on his glasses, coming out from behind his desk. "Sorry to take so long. What have you brought me?" He glanced at the file. "Beltran Plastics. Yes. What's up?"

He knew the facts, so Gail got to the point. "The other side is offering to settle. Bottom line, $175,000, everybody takes care of their own costs. I think it's reasonable, given what we have to work with. Did you read Oscar Beltran's deposition? I told Miriam to give you a copy." Gail pulled hers out of the file.

Larry made a cursory nod toward the papers stacked on his desk. "It's here, but I haven't had a chance to review it."

"The man sounds evasive. He mumbles and speaks in monosyllables. I've worked with him, but he isn't going to impress the jury. They want what they see in movies."

9

Larry flipped through the onionskin pages of the deposition. "Are we ready for trial?"

"Absolutely."

"What are we asking for in the complaint?"

"Four hundred thousand."

His thin face went into a grimace. "Ouch."

Gail said, "They've got a counterclaim for two-fifty. Beltran could wind up eating it."

"What about fees?"

"We bill our own. We've collected about fifteen thousand so far, with maybe another two outstanding. We're ahead on the cost deposit. I don't think it's worth the risk of a trial."

"So you believe it's a decent offer."

"I'd grab it before they change their mind."

"All right." He took off his glasses. "You know the situation better than I do. Just make sure the client approves."

Clients were often the last to admit they had a lousy case, particularly if they had paid a law firm thousands of dollars in fees. On the eve of trial, adrenaline pumping, they would die for principle.

"I've already explained it to him," she said. "He understands."

"Good." Larry swung around to check the clock. "Uh-oh. I forgot to call Dee-Dee. We're supposed to go out to dinner tonight."

"Larry—"

He stopped, waiting for her to go on.

She took a breath. "Trans-State Bank. I understand they're not happy with their bond broker." His creased brow said he hadn't heard of this. "They lost close to eight million on some muni bonds in Illinois, a real dog of a deal. They say fraud was involved. If it's going to wind up in litigation, I'd like to take it on."

"Oh, that." He folded his glasses, came back across his Oriental rug. "Yes, someone mentioned Trans-State in the last management meeting. And you want to do this case?"

"Why not? I've worked for them before. They know me. But they're Paul's client. Would it be better if you talked to him?"

Paul Robineau represented banks, but he didn't do litigation. He and Gail rarely spoke, except on business. He was the firm's managing partner and grandnephew of a founding member. She couldn't imagine dropping by his vast office upstairs and casually asking for a multimillion-dollar case.

Larry was mulling it over, his eyes fixed somewhere past the windows. "You want me to talk to Paul for you?"

"Would you mind?" She noticed her hands had gone weak.

"Mmmn. We're going to have federal banks, out-of-state counsel, claims and counterclaims all over the place. I assumed Paul would give it to one of the senior attorneys. Jack, for instance. What about a spot as co-counsel?"

Jack Warner ran the litigation department. Not hard to work with, but he would take all the credit.

"No. Give me the staff. With Beltran settled, I've got the time." After a moment, she said, "I need this case, Larry." When his forehead creased again, she said, "Forget talking to Paul.

11

You don't have to. Knowing Paul, he'd probably think I was going behind his back."

He looked at her reproachfully. "Gail. Are we friends or not?"

"I don't like to ask for favors, so I won't. Just—" She managed a smile. "Well, maybe this once. I could work the hell out of a case like this, Larry. You know I could."

He nodded. "You'd do a fine job. You've had some . . . personal crises, but they're behind you now."

"Yes. Absolutely."

"All right. I'll ask Paul about it. Lead counsel on Trans-State."

She wanted to hug him, but didn't. "Larry, you're a peach. But don't tell him it was my idea. Oh, that sounds gutless, doesn't it? Tell him whatever you want to."

"I'll say I thought of it."

She went to gather up the Beltran file. "Better call Dee-Dee. It's getting late."

"Yes. I will." He was looking at her closely. "Are you all right?"

"Of course."

"If you need anything—" He touched her arm.

"Larry. I'm fine. Really." She waited for him to nod. "If Paul says no, I'll take your suggestion and talk to Jack Warner, okay?"

"You sure?"

She laughed. "Yes. Enough already."

No one was in the corridor outside her office, and the room itself was dim. It faced north, and the sun had dropped behind the adjacent building. Gail stood just inside the doorway for a while, replaying her conversation with Larry Black.

"Stupid," she finally muttered, and flipped on the light. Miriam had left a few messages on her desk. There was a note: *Have taken the Acosta Realty motions home with me, will work on them. ¡Hasta mañana!* And then a loopy letter M and a happy face, which made Gail smile.

She shuffled through the messages. A client wanting his deposition reset. A witness returning her call.

Nearly eight years at this law firm. She might have been a partner already, except for . . . personal crises. Larry's polite term, which didn't quite catch the reality of death and divorce falling like double hammer blows.

Her sister Renee had not just *died.* She was slashed and left to bleed to death, and Gail had been accused of murder. One hell of an inconvenience for Hartwell Black. They took away her major cases for the duration. Not a judgment about her work, of course. Only a PR move, to keep the clients from getting nervous until she was exonerated.

It might not have been so bad if Dave hadn't walked out two weeks before that. She woke up one bright Saturday morning and he said it was over. He couldn't explain why, except that half his life was gone and he couldn't breathe. And anyway, they weren't suited to each other, never had been. But she would be all right, he was sure of it. She was the strong one. And Karen would be better off, not hearing her parents yelling at each other. And so Gail's marriage had bled to death too, and it was somehow her fault. Now Karen was in therapy and Dave was giving tennis lessons to tanned, fortyish wives of corporate executives on vacation in St. Thomas or St. Croix or wherever.

Personal crises. Larry Black didn't know how close she had come to losing it. Nobody knew. It was funny now. That time she had looked through the windshield of her car and realized she was in Key Largo, for God's sake. Or couldn't remember her daughter's name. Or sat on the floor of her closet for over an hour, unable to decide what to wear.

A waste of time thinking about it now. Gail flipped through the next few messages. *Dry cleaning ready. Hearing on Thursday canceled.* At the last piece of pink paper she stopped. Miriam had decorated its border with little red hearts, arrows shot through them. *Anthony Q. Call when you can.*

Dropping the other messages on her desk, she reached for the telephone and dialed. The answering machine picked up. *"Esta es la oficina de Ferrer y Quintana.* This is the office of Ferrer and Quintana. *Al sonido electrónico, deje su mensaje—"*

"Drat." She switched lines and punched his home number. After four rings his voice told her in English, then Spanish to leave a message. She laughed aloud. "Anthony, where are you? Is this all I get, a phone call? Would you like to know how long it's been since we've seen each other? *Two weeks.* Call me after I'm in bed tonight, *querido,* and we'll make heavy breathing noises." She made a kiss into the phone, then hung up.

In a neat row on her desk were the files Miriam had set out for her to take home. Gail crammed them into her briefcase, then threw her time sheet in as well. She had been too busy to record her activities today, how many hours and tenths of hours spent on this pleading or that telephone call. She would have to reconstruct the day and invent what she could not remember.

As soon as Gail pulled into the garage, the jalousie door to the kitchen swung open. Phyllis must have heard the engine, and now waited on the second step with her arms folded just under her wide bosom. Phyllis Farrington, close to seventy, came in every afternoon, weekends if needed. Arthritis in her knees kept her from doing much housework. That didn't matter; Phyllis had a way of making Karen toe the line. Gail had told her she didn't have to wear a uniform, but Phyllis said it made her feel more professional. She wore pink today; her apron had a design of wild roses.

Gail hit the button on her dash to send the automatic door down, then got out of her car, maneuvering past a stack of cardboard boxes and assorted junk taking up half the space in the double garage. "Phyllis, I'm sorry it took me so long to get home. I had to stop for gas or I'd have stalled out halfway here."

She came down a step. "Don't go in yet. I got to tell you about Karen. The school called this afternoon, said they couldn't get you. She had

15

herself a fight on the bus with a boy named Javier, laid him out cold."

"Oh, my God. *Why?*"

"He was teasing her, she said. She punched him in the stomach and he fell down and hit his head on a seat."

"Is he okay?"

"The boy's all right. He woke up before they called Fire-Rescue, or else your baby would be in big trouble. They want you to go by there in the morning and talk to the principal."

Biscayne Academy was one of the best private schools in Dade County. It cost $12,000 a year in tuition, fees, books, field trips, and assorted amenities. There were no metal detectors at the door or drugs in the lockers. The students were individually tutored. They raised money for the children of Bosnia and sang songs about the Earth. And Karen had just beaten the crap out of another fourth grader.

Gail could feel the tension creeping up from her shoulders. "I should call Dr. Feldman tomorrow."

Phyllis snorted. "Dr. Feldman. Baby come out of her appointment last week, don't say two words. We get home, she say she's the child of a divorce, and that's why she can't clean up her room. I want to shake him by his skinny neck."

A corner of Gail's briefcase nudged a can of tennis balls, and it hit the floor. The lid came off and three yellow balls rolled in different directions.

"When you going to get this stuff out of here?" Phyllis said.

16

"Dave said he'd take care of it by the end of the month."

"Uh-huh."

He had sailed out of Miami in July in a forty-foot sloop, leaving in the garage what wouldn't fit in the sailboat—boxes of winter clothes, a small boat trailer, tools, golf clubs, a machine to string tennis racquets, odds and ends of furniture.

"He's got a free storage shed is what he's got. You ought to give him one week to get hisself up here and find a warehouse, or you'll call Goodwill."

Gail picked up two of the balls and tossed them into a box. "I can't do that. It would be like getting rid of Dave completely, and Karen needs to feel his presence in some way. She already blames me that he left."

"Dr. Feldman tell you that?"

"Phyllis—" Gail pressed the heel of her hand into her forehead. "I can't talk about this right now."

"You better think about it, though."

"I will."

Phyllis opened the door and they went up the steps into the kitchen, Gail following Phyllis's heavy white shoes. She dropped her briefcase and purse on the kitchen counter. A piece of paper was lying there.

"What's that?"

"Roof man came by."

Gail picked up the estimate. "Twenty-five hundred dollars? For three leaks?"

"He can fix it, but he won't give you no guarantee. Says you need a new roof."

17

"Oh, great. Did he tell you how much?"

Phyllis pursed her lips. "About twenty thousand. That's with the same red barrel tile. Less for asphalt shingles."

"Asphalt shingles? The neighbors would kill me."

"Man's a thief." Phyllis checked her watch and untied her apron. "I got to go. The association's having a meeting tonight." Phyllis belonged to a homeowners' association in Coconut Grove. Not the chic part of the Grove, with its boutiques and sidewalk cafés, but the older black Grove, settled around the turn of the century when Phyllis Farrington's grandfather came over from the Bahamas to help build Miami.

She stashed her neatly folded apron in her big purse. "We got a crack house we want to get bulldozed. We'll go on down to City Hall with picket signs if we have to, get on the news. We won't have that trash around, no thank you."

"Go get 'em, Phyllis." Gail poured some ice water from the refrigerator and opened the cabinet for aspirin. "Where is our little angel?"

"In her room. I said go do your homework. She had her bath already. Supper too." Phyllis started toward the front door, then looked back at Gail, keys in her hand. "There's leftovers in the microwave. You don't eat, you're gonna make yourself sick, you hear?"

"Thanks, Phyllis."

She let herself out and locked the door behind her.

Gail found Karen at her desk. When she came

in, Karen slid a *Cracked* magazine under her math book.

"Doing your homework?"

"Yes." She flipped a page and twirled her pencil.

"Really. Can I see?"

"When I'm finished." Karen bounced her canvas sneakers on the legs of the chair. The toes were wearing through and the laces were gone.

Gail sat on the end of Karen's bed, which was covered with a faded dinosaur quilt. "I heard about your fight with Javier."

One shoulder rose.

"You want to tell me about it?"

Karen spun to face her, long brown hair swinging. "Javier is a major geek. All the girls hate him."

"And that's a reason to punch him out?"

She narrowed her eyes. "He said I have no boobs and I'll never have any."

"But you can't go around hitting people you don't like. Let Mrs. Johnson deal with Javier."

"She won't do anything. She only talks to him, and he laughs behind her back. Butthead."

"They want us to see the principal about this, you know."

"I hate that school," Karen said tightly. "I wish you didn't make me go there."

"It's a great school."

"It sucks."

Gail's voice rose. "Don't you dare use that kind of language in Mr. Alliston's office. You'll be a perfect lady. If he says to apologize to Javier, then you will, and nicely."

19

Karen picked at a small mole on her arm. Her hair hung over her face, and the light from the desk lamp shone through it.

"Did you hear me?"

"I'm not sorry," she mumbled. "I hate boys. They're all buttheads. Especially Javier. His dad is on a stupid *telenovela*. Javier is always saying how his dad is so-o-o famous."

Gail sat for a while with her hands on her knees, then pushed herself up, taking a breath. "All right. We'll talk about it later. Go on and finish your homework." She lifted the math book to find the issue of *Cracked*. "You won't need this."

"Daddy said maybe I could go to school in the Virgin Islands someday."

"Did he?"

Karen looked up at her with blue eyes surrounded by blond lashes. Like Dave's. "Not all the time, I mean. I could live here too. My friend Marisol lives in Bogotá and Miami, and she goes to school here and also to her school down there. Her parents aren't even divorced."

"Well. Lucky girl. When did your dad call?"

"Labor Day, remember?"

"That was three weeks ago."

Karen shrugged.

Gail bent to kiss her. "I'm going to see what Phyllis left in the microwave. You want to bring your homework out to the kitchen?"

She shook her head.

"Come see me when you're finished then."

Gail closed the door behind her as she left Karen's room. Damn him. Dave rarely called, but he would send Karen postcards—beaches and sleek hotels and whitewashed little towns close to the sea. What fun. *Can't wait till you can come see me. You're my best girl.* Such sweet lies.

You think you know someone. Married twelve years and not a clue.

Lying on the sofa in the family room, Gail heard a telephone ringing somewhere. Groggily she opened her eyes, reached toward the noise. A file slid from her lap, papers ruffling to the floor. It would be Anthony.

She brought the phone to her mouth, said hello. But the voice was unfamiliar. She struggled up. "I'm sorry, what did you say your name was?"

"Patrick Norris." There was a pause. "Gail? It's me. Patrick."

She blinked, disoriented, past and present clashing in her mind. "Patrick?"

"Don't you remember me? Now I'm embarrassed. I was sure you would."

Finally she said that yes, of course she remembered. It was just such a surprise. A long time. Since law school, at least.

"Your mother very kindly gave me your number at home. I called before and left a message with your daughter. I guess she didn't tell you."

"No." Gail tried to make out her watch. "What time is it?"

"About nine-thirty. Were you asleep?"

"Not exactly."

"I'd like to see you tomorrow morning, if that's at all possible."

21

She couldn't recall her schedule. "What about?"

"It has to do with my aunt, Althea Tillett. She passed away two weeks ago last Friday."

"Oh, yes. I'm so sorry, Patrick. She was one of my mother's best friends." Gail had thought of Patrick when she had heard about Mrs. Tillett's death, remembering he was her nephew. Her mother had told her what had happened. Irene Connor had been playing bridge at Althea Tillett's house that night. Irene had heard it from her friend Edith, who had heard it from Jessica. The police had found Mrs. Tillett at the bottom of the stairs in her living room. She had been drinking heavily, and must have caught one of the wooden clogs she was wearing on the hem of her robe.

"I need to talk to you about her estate," Patrick said.

Gail told him she had an early meeting, but to come around ten o'clock.

"It'll be good to see you again, Gail."

"You too."

She hung up and sat staring at the telephone. Patrick Norris. After all this time.

The memories came rushing back.

chapter two

Slipping out of a litigation department meeting that threatened to drag on, Gail glanced into the lobby to see if Patrick was there. He was. He stood in a square of sunlight, staring out at Biscayne Bay. His image reflected like a ghost in the window: beard and wire-rimmed glasses, light brown hair falling past his ears.

Clients liked to wait where Patrick stood now. They liked to watch the traffic fourteen floors below, or the boats skimming across the bay between the city and the Port of Miami. Patrick was probably contemplating the quirks of economics that gave one man a suite on the Emerald Seas and another a flattened cardboard box under the expressway.

Two months into their senior year in law school at the University of Florida, Patrick had walked out of a class on corporate taxation. The students had sat at long, curving tables, rows of them that ascended from the podium in the center. When the professor suddenly stopped speaking, Gail looked up from her notes. Patrick was out of his chair, gathering his books under his arm. Without a word he walked down the steps of the aisle and dropped the books on the floor in a neat stack at the professor's feet. He let his gaze sweep over the faces of the students in wordless judgment. Then he was gone, the side door clicking shut behind him. The professor rapped with his pen to still the murmurs. "Anybody else care to throw in the towel? No? Then let's continue. Under the Revised Code of 1976 . . ."

Gail begged him not to quit, but it didn't do any good. He had been born in Miami, but headed his car in the opposite direction, winding up somewhere in the Southwest. An Indian reservation. He called her a few times. He was working at a hospice, a construction site, a diner in Gallup. He drifted to California. Gail was hired as an associate by Hartwell Black. A year or so later Patrick sent a letter from Mexico, then a string of postcards from South America, none with a return address. Then nothing. Patrick Norris gradually receded into memory, becoming another face in the photos from law school, buried with others in a drawer.

"Patrick?" When he only turned and looked blankly at her, she laughed. "It's me."

His sharply boned face softened in a broad smile. "Gail." He gave her a hug, leaving his arm around her shoulders. "It is you. All sleek and prosperous. I should have known." He ruffled her perm. "You've cut your hair. But I like it. It's nice."

She patted his chest. "Are you home for good and didn't tell me?"

"Since last winter."

"Last winter!"

"I know, I'm such a dog." He grimaced as if expecting a blow. "I moved back to Florida a couple of years ago to help on a lawsuit for the migrant workers up in Belle Glade. Now I'm counseling at a drug rehab center in Miami. Plus odd jobs here and there. Carpentry, whatnot. I'm one hell of a framer." He smiled again. "We'll trade stories sometime."

"Mine won't be as interesting as yours, I'm afraid." Gail nodded toward a walnut-paneled door past the reception desk. "Come on, I'll show you my office."

Patrick picked up a heavy mailing envelope from a chair and followed her inside. Carpeted corridors ran left and right, winding past glassed-in secretarial areas, long metal cabinets, framed lithographs, and murmured conversations. One of the partners' doors was open. Patrick slowed as he walked by, taking in a glimpse of beveled glass bookcases and thick carpet.

Gail waited until he caught up.

His voice dropped to a conspiratorial level. "We are now making our way into the belly of the legal beast."

"God. You haven't changed." She slipped an arm around his waist. Patrick was thin as a hermit. She could feel his ribs through the plain blue shirt he wore. In law school he would buy his clothes at thrift stores.

She led him into her office and closed the door. The office was full of furniture she herself had purchased, white oak with softly upholstered chairs. Pink bromeliads flowered from clay pots on the windowsills. Patrick glanced around, running his hand along the practice manuals on the bookcase. He checked the labels on the heavy accordion folders and with his knuckles lightly tapped the computer monitor on her desk. He flipped the cover of a *Southern Reporter* open, shut. "Looks like you've done well for yourself," he said. He focused on the framed diplomas and certificates on the wall. "Very well."

"Did you ever think of going back?" she asked.

Still reading, he shook his head. "No. I didn't belong in law school. I could never learn to argue convincingly for either side. They're so good at turning out moral ciphers." He smiled at her. "Not everybody. Not you." He came around one of the client chairs and sat down, pushing his hair off his forehead. It fell loosely from a center part.

Patrick looked at Gail a minute, then said, "I read about your sister in the paper. Damn. I should have called."

She gave a slight shrug.

"And then Dave. I thought you two would make it."

"Who told you?"

"Your mother. I saw her at my aunt's funeral. She said you were all right." Patrick's expression said he wanted to be sure.

"I'm fine. Really. The divorce was overdue."

He nodded. "Irene showed me some photos of Karen."

"You remember Karen?"

"Sure. She's a great-looking girl. Tough like Mom, I bet."

"Well, she has her moments. What about you? Married?"

"No. With the kind of life I've led the past few years, it would have been impossible. Wife, kids, all that. I don't think so." His crooked smile was half hidden by the beard.

With a funny little twist in the pit of her stomach, Gail remembered how Patrick's beard had felt under her lips. Springy, soft. The first time smelling faintly of woodsmoke from a fire in his backyard. He was the only man with a beard she had ever made love to. An impulse, acted upon. A guilty-sweet little affair, like seducing a seminary student. It had happened, then it was over. She had never told Dave.

"Well." She laughed softly. "Here you are. I don't know why I didn't phone your aunt and ask about you. I could have."

"Hey, half the time she didn't know where I was."

"You weren't close?" Gail thought back. "You never talked about her."

"No, we didn't have a whole lot to do with each other then. It got better. We both mellowed out, you could say." He propped one foot on his knee. He wore heavy brown sandals, and the skin of his ankle was pale and delicate, blue veins beneath. He concentrated on straightening his pant leg. "I keep imagining that if I go over to her house, Aunt Althie will still be there, telling dirty jokes and playing her stereo too loud. Whatever else you say about Aunt Althie, you've got to give her that. The woman didn't hold back."

"You wanted to talk to me about her estate. How can I help?"

Patrick handed her the heavy envelope he had brought with him. "Start with this."

27

Gail unbent the prongs holding the flap. She reached inside. There were several documents, each consisting of copies of typewritten pages stapled together. The words at the top of the first one read "Last Will and Testament of Althea Norris Tillett."

"A copy of your aunt's will." She shuffled through them. "What are these, prior versions?"

"Yes. These copies go back to 1981." Patrick pulled his chair closer. "That one on top. I got that last week in the mail from Monica, after a lot of whining."

"Monica?" Gail looked up.

"My cousin. Rudy's sister. You know Rudy and Monica. You went to the same prep school."

Rudy and Monica Tillett. Brother and sister. Wavy black hair. Fraternal twins. She said, "I think they were two or three years ahead of me at Ransom-Everglades."

"Where the rich white kids go to avoid the dregs in the Dade County public school system. Present company excepted, naturally."

"Didn't you all live together?" Gail asked.

"Correct. After my parents died, Aunt Althie took me in."

His parents had run a church in El Salvador, a tiny mission in the backcountry. Gail had thought, when Patrick told her the story, that the manner of their death embarrassed him. They had not been martyrs to the death squads. They had not even been good missionaries. Their car had hit a cow and spun off the road in a rainstorm. At age eleven, Patrick had been sent back to Miami.

He took off his glasses and reached into his pocket for a handkerchief to clean the lenses. "Have you ever been to Aunt Althie's house?"

"Probably," Gail said slowly. Althea Tillett had been a friend of Gail's mother, but Gail had not known the woman well. She had never met Patrick until they both wound up in the same class at law school.

Patrick prodded. "North Bay Road? Mediterranean? Fountain in the driveway?"

"Oh, yes." One of the older waterfront neighborhoods on the bay side of Miami Beach. She and her mother had picked up Mrs. Tillett one evening to go to the opera. "It's been years, though."

Patrick squinted at his glasses and rubbed another spot. "I went over there after the funeral. Rudy and Monica were throwing a sort of bon voyage party with the guest of honor already departed. They had champagne and male-model types from South Beach serving hors d'oeuvres. I practically had to show my ID at the door."

He put his glasses back on, tucking the earpieces carefully over his ears, moving strands of hair out of the way. Gail rocked in her chair, waiting.

"Rudy and I got into a disagreement. I told him it wasn't his house. He said it was. He said Aunt Althie left it to him in her will. To him and Monica. Then he and a couple of his buddies kicked me out."

"You're referring to this will?" Gail held up the copy. "Signed August third."

29

"I don't know when it was signed," he said quietly. "I do know it's a forgery."

"Why do you say that?"

Patrick got out of his chair. "First of all, the signature." He ruffled forward through the pages. "Close, but not good enough." Gail barely had a chance to see it before he thumbed backward. "Now read this. 'Two hundred and fifty thousand dollars to my beloved nephew Patrick Norris.' No way."

"No way?"

Patrick pulled another will from near the bottom. "You want real? How's this? 'To my commie nephew Patrick, a one-way flight to Havana so he can visit his hero Fidel.'"

Gail's eyes shifted to look up at him.

"That was when I marched on Calle Ocho to protest the U.S. embargo. The Miami Cubans beat the shit out of us. And way before that, when I said I didn't want to go to college, Aunt Althie left me a million dollars in trust, to be released upon my graduation. I've got a copy of that one too. She revoked the trust when she got pissed off at me again. I've forgotten why."

Patrick dug through the stack. "Look. 'To my darling nephew, the joy of my life, three million dollars.' Now what was . . . ? Oh, yeah. That's when she had the flu and I came back from California to stay with her. And this: 'To my dear nephew Patrick, five million dollars.' That's earlier, when I enrolled in law school. That sent her into raptures. But the codicil—'To my idiot nephew who is throwing away the education I paid good money to give him, five thousand dollars in his name to the United Negro College Fund.' And here's the one before the one Monica gave me. 'Fifty dollars for membership in the ACLU.'"

Now the wills were spreading out to cover Gail's desk.

"She thought she could control me with her money, like I was fourteen years old and too big to spank. I said 'Aunt Althie, stop. I don't give a damn about the money.' But she didn't stop."

Patrick flipped the next-to-last will onto the rest of them. "The woman was incredible. When she was happy with me, she'd write me into her will big time. If not—well, you saw. A joke. But a quarter million? Way too sane for Aunt Althie. She thought she was always going to be around to make another joke. Aunt Althie never considered anything like a heart attack or lightning, much less falling down her stairs. Never. Trust me, I knew this woman." He sank into his chair. "It's a forgery. A brilliant, elaborately executed forgery."

"Where's the prior will? The one leaving you fifty dollars for the ACLU?"

"Who knows? Burned, probably. That's what she usually did."

"All right, let's assume you're right, and the judge throws out the August will. And assume no prior original will can be found. That means Mrs. Tillett died intestate. A copy doesn't count. If there's no will, everything goes to her children. A nephew would inherit nothing. You remember enough probate law to know that."

Patrick gave her a blank look. "What children?

Rudy and Monica? They aren't Althie's kids. They were her late husband's children. I'm all she had."

"But you called them your cousins."

"Yes, but they aren't. They're . . . what? Stepcousins."

It took a few seconds for Gail's mind to switch tracks. "You're her only heir?"

"Correct."

"How much is her estate worth?"

"I don't know exactly. Ten million? At least that."

"Lord." Gail picked up the copy of the latest will and looked at what was printed in small type at the bottom of each page: the name of a law firm on Miami Beach. "Weissman, Woods, Merrill and Sontag," she murmured. "I know Lauren Sontag. She's running for circuit court judge in November."

"Good for her. Her partner Alan Weissman was Aunt Althie's attorney. I'd like to know what he got for doing this."

Gail gave a short laugh. "Alan Weissman? He's a past president of the Florida Bar. He's in the Miami Beach Chamber of Commerce."

"Well, golly gee. I guess that makes him honest."

"Most attorneys aren't into professional suicide, Patrick. Is Weissman handling the probate? Do you know?"

"According to Monica, he is. The estate was filed about a week ago."

Gail went back to the will, scanning the list of beneficiaries. The housekeeper. A gardener. The

Miami Shores Presbyterian Church. The Miami City Ballet. The list went on. She was relieved not to see her mother's name. That would be another problem in advising Patrick, and there were already plenty.

"Where are Rudy and Monica in here?"

"Page four. They got the house and art collection."

"That's it?"

"It would have been too obvious if they'd given themselves everything. They got what they wanted. They have a gallery on Lincoln Road for the art. The house was in their family from way back, but R.W. had Aunt Althie's name put on the deed, so it went straight to her when he died. He left Rudy and Monica some money—a lot of it—but they've probably gone through that."

"Didn't your aunt make any provision for them in her other wills?"

"Yes, the collectibles and paintings that used to be their mother's. Kitsch and sofa art, to be honest about it. That was her way of getting back at them. When she married R.W., Rudy and Monica made her life hell. Mine too, when I came to live with them. Then after R.W. died, they started sucking up to her, afraid she would cut them out."

Gail paged through the prior will. "Here she leaves her collection to the Bass Museum of Art on Miami Beach."

"That's how she usually did it. She and R.W. traveled a good deal together—Europe, the Orient, Egypt. She would never have given it all to Rudy and Monica."

Gail returned to the August will, curious to know who would get the leftovers—whatever property had not been specifically listed. She found it: another charity. No surprise.

"What is this Easton Charitable Trust? Are they local?"

Patrick shrugged. "I don't know. It's in all the wills as the residuary beneficiary. Rudy and Monica didn't change that either."

Bouncing her pen on her still-empty legal pad, she asked, "What did they have to say about the new will? I assume you asked them."

"Sure. Monica asked me what I was bitching about, since I got a quarter of a million dollars. I finally got in touch with Rudy." Patrick's mustache lifted over a smile. "He told me to fuck off."

"Nice." Gail kicked off a shoe and curled one leg under herself. She compared the signatures of Althea Norris Tillett on three of the wills, a bold, flowing hand. She studied the latest version. Mrs. Tillett's signature was followed by those of two witnesses, then a notary's acknowledgment, swearing that the testatrix and the witnesses had signed in her presence and the presence of each other. The copy machine had picked up the faint shadow of the notary seal of one Carla Napolitano. Then Gail must have let out a sound, because Patrick stopped rubbing his fingers across his forehead.

She held the will up so he could see it. "Do you know these people who signed as witnesses?"

He read. "Jessica Simms and Irving Adler. No."

34

"I do. She's the president of Friends of the Opera. And Adler—I think he was once the mayor of Miami Beach." She waited for Patrick to respond.

He sat silently for a moment, then pointed. "Check the list of beneficiaries. The opera's mentioned."

She paged backward through the will. "So it is. Fifty thousand dollars to the Greater Miami Opera. I can see the headlines now. 'Elderly Miami Beach Socialites Charged in Forgery Conspiracy.' Not likely." She turned the will so he could see it. "Look at these charities."

"What about them?"

"Try to imagine a judge ruling against the University of Miami or Big Brothers and Sisters of Dade County." She raised her brows. "We still elect judges in this state, remember? And tell a judge that one of Miami's most respected probate attorneys took part in this."

Arms skyward, Patrick abruptly stood. "Our American legal system. Oh, ain't it just grand?"

"Come on, Patrick. The judge will look for facts to fit his opinion. We all do."

"Then give him the truth." He leaned his fists on her desk. "We can get a handwriting expert!"

"So can they! For ten million dollars, experts lined up from here to the county line."

"Take depositions! Hire an investigator, I don't know. You're the lawyer."

Gail looked at him.

Patrick slumped, head bowed. "Sorry. I am sorry. This has got me so . . . wired." He took a breath. "Gail. I need your help. I can't let those bastards get away with it."

"Bastards get away with things all the time."

"No. Not always. Not always." Then he came behind her desk and sat on its edge, taking her hand in both of his. "Know what I'm going to do with the money?"

Gail shook her head.

"Guess."

"Guess?"

"Sure. What did I always want to do? You remember. I talked to you about it. Said wouldn't it be nice if . . ."

She laughed. "You didn't exactly talk to me yesterday, Patrick."

"I know that. Come on. Guess."

"Well." She swiveled her chair. "I doubt you'd buy a yacht and sail to the Riviera."

"Way off." His eyes danced.

As she continued to look up at him, it began to come back to her. "You were going to . . . something about building a new community in the inner city. Oh, lord. Patrick, you've got to be kidding." But he was still smiling. "What? You're going to drop ten million dollars into Overtown?" She pulled her hand away.

"Not exactly. Anyway, there wouldn't be that much after the IRS took its bite. I'm thinking a bit farther north, up around Sixty-second Street west of Biscayne, where I work. There are some vacant lots, mostly overgrown with weeds, and some buildings that were burned out in the '89 riots. I've got some friends up there, and we talk about it. What if. What if we could clean it all

36

out and start over. Put in some trees and a park. Build a community center, a medical clinic. Even a legal clinic. There are ten thousand attorneys in Dade County. If one out of a hundred donated a day a month pro bono—"

"Patrick. You are out of your mind."

"Do you think so? Really?"

She considered. "No. It's exactly what I would expect from you."

He walked back around the desk. "How much are you charging me for this, anyway?"

"Assuming I would take the case."

"Let's say you did."

"And assuming you even have a case."

"Which you won't know unless you look into it."

She said, "No way this firm would do it pro bono."

"I didn't think so."

Gail flipped the pen back and forth between her fingers. "We'd probably ask you to sign a note against the amount you have coming under the will, as security. Two-fifty an hour office time, three hundred in court, if it got that far. Say a cost deposit of . . . ten thousand dollars."

Patrick pulled down the handle of an imaginary cash register. "Ca-ching!"

She shot him a look, then doodled on her legal pad. A long spiral. "I could recommend some other firms."

"No." Patrick sat back down, studying his interlaced fingers. "I want Hartwell Black and Robineau for two reasons. One is you. And second—this firm has the clout to go up against the establishment."

Gail smiled. "Patrick. I don't think you get it. We are the establishment."

"This law firm is, but not you. I know you, Gail." For a long moment his eyes gazed steadily into hers. Finally he nodded toward her legal pad. "Aren't you going to take some notes?"

She said, "This is the worst set of facts I've seen in years."

Patrick shrugged. "Check it out. If I'm wrong, I'll take whatever advice you give me." His hands lay stilled in his lap, all pale angles.

"No promises," she said.

"I know."

Gail tapped a rhythm with her pen, then began to write.

chapter three

In the rudderless days after her divorce, Gail learned to make checklists to keep herself from getting lost. The habit stuck.

Now, at 8:15 A.M., one of the younger associates was taking notes as she ticked off things for him to do: Review this crossclaim and draft an answer. Where's the research I asked for? File an objection to that motion to compel production and set it for hearing.

Eric J. Ramsay, a second-year associate, sat in

a client chair with a legal pad. One of his knees was bouncing impatiently.

Gail went to get the heavy accordion file from her bookcase. "I've got the correspondence in here. See if you can find that letter they're talking about in the cross- claim." The file thudded onto her desk.

Eric scrawled *Locate Nov. 2 letter.* Gail saw that his tie had slipped below the back edge of his shirt collar. She wanted to poke it into place and fasten the little button, but didn't think he'd appreciate the gesture. At twenty- eight or so, he had the hard body of the linebacker he claimed to have been at Ohio State, but with a cowlick in his sandy hair. His rosy skin had probably freckled when he was a boy. He wore pinstriped trousers, suspenders, and wing tips, trying to fit in. He was a top-five-percent graduate of Michigan Law, one of the country's best law schools, but how he had sat still long enough to get a specialty in tax she couldn't imagine.

They said he had a Pentium chip in his brain. But they also said he had pissed off the senior partner in the department, a genius-level woman attorney, by pointing out her mistakes. A few weeks ago, when Gail had asked for a trial associate, they sent her Eric. Gail didn't need a tax attorney; she wanted a litigator. After they cleared up this one last case, she would bump him to somebody else.

Standing at her desk again, she flipped through a file, the pleadings attached with a binder at the top. "You're pretty good on computers, aren't you?"

Eric raised his pale green eyes from the legal pad. "Fair. I've done some programming. What do you need?"

"We've got about twenty boxes of documents coming in on Friday. I'd like you to get together with Miriam and work out a system for retrieval. She's going to do a computer index."

He seemed to smile. "You want me to work on document retrieval. One would think a paralegal could do this more efficiently, in terms of billing."

"Well . . . one might think that, if one were sure a paralegal were available who knew what the case required."

"What would be wrong with finding a paralegal and giving her the appropriate instructions?"

"You know, Eric—" Gail directed a smile at the papers in front of her. "When I came here, if a senior associate asked me to do something, I did it. I figured it would create a good working relationship. Do you understand what I'm saying?" The intercom line on her phone buzzed, but Gail concentrated on opening a paper clip with her thumbnail, wanting to pop him with it. Instead she attached a pleading to the file. "Just supervise, okay? Make sure the system fits our needs. I don't expect you to be the one with the numbering machine."

Eric ran his tongue around the inside of his cheek, then put his pen to the paper and made a note.

Gail picked up her telephone. "Yes, Miriam?"

"It's Karen's school. Something about no lunch?"

"She forgot *again?*"

"That's what they told me."

"Damn. All right, put them on." She heard a click. "Hello."

"Mrs. Metzger?" It was the soft Southern voice of Karen's fourth-grade teacher.

Gail sat down, sighed. "This is Ms. Connor. Karen's mother." Several times she had told them her name— Connor. She had never used her ex-husband's name, but they couldn't seem to remember. The switchboard knew where to direct the calls.

"This is Mrs. Johnson. Did you know that Karen came to school again today without her lunch?"

As if Gail had done it on purpose. "No," she said. "I didn't." This morning Gail had left the house at seven, putting Karen's lunch box by the door so she would trip over it if she didn't pick it up. The bus came at seven- thirty. Gail scooted a stray, bent staple along a curve of wood grain in her desk. "You know, Karen has done this three times already since school started. Maybe it's better if she skips lunch this time. She might learn."

There was an accusatory silence. "Mrs. Metzger, a child can't concentrate when she goes hungry. Karen said she didn't have breakfast."

"She had cereal. Cheerios with a banana." At least it had been sitting on the table when Gail had kissed her good-bye. "Fine. I'll take care of it . . . . Yes, before eleven."

Gail swiveled her chair back around. Eric Ramsay was watching her, as if waiting for Gail to tell him to run out and buy lunch for her kid

41

at a convenience store and deliver it to Biscayne Academy.

She said, "Well. I guess that's it for now. Any questions?"

"Nope." He stood up.

Eric left with a stack of files and Gail dialed her mother. Irene Connor was just on her way out. *Again? Well, all right, if the poor little thing doesn't have any lunch. Really, Gail, you need to make arrangements—*

Gail hung up and closed her eyes on her fists for a moment, wondering if she should call Karen's psychologist about this. Later. She went to the door of her office, leaning forward into the corridor, her hands on either side of the frame.

"Miriam!"

There was a hearing scheduled at the Dade County Courthouse at ten-thirty, and she wanted to make sure all the documents were ready. Miriam said of course they were, and opened the file to show her: motion, exhibits, and cases to support her position, with copies for the court and for the other party. As if Miriam would ever forget anything. She had put them all in the file, neatly catalogued with sticky notes.

"Excellent." Gail made another checkmark on her list.

Miriam was a petite twenty-one, with curly brown hair to her waist, fluffy bangs on top, and bright red lipstick. She went four evenings a week to the local state university, making straight A's in accounting while her husband Danny worked twenty-four on, forty-eight off with Hialeah Fire-Rescue and her parents kept the baby. Miriam was second-generation Cuban-American, a fizzy blend of two cultures. She had romantic ideas about lawyers and wanted to go to law school. Gail didn't have the heart to remind her what the public thought of lawyers these days.

"There were some phone calls while you and Eric were talking." Miriam dug into a pocket of the sweater she wore. She had put on one of Gail's with the sleeves rolled up. The lower edge reached to the hem of her miniskirt. Miriam wasn't supposed to wear miniskirts to work, but as with other *ridículo* Hartwell Black policies, she paid no attention. She wasn't supposed to speak Spanish on the job either.

She pulled out a stack of messages.

"Holy God," Gail said. She shook two Excedrin out of the bottle she kept in her top drawer and downed them with the last of her coffee, cold as tap water. Miriam read the messages. Some were leftovers from two or three days ago and could wait. Others couldn't.

"Where in hell is that part-time girl we were supposed to get this week?" Gail grumbled.

"Still working on the AeroMexico case. I could call a temp agency."

"And I'd have to pay for it myself. Never mind. What else?"

"Paul Robineau called."

"Oh, good. Did he say what for?" Nothing came to mind but the case she wanted. Larry must have come through.

"He just said come up and see him when you have the chance." Miriam's expression said she would like to know what that was about, the managing partner summoning her boss to his office, but Gail did not elaborate.

Miriam pressed the last message to her small bosom. "And this is from *tu novio.*"

Gail waggled her fingers and Miriam handed it over. "He is far too dignified to be referred to as a *boyfriend.*" She read it. Anthony, calling to confirm lunch, which was the best they could do. He had a trial in federal court to prepare for; she was in her usual midweek crush.

"When he called back I told him yes," Miriam said. "Is that okay?"

"Indeed yes. We're even going to discuss business."

"*Mentira-a-a-a.*" Lie. She grinned and busied herself collecting letters Gail had signed.

Twenty minutes later Gail had worked her way through half of her messages. She had her pumps off and her toes curled over the edge of a lower desk drawer pulled halfway out.

Miriam had come back in to clip papers into the files scattered around the office.

Gail was on the telephone. "Go ahead and appeal it, if you feel that strongly . . . An extension? Don't ask me that. You're past the deadline already . . . Marty, listen to me. Listen . . . Fifty. I think it's more than reasonable . . . No, we can't."

At the edge of Gail's vision, the flutter and shift of papers in and out of files gradually stopped. Often Gail would become aware that Miriam was intently watching her, as a young dancer offstage might watch the ballerina in the lights. Close enough to see the sweat and concentration, too far to know the ache of muscles and tendons.

"Seventy-five? Uh-uh. Can't do it." She sighed. "Maybe. But you pay the costs . . . Well, I hope so, Marty . . . you too."

She hung up. Miriam was still watching. "When you become a lawyer, *niñita,* keep a copy of the Rules of Civil Procedure in your purse and learn them by heart. Our esteemed opposing counsel forgot to file his amended counterclaim, and we've got him in the crosshairs."

"So he's lost the case?"

"Well—" She reached for her time log. "Marty Gerson is a decent guy. If I screwed him over, he'd do the same to me one day. There's no point in being a complete meanie."

She wrote the code for *Tel conf w/opp atty.* Then she wrote the amount of time that would show up on the bill: .5—half an hour. It hadn't been half an hour, but point-one would look silly. Point-five was better. $125. She visualized Jack Warner, head of the litigation department, putting down 1.0 at his $500 rate. Jack would get huffy if you asked him why. *Why? Because I just kicked the other guy in the nuts, and I deserve it.* So point-five was an acceptable middle ground, Gail decided.

She tore off the time slip.

Sometimes gifts would drop from heaven like that, another attorney's lapse. Sometimes—more often—she would have to wrench them out of stone. Either way, she would feel a giddy rush of satisfaction.

"Miriam. How would you like to go with me

45

to the courthouse? I need you to copy the probate file on Althea Tillett."

"Sure. I could do that."

Gail said, "I'd use the regular runner, but this isn't a case yet, and there's nothing to bill it to." She picked up a folder from her credenza. No file number, just a handwritten name: *Norris.* "Get me the Petition for Administration, Appointment of Personal Representative, whatever they've got." She slid the folder across the desk. "And find out how we file this thing. A collateral action in Circuit Court? Petition in Probate? I've never done one of these."

"No problem. I'll ask Claudia in the probate department." Miriam had it figured out: Don't waste time in the library when you can ask a head paralegal, who usually knows procedure better than an attorney.

Gail said, "All right, but don't tell her what it's for. I'd like to keep this buried for a while. Also get me a copy of the Probate Code and the statutes on wills."

Miriam didn't write it down. She would remember everything, point by point. She looked up from the notes Gail had made in the conference yesterday with Patrick, and her brown eyes widened. "*¡Mira!* Ten million dollars! Is that how much this old lady had? Patrick Norris doesn't look like he comes from a rich family."

"Surprise, surprise."

Miriam left the room still reading, turning to the next page of notes. Gail opened the file on the case set for hearing at the courthouse.

★   ★   ★

Thinking about Patrick for the past couple of days had convinced Gail that he had been right to leave law school. He'd never been meant to play a lawyer's game of bluff and threaten. Jack Warner squashed opponents simply because he *could,* and the other side expected that from a top trial attorney. Patrick would extend the deadline to Marty Gerson; he would be trampled. Patrick would suffocate on time sheets and staff meetings and budgets and personnel complaints and the dozens of other nitpicking details of a law practice.

This wasn't what Gail had pictured either, entering law school. Then she had been as naive as anybody. She had wanted to work at the EPA. Or in the juvenile courts. Or the Florida Department of Consumer Affairs. She and Patrick had hit it off immediately.

She had gradually become one of the friends he invited to his wood-frame cottage a few miles north of the university. On Saturday afternoons everybody would sit by the lake, drinking jug wine, arguing happily about the law and justice while the sun went down. Then they built a fire and drank more wine and argued some more. Patrick's spare, angular body seemed to quiver with conviction, and the flames danced in his eyes.

When Gail learned that Hartwell Black and Robineau wanted her for a summer clerkship, she waited till the other students had left before telling Patrick. She expected a comment about going over to the enemy, but he only said it was great news and squeezed her shoulder. Gail could feel his hand through her sweater. Could feel the bones and the light pressure of fingertips. Her wine was rocking in the glass, dark red in the firelight. She turned to Patrick, slid her fingers up his cheek through his beard, and kissed him.

She went alone to Patrick's house by the lake two or three other times that semester, looking in the rearview mirror before she turned onto the dirt road where he lived. Dave had been home in Miami selling powerboat parts and taking care of Karen, so that Gail could concentrate on her studies. Wretched with guilt and desire, she hadn't expected it to last with Patrick. When the affair sputtered out, she thought he was as relieved as she.

Dave had never known, but she tried to make it up to him anyway. She worked hard at Hartwell Black, joined the PTA, and helped Dave start his own business. She was as good a wife and mother as she knew how. Gradually their marriage turned brittle and joyless. It tottered along for a while on habit, then fell over stone dead when Dave left her.

Relationships don't last, her women friends had said, consoling. Count on your kids, your friends, your job, because men will leave you. Some do it by walking out, others in their minds, but eventually they all leave. Gail didn't know if that was true or not. She suspected her friends might work themselves into a melodramatic funk when they all got together and talked about men. Perhaps each still had more hope than she would admit.

Today at noon, upstairs in the law firm's

elegant private club, Gail would have lunch with her lover, a man who could still do his half of the pre-liberated dance of the sexes: male pursuit. Anthony Luis Quintana Pedrosa liked silk boxers, Spanish cognac, and illegal Havana cigars. And—most wondrous of all—she believed him when he said no, he didn't have some other woman to go to when Gail was in trial for two weeks straight. She didn't tell her friends everything for fear of making them envious.

They had not known each other long. Last spring, when Gail had been accused of murder, Anthony was her defense attorney. That arrangement ended quickly: Legal ethics don't allow sleeping with a client. He turned her case over to another attorney and waited for it all to be over. When the charges were dropped, Anthony had taken her across the state to Captiva Island, where they came out of the room only long enough to watch the orange sun settling into the Gulf, the sky slowly turning velvet blue and starry.

Now they saw each other a dozen times a month, if that. Their schedules created Byzantine complications of timing. He was open one weekend; she had to prepare for trial. She had an evening alone; he had to fly out of town. Gail suspected it was better that way. When they did make love, it was magical; nothing existed but the two of them. See someone every day and God only knows what accretion of annoyances will finally outweigh the magic. Soap film on the shower doors. Leaky roofs. Chinese carry-out for dinner instead of risotto. A ten-year-old girl who didn't want him around. Then the regretful shrug, the murmured assurance that he still cared for her, would always care . . .

With a sudden sharp intake of breath, Gail stood up from her chair, heart racing.

For one awful, panicky moment, she could not remember where she was supposed to be. The clock on her bookcase said 9:42.

She sat back down. The hearing was at ten-thirty. Good. Plenty of time. Miriam would have come in. Miriam had kept her from disaster more than once.

But over half an hour had ticked by, Gail staring at the heavy brown file, doing nothing at all.

Paul Robineau had a corner office on the sixteenth floor, with round-edged furniture and ivory carpet, the monochrome broken by a vivid abstract painting in the colors of Biscayne Bay. From where she sat, Gail couldn't see the bay, only the sky and the puffy white clouds reflected in the windows of a nearby bank building. At the opposite end of the room, the CNN Business Channel was playing soundlessly behind Robineau's desk, stock prices sliding along the bottom of the screen.

He stood halfway in the corridor speaking to his secretary, telling her to hold his calls, he wouldn't be long. He came back in and closed the door.

If he had possessed the least scrap of humor, Paul Robineau would have been an attractive man. He had a strong jaw, heavy shoulders, and thick gray hair. The points of his starched, white collar were secured by a gold pin. That he had become the managing partner of a major Miami law firm in his mid-forties was due to an uncanny knack for keeping his clients dazzled and the staff in line.

"Thank you for coming up on short notice." Robineau walked toward his desk, a slab of smoky glass supported on polished limestone columns.

"I had a few minutes." She smiled.

He sat down. "There are two matters I wish to discuss with you. First, this Trans-State case you wanted to take. Larry Black spoke to me about it. I'm going to say no, and I want you to understand why. It's not my policy—"

"Paul, before you—"

"May I finish?" He waited. "As I said, it is not my policy to make associates at this firm guess why their requests are turned down. Larry didn't tell me you had asked him to intercede on your behalf, but I assume that is the case."

His thick brows rose; he expected a response. Gail drew a breath. "'Intercede' isn't accurate. I mentioned the case to Larry and he said he would speak to you."

"Next time I suggest you try the direct approach in dealing with another attorney's clients."

Gail felt her cheeks flame. "All right. I don't see that it matters, but if that's what you prefer, fine. As for Trans-State, I believe that I can do a good job. Larry knows my work and he agrees. Apparently you have reasons for giving it to someone else. If so, that is certainly your decision."

Paul Robineau slid his fingers down a black and gold pen, upended it, then turned it again. He wore cuff links of a striated gray stone that glittered with the movement of his hand. "Let me raise this other matter, which may help you understand my position on Trans-State. Jack Warner told me about Beltran Plastics. Apparently you've arranged a settlement. Correct?"

"Yes." Something else was coming.

"We've got a—what?—$400,000 case ready for trial and you let it go for $175,000. That's quite a hit."

"What do you want me to say? It was my case and I made the call. And not in a vacuum. Larry and I discussed it." She could feel herself sliding backward down a long slope. "It was a loser, Paul."

"Is that right? A week before trial and you know it's a loser."

"And you're in the banking division, not litigation. Give me some credit for knowing how to do my job."

He pointed at her with the black pen. "Don't tell me, Ms. Connor, what should or should not be of concern to me." His voice was rising. Anyone standing in the hall must have heard. "I suggest that if you want to become a partner of this or any other law firm, you pay more attention to winning cases than settling them for less than half of what they're worth. Is that understood?"

The clouds were moving from window to window on the shiny panes of the building to the south. Gail felt her stomach floating. Her mouth was dry as a stone, and her tongue clicked when she spoke. "You probably don't know what was involved. Oscar Beltran isn't—"

"Forget it." Robineau shifted his shoulders in the chair. "Look. I'm not trying to be an SOB. You're a good lawyer, I'll be the first to say so. But here's what I see. I see a tendency to compromise too quickly, and I think it goes deeper than your recent personal problems. You want to be more than just a good lawyer? You need a set of *cojones*, so to speak. And this is not—I promise you—a gender issue. I think you can be taken advantage of. And if you can, so can your clients. And ultimately, so can this law firm." He stared impassively at her. "And that is the basis of my decision on Trans-State. It would please me greatly to be proved wrong."

After a few seconds, she stood up, the muscles in her legs shaking. She gave him a polite smile. "Is there anything else? I have to be in court."

"No. That's it."

At the door she turned around. "You are wrong about me."

He lifted his palms momentarily from the desk. "I hope I am."

In the ladies' room on the fifteenth floor, with its beige marble and faux gold faucets, Gail took the box of yellow tissue into the last stall and threw up until her stomach cramped and the sharp taste of acid was in her mouth. Shaking, she came out and patted her face with a wet paper towel.

She went the back way down another floor to

53

her office and closed the door. At the bottom of her purse was one lint-covered Xanax. She swallowed it dry, then repaired her makeup before Miriam could buzz her and say it was time to leave for court.

chapter four

A table by the windows in the Hartwell Building's luncheon club usually gave a stunning vista of shimmery blue water curving into haze at the horizon. Today a downpour had turned the scene gray and indistinct. Palm fronds hung limply along the shiny streets. On leaden water a cruise ship pivoted slowly in the turning basin at the Port of Miami. Along the railing, passengers huddled under their umbrellas, little dots of color.

Gail wished she had told Anthony to meet her somewhere else, a restaurant with a booth in the back, a dark one. She wanted to sit next to him and lean against his arm.

A waiter with a tray backed out of the partners' private dining room, and for a second Gail could see rosewood paneling and a flash of crystal on white linen tablecloths. As a guest there herself, it had occurred to her that hanging out too long at these altitudes could make you think you owned the city—you and people like you. Maybe it was true.

This morning the power of the luncheon club

had reached into the courtroom. The judge was a fiftyish blonde whose husband was an executive at First Union Bank. The other lawyer was a partner in a small firm in North Miami, a Ms. Rosenbloom—a smart woman, but struggling to make it, clothes showing some wear. Maybe the kind of lawyer Gail would be if she ever left Hartwell Black and tried it on her own. Ms. Rosenbloom was arguing against the admission of evidence in an insurance case. Gail had points on the other side, and cited cases one of the law clerks had found in the firm's research computers with **CD-ROM** laser disks, cross-checked through Westlaw, with the latest appellate court decisions attached. At some point Miriam came in quietly and sat in the last row of benches. She curled her fingers over the back of the next bench, chin on her hands.

The case might have gone either way on the law, but Gail could have bet, before the judge opened her mouth, how she would rule. Later in the elevator Gail explained it to Miriam: It was theatrics, in a way. You know the moves, the tone of voice; you hint you might appeal if the judge rules against you. And it didn't hurt that this particular judge belonged to Temple Beth Am, from which Hartwell Black regularly purchased a large block of tickets for the annual concert series.

She and Ms. Rosenbloom had shaken hands, being polite. Ms. Rosenbloom wasn't the kind to ride the case for the fees, telling her client when they lost, *Look, juries are unpredictable, I told you.* Gail wondered about putting Ms. Rosenbloom on the rack when it came time to settle. How tough would she be with her? How big a set of *cojones?*

Walking back to the office, Miriam showed Gail what she had copied from Althea Norris Tillett's file in the probate division. There were only a few documents so far, plus a copy of the will. No inventory yet, and when it was filed, they would need the judge's signature to see it. Gail noticed that Alan Weissman had not signed all the papers. One had been signed by his partner, Lauren Sontag. She and Gail had served together in the Dade County Bar, had spoken on seminars at the state conference. Gail had meant to call Lauren to wish her luck in her run for the circuit court bench. What would she say now? *Good luck, Lauren. So tell me, did Alan help forge Althea Tillett's will?*

Gail felt a hand on her back and looked up from her empty wineglass. Anthony. He bent to brush her right cheek with his lips, and she breathed in the light scent of his cologne. "I am so incredibly glad to see you," she whispered.

Anthony kissed her on the mouth. "I've missed you too." He propped a furled umbrella against the wall. The shoulders of his deep-green, double-breasted suit were spattered with raindrops. Tall and slender, he moved like a cross between a tango dancer and a Spanish duke. The gray was just beginning to show in his rich brown hair. Sometimes she had to look away from him; his dark eyes were that intense.

Gail said, "Lunch is my treat today, *quid pro quo* for your legal expertise, although I think I'm getting the better of the bargain." She caught the waiter's attention and asked for another glass of chardonnay—the first had just begun to ease her headache.

Anthony ordered mineral water and lime, then leaned back in his chair, looking at her. She had undone the top two buttons of her blouse. His eyes climbed to her face. "Where have you been? Two weeks. Gail, no one's schedule is that impossible." Adulthood in Miami had softened his Spanish accent.

"I don't suppose you want to come over tonight? I'm helping Karen do her science fair project."

He faked a sigh of regret. "Oh, what fun. Unfortunately, I have a meeting to go to."

No surprise. Whenever he came to her house, it was only to pick her up. He would sit in the living room tapping his long fingers on the arm of the sofa, Karen would stay in her room with the door shut. He had conspicuously made no comment about the pile of Dave's things in the garage.

Gail said, "Just don't disappear completely." Anthony gave her a slow smile that made her insides feel like the elevator cable had snapped. She leaned across the table. "Do that again and I might forget there are fifty other people in here."

"So." He flipped back the napkin from the basket of rolls. "What is this case we are supposed to discuss that entitles me to lunch at the Hartwell Club?"

Gail said, "An allegedly forged will in a multi- million- dollar estate. I'm not sure yet how multi.

The decedent is Althea Norris Tillett, lately of North Bay Road, Miami Beach. She was a widow, a friend of my mother's, as it happens. She died in a fall down her stairs about three weeks ago."

"That's too bad." Anthony broke open a roll, still warm enough to steam. Under spotless white cuffs he had a lizard-strap watch on one wrist and a link bracelet on the other. "Who is your client?"

"Patrick Norris, her nephew. He claims that her late husband's children—a brother and sister—forged the will. They get the house and Mrs. Tillett's art collection and Patrick gets a quarter of a million dollars. Unless the will is a fake, then he collects everything, ten million dollars, maybe more."

"So naturally he wants to hire an attorney. What does he do?"

"He counsels at a drug rehab center. Works as a carpenter. I'm not sure what else. Patrick and I knew each other in law school, but he quit after two years. He said it was warping his moral judgment."

"What that usually means—" Anthony shifted the bread basket to find the butter. "—is that he was going to flunk out."

Gail shook her head. "You don't know Patrick. He said law school in the mid-Eighties was like getting an M.B.A. He didn't care about making money."

Anthony buttered his roll. "He cares about his aunt's estate, no?"

"He says if he wins, he's going to build a model community in the inner city."

"Que santo."

"Not a saint. But he is untouched, in a way. His values are different from most people's."

"Evidently. Tell me about the stepchildren."

"Rudy and Monica Tillett. Twins. You might know the names if you were into the South Beach scene. According to Patrick, Rudy organizes activities for European tourists while they're in South Florida. Exotic diversions, and I don't mean a tour bus to Disney World. Rudy also designs parties for nightclubs. He did a jungle theme with everybody half naked and carrying spears, and an outer space *Cage Aux Folles* party. Monica is an artist, so she and Rudy often work together. I don't know how good she is. Anyway, they own a gallery on Lincoln Road. That's why they got creative with the will. They wanted Mrs. Tillett's art collection. Also her house, which they grew up in."

The waiter came back with wine and a green bottle of mineral water, which he poured into a stemmed glass. They ordered lunch, and when the waiter was gone, Gail reached into her purse for a copy of the will, asked Anthony to read it, and sipped her wine while he did so.

One elbow on the table, he slowly turned the pages. "If this is a forgery, it's damned convincing."

"Isn't it, though?"

"Where was this found? In a safe deposit box? Her lawyer's office? It could make a difference."

"True, but Patrick doesn't know. His stepcousins wouldn't talk to him about it." Gail explained why Patrick thought it was a forgery:

59

the signature, the odd bequest of $250,000 from a woman who had never written a will in that way before. She explained the prior wills, how Althea Tillett had hoped to separate Patrick from his radical politics.

Anthony smiled a little at that. Gail could imagine what he was thinking of: family and politics. His father was still in Cuba, a hero of the revolution, blind now and growing old. His maternal grandfather, Ernesto Pedrosa, once a banker in Havana, had made a second fortune here. Anthony stayed out of politics but refused to denounce his family in Cuba; the ones in Miami pretended not to notice his occasional trips to the island. Gail wondered how he did it, walking that narrow line, pulled by both sides, keeping his balance. Quite a trick.

He asked, "What about these other signatures? Are they supposedly forged too? Witnesses, notary?"

"Patrick thinks they were in on it with the Tilletts."

The waiter returned with a tray. Gail ate her fruit salad and watched Anthony read. His grilled yellowtail sat untouched in front of him. A minute later he said, "Perhaps Patrick wants a good settlement. He'll go away if they give him a million dollars."

"Not Patrick. He truly believes someone forged his aunt's will. He wouldn't ask me to do this otherwise."

"*Claro que no.* Pardon me." Anthony lifted a bite of fish to his mouth, then made a little noise of satisfaction, a rumbly growl in the back of his throat.

"I love it when you do that," she said.

He looked at her, smiled, and leaned closer, speaking nearly at a whisper. "On the way here I thought, Oh, lunch at the Hartwell Club. How tiresome. Except that I would see you, of course. I thought of calling you from my car. Gail, meet me at the Hotel Intercontinental. But then I would take you upstairs."

"And miss lunch?" Gail left her shoe on the floor and slid her toes up the inside of his calf.

"I'd have you instead." He clamped his knees on her foot.

"You for dessert."

"Tell me yes, we can go now."

"Yes, yes."

He put his napkin on the table. "Let's get out of here."

"Are you crazy? I have a client coming at one o'clock."

"Say you're in conference." Under the table his hand skimmed over her instep, around her ankle, as far up her calf as he could reach.

"Don't do that." She tugged and looked to see if anyone was watching.

"Half an hour, touching you. It's worth it."

She pulled her foot away, then laughed. "If I thought you were serious—"

"Your face is red."

"I'm sure it is." She put her shoe back on.

His eyes moved upward, to a place behind her. At the same moment she heard Larry Black's voice saying her name.

She turned. "Hi, Larry."

He nodded and smiled, then his attention went to Anthony. "Larry Black. We met at the Bar conference in Tampa in July."

Gail became aware of another man. Late forties, a custom-tailored suit and a fifty-dollar haircut. He smiled broadly. And excellent dentistry. She had seen him before. Theater openings. Or the opera. She couldn't remember.

"Yes, of course," Anthony said. The men shook hands. Althea Tillett's will lay facedown on the table. Anthony didn't invite them to pull up chairs—his way of saying he didn't want to be disturbed.

The second man's hand went out. "Tony, good to see you. I said to Larry, look who's here. Got to go over and say hi." The man's voice was a rich bass. He could have announced golden oldies on a wee-hours AM station.

Larry said, "Gail, this is Howard Odell. He's in business in the area. Gail Connor's an associate in our litigation department."

"Gail." Howard Odell gave her a subtle wink when she said hello. Part of his routine with women, no doubt. Like a tic. Somebody ought to tell him, she thought.

Odell braced one hand on the back of Anthony's chair, the other on the table. Some chitchat about the economics in downtown Miami these days. A comment to Gail to make sure she didn't feel left out. Odell said he'd like to get together, how about lunch next week at his club. Anthony said he would check his schedule. Howard Odell gave him his card, then smiled at

Gail. "I'll let you get back to this lovely lady." Wink.

When the two men were out of earshot, she said, "I remember now. The last time I saw Howard Odell, he was in a tux, with the CEO of a cruise line and a bunch of society types."

"What do you downtown attorneys call it? A schmoozer."

Gail saw the door to the partners' room close. "You were being seduced."

"Not me," Anthony said. "He wants one of my grandfather's restaurants."

"And? Ernesto doesn't want to sell it?"

"Ernesto doesn't care for Mr. Odell's friends."

"What friends?"

"One of whom I represented."

"You're kidding. An upstanding businessman like that, consorting with criminals?"

"Gail, you don't become wicked simply by knowing people who have been accused of crimes. What would I be, if that were true?"

"Even wickeder than you are." She made an air kiss.

Smiling, Anthony picked up Odell's card and folded it in half. He started to drop it tented in the ashtray.

"No, let me see that." He gave it to her and she unfolded it, a cream-colored card with the name *G. Howard Odell* embossed in gold.

Anthony went back to his lunch. "Do you want his investment advice?"

"No. Look at the address. The same address on Brickell Avenue as the Easton Charitable Trust."

He tapped the will. "Althea Tillett's residuary beneficiary."

"Exactly." Gail flipped the card between her fingers. "I wonder what G. Howard Odell does for the Easton Trust. Tell me more about him."

"I don't know much. We met through my grandfather. When one of Odell's acquaintances—a Cuban—was arrested, he told him to call me."

"Arrested for what?"

"So inquisitive."

"And you're such a tease. What difference does it make if you tell me? Do I know him?" Anthony rarely talked about his clients.

"No. He owns a dry cleaning business in Hialeah, and he was arrested for selling pornography out the back."

"And you represented this man?" Gail asked.

"It's what I do. I defend people accused of crimes."

"Pornographers? Okay, okay. The First and Sixth amendments to the U.S. Constitution. You've told me." She nudged his leg under the table. "You wouldn't be half as much fun if you were a real estate lawyer."

"It's why you love me."

"Was he guilty?"

"Who? The dry cleaner?"

"Yes, Anthony. The dry cleaner."

"Guilty? Not officially. The judge granted my motion to dismiss. The police improperly searched the premises." Smiling, he lifted his glass. "Fourth amendment."

Gail had once asked Anthony Quintana why

64

he practiced criminal law, where almost everyone was guilty as charged. He had told her there was no more guilt in criminal law than in civil practice. Civil practice was taken up with lawyers who didn't like to associate with semiliterate persons of another social class. Anthony said he didn't mind this. His clients could come from the most sordid conditions; at least they weren't hypocrites. In civil practice, he said, both lawyers and clients claim perfect innocence.

She tucked Howard Odell's business card into her purse. "Howard isn't going to like me very much when I tell him Patrick is going to get the money meant for the Easton Trust. Speaking of which—" She tapped the will Anthony had left upside down on the table. "You still have to earn your lunch."

"What do you want me to do?"

"Not much. Tell me how to go about investigating a case like this. Felonies are your territory. I could use one of the P.I.'s we hire for insurance defense work, but who pays? The firm isn't going to authorize an advance, not on these facts. Not with this list of well-connected beneficiaries."

"Start with your mother," Anthony said. "She and Althea Tillett were friends. Maybe they discussed her will."

"I'd thought of that."

"And talk to the witnesses. You said you knew them."

"Could you recommend an investigator, if I need one?"

"Yes, several."

"Another question. If Patrick is right that the

will was forged, what about the people who did it? What would they be charged with? Grand theft? Fraud? What would the State Attorney's Office do to them?"

"Probably nothing."

"Nothing?" Gail asked, hardly believing this. "Why? Because of who they are?"

"No, because the State Attorney doesn't usually care about civil matters. Who is the victim? Patrick Norris? They have their hands full prosecuting thieves who carry guns." He added wryly. "My clients."

"But I could use threat of prosecution to make them nervous."

"Be careful." Anthony folded the will and handed it to her. "You could get burned."

"I don't see how, just by asking a few questions." She put the will back into her purse. "Maybe Althea Tillett did sign this, all witnessed and notarized right in Alan Weissman's conference room. Patrick can accept that, if it's the truth. I owe him my best shot at finding out."

Anthony frowned slightly. "You owe him? Why?"

"Because . . . he's a friend. Or because of what he represents."

"Which is?"

Gail thought for a minute. "I'd say commitment. Patrick might be a little extreme at times, but at least he knows where he stands. I admire him for that. I always have. In law school, he made me ask myself, What am I really doing with my life? What's the purpose? You know— typical first-year law school idealism. When you are dying to do something great and wonderful. But then you graduate and go into practice. You find out what a muddle the law really is. You're just there to push and shove, and whoever can push harder wins. The times where you've really got something to fight for are so rare."

Anthony looked at her for a while, then said, "Whenever you have a client, you have something to fight for."

"Of course. ~~But~~ why? Because you get paid? Or—as Patrick might say—for a greater good?"

"Ten million dollars is pretty good." Anthony picked up his fork and cut a piece of asparagus. "I've learned one thing: It's not wise to represent friends. Send him to someone else."

"No. He wants me. And frankly, I need a case like this."

Anthony gave a short laugh. "This is the last thing you need."

"I'd appreciate your not telling me how to run my own law practice. Please?" She smiled.

"Ah-ha." He patted his mouth with his napkin. "And you expect Hartwell Black will take this case?"

"Yes, if I find evidence of forgery. If we can prove—"

"Gail, they won't let you. They can't. How would it look, trying to break a will where a woman left most of her estate to charity? Very bad. And here's another point. Patrick Norris, from what you tell me, is a socialist, and in Miami—"

"Oh, for God's sake." She had to laugh. "What an outdated concept. Like one of those Little

67

Havana radio hosts, calling everyone to the left of Ronald Reagan a Communist."

"I don't care if the man is a flaming Marxist, but other people might. There could be publicity."

Gail said, "Look. Hartwell Black is more interested in fees than in anyone's political persuasion."

"Only if you can win."

"Well, that depends on what I find out, doesn't it? I told Patrick I'd help him, and I will."

For a few seconds Anthony said nothing. Then he sat back in his chair. He smiled. "Did you sleep with him?"

She tilted her head. The words had made no sense. "What?"

Lifting an eyebrow, he restated them. "Did you sleep with Patrick Norris? When you were in law school?"

"Oh, I see. If a woman feels any sense of loyalty at all for a man, it must be because she slept with him."

"Did you?" His eyes fixed on her.

"No, I did not."

It was said before she could think, as quick as ducking a rock. For an instant she considered taking it back. But how would that appear to him? And what was there to tell? An event so many years ago that it didn't matter anymore? Or the reality of what they had here, now? One thing she had learned was that complete honesty between men and women was dangerous, unless you had nothing to lose.

She whispered across the table. "You're

jealous. This is incredible. You don't want me to represent Patrick because you're jealous. I've heard about Latin men, thinking they can—"

"This is not because I am Latin! Don't make me into a stereotype."

"Then stop acting like one. My God."

He turned sideways in his chair and glared out the window.

The waiter came then, asking if they wanted anything else. Only the check, Gail told him. He took their plates and went away.

Through the rain-streaked glass she could see that the cruise ship was gone, its berth empty. In a moment Anthony would thank her for lunch and offer to escort her back to the fourteenth floor, not wanting to make her late for her clients. Impeccable manners.

Close to despair, she slid her hand across the table to touch his wrist. "I should have been glad you care, instead of yelling at you."

Anthony's head turned slightly. He let out a breath. "Why do we do this?"

"I don't know." He wore a ring with a curve of jade set into it. She traced the curve with her thumb.

"Gail."

She raised her eyes.

He had turned back around, and took both her hands. "There's a handwriting expert you should see. I'll have my secretary give you his phone number. He's expensive, but I think as a favor to me he'll give you a preliminary opinion."

"Thank you." She entwined their fingers.

He tightened his grip. "Let me take you to dinner after work tomorrow."

"I'd love it. Oh, wait. No. I have a hearing early Wednesday."

"This law firm takes your life."

"Not forever," she said. "How about this weekend? Saturday. I promised to take Karen to the Museum of Science. Come with us."

"I have a client to see in Fort Lauderdale. What about dinner on Saturday night, the three of us, at my house."

"Karen too?"

He shrugged. "Why not?"

"I can't stay over," she said. "You know. Not with Karen."

"I know."

"But she has a birthday party to attend on Sunday afternoon."

"Good. Come back on Sunday."

"Very good. But I'll have to leave by four."

He laughed softly. "Then we have whatever time there is." Standing up, he went around to pull out Gail's chair, then put his back to the room and lifted her hand from the table. She felt the moist warmth of his lips on her fingertips.

"Anthony." She glanced past his sleeve. "What are you doing?"

He bent close to her ear. *"Esta noche, quiero que pongas tu mano donde yo quisiera poner mi boca ahora."*

Her mind worked to translate: Tonight, put your hand where I would like to put my mouth right now.

She whispered, "You are so bad."

70

chapter five

Gail's mother, Irene Connor, did volunteer work for a few of the charities around Miami, including Friends of the Opera. On Saturday Gail took Karen along to the new performing arts center downtown. They stopped to look inside the auditorium. Onstage, bits of Egyptian backdrop leaned against bare walls. From the wings came the whine of a power saw. *Aïda* would open in two weeks.

Karen craned her neck around to see up in the ceiling, where a man crawled along a catwalk, unrolling cables. "What are they doing?"

"Looks like they're working on the sound system."

"Mom, I want to stay and watch." Karen faced Gail squarely, the bill of her Miami Hurricanes baseball cap low and level.

"No, come with me. I don't think they want people watching."

"It's okay. If anybody tries to kick me out, I'll tell them my grandmother Irene Connor works here." She pushed a seat down and sat on the edge of it.

Gail glanced around. Two stagehands were carrying a wall painted to look like the inside of a temple. "All right. But don't run up and down the aisles or go into the balcony."

Karen sighed. "I won't." She scooted back, the toes of her ragged sneakers touching the slanted floor. For ten years old, she had long legs. Karen would be tall one day, like Gail. She pulled her purse around so it lay in her lap. It was a small alligator handbag that she had found in a cedar chest at her grandmother's house. Irene had let her have it, perhaps in an attempt—useless, so far—to encourage some femininity in the girl. Gail remembered Irene carrying the bag years ago. Alligator purse and shoes, mink stole, gloves. The strap was short, so Karen had made a new one with a snakeskin belt, and now wore the purse crossways over her chest.

Karen didn't say what she kept in there, and Gail had never opened it, respecting her privacy. But she wondered. Miniature unicorns with long pink manes? Dead bugs and a magnifying glass? Pictures of her father? Or things she would need to survive in the woods alone, which she could probably do as well as most adults.

Ten years old. She did what she wanted and Gail would find out about it later. A strange child, Irene often said in a tone that carried a hint of censure for the mother who had let her get that way.

Gail tugged on her ponytail. "Be good."

In the administrative office, Gail's mother waggled a finger toward an upholstered bench by the window. She was on the phone, checking hotel prices for someone flying in from New York. On her desk a tiny fan whirred in a smokeless ashtray.

Irene Strickland Connor was a petite redhead who favored colors bright enough to induce eyestrain. Today she was wearing a parrot-green pullover cinched at the hipline and matching jersey slacks. Her Yankee grandfather had come down in 1882 to hack a homestead out of scrub palmetto and eventually get rich in land sales. Her husband died before he could run through her entire trust fund. Even so, Irene was part of the right group, and she liked to do her bit for the arts. She had often said that Miami's high culture—such as it was—would disappear entirely if the three or four dozen ladies behind the scenes suddenly moved out of town.

When Irene hung up she asked, "Where's Karen? You said you were bringing her."

"She wants to watch what's going on in the auditorium." Gail scooted over and patted the seat. "Talk to me a minute."

Irene took a final drag off her cigarette, then twisted it into the ashtray. "Crank the window open, will you? If Jessica catches me, I'm in deep caca."

"Is she here?" This was someone else Gail wanted to talk to, but not necessarily today. Jessica Simms. A witness to Althea Tillett's will.

"She should be here. There's a meeting." Irene brightened into a smile. "Hey. Why don't you girls let me take you out tonight?"

"Ah—"

"Nothing fancy. Miniature golf. Karen likes that." Irene laughed. "I lost two bucks to her last time we played, the little hustler."

"Maybe next weekend? We're having dinner

73

at Anthony's house. And don't say anything, Mother, I mean it."

"At his house? Is she ready for this?"

Gail gave her a look.

Irene raised her hands. "Never mind. What did you want to talk to me about?" She sat down.

Already Gail had considered how to say enough without setting off bells and whistles. "I have a case involving a document that might have been written by Althea Tillett. I need to see a sample of her handwriting to make sure. There must be some letters or memos around the office here, something with her signature on it."

"A case? What do you mean?"

"I'd explain, but I can't right now. It's a matter of client confidentiality. Could you take a look without letting anyone know?"

"Goodness, you make me feel like a spy. What is this document? Let me see it. I could tell you if she wrote it."

"No, it has to go to a handwriting expert."

"Darling, you're so secretive. I'm your mother. I wouldn't tell."

Gail shook her head. "I can't discuss it. Not yet."

"Uh-oh." Irene stood up suddenly, looking through the window. She rushed back to the desk, grabbed the ashtray, and pulled open a bottom drawer. She dropped the ashtray inside and took out a can of air freshener, laughing at herself. "I've really got to stop this. Jessica has a blue fit if she catches anybody smoking in here." Two quick sprays left the scent of roses.

Gail looked out. A white Lincoln had stopped

under the portico fifty yards farther toward the rear of the building. A man in a dark suit opened the rear door of the car. His hand went inside. He steadied himself and pulled.

Jessica Simms, her face obscured by big round sunglasses, emerged slowly, ducking her head to keep her straw hat from catching on the door frame. As she stood up, she shook the folds of her dress, a muumuu with short, puffy sleeves. The flowered cotton could have upholstered a chaise in a lady's boudoir. Her legs, clad in off-white hose, tapered into tiny green flats. She glanced at her watch and said something to the chauffeur, who nodded and closed the limo door. Jessica Simms disappeared into the building.

Gail waved a quick good-bye to her mother and caught up with Jessica in a corridor leading to the backstage area. "Mrs. Simms?"

She turned slowly, all bosom and hips, a head shorter than Gail. The sunglasses were off now, perhaps stowed in one of the patch pockets of her dress. The brim of her green straw hat tilted upward. "Yes?"

"I'm Gail Connor, Irene's daughter."

"Indeed. The lawyer. How are you, Gail. Is Irene here?"

"Yes, in the office. Mrs. Simms, I wonder if I could talk to you for a moment. It's about Althea Tillett."

"Althea?" She frowned at the double doors at the end of the corridor. Beyond them a piano was playing, the notes muffled. "I have a meeting with the production staff. What about Althea?"

In the thirty seconds it had taken to dash along

the hallways, Gail had decided what approach to use with Jessica Simms. Lie.

"Her nephew Patrick Norris came to see me this week. We knew each other in law school, and he had some questions of a legal nature. Perhaps you have met Patrick?"

Jessica Simms's pink mouth made a little smile. "I have."

"He asked me to look into the circumstances surrounding the signing of his aunt's will. He wonders if she might have been under a strain at the time. You were one of Althea Tillett's friends. She asked you to witness her will. You could tell me what occurred that day."

"Does he believe that Althea was . . . incompetent?"

"He is concerned about that, yes."

From the auditorium a tenor began to sing. Gail recognized the piece: the death scene in the final act. For a few moments Jessica Simms looked down the corridor, then shifted her eyes back to Gail. "He is concerned, is he? I would venture to say that what concerns Patrick Norris is the fact that Althea did not leave enough money to suit him."

"Are you aware of the amount?"

"I believe it was well over two hundred thousand dollars. Forgive my candor, but I personally would not have left him a dime. He should be grateful."

The piano stopped. There was laughter, then piano and tenor resumed. Gail said, "What about her stepchildren? How was her relationship with Rudy and Monica Tillett?"

Mrs. Simms smiled. "I really couldn't say."

"She didn't talk about them?"

"Now and then she might have. Nothing I could recollect now."

"You're aware she left them her house and her entire art collection."

"Is that so?"

"Althea didn't discuss the contents of the will with you?"

A steady gaze. "I only witnessed the will. I was not aware—Althea did not tell me, nor did I ask—what was contained in it."

"Then how did you know about the bequest to Patrick?" Gail asked.

"How? I presume it came up in conversation."

Gail hesitated. She had too few facts to start pushing hard on Jessica Simms. "Could you tell me where the signing took place?"

"Alan Weissman's office," Mrs. Simms said patiently. "He was Althea's attorney. Mine too, in fact. He represents many of our friends. If Althea had been under a strain, Alan would never have allowed her to sign the will." She gave Gail another smile.

The tenor aria ended with a soaring flourish, followed by scattered applause. Then came the sound of something heavy being winched upward.

Gail asked, "Who else was present? Besides you, Althea, and Mr. Weissman?"

"Irving Adler. Irving was once our mayor, you know." Mrs. Simms lifted her arm to see her watch—gold with diamonds around the face. Her wrist was no more than a crease. "I really must go. They're waiting for me."

"Do you recall what Mrs. Tillett was wearing?"

"Wearing?"

"Yes. What did she have on?"

Mrs. Simms gave her a long look. "Why in the world would you care what she was wearing?"

"Well . . . it could show her state of mind." Gail had to walk alongside Jessica Simms now, because the woman was heading toward the end of the corridor.

"Good heavens. I really don't remember. A dress, I assume. Althea always wore a nice dress when she went out."

"Was she able to drive?" Gail leaned a shoulder on the door. "Or did you all arrive together? She didn't live far from you, did she? Perhaps you picked her up."

"Pardon me." Mrs. Simms gripped the handle of the wide steel door and waited for Gail to move out of the way. "Please assure Mr. Norris that his aunt was perfectly sane and that if he tries to break the will on those grounds, he will be wasting his time. And yours." She opened the door and Gail could see the stage blazing with light. Jessica Simms went through, then turned back, filling the crack in the doorway, speaking in a low voice.

"Gail, dear. You should know that Althea gave your mother a ring. Althea and I discussed it. Irene always admired her emerald dinner ring. Four carats, with a spray of diamonds. My goodness, it must be worth twenty thousand dollars. Althea said she would leave it to her."

Gail frowned. "It isn't in the will."

"Oh, but it is, indirectly. Althea kept a list in her safe deposit box, naming friends who would receive various items of personal property. Mr. Weissman sent out letters last week. Irene didn't tell you?"

Gail knew it was true, about the list. People did that sometimes, keeping a list in a separate place, changing it when they wanted to, rather than redoing an entire will or making a codicil. Althea Tillett had mentioned such a list on page five. Gail had crossed her fingers, hoping her mother's name wasn't on it. She should have known better.

Now Jessica Simms's round face drew closer. She smiled. "That was Althea's last wish, to remember her dearest friends. So you think about that the next time you talk to Patrick Norris."

She drew back, and with a hollow clank, the door closed firmly behind her.

"Mother?"

When Gail came in, Irene was standing over a map of the auditorium spread out on a table, the sections colored with various shades of marker—pink, yellow, blue. "You certainly ran out of here in a hurry."

"And I have to go again. Could you watch Karen for a while? I won't be long." She picked up her purse from the bench by the window. "If Jessica Simms says anything, pretend to be surprised."

"I won't have to pretend. Where are you going? But I suppose it's none of my business." Irene capped her yellow marker.

79

Gail came back in. "All right. Althea's nephew Patrick came to see me. He says Rudy and Monica Tillett forged her will. I was asking Mrs. Simms about it. She was a witness. Supposedly. I need the signatures for comparison."

"Are you sure?" Irene whispered.

"I'm sure Jessica Simms was lying. Please don't say anything about this, Mother. I'll explain it to you later."

Irene could only shake her head.

Gail put the strap of her purse over her shoulder. "Did Althea ever discuss her will with you?"

"No, never."

"Was she on good terms with Patrick?"

"Patrick?"

"Her nephew."

"I know who you mean." Irene sat down heavily. "Well, she didn't talk about him much—not to me, anyway. I heard her yelling at him on the phone once, but not as though she didn't love him. Some people express love in the oddest ways. Outsiders might not understand it. One time Althea said, 'Would you believe what that blankety-blank has done now?' The way she said it made me think she admired him for doing what he wanted, regardless of how much money she had. Althea sounded hateful sometimes, but she wasn't."

Irene smiled. "Oh, Althea could rant and rave. But she was never petty about it, never selfish. It's hard to explain. I've never known anyone who cared so little what people thought of her. She was about to fly off to Greece all by herself and have an adventure." Irene looked into her lap. "I think about her a lot."

Gail scooted her mother over to sit on the same chair. "Jessica said Althea left you an emerald ring. Is that true?"

"Well . . . yes."

"You didn't tell me."

Irene raised her chin. "I haven't seen you. And anyway, I didn't want to be disrespectful to Althea by being glad she left me something." She extended her arm and studied her small hand. "It would be lovely but . . . I'll probably sell it. Is that awful of me? I could redo the kitchen and replace the tile on the back porch." Then her eyes welled up. "Poor Althea. I'd so much rather have her than a new porch."

Gail hugged her. Her chin fit on top of her mother's head. "Don't. Althie would like knowing you could sit out on a new back porch and watch the water and think of her."

"That's just what I would do." Irene laughed. "I'd fix a pitcher of martinis in her memory." She added quietly, "But if the will isn't any good, I guess the list isn't either?"

"I'm sorry."

Irene bit her lips, trying not to smile. "She left Jessica a chair. A very nice chair, from a palace in Venice."

"I hope it's sturdy."

"Now, now."

Gail whispered, "Althea liked you better."

"Oh, she did not." But Irene was smiling.

★　★　★

It took Gail fifteen minutes to cross the Julia Tuttle Causeway, find Irving Adler's house, and park under a shade tree in his front yard. She wanted to get to ex-mayor Adler before Jessica Simms finished her meeting and thought to call him. The house was a one-story stucco on a street laid out in the Fifties, more or less unchanged thanks to a waterway separating the neighborhood from a row of big hotels to the east. Across the street a crew of black men in matching green T-shirts was mowing and edging a lawn. Other than that, the neighborhood was quiet.

On the porch Gail rang the bell and from the other side of the door came a sharp yap, then high-pitched snarls getting louder, then little thuds, as if some small animal were throwing itself against the wood.

The inner door opened, leaving a storm door between Gail and an aged, pop-eyed toy poodle yapping through the glass. A red bow quivered in its topknot.

"Mitzi, be quiet!" A stoop-shouldered man peered out. "Who is it?" The dog stood trembling between his feet.

"Mr. Adler? It's Gail Connor, Irene's daughter." She spoke over the rattle of the lawn-mower. "I'd like to talk to you about Althea Tillett. I'm an attorney. I represent her nephew, Patrick Norris." The sun reflected off the white paint. Gail was wearing tan slacks and a cool top, but she could feel the sweat tickling down her back.

Adler tilted his head to get a better fix through

his glasses. "Irene said her daughter was a lawyer. Is that you?"

"Yes. May I come in?"

He hesitated. "What's this about Althea?"

The poodle snarled. One eye was clouded with cataract. Except where the clippers had left a patch of fur around its shoulders, puffy as a life vest, the dog's skin was a mottled bluish gray. There was a ball of fuzz over each foot and one at the end of its tail.

"If I could just talk to you for a minute, I could clear up some of Mr. Norris's concerns." Gail gave a reassuring smile.

After a second or two, he unlocked the storm door. The poodle rushed at Gail's toes. She wished she were wearing tennis shoes instead of sandals. "Quite a watchdog you've got there," she said, pulling her foot out of the way.

"She won't bite you. She's a little love. She loves her papa." Adler bent over and scooped up the dog, kissing its walnut-size cranium through the furry topknot. "Mitzi was my wife's dog, but my wife is gone now."

"I'm sorry to hear that, Mr. Adler." There was a cold breeze coming through the AC vents.

Irving Adler was wearing a warm-up suit, gray with red piping, and spotless white running shoes that seemed too big for his feet. There was a towel tucked around his neck. He led Gail into a living room with blue brocade furniture and a fireplace whose mantel held family photos in gold frames.

"Have a seat." He pointed to the sofa. A

stationary bike faced the window, a shiny model with a front wheel like a fan.

"Did I interrupt your workout?" Gail asked.

He waved a hand. "Hadn't started yet, don't worry about it." Adler let himself down into a chintz-covered armchair and Mitzi stood in his lap, teeth bared. "I wouldn't ride the thing at all, but my doctor says I have to. When the weather lets up, I'll walk. I went into the hospital last year." He tapped his chest. "Triple bypass at Mount Sinai, Dr. Fishbein. He put in a pacemaker and told me to exercise and watch what I eat. You look in pretty good shape. Do you take exercise?"

"When I have the chance."

"Good. Live longer. You tell Irene I said hello. I saw her at the funeral. What do you want to know about Althea? I don't have much time. My niece is coming over. She's about your age."

Gail said, "As I said, I represent Patrick Norris—"

"Patrick. Her brother's boy. Her brother is dead."

There was a crocheted afghan folded at the end of the sofa. Gail wished she could wrap it around herself. The house was frigid. She rubbed her arms. "You may have heard that Patrick was Althea Tillett's only relative."

"Yes. And a bum. Excuse me if he's your client, but the man is a bum."

"Why do you say that?"

"I know what he is. Kids like that expect to live off the rich relatives, so they don't do anything for themselves. He's a dropout, did he tell you that?"

Gail started again. "Patrick is afraid that Mrs. Tillett may have felt pressured into writing her will as she did. You were there at the signing, correct?"

Adler looked at Gail through his glasses for a while, then said, "Who does he say pressured her? Nobody pressured her."

"Maybe no one did. He wants to make sure."

"This is very strange. Why are you asking me these things?"

"Because you were there." Gail had the sense that she was treading water. "Weren't you?"

Adler's neck was craned forward, his heavy lower lip drooping. "Yes. I was there. You want to know what happened, I'll tell you, no big deal. We all went to Weissman's office on Alton Road. You know Alan Weissman?"

Gail asked, "Was Mr. Weissman present?"

Irving Adler looked at her through his glasses. "Yes. Althea's lawyer."

"Who else was there?"

Mitzi's lips curled back and she growled in rapid spurts. Adler squeezed her muzzle gently with a big-knuckled hand and told her to be quiet. "Jessica Simms. You know Jessica? And Althea, of course. So Althea signs it, I sign as a witness, and Jessica signs after me. Done. Nobody pressured her."

"Was there a notary?"

"Notary? Sure. You gotta have a notary."

"That was Carl Napolitano, I believe?" Gail asked, knowing it had been a woman. Carla.

"Who remembers?"

"Did he work in Mr. Weissman's office?"

85

"I don't know, maybe."

Gail rubbed her arms, shifting a little on the sofa to avoid the vent in the ceiling. "What day of the week was this? Do you recall?"

"The day? Whatever it says on the will. I don't know what day."

"Was it the weekend?"

"Maybe. I'm retired, I don't know." He pushed the poodle's hindquarters down so she would sit. "Althea died three weeks ago. She was a hell of a girl, Althea was. A hell of a girl."

"How long had you known her?"

"A long time." Adler patted the dog, and the weight of his hand bobbed its head up and down. "I met her when she married R.W. Tillett."

"You were a friend of his?"

"R.W. and I were in the army together. Kids. We were in Italy in 1944. I was wounded and they sent me home."

Gail watched the poodle stretch out flat on Adler's thigh and close its eyes. "Do you know her stepchildren? Rudy and Monica?"

"Those two. You can't tell which is which. I don't think they can either." Adler laughed, then coughed into his fist.

"Did they get along with Althea?"

"Aaah-h-h." He waved a hand. "She put up with them."

"When did she ask you to be a witness?"

"When?" Adler was concentrating. "I don't know. A day or two before it was signed, I guess."

"Did Althea leave you anything in her will?" He shook his head. "Nothing? Maybe on a list she kept in her safe deposit box?"

"I don't know about a list."

The telephone rang then, a blue princess phone across the room near a lounge chair strewn with the morning paper. Mitzi stiffened, threw back her head, and gave a howl like a cat with bronchitis.

"Mitzi, hush!" Adler got up, cradling her in the crook of his arm. He crossed the room and picked up the phone. The expression on his face a few seconds later told Gail who was on the other end. Adler looked at her then walked the phone as far as the cord would reach, through an arched opening into the dining room, where an ornately carved table held a silver bowl of wax fruit.

By the time he returned, Gail was standing.

Framed in the archway, Adler glowered. "You'd better go."

"I suppose that was Jessica Simms." Gail said.

He took a breath, then another, and set the phone down on a small table. "I let you in my house and you try to trick me, asking questions about Althea. You're working for Patrick Norris, I should have known. He's a no-good bum, you can tell him I said so."

Gail said, "I'll have to see you again, Mr. Adler. Please don't make me do it with a subpoena."

"You ought to be ashamed of yourself. I should tell Irene. Go on now. I'm upset." He waved a hand toward the front door. "Go on." Mitzi growled and struggled to get down.

Gail didn't move. "Mr. Adler, I'm sorry. Whatever happened, maybe you were talked into it. Tell me if that's how it was."

His face was red. "Go on. Get out." He bent and released Mitzi. She streaked across the room toward Gail, yapping, the red bow in her topknot streaming like a battle flag.

Gail scooted the dog away with the side of her foot. Mitzi rolled.

With a cry, Adler started forward.

"I didn't—" Gail shook her head and left the house. She could still hear the howling and the little thuds against the door.

chapter six

"Sweetie, hand me my sunglasses out of my purse, would you? And find that little memo book. I want you to write something down for me before I forget."

Gail put on her sunglasses one-handed and whipped the car around the corner past the First Union building. The downtown streets were nearly empty on Saturdays.

After leaving Irving Adler's house, she had gone back to the opera offices to pick up Karen. Now both of them were on their way to the Museum of Science, a few miles south of downtown. Her car buzzed over the metal bridge at the Hyatt Regency then came down onto Brickell Avenue with its glass office towers and shady banyan trees. Gail had the afternoon laid out: an hour for the show at the planetarium, home by one, then work a few hours before they had to get ready for dinner at Anthony's.

Karen held up the memo book. There was a pen clipped inside.

"Okay, write 'Norris N-o-r-r-i-s.' Then under that put 'Two hours, Simms and Adler—' That's A-d-l-"

"Mom. I know how to spell."

"Yes, you're very smart," Gail said. "And add 'including travel time.'" Hours for Patrick Norris were beginning to accrue. If this turned into a case, Gail would bill starting today. "Thanks."

Karen muttered something and put back the memo book.

Gail patted Karen's bare knee. There was still a scab on it from falling out of a tree last week. "Well. We're going to learn all about the Mayan calendar today."

Karen cut her eyes over to Gail. "I already saw it."

"You did? When?"

"My class went last week. You signed the permission slip."

"Well, we could go into the museum. They've always got a special exhibit, don't they?" Gail adjusted the vents on the air conditioning. "What is wrong with this thing?"

She zipped around a van ahead of her—in, out, feeling like a cop in a car chase. There was still that adrenaline rush from getting thrown out of Irving Adler's house. And then returning to the opera building, expecting Jessica Simms to be lying in wait for her.

Irene reported that Mrs. Simms had indeed

come into the office in a snit, but Irene had feigned ignorance. After Mrs. Simms left, Irene pulled a dozen samples of Althea Tillett's signature from the files, most of them original memos, others copies of letters. Now they were all in a folder in the backseat. On Tuesday Gail would take them to the document examiner Anthony had recommended.

She held her hand in front of the AC vent. "Please God, don't let it be the compressor. Roll your window down, Karen. Nothing's coming through."

If Dave was still around he could check the freon. It was funny, Gail thought, how you miss things like that. Freon and oil changes and sprinkler heads. She tried to imagine Anthony Luis Quintana Pedrosa on his hands and knees in the backyard, fixing the sprinkler system. She had never even seen him in shorts. Cuban men of his generation didn't wear shorts, she had heard. The younger guys, sure, but anybody over forty . . .

She hung her arm out the car window and let the air rush up her sleeve. The museum would be half a mile farther ahead on South Dixie Highway.

"You know, I haven't heard much from you about school this year. Except that you forget your lunch. But otherwise, how's it going?"

"Okay."

"Just okay? Are you making any new friends?"

"No."

A Metro bus stopped ahead, letting someone off, and Gail slowed down. "Mrs. Johnson is nice, isn't she?"

"She's a dork."

"Why?"

"She just is."

Gail hoped Karen's mood would improve by tonight. Karen and Anthony had never spent more than ten minutes in the same room together. If this kept up, they never would.

She reached down and pulled her memo pad out of her purse. She wrote *oil change,* ripped out the page, and stuck a corner of it on the ashtray so she could see it. A horn blared behind her. She stepped on the gas, tires squealing on the pavement.

At the museum, a one-story building with a dome at one end, Gail parked in the shade. The engine went quiet, and for a few moments she held her keys in her hand, listening to the birds. A gray squirrel clung to the oak tree by the front bumper, its tail twitching.

Gail said, "Well. Here we are."

Karen was looking into the middle distance beyond the windshield. "Yep."

"All right, then." Gail rolled up her window and opened her door, but Karen hadn't moved. "What's the matter?"

"Nothing."

"Do you want to go or not?"

"You don't want to," Karen said. "You'd rather be working at your office."

"No, I wouldn't. Come on."

Karen clicked the catch of her alligator purse open and shut. "You said it was boring."

"When did I say that?"

"You said it to Daddy, before he went away.

He asked if you wanted to go with us to the museum, and I heard you say it was boring."

Gail remembered. Dave had invited her to go along on Saturday. That was during a brief period when he felt guilty. She had told him to leave her alone, and a week later he was on his way to the Caribbean.

She said, "Well, I must have meant the exhibit they had at the time was boring."

Karen swung her head around, tilting her hat brim up far enough to glare at Gail. "This is the same exhibit."

"It is?"

"I told you last night. It's the cavemen."

Gail looked for the banner at the entrance. It read HUMANITY AT THE DAWN OF TIME, THROUGH SEPTEMBER. "You saw it already with your dad?"

Karen shook her head. "We went to the Seaquarium instead."

"So do you want to see it now?"

"I want to go home."

"Damn it!" Gail grabbed the steering wheel so hard she felt the jolt all the way up her arms. "I'm sorry I can't be your father! I'm sorry he decided to go off and play on his damn boat, but there is *nothing I can do about it!*"

Karen stared at her.

Gail dropped her forehead onto her hands.

The sun flashed off the windshield of a minivan parking nearby. The doors opened. A man and a woman and two kids got out. The woman unfolded a stroller and set the smaller child into it, and the man swung his son onto his hip. They all headed toward the museum. Gail closed her eyes. Her throat ached.

Before Dave left, the three of them had developed a balance, like equidistant points on a circle. Not necessarily happy, but at least they all understood where they were. Now the thing was out of whack. All the moves were wrong.

"I'm sorry for yelling at you, Karen. It wasn't your fault."

Karen was playing with the catch on her purse again. Her hair was in her eyes. Stringy, Gail noticed. She took off Karen's hat and combed through her hair with her fingers. Her forehead was sweaty.

"Let's trim your bangs before we go to Anthony's tonight."

Karen pulled her head away.

A desultory breeze shifted the branches, making a pattern of lacy shadows on the hood. At the entrance to the museum people were going in and out. Bright colors, kids running, a cart selling snow cones. The family she had seen earlier went inside.

"Never mind the museum. We'll come back when we feel like it."

"Okay."

From overhead came a raucous screech—a parrot of some kind. A twig dropped onto the roof of the car.

"You want to go somewhere with me?"

"Where?"

"We're going to play detective."

The blue eyes turned to her.

Gail took two dollar bills out of her wallet.

"Here. Buy us some snow cones while I make a phone call. Get me lemon. I don't want my mouth to turn purple."

Over the phone, Mark Brody said it was lucky she caught him. He was just leaving for lunch.

South Florida Forensics, owned by Brody and a partner, was located in a semi-industrial area west of the airport. Gail didn't think much of the flat-roofed, dusty building until he took her into the back and she saw the lab equipment and the shiny floors. It reminded her of college chemistry class—except that behind a soundproof steel door, there was a firing range and a stunning collection of weapons. Karen wanted to touch the MAC 10 and AK-47, which she recognized from TV. Gail had asked him to close the door.

Now she sat at a white-surfaced work table while Brody bent over the wills and letters she had laid out. He had a lighted magnifying lens the size of a saucer supported on a goose-necked stand.

She fidgeted on the hard lab stool. "Can you tell if it's her signature?"

His nose was six inches from the table. "Give me a minute." Brody matched the lab: smooth-surfaced, precise. Graying hair clipped military style. Short-sleeved white shirt, no tie. Gail supposed he played with computers when he got home at night.

She spotted Karen adjusting the focus on a microscope. "Karen, don't touch that."

Brody didn't look up. "She won't break it.

Now, the electron microscope I would worry about."

Karen said, "I know how to do it. We have microscopes at school."

"Go get some sugar crystals. Or a bug. There's a roach trap under the coffee machine."

"Cool." She vanished into the other room.

"Karen—" But she was gone.

Brody looked up at Gail. "Roach traps aren't toxic to humans, unless you eat them."

"Well. That's good to know." She glanced around the lab. "So. Did you get a degree in this? Examining documents, I mean."

"Not really." He moved another of Althea Tillett's letters under the magnifier and peered at it. "You learn as you go." His eyes moved to her for a second, then back to the paper. He smiled. "Degree in chemical engineering from Georgia Tech. Six years Naval Intelligence, fourteen with the Miami P.D. crime lab, then five as chief document examiner for Metro-Dade. Now I'm over there three days a week, the rest of the time here. I've taught at the FBI, the Treasury Department, the Florida Department of Law Enforcement. Member, American Academy of Forensic Scientists, Southern Association of—"

"Okay." Gail laughed. "I submit the witness as qualified, your honor."

He settled the glasses back down on his nose. "Now then. About this will. What I usually do is submit a written report. However, my buddy Anthony Quintana said to be nice to you."

"Thank you for doing this," Gail said.

"He's good people," Brody said. "One of the

95

few criminal attorneys I have any respect for, to tell you the truth." He set the magnifier aside and leaned an elbow on the table, loosely clasping his hands. "Got a few questions about Mrs. Tillett. Age?"

"Fifty-eight."

"How was her health as of August third?"

"Fine, as far as I know."

"No drugs, no medication?"

"I don't think so," Gail said.

"Did she drink?"

"A social drinker. She was drinking the night she died."

He turned the papers around so Gail could see them. "These memos and letters are in Mrs. Tillett's own handwriting, so they're our standards. Likewise the signatures on the prior wills. Notice the variation in the memos and the wills. That's because people sign their names differently, depending on what they're signing. For example, you zip through a check, and you take more time with a business letter. Now, if you're signing a will, that's an important occasion." Brody smiled. "Although maybe not for Mrs. Tillett, since she wrote a will every other year."

"Three in the last year alone," said Gail. "Assuming the August will is genuine."

"The point being," Brody said, "the memos aren't going to look like the wills, but you expect that, so you don't get thrown off. You look for the subtleties, like the angles and the distance between letters. Or the height ratio—height of capitals compared to lower-case letters."

He laid half a dozen memos side by side.

"These standards are originals, not copies. You can see that Mrs. Tillett had her own characteristic way of writing, as we all do. The angle, the amount of pressure we use, where we lift the pen, and so forth. It's automatic. We write and we don't even think about it. Mrs. Tillett took more time with her wills, but that ingrained way of moving the pen across the paper is still going to be there."

He nodded to the papers within Gail's reach. "Let me have the three most recent wills, but not the August will. Not yet." Each copy was already flipped to Althea Tillett's signature, and Brody put them in a row. "Look at the angle of the capital letters—the T particularly. You get some variation, but not much. The memos are signed faster—see how the pen lifts?—but there's that same angle, still more or less the same height ratio. Now hand me the August will."

Gail put it to the right of the others. "I don't see much difference."

"If we had the original in front of us, we could look for variations in pen pressure and speed. You'd see the actual indentations in the paper. But you're right. This signature on page six— rather, a copy of the signature on page six—is consistent with the standards. However—" He flipped to the beginning. "She also signed the bottom of every page. The usual practice with wills, right?"

Gail bent closer. Brody overlapped the pages of the August will so that all the signatures showed. Six of them.

"Let's say you're going to forge a will," he said.

"You spend time on the last page. In fact, with these laser printers now, you can spit out fifty copies of page six and sign until it looks perfect. But say you get a little lazy with the other pages."

His forefinger landed beside *Althea Norris Tillett* on page three.

"Ahhhh. The double R's. No loops at the top."

"Not just that. The angle is different." His finger moved to page five. "Here the spacing is off. And there are a few other points I could mention."

Gail straightened slowly. "It's a forgery. Is that what you mean?"

"No, I never say that. What I can tell you is that one of the signatures on the August third will is consistent with the decedent's standards, two are indeterminate, and three are not consistent."

"Mr. Brody. You sound like you're testifying for the defendants."

"Ms. Connor, only God almighty or the people in that room could testify that Mrs. Tillett did not sign this will."

"All right, then. I'll rephrase the question. Mr. Brody, as a document examiner qualified as an expert by this court, do you have an opinion as to whether Althea Tillett signed this will?"

He fell into the game. "Yes, counselor, I do."

"And what is that opinion, sir?"

"My opinion is that she did not." He raised a hand. "Given that I haven't examined the original August will, you understand."

Gail leaned against the edge of the table, the

implications of this beginning to hit her. "Could that change your opinion, sir?"

He dropped the persona of expert witness. "Between you and me? I doubt it."

Across the room Karen stood on her knees in a chair, squinting through the microscope. Brody called to her. "What have you got there, assistant crime tech? Find any bugs?"

She grinned at him. Her lips were still red from the cherry snow cone she had bought outside the Science Museum. "Roach legs."

"Some kid you got there," Brody said.

Gail rested her forearms on the work table and stared at the will. "They did a good job, didn't they? Signed, sealed, and notarized. How hard is it to forge a notary seal, by the way?"

"Don't do that. Pay the notary, it's easier."

"And the attorney?"

Brody shook his head. "Mine is not to reason why, counselor."

She ran her finger along the name of the law firm printed at the bottom of the pages. "I suppose it's possible Rudy and Monica Tillett stole the paper from Alan Weissman's office."

"So why isn't Weissman screaming?"

After another moment, Gail said, "Maybe it wasn't Rudy and Monica at all. Maybe it was one of the other beneficiaries. Maybe it was Jessica Simms. What do you think?"

"I don't like to speculate, but—" He shook his head. "I'd start with the stepkids."

Gail asked, "Have you ever seen anything like this before?"

"In twenty-seven years? You bet. And good

luck getting these folks to admit what day it is."
Brady's stool creaked a little when he reached
over to turn the light on his magnifier off.
"Another question for you. Mrs. Tillett alone
when she died?"

"Alone? Yes. My mother and the two other
women had already left. The housekeeper found
her body in the morning."

"Is Miami Beach P.D. investigating?"

"They did at one point. My mother said they
questioned everybody who was there that night.
They told her it was routine. They even took her
fingerprints."

"Uh-huh. For elimination, matching against
others they might have found in the house. What
does the death certificate have for cause of
death?"

"Well . . . accidental, I suppose."

"You suppose? See if it says 'pending.' That
means they haven't made up their mind yet if she
fell or if somebody helped her down the stairs."
When Gail only looked at him, he added, "Well,
it's a big estate. You know. Makes you think."

Finally she said, "No. I didn't think of that."

"One thing I've noticed about people with
money. The more they have, the more other
people will do to get their hands on it."

"You mean Rudy and Monica Tillett—"

"Or whoever stood to benefit. Could be
anybody. I'm a frustrated detective, what can I
tell you?" He gathered the papers. "Let's fire up
the copy machine. You want the originals back
or do I keep them?"

"I'll keep them for now," Gail said. She

followed him across the room, mulling over the thought of someone shoving Althea Tillett down her stairs. Unlikely. If the police thought that, it would have hit the news by now. If Patrick had been questioned, he would have told her.

Brody pushed a button, and the copier began to whirr. "So Gail. What do I do, wait to hear from you?"

She knew her next step: persuade the management committee at Hartwell Black to give her the green light. She said, "I'll be back in touch next week. What's the procedure if we hire you?"

"We charge one seventy-five an hour, four hour minimum, plus costs. Is that acceptable?"

"Certainly." If the firm let her take this case.

"Usually we require an advance, but since Quintana thinks you're okay, I'll send a bill." Brody stood by the copier, one hand on his hip. A narrow belt ran through the loops of his brown polyester slacks, and he had the girth of a man over fifty. But not sloppy. Solid.

He seemed to be thinking, then said, "I'll photograph the original with a macro lens so we can blow it up for demonstrative evidence in court. And I may ask you to get a subpoena so we can snip a tiny piece of the paper, to see if it matches paper from Mrs. Tillett's lawyer. You'll need to subpoena some samples from Weissman too. Doubt he'd give them to you voluntarily."

Brody laid the will facedown and hit the button.

"Who do you think the other side will hire?" she asked.

"Don't know. There aren't too many qualified

people in the area. Three or four in Dade County, a couple up in Broward. Excuse the way this sounds, but most guys, they know my partner and me are on one side, they don't like to get on the other. So maybe your defendants will get somebody from out of state." His hands had become like machines, flipping pages, pushing buttons, an effortless rhythm.

"But it says something to the judge when they can't find someone local. One thing you can be sure of. With this amount of money, they'll keep looking till they find somebody who'll say what they want to hear."

"I'm lucky I got you before they did," she said.

"Doesn't matter who calls me first. That won't change my opinion."

"Unlike hiring an attorney?"

He laughed. "Hate to say it, but you're right about that."

chapter seven

By the time they arrived at Anthony Quintana's townhouse on Key Biscayne, it was nearly six o'clock. Karen had dawdled in the bathtub, then complained of a stomachache. Finally Gail had lost her temper and yelled at her. They had hardly spoken on the drive.

Gail kissed Anthony's cheek at the door.

"Sorry we're late. You know. Traffic on the causeway."

"You should have a phone in your car."

"Oh, stop. You and my mother."

Karen had gone past them and now stood at the edge of the living room, looking around. The house was immaculate, with a dark green, L-shaped leather sofa, area rugs on Mexican tile, and track lighting over the bookcases. Karen wore a fresh T-shirt and shorts, but her usual grungy, unlaced white sneakers. The alligator purse was slung across her chest, and her green and orange Hurricanes baseball cap sat squarely on her head, the ponytail hanging out the back.

Anthony walked over to her, his hand out. "Ah, Karen. *Bienvenida, mi cielo. Cómo estás?*" After a second, she shook his hand. He smiled.

"It means welcome, and how are you? Your mother says you are studying Spanish in school."

Gail gave her a hug around the shoulders. "And getting an A, too."

"*Que bueno.*"

"But I prefer to speak English," Karen said.

He glanced at Gail. "All right. English." Another smile at Karen. He gestured at the purse. "You are a young lady now. I see, carrying a handbag."

She only looked at him.

"Ah . . . ha. Well." He clapped his hands together, as if he had remembered something. "I have a surprise for you. And for your mother, of course. We're going to have dinner at Biscayne Billy's and tie up at the dock. Look." He moved to the French doors at the other end of his living room, gesturing as he walked. "A boat."

Gail followed him. "So this is why you told us to wear something casual." She could see past the screened patio to the inlet behind his house, where a sleek red and white speedboat waited at the sea wall. Not just a speedboat. A Cigarette offshore racer with a radar arch over the stern. "My God. You didn't buy that, did you?"

"No, no. It belongs to Raul." His law partner had a waterfront home near Coconut Grove. Gail had met Raul Ferrer. He was married and middle age, with four kids. She would never have expected a boat like this.

"What do you think?" he asked.

"It looks awfully fast. He showed you how to handle it, didn't he?"

"Gail, please. Of course."

Karen was still standing by the sofa. Anthony walked back to her. "Would you like to see the house? I'll take you on a tour when we come back. I rented three videos in case we want to watch a movie later. *Beauty and the Beast*. And two more they gave me, I can't remember which. But we should leave now, so we can watch the sun set while we eat."

Gail bit her lip to keep from smiling. She had never seen Anthony Quintana remotely nervous, ever.

Karen turned to her. "May I use the rest room, please?"

Gail took her to the one in the hall, closed the door and lectured her about her manners, then left her there. She found Anthony in his kitchen packing a zippered bag: cookies, sodas, a Thermos, cups and napkins. All this for a two-mile boat trip. He wiped a smudge of something off the counter and hung the towel neatly by the sink. He had Belgian cookware, spices she had never heard of, tiled countertops, and solid oak cabinets. An espresso maker gleamed from one corner. There were no spatters on the stainless steel stove, no drips of jelly on the floor, and no dust kittens under the refrigerator.

Gail leaned against the end of the counter, which had four chairs at precise right angles to the other side. She watched him zip the bag.

"Sorry Karen's being so bratty," she said.

He turned around. "Ah, well. This is new for her. And for me, having a child here." His own children, teenagers, had both moved to New Jersey with their mother four years ago. He saw them when he could.

"You're a grand host," she said.

He shrugged. "I hope she has a good time tonight. By the way, what does she keep in that purse?"

"I have no idea." Gail smiled. "Why, Antonio, your *rodillas* are showing."

Puzzled, he looked down. He was wearing a white pullover and crisply pressed, navy-blue shorts, revealing pale skin and a fuzz of dark hair down to his boat shoes. "My knees?"

"I thought Cuban men didn't wear shorts," she said.

He shook his head slowly. "Where do you hear such things?" His eyes came back to hers, deepest

105

brown, shadowed with black lashes. He had just shaved; his skin glowed.

She felt a flutter low in her belly and let out a breath.

They met halfway across the kitchen, diving into each other. She locked her arms around his neck, and he slid his hands down to cup her backside. He squeezed and her heart rate shot up. His lips found her ear, then her mouth. They broke from another kiss then noticed Karen standing by the refrigerator with her eyes narrowed.

Anthony took a step backward. "Well. Are we ready to go?" He smoothed his hair and put on a turquoise Florida Marlins baseball cap. He patted her on the head as he walked by. "The 'Canes aren't bad for a college team."

Karen glared at him behind his back. Gail whispered, "Don't say a word. I mean it."

After setting the burglar alarm and locking the doors, he led them down the rear steps and across the thick grass. His townhouse was one of a dozen that curved around a quiet inlet in a canal that led west to Biscayne Bay. Two sailboats and a sportfisher were tied at other docks. Raul Ferrer's boat had a stiletto prow, two form-fitting white seats in front, a padded bench just behind, a dashboard like an airplane, and four chrome exhausts at the stern. A hatch led to a small cabin below. The boat seemed to crouch by the dock like a feral cat, ready to leap.

When Karen jumped aboard Anthony handed her a bright orange life vest. "Here. This should fit. Raul has a daughter about your size."

Karen didn't take it. "Are you and Mom wearing one?"

"No. We're adults and we can swim."

"So can I."

"Look, it's the color of the Miami Hurricanes."

"I don't want to if nobody else is."

He turned his face to Gail, eyes shaded by his cap. Gail said, "Put it on, Karen. I'll wear one too."

For a few seconds Anthony said nothing, then announced he would go below to find one more. Gail took Karen's hat off, dropped the vest over her head, and helped her adjust the buckles.

"How come he doesn't have to wear a life vest?"

"Because it's his boat."

"No, it's not."

"Stop it, will you?" Gail fluffed Karen's bangs. She hadn't meant to cut them so short, halfway between eyebrows and hairline. "Please? For me?" She handed back the hat.

Anthony gave Gail a life vest, then stepped back to the dock to untie the lines at bow and stern and flip the ropes onto the boat. Gail wanted to tell him somebody else should do it while he started the engine, or they would drift away, but he was already coming back aboard, sliding into the captain's seat on the right.

Gail cinched the straps on her vest, a slick yellow ski vest with reflective stripes at the neck— in case the wearer fell overboard at night, she supposed. She wished the boat had seat belts.

From the front passenger seat Karen watched

him turn one of the keys. There were two of them. Two monstrous engines, Gail realized. The starter whirred. He tried again. Karen swung her legs. "My father used to have a lot of boats. He's in St. Thomas at the moment. That's in the U.S. Virgin Islands."

Anthony smiled at her. "Yes. I know." He turned the other key. Another whirr. They had drifted halfway across the inlet. Gail was standing now, ready to push them away from the sportfisher.

Karen said, "He has a sailboat, a forty-foot sloop. It's bigger than this boat. He lets me sail it. I think he'll be back around Christmas."

"You can be my special boat consultant." Finally the engine snarled and spat, then settled to a low growl. He gave the other key a turn, and that engine also began to rumble.

Gail tapped Karen's shoulder. "Sit in the back. I get the front seat. Privilege of age."

In the bright orange vest, Karen climbed over the rear seat, then sat on the long, padded rear deck that covered the engines.

"You should sit on the seat." Anthony said.

"I won't fall off. We're not even making a wake." She held on to the stainless steel railing along one side.

Anthony's fingers drummed for a second on the wheel. He shrugged and put the boat into gear. Slowly the ridiculously long bow swung around. Gail could feel the heavy vibrations through her feet, as if there were a beast underneath the deck gathering its muscles to break through the fiberglass and steel. She straight-armed the dash, checked Karen, then said, "Take it easy when you give it the gas, okay?"

Muttering in Spanish, Anthony sat back down. At no-wake speed they maneuvered out of the inlet then along the canal. The air was sticky with humidity but not as hot. The sun was turning orange above the horizon.

Gail said, "She isn't usually like this. I don't know what's the matter with her."

"You don't?"

"Be patient, will you?"

"I am." Anthony's eyes flicked to the rearview mirror. "I'm very patient."

Gail stood up, crossing her arms on the wrap-around Plexiglas windshield. Karen was a hard topic, better avoided. She took off her sunglasses and tilted her face into the breeze. A smaller boat putted past and the couple in it waved cheerily. Gail waved back. Water gurgled in the channel, sparkling in the lowering light.

She looked around at Anthony. He was watching her and reached over to pull her closer with an arm around her waist. Gail lifted off his cap to kiss him on the top of his head. His hair was thick and wavy and smelled of spicy shampoo and fresh air. He leaned his cheek against her chest for a moment, then let her go.

"Guess who I saw today," Gail said. "Your pal Mark Brody."

"Pour us a daiquiri, why don't you? What did he say?"

She found the bag Anthony had brought, Thermos of frozen daiquiris inside, then told him the gist of the conversation: the signatures didn't look like Althea Tillett's. It wasn't enough to guarantee a win, but enough to start digging.

She sipped her drink, then set the insulated glass into the holder on the dashboard. Polished chrome, designed to swing when the boat moved. She wondered if anyone had ever baited a hook in this floating rocket. Behind her, Karen was flat on her stomach, barefoot, watching the water churn slowly past the stern. She had a little stack of cookies beside her.

Gail turned around. "Next week I'll talk to the management committee about letting me take the case."

"You'll make some money," he said.

"Maybe a few extra thousand dollars at the end of the year when they hand out bonuses."

"That's it?"

"The partners get a percentage, not us poor associates."

Anthony squinted into the sun, pointing the boat to the north. They were coming into Biscayne Bay, and the boat moved with the deeper swells. "I don't understand. Why do you work for a law firm which pays you so little, tells you what cases you may have, robs you of your family life . . ." He lowered his voice. "It doesn't surprise me she is so jealous. She has too little of you as it is."

"Make me feel guilty. Look. I've worked for Hartwell Black since before I graduated from law school. Yes, the pressure can be murderous, but finally it's coming together for me. Partners can set their own schedules, hire extra staff. My God, I might even be able to work normal hours."

"Then you tell them—" He turned the wheel a little, watching ahead. "Tell them if you win this case, you want a partnership. Make them do that for you. Otherwise, you leave."

She took a swallow of daiquiri, the slushy ice chilling her mouth. "I'd almost say it just to see Paul Robineau's reaction."

"And what will you do if they don't accept the case?"

She laughed. "Maybe show up at your office, how about that? You and Raul need a good civil trial attorney?"

Under the hat brim Anthony's face was bathed in gold light. He didn't answer right away, then said, "Is this something you've been thinking about?"

"No. Not really." She finished her drink and dropped the empty glass into the holder. "I do appreciate the enthusiastic response, though."

"Gail." His look was gently chastising.

She grinned at him. "Would I get to bring Patrick with me?"

"No."

A little way past the mouth of the channel he turned around in his seat. "Karen! Sit down. I'm going to go faster, and I don't want you to fall out."

She scooted forward to the edge and put her bare feet on the bench seat. Her sneakers lay upside down on the deck behind her.

"On the seat, please."

"I can't see from down there."

Before Gail could speak, Anthony took the boat out of gear, stood up, and pointed. "Sit on

the seat. Now. And put your shoes on the floor."
Chooz. His Spanish accent came through when
he was angry.

The two of them glared at each other from
under the bills of their baseball caps. Then Karen
retrieved her shoes and slid down into the seat.

Gail held back a laugh. "Aye, aye, Captain.
Karen, come up here with me." She stretched
around the front seat to take Karen's arm and
pull her into her lap. The life vests were bulky
between them.

Anthony pushed forward on the throttle. The
pitch of the engines rose from a deep growl to a
roar. The stern sank and the bow shot upward.
The Thermos of daiquiris flew off the dashboard
and bounced on the carpeted deck.

Gail shrieked.

Karen swung her head around to look at her,
laughing. Her ponytail whirled under her hat.
After a second the boat leveled out, but the water
was a hissing, foaming rush. Gail clutched Karen
around the waist.

"Mom. Mom! Let go!" She pointed at the
speedometer and yelled, "It's only thirty miles
an hour!" The speedometer, Gail noticed, went
all the way to eighty.

"Oh, God." The shoreline was scrolling past
on their right, tile-roofed houses and green lawns.
Kids playing in a pool. A woman trimming her
roses. The sea beside the boat was a blur.

Karen tugged on Anthony's arm. "Go faster!"

"We can't, this close to shore."

She bounced up and down on Gail's lap,

shouting over the roar of the engines. "Anthony, let me do it! Please?"

"You know how?"

"Yes! Yes!"

Gail yelled, "No!"

Karen wriggled away. Anthony stood her between his knees. "Turn it south. Let's go around the ocean side."

"We're going into the *ocean?*"

"Gail, don't worry, it's okay."

The horizon tilted. The Miami skyline moved around the bow, then swung to the stern. Anthony stood up behind Karen and his hat flew off, sailing up and back, a spiraling dot that bounced once on the wake, then vanished. He looked after it for only an instant. The wind whipped through his dark hair. He pushed Karen's hat down on her head. She was holding on tightly to the wheel, squinting over the top of it, flexing her legs with the rhythm of the boat. The water hissed under the hull.

"Oh, God!" Gail clamped her fingers into the armrests.

The boat skipped from one crest to the next, the seat rising and falling.

Anthony shouted, "Gail, look at her. She can do it!" His arms extended around Karen, not quite touching, and his hands were poised at the wheel.

chapter eight

The management committee of Hartwell Black and Robineau was comprised of six of the seventeen partners. Gail tracked them down at lunch, in the corridors, or in their offices. More law firm business got done that way than in formal meetings. She told them about Patrick Norris and the phony will.

Larry Black had been surprisingly noncommittal. Jack Warner, head of litigation, wanted to hear more. Paul Robineau, with no time to listen, requested a memo. Cy Mackey from real estate and zoning had laughed. He said, "Hey. Rock and roll." The head corporate lawyer, Bill Schoenfeld, said he would wait to hear what everyone else thought. Forrest Putney, the oldest member of the firm, had invited Gail to attend the meeting.

The committee convened late Monday afternoon, their regular month-end get-together. It was nearly six o'clock before they called Gail in to explain why she wanted the firm to take on Patrick Norris as a client.

Paul Robineau, who might have been counting the little holes in the acoustical ceiling tile as she spoke, swung his chair back toward the table. "Questions? Anyone?"

The six men looked tired, and the room stank

of cigarettes. Papers, coffee cups, calculators, and files littered the polished oval table. Gail sat next to Larry Black along one side.

Cy Mackey grinned at her from under his brushy, gray-streaked mustache. "Jesus. Fifteen mill. You sure about that?"

"It's a fair estimate. I did a real estate title search and came up with a list of holdings Patrick Norris didn't know about. Without the inventory, this is the best we can do for now. It could go higher."

"Rock and roll. Hey, Jack." Cy Mackey tapped a rhythm on the table. "What are the numbers on a case like this? I'm talking fees."

Warner, tie loosened and jacket off, was reaching around to refill his coffee cup from the pot on the credenza behind them. In his late fifties, one of the state's top litigators, Warner had to be pulling down well over a million a year. He could walk into a courtroom and hypnotize a jury. Uncanny. Lately the talk was that if Jack Warner had his way, he and Paul Robineau would move the firm out of the cramped quarters on Flagler Street and into one of the sparkling towers on Brickell Avenue.

Warner was a tall, slender man with thinning gray hair and heavy-lidded eyes, which now moved toward Cy Mackey. "I'd want to go with the standard contingency fee. Thirty percent if settled, forty if it goes to trial, fifty on appeal."

"Excuse me?" Gail said. Everyone looked at her. "Six million dollars for a trial? Isn't that a bit much? I quoted the client an hourly rate."

Warner smiled slightly. "Hourly?"

"Two-fifty office, three hundred in court."

He and Robineau exchanged a look.

Paul Robineau said, "Gail. Please don't tell me that you agreed to a fee before you discussed this matter with us."

"No, I gave Mr. Norris an estimate. But I in no way intimated that he'd be paying a standard contingency fee. I've never used that for commercial litigation. It's for tort cases. Personal injury."

Robineau raised an eyebrow. "I believe fraud is a tort. Have they changed the law?"

Larry Black said, "Lay off, Paul. You know what she means."

Three of the lawyers started talking at once. From the other end of the table, Forrest Putney tapped the bowl of his pipe on his coffee cup and waited for quiet.

"Ms. Connor is correct," he said. "It's exorbitant." Putney's hair stood out from his pink scalp like dandelion fluff, and age spots dotted his forehead. He was wearing a seersucker jacket and a red bow tie. Fifty years ago, returning from the war with a Navy Cross, Putney had clerked for the firm's original founding members.

"You'd be in probate court, gentlemen. The probate judges don't like big fees. Takes money from the heirs." He gripped his pipe in his teeth and felt around in the inside pocket of his jacket, retrieving a thin green book. He thumbed through the tattered pages. The title read *Florida Bar Minimum Fee Schedule 1970*.

Putney spoke around his pipe. "The old guideline for contingency fees in will contests is fifteen percent. I wouldn't go over that."

116

Mackey snickered. "Fuckin' book's a little out of date, isn't it, Forrest?"

Robineau raised a hand. "We'll get to this later. Are there any more questions for Ms. Connor?"

"If I'm going to do this case," Gail said, "I expect to have some input as to what we charge."

Cy Mackey grinned. He glanced at Robineau, who was playing with his pen. Robineau said slowly, "Ms. Connor. On major cases, this committee assigns counsel and determines the amount of attorneys' fees."

She felt her stomach tense. "I know the policy. I also know that Patrick Norris will go somewhere else if he thinks we're overreaching."

Robineau made a smile. "Something of a conundrum, isn't it? He wants you. He doesn't want you if you charge the going rate. What do you suggest?"

"Fifteen percent would probably be acceptable to him, against an hourly rate of three hundred. Ten percent if it's settled, twenty on appeal. Plus costs. If other attorneys at the firm become involved—Mr. Warner, for instance—the hourly rate would go up accordingly."

Jack Warner asked, "Is it winnable at trial?"

"I never guarantee—"

He swiveled his chair around. "I'm not a client you're talking to. You want a twenty grand cost advance. I want to know what we get for it. Do you believe the case is winnable or not?"

"Winnable, yes," Gail said. "I wouldn't recommend it otherwise. And remember we have security—the $250,000 cash bequest to Patrick

Norris." She casually poured herself a glass of water. Her mouth was going dry.

Mackey laughed. "Come on, Jack. This kind of fee potential and you've got a bug up your ass about twenty grand?"

Schoenfeld took another pull on his cigarette. He was pushing sixty and overstuffed on deli food from years in smoky conference rooms. "So even if we lose, we can't lose. So to speak."

Larry got out of his chair and took his coffee cup to the insulated pot on the credenza. The curtains were drawn. Already the light behind them was fading. "I don't like it." He glanced at Gail—apologetically, she thought. He said, "We'd catch more hell than it's worth."

"Who from?" Mackey asked. "What are you talking about?"

"I'm talking about the charities who'd think we were taking their money." He lifted the top off the porcelain sugar bowl. "They'd be right too."

Gail had expected opposition, but not from Larry. Warner's gaze was fixed on the opposite wall. The two men worked together, but apparently they had not agreed on this one.

Larry measured two level teaspoons of sugar. "Yes, we might collect a sizable fee. But this is one case. What about the long term? My God. Killing a half-million-dollar bequest to the University of Miami? I'm on the Orange Bowl Committee, let me remind you." He laughed. "They'd cancel our season tickets. Oh, hell. It isn't that. The point is, you don't screw the people who count in this town. You don't even allow

118

the perception that you're screwing the people who count."

Schoenfeld chuckled. "I'm worried what my wife would do to me. She plays golf with Weissman's wife, Mona."

Jack Warner leaned back with his hands locked behind his head. "You know, Alan and I did a seminar for the Bar a couple of years ago. I think he was slipping, even then."

Mackey poked Schoenfeld. "I was in Sally Russell's the other day at lunch and he was slipping off his fuckin' barstool."

"Yeah, but forge a will," Schoenfeld said. "What a dumb-ass thing to do. He drinks, but he's not stupid. Is he on coke or something? Is he screwing Monica Tillett? What?"

"May I remind you, gentlemen—" Forrest Putney's voice, honed on forty years of trial work, could still resonate. "We in this firm do not question the integrity of fellow members of the Bar without cause."

"Sorry, Forrest." Mackey smoothed his mustache, trying to look serious.

Schoenfeld spoke to Gail over Larry's empty chair. "What about conflicts? Did you run all these names through the computer? I can't believe we don't represent at least one of the beneficiaries. I'm not talking about your mother. She's willing to let the ring go. We've got no problem with that."

Gail said, "There is one minor thing. We advised the YMCA last year with relation to renewal of their lease."

Paul Robineau asked, "Are we on retainer?"

119

When Gail shook her head, he added, "So they aren't a current client."

"Paul." Forrest Putney looked pained.

"Forrest is right." Larry Black set his cup down on the table but remained standing behind his chair, stirring, the spoon clinking, clinking in the cup. "It's a conflict." He looked at Gail. "Did they send us a letter terminating our representation? Anything?"

She had to admit she didn't know.

Warner sighed. "Larry, forget it."

Gail could guess what Warner would do. If the YMCA complained, he'd ask Patrick to pay the amount listed in the will. Five grand. A cost of doing business.

Mackey said, "Hey, Larry, you going to drill a hole in that cup or what?"

Still frowning, Schoenfeld tapped his ashes into a cut-glass ashtray already full of butts. "What about this residuary beneficiary? What about that?"

Gail said, "The Easton Charitable Trust. They get the leftovers, whatever's not otherwise mentioned in the will, which should amount to quite a pile of cash, even after the other beneficiaries collect. Easton has an office on Brickell Avenue and a phone number in the book."

"Which I assume you called."

"I did. A woman answered—very cultured voice. I pretended to be doing an article on local charities for the *Miami Business Review*. She told me that the Easton Trust was established in 1937, that their projects are strictly confidential, and that the man who runs it is G. Howard Odell. The executive director."

She glanced at Larry, who was hiding behind his coffee cup. He knew Howard Odell, but he wasn't going to say so, and she wasn't going to bring it up first, not here. "Howard Odell was out of the office. The woman offered to have him call me, but I said no. I'd given her a false name."

Cy Mackey laughed. "Hey."

Gail went on, "The chairman of the board is Sanford V. Ehringer, currently residing on South River Drive." She added, "Ehringer is also the P.R. of the estate."

Larry lowered his cup. "Say again?"

"Sanford Ehringer is the personal representative. The executor."

Schoenfeld said, "Sanford Ehringer. Shit."

"What's the deal? Who's he?" Mackey asked.

Larry looked at Paul Robineau. "We'd be suing Sanford Ehringer."

"In name only, Larry. Don't get into a panic. His legal expenses would come out of the estate."

"I know that, dammit."

Mackey repeated, "Who's Sanford Ehringer?"

Larry walked to the end of the table and smiled, making an effort. "Paul. Tell me. What is Ehringer going to think if we try to grab the money Althea Tillett left to his favorite charity?"

"He'll think it's business. I'm not going to sit here worrying what the hell Sanford Ehringer will think. If we don't take this case, another firm will."

"Of all the asinine—" Larry's cheeks flushed. He thought better of whatever else he had to say and stalked to the other end of the room. Gail had suspected these men resented each other, but she hadn't known until now how much. They weren't fighting over Althea Tillett's will. They wanted to control the law firm. Blood was beginning to spatter the table.

Mackey said, "Ehringer lives on South River Drive? Nobody lives there. It's a bunch of boatyards and scuzzy apartments."

"You are mistaken, Cy," Forrest Putney announced. "If you had been reared here, you might know. At one time, South River Drive was home to some of the most exclusive estates in Miami. Most have been sold off and divided. Ehringer's remains."

"Okay, I'll ask one more time. Who the hell is he?"

Putney took time to relight his pipe, then expelled a puff of smoke upward. "Sanford Vanderbilt Ehringer served as ambassador to Greece after the war. He has been a guest of royalty. He speaks five or six languages. He plays the violin, writes poetry, collects rare tropical plants. He owns—" Putney seemed at a loss. "God knows what he owns."

Gail exchanged a glance with Mackey across the table. "Vanderbilt? As in, *the* New York philanthropist Vanderbilts?"

"Yes. A cousin." Putney spoke around the stem of his pipe. "Perhaps because of that, or from a natural distrust of publicity, he places great value on anonymity. His family wintered here and in Palm Beach. Sandy stayed, didn't like the cold. I've advised him from time to time.

Nothing within the last few years, however." Putney cocked a bushy white eyebrow at Gail. "If you need his phone number, I have it."

Warner said, "I met Ehringer at a reception when President Bush was in town. He was old then. What is he now, Paul? Eighty?"

"At least." Paul Robineau seemed to be watching Larry Black pace along the narrow room. In his dark suit, Larry could have been dressed for a funeral.

Mackey asked Gail, "Who was Easton?"

"I don't know," she said. "I couldn't find a record of anyone by that name." She looked around. "Do any of you know?"

There were only blank stares, even from Forrest Putney. Gail wasn't certain what they meant. Ignorance or an unwillingness to say?

Schoenfeld lit another cigarette, then played with the matchbook cover. "Easton. I know where I heard the name now. My department did some work for somebody from Easton."

Gail said, "Howard Odell?" She looked at Larry, but he was still pacing.

Schoenfeld exhaled smoke. "Well, shit. I can't remember if it was the Easton Trust or Odell. If it was the trust, we'd have a problem."

"We would indeed," Larry noted. "A clear conflict of interest."

"That kid from Michigan Law handled it. Ramsay. Let me see if I can track him down." Cigarette in a corner of his mouth, he heaved himself out of his chair and reached for one of the three phones in the room, got through to the receptionist and asked her to find Eric Ramsay,

123

if he was still around, and have him call the conference room on fifteen.

Jack Warner was annoyed. "If we refused every case where we were remotely connected to anyone affected by the outcome, we'd lose half our client base. So would every other large firm in Miami."

Still standing, Schoenfeld leaned his forearms on the back of his chair, belly hanging, and passed a hand over his bald head. "It's not just conflict of interest I'm worried about. I think we could get around that and take the damn case if we want it. What I think is, we're going to get our asses kicked out of court without the proof. I want more than some ex-cop saying Althea Tillett didn't sign the will. I want carved-on-stone, appeal-resistant proof."

Hand cupped at his mouth, Cy Mackey made a stage whisper. "Hey, Bill." He pointed at Gail's file. "We've still got the quarter million bucks."

Gail gave him a look. "No. That isn't a good enough reason to take this case. It isn't only about money. And if we turn it down, it shouldn't be because of who we're afraid to offend. Althea Tillett's will was forged. Someone screwed Patrick Norris out of his inheritance. He came to me—to us—for help."

"Bravo!" Putney laughed, his pale, mottled cheeks growing ruddy. He leaned over and squeezed her shoulder. "Good for you."

Robineau asked her, "What are the chances of settlement?"

"Depends on what I can find out, who did what. Possibly Rudy and Monica Tillett would pay Patrick fair market value for the house and art collection. If Weissman had a hand in this, he'd have to kick in. I don't know what Patrick would accept. Fifteen million dollars is a lot to lose. Even half that, after taxes."

There was silence around the table. Putney finally said, "If Alan Weissman did participate, we are obliged to notify the Bar."

Bill Schoenfeld dropped back into his chair. "Who gets that honor? You do it, Forrest. You're retiring."

Larry Black said quietly, "Poor Alan. I hope he wasn't involved."

"Shit. Tell me how he couldn't be," Mackey said.

A knock sounded on the door, and Robineau swung around in his chair, annoyed. "Who is it?"

It was Eric Ramsay, pinstripes and suspenders, his sandy hair as rumpled as his long-sleeved white shirt. "Mr. Schoenfeld, you were looking for me?"

"I said call. You didn't have to come up."

"It's okay. I was just in the library."

Schoenfeld said, "Last year we did some work for somebody connected to the Easton Charitable Trust. Who was it?"

Eric took a second, looking at the faces turned to him. "Howard Odell, I believe."

"What about?"

"He was selling some real estate and I reviewed the contract for tax consequences."

"How did he happen to ask you to do that?"

"We met playing racquetball. I said I had some

125

ideas that he could use. He was interested and we talked."

"Did it involve the trust in any regard?"

"No, it was his own personal business."

"Anything to do with Sanford Ehringer or Althea Tillett?"

"I don't recall those names."

"Is Odell still our client?"

"No, I only handled that one matter for him."

"Okay. Thank you."

Eric looked around the room again, apparently mystified. When Bill Schoenfeld told him that was all, he nodded and went out, closing the door.

Robineau announced, "No conflict there."

"No, not there," Larry said. "Just with our existing clients. I hope you can explain it to them when this hits the news, as it surely will. Explain why we want to take the millions of dollars that Althea Tillett left to charity and give it all to her estranged nephew."

Robineau pinned him with a hard gray stare. "Speaking of conflict of interest, Larry. Didn't you and Althea Tillett belong to the same church?"

"Yes. Miami Shores Presbyterian."

Gail hadn't heard this before. Larry had known Althea Tillett.

He went on, "And yes, Paul, she made a bequest of two hundred thousand dollars. Which is precisely the point. Do you have any idea how many of our clients attend that church?"

"What are we? A law firm or a country club?"

126

"You don't survive by alienating prominent members of society."

"What society? The only society we're going to alienate is Rudy Tillett and his sister and the South Beach-Warsaw Ballroom-afternoon tea dance crowd."

"Watch it, Paul." Cy Mackey snickered. "You're making politically incorrect statements about persons of another sexual orientation."

"Cy, shut up," Schoenfeld said tiredly.

"You're going to regret pushing us into taking this case." Larry was standing over Paul Robineau's chair. "I swear you will."

"You swear." Robineau's eyes gleamed coldly, but his body showed no sign of tension. He shook his head, smiling. "Larry, your trouble is, you're too much of a pussy."

Larry said, "Screw you, Paul."

"And fuck you."

Mackey gave a delighted laugh, as if he would shortly see someone knocked across the room.

"Gentlemen!" Putney rose magisterially from his chair.

Robineau made a shrug of apology in Gail's direction, apparently remembering there was a woman in the room.

"You miss the point," Putney thundered. "*I* am offended as well. As a member of this law firm I am offended."

Larry retreated, squeezing the bridge of his nose, mumbling.

The smirk was off Mackey's face. "Sorry."

Putney glared around the table, then straightened the front of his seersucker jacket and sat down.

Robineau said, "Ms. Connor, that will be all. Thank you for coming in."

Schoenfeld lit another cigarette. Warner seemed to look through the wall with his hooded eyes. Cy Mackey picked something out of a front tooth with the nail of his little finger. Larry hid his face in his coffee cup.

No one spoke. Gail drew her notes together and tapped them into a neat stack. After she was gone, the committee would talk about what to do. She would find out tomorrow. If they took the case, then she would ask to handle it. Insist on it. But not now. They weren't in a good mood, any of them.

She stood up to go. Then stopped, knowing beyond doubt that her future at the firm depended on what happened in the next few seconds.

Paul Robineau asked from the far end of the table, "Is there something else?"

Her heart raced erratically, as if a hand were trying to pull it out of her chest. She said, "Yes. Patrick Norris wants me to represent him. If you decide not to take the case, then I'll have to decide what to do about that. I have no current plans to leave this firm, but I do feel some obligation to Mr. Norris. If you want the case, then I would like a percentage of the fees. And I would like to apply that to a purchase of an equity partnership."

There was dead silence in the room. Finally

128

Robineau said, "You're assuming a great deal, aren't you, Ms. Connor?"

"After almost eight years, Paul, I have a right to make assumptions. I assume I'm a good attorney. I assume I belong here."

Cy Mackey's teeth were showing again. "Gee. And I thought you wanted the case because the guy came to you for help."

Gail forced herself to smile at him.

From where he leaned on the sideboard, Larry said, "Gail is right. It's past time."

Most of the other attorneys were looking into space. Putney chortled silently, the loose skin of his neck shaking. "Here's a young woman with chutzpah!"

Robineau's pen turned over and over in his fingers. Finally he said, "Thank you, Ms. Connor. We'll let you know."

When she got back to her office, shaking so hard she had to sit down, there was a message from Anthony. She called. He was home. A second-degree murder had pled out to aggravated battery. Could she come over for dinner?

Gail called Irene next and talked her into taking Karen for a round or two of miniature golf. She drove straight to Anthony's house from work, unbuttoning her dress on the way up the stairs.

Now the smoky baritone voice of a Spanish ballad singer was winding upward from the stereo in the living room. A candle flickered in the mirror. The bathroom was dark; Anthony had pinned a towel over the window to keep out the late-afternoon sun.

It was a big bathtub, shiny black, with water jets to turn on and a ledge along the wall for scented soap and bath oil and loofah sponges. Anthony reclined against the back of the tub, Gail between his legs, eyes closed, head on his shoulder. He was soaping her breasts, making designs.

She said, "I thought I was going to die."

"No." He nudged aside her hair with his chin to kiss the back of her neck. She felt the rasp of beard.

"Really. I thought my heart would stop and they would have to call 911. Then I said, Well, if they can be such pricks, then I can too. So I went for it."

"Soon you'll be too much for me, do you think?"

"Damn right. More macho than even you." Gail rolled over, slippery in the perfumed water, then held on to his shoulders and pulled slowly up his body, feeling his chest hair on her skin.

He whimpered. *No puedo más.* Gail, please."

She ran the tip of her tongue along his teeth until he gave in and opened his mouth. His hands slid under the water, parting her legs, shifting her on his lap. The water rose and fell on the sides of the bathtub.

He had the pale skin of northern Spain, the long nose and aristocratic bearing of his maternal grandfather, and the dark eyes of his father's people: ex-slaves, santeros, and worshippers of Santa Bárbara, who under a full moon gave herself to Changó, god of lightning, thunder, and virility. That would make Anthony an octoroon,

Gail thought. The word rolled around in her mouth. Octoroon. Like macaroon. Or full moon. One-eighth Afro-Cuban, mambo and cha-cha and *ritmo latino*, timbales and congas pulsing in his blood.

A while later, she sank onto his chest.

"*¿Quien es más macho, mujer?*"

"I am," she said.

"Who?" She shrieked when he tickled under her arm. "Who's more macho?" He poked at her ribs. "Say it."

"Oh, stop. Anthony!"

"*¿Quién es? Dímelo.*"

"You! You are." She slid under the water, her laughter turning to bubbles. Anthony pulled her up by an elbow and swept the hair out of her face.

He kissed her, hard, then put his arms around her back.

For a few minutes she closed her eyes. "Imagine. Anthony Luis Quintana Pedrosa and a skinny-assed *Americana* with her bad-mannered kid. Can't cook, doesn't clean. Every Cuban mother's nightmare. God. Who could have predicted this? Could I? Not in a hundred years. Could you?"

His breathing was slow and steady.

"Not in a thousand." Then she whispered, "Are you asleep?"

"No." He moved his arms and cool air from the vent in the ceiling hit her back. "Gail. It's late. Eight-thirty. You wanted me to remind you."

She looked at the clock on the vanity. "I could stay a little longer. We haven't eaten."

131

"I'll fix something later." He patted her bottom. "You should go."

They stood carefully and got out. Anthony dried off, singing softly in Spanish the words of a song from downstairs.

Gail wrapped a towel tightly around herself as she watched him—the long lines of his back and legs, the muscles moving under the skin, the dark hair on his chest and groin. Soon he would kiss her goodbye at the door, and at midnight they would both be reading their office files, a cup of tea or *café* on their respective night tables.

She stifled a sob and sank down on the edge of the bathtub.

"What is it? Gail?"

"Nothing." She laughed, wiping her cheeks with a towel.

"Nothing?" He sat beside her.

"God, it's—too much to do when I get home. I don't know." She stood up. "I'll call you during the week, all right?"

"We'll talk about it now."

"Talk about what? I'm fine."

Still sitting, he looked up at her. "You make me crazy."

"Do I? Well, good." She lightly kissed his mouth. "As long as you're not crazy for anyone else."

chapter nine

Two days later Gail got the news from Jack Warner, head of litigation. She could do the Norris case. They haggled for a few minutes over details of the fee agreement, but in the end he gave her what she wanted. He hoped she would allow him to assist. She would. She asked about a share of the proceeds. He said she could have it, five percent of recovered fees. And if all went well, they would apply that percentage to her purchase of a partnership in the firm. He shook her hand as she left. It seemed to Gail that the men on the management committee hadn't held it against her that she had pushed. If you're afraid to use your cleats you don't belong on the team.

Walking out of Warner's office she felt an odd mixture of exhilaration and dread. Five percent of legal fees of 15 percent on fifteen million . . . if she won the case.

Now Gail stood at her desk dividing files and correspondence into two stacks—urgent and pressing. Miriam's head was bowed over a legal pad, her pen flying. There would be a heavy schedule in the morning, then at one o'clock Gail would meet with Patrick Norris and he would sign some papers.

At a stopping place she glanced at her watch.

Eight-fifty. "Can you get all that done before noon?"

Miriam flipped her hair back over her shoulder. She had loop earrings with little gold hearts that swung on tiny chains. "Sure, but not if you still want me to take that letter to Karen's school this morning."

"Call a courier service, then. I can't think of what else to do."

Karen had forgotten her permission slip for a school choral concert at the Holocaust Museum on Miami Beach, and the bus would leave at ten. Karen was doing a solo. Otherwise, Gail might have been tempted to teach her a lesson.

"I was wondering," Miriam said. "I've got a finance exam tonight. Could I leave an hour early? I didn't have a chance to study last night because Danny was working and couldn't watch the baby."

"Sure, go ahead." Gail stood on tiptoes to reach a heavy box on her bookcase. "Your schedule is as bad as mine. Danny doesn't complain?" She dropped the box on a chair.

"Not so much. I know how to handle him." When Gail looked around, Miriam laughed. "Men are like that! They give you anything you want at first, then"—she snapped her fingers— "they turn into husbands. They try to order you around. But I never let Danny do that, _¡olv,dalo!_ He won't be like my father. He makes my mother ask permission for everything. Papi is very old-fashioned, you know?"

"Hmmm."

Miriam uncurled herself from behind the desk,

a flash of knees and bare legs. "Anthony? Don't worry, he's not as old as my dad. You can probably teach him to do things for you."

Gail rummaged in the dusty box. "I can't imagine."

"You don't just *tell* him to," Miriam said, as if astonished that Gail could be so dense. "It can't be stuff he won't do anyway. But sometimes he'll only say he won't, so he can think he's in control. Danny does that. I say, Please, Danny. *Por favor, papi.*"

"Ick."

"No, it works, *te juro.* I swear to God. If you don't make him do things for you, how does he know you love him?"

Gail stared at her. "You actually do this?"

Miriam burst into giggles. "Oh, Gail. You are so funny." She gathered up an armful of files, then said, "You should let me take you shopping sometime. It's okay to look like a lawyer at work, but if you're going to go out with a Cuban guy, you have to know how to dress. For one thing, you ought to wear tighter skirts."

"Miriam, please."

She shrugged and vanished into the corridor.

A moment later Gail heard a knock at the open door. Eric Ramsay stepped inside. He said, "Got a minute?"

"About that much. What do you need?" Gail headed back toward the bookcase with the box.

Eric shut the door. He wore cuffed trousers and blue suspenders. The shirt was snug across his wide shoulders. "I thought maybe you could use some help with the forgery case."

She looked at him. "The forgery case?"

He took the box out of her hands and tossed it easily on the top shelf. "It is your case, isn't it? Tillett?"

"Where did you hear that?" The partners had agreed to keep it quiet for a while, until Gail had formed her strategy.

His smile faded. "A couple of paralegals were talking about it in the coffee room."

"Oh, great."

"They said you've just taken a will forgery case. Alice Tillett?"

"Althea."

"Right. Althea. The name sounded familiar. Bill Schoenfeld asked me about Althea Tillett at the meeting on Monday. When I heard the paralegals talking, it hit me as something I'd like to work on."

"Why?" Gail asked.

"Why?" One corner of his mouth lifted into a smile. "Because they say it's going to be one hell of a trial. Except for moot court in law school, I've never argued a case. You know why Hartwell Black hired me. Taxes. At Michigan I specialized in tax. I wrote articles on tax shelters and offshore investment. At Hartwell Black I do corporate tax evaluations. Tax."

He leaned on the edge of her desk. "Frankly, I'm sick of it. It's numbers. No soul. You know what I'd like to do? I want to be a trial attorney. That's a one-eighty turn, but I've felt it pulling at me ever since I saw the inside of a courtroom."

"Really."

"Really." He smiled again. "And who better

136

to teach me trial tactics than Gail Connor? You're one kick-ass lawyer."

She made a little moan and crossed her office. "Eric, please. I can't take bullshit this early in the morning."

He blinked. "It wasn't bullshit."

"All right. Thank you for the generous offer of your time, your compliments, and so forth, but I don't need any assistance."

"Look at this." He motioned toward the files stacked on her desk. "You've already got too much to do. How are you going to take on a major case by yourself?"

She folded her arms. "Okay. I'm going to be real honest here. Remember that complaint in the Aventura Mazda case I asked you to do a couple of weeks ago?"

"It was the beginning of September."

"A month ago, then. Whatever. Frankly, I was disappointed. I had to do it myself and nearly missed the filing deadline."

"Gail, you dropped it on me without any instruction except 'Draft a complaint.'"

"I should hold your hand?"

He stepped in front of her, lifting placating palms. "Okay, I messed up. I'm big enough to admit that."

"Great. I still don't need your help."

"I need yours. Please. Gail—" He dropped into one of the client chairs. "They're going to let me go. I'm on probation now, and I don't think I'm going to make it."

Gail stared down at him.

"Gone. My career. Everything."

"Eric. I'm so sorry. Are you sure? Who told you?"

"The man himself. Paul Robineau. Christ, they're such jackals in this place."

"No, not everyone." She sat down next to him. "Eric, can I make a small suggestion?"

"Sure."

"It's your attitude. As if nobody knows as much as you do. People don't like that. Senior partners particularly don't like it."

He sat silently, then nodded. "Maybe I'm over-compensating. See, I didn't have things handed to me, like most people around here. My mom died when I was a kid, and my dad worked double shifts putting us through school—my sister and my kid brother and me. We lived in a trailer. All I remember is snow and rain. I didn't want to end up like that. I studied and got out. I promised to put my kid sister through college." He sucked in a breath. "What the hell am I going to do? What can I tell my father?" He squeezed his eyes shut.

Muffled voices passed by the door. Gail put a hand on his shoulder. "They haven't fired you yet."

He lifted his head from his fist. "If I could prove myself. Let me do this. Just give me a chance. That's all I'm asking. One chance."

She slid her eyes away from him. She didn't like hearing a grown man beg. Or knowing that she cared about how it would look to the partners if she took on Eric Ramsay, the top-five-percent tax whiz whom Paul Robineau had just put on probation.

Screw Paul Robineau.

She said, "What's your schedule this morning?"

"Whatever you want it to be."

"First, calm down. Second, go tell Miriam to show you the Norris file. By noon I want a draft of a petition for revocation of probate."

He grabbed her hands and rose slowly to his feet. "Thank you, Gail. Thank you so much."

She retreated behind her desk, afraid he was going to put his arms around her. "You're going to have to get along with Miriam. She has her own way of doing things, and I don't want her to feel pushed aside."

"No problem. You're the boss." He opened the door, then stood there a moment. "You won't be sorry, I promise."

Patrick had suggested yesterday that Gail bring the papers to him to sign. That way she could take a look at the neighborhood where he wanted to put his inheritance, if he got it. Gail asked Eric Ramsay to come with her. She wasn't sure if she wanted to go into that area alone. Besides, the AC in her Buick still wasn't working, even after three hundred bucks to the mechanic.

Eric's car turned out to be a silver Lexus coupe with a cellular phone and a $2,000 sound system. As they corkscrewed their way down the ramp of the parking garage, tires singing, he grinned at her through his gold-framed, leather-trimmed sunglasses. "What do you think? Is this great?" She gripped the handhold and agreed that yes, it was a very nice car. He explained how he could afford such a thing: long term lease/ buyout plan. She ought to consider it.

They drove north on Biscayne Boulevard, past the shabby urban shopping center that had tried but failed to lure people downtown, then past Belle Mar, the walled subdivision where her mother lived, with its waterfront houses, profusion of flowering trees, and private security guards.

"When do we file the petition?" Eric asked.

He had absorbed the Norris file with startling speed. He knew the smallest details of Althea Tillett's will better than Gail did, and had roughed out a fairly good draft of the petition for revocation.

"Well, first," she said, "we're going to make damn sure we have a case. If I can show Weissman and the Tilletts that we've got them dead to rights, they might give up without fighting. Do some emergency motions for deposition. I want to nail these people before they can get their stories straight." Gail rested her elbow on the bottom of the closed and tinted window. "My God. Taking Alan Weissman's deposition. That's going to be exciting."

At a traffic light Eric came to a stop and glanced out the side window, mumbling something about the lousy neighborhood.

"Here's something else you can do," Gail said. "Find Carla Napolitano."

"The notary."

"Yes. I thought she'd be in Weissman's office. Miriam called on a pretext yesterday, and they said she didn't work there."

"So where is she?"

"Miriam can find her through state records. I want you to check her out. Just see where she works, what kind of place it is. Then go by her house. Find out what she drives and write down the tag number. We'll get her driving record. Maybe a credit check too. But don't let her see you."

"I can handle that." Eric looked through the windshield at the street signs. "Where do we turn?"

"Left on Sixty-second," she said.

It was just ahead. He put on his blinker, waiting for traffic, then hit the button for the automatic door locks.

They turned west, passing a triple-X movie house on the corner. *The Reel Stuff. Adults Only, 24 Hrs.* Half the flowing yellow lights around the marquee had burned out. Gail watched the tacky motels and run-down storefronts on Biscayne turn into squat, concrete block houses behind chain-link fences, then into two- or three-story tenements, some with plywood over the doors and windows. Children played on tattered lawns. A rotting sofa, scorched on one end, lay halfway in the street. She remembered that a child had died near here, hit by a stray bullet.

Three teenagers wearing baggy jeans and sneakers as big as buckets watched them pass. Gail was aware of drawing away from the window, as if someone were going to run up and hit the glass with a spark plug. She had heard that was the method for smash-and-grab.

She put her purse on the floor.

"This is nothing." Eric snorted. "Visit Detroit."

"Patrick wanted me to see the neighborhood, so I'd feel a personal connection." She watched a skinny girl pushing a stroller along the littered sidewalk.

"Personal connection," Eric repeated.

"Take the next right."

Three blocks to the north she pointed. "There. That must be it." The two-story building was sandwiched between a Laundromat and a hardware store with bars on the window. The white paint was smudged and flaking. A sign beside the door announced CENTRO RENACER, COUNSELING AND JOB PLACEMENT. *Archdiocese of Miami.* Eric parked in the pitted lot beside the Laundromat. He got out, waited for Gail, then aimed his key ring. The Lexus chirped twice, and a tiny red light blinked on the dashboard.

Two spaces away a barechested young man sat on the trunk of a faded green Plymouth, drinking a Jupiña pineapple soda.

"Hey! Bro!" Eric motioned for the young man to come over. "How'd you like to watch my car for me?" He extended a twenty-dollar bill folded lengthwise. "Twenty more when I come back, what do you say?"

He looked into Eric's sunglasses for a while, then smiled and took the money. He was wearing a heavy gold crucifix. "Okay. *Bro.*" He jumped back onto the trunk of the Plymouth.

Gail whispered, "Eric, I don't know."

"Don't worry about it," he said, and took her arm.

When they reached Centro Renacer, a black man with an island accent invited them to be seated, he would fetch Mr. Norris. The narrow room, which smelled vaguely of disinfectant, was sparsely furnished with a green leatherette sofa and several metal chairs. An aquarium with yellow striped fish and bright blue rocks buzzed on a folding table by the window.

The wait was short. Patrick Norris came in, smiling at Gail. He seemed thinner than before, if that was possible, but now he moved with assurance. His eyes shone behind the wire-rimmed glasses. He took both her hands, then said to the other man, "Trevor, this is Gail."

The man showed a wide white smile. "Patrick has spoken of you, miss."

Murmuring her niceties, Gail wondered what Patrick had said about his case. It would be better if he kept his mouth shut before he raised anyone's hopes. She introduced Eric Ramsay and the two men shook hands. Then Patrick said, "Come to my apartment. It's half a block away. We'll have tea."

He took Gail's arm and Eric followed, carrying her briefcase. It wasn't bad, walking. The weather had finally broken, the temperature dropping to the mid-eighties. Patrick smiled and nodded to people along the sidewalk, and one older man tipped his hat.

"Imagine this neighborhood in a few years," Patrick said. "New businesses, day care, a community center. These are decent people. They want the trash picked up as fast as in the suburbs. They want to get rid of the drug dealers and the porno movie theater."

"That place on the corner of Biscayne?"

"Prostitutes hang out there."

"You should report it to the police."

"This isn't Coral Gables," Patrick said, practically patting her on the head. "The cops don't give a damn. We're on our own."

He led them through a gate into a yard green with banana plants and riotous with flowers. Half a dozen chickens were pecking in the dirt beside a white frame house. A woman with a kerchief tied around her head sat on the porch. A radio played on a table at her elbow, a talk show in Creole. Seeing Patrick, she smiled and nodded to him. *"Bonjour, m'sieu."* Gail wondered if everyone in the neighborhood had heard what he intended to do here.

"Bonjour, Madame Debrosse," Patrick called out, then said to Gail, "My landlady. She's from Port-au-Prince." He lowered his voice still further. "She's part of a network, helping to get people out of Haiti. You know our good old American immigration policy. Bring me your tired, your poor, your huddled masses—as long as they aren't too poor and huddled."

Eric had been looking at the chickens. He moved closer to Patrick. "What are they for, voodoo sacrifice?"

Patrick smiled patiently. "For eggs."

His apartment was built over a single-car garage. He led them up some wooden stairs and unlocked a metal-plated door. Inside, carpentry tools were neatly arranged along the back wall.

A pair of laced boots sat by the door to a small bathroom. The kitchen consisted of a table, a refrigerator, and a two-burner hot plate. A woven cotton rug of Mexican design indicated the living area: single bed with a thin brown blanket, big pillows on the floor, one wooden chair, and a desk over which bare pine shelves sagged with the weight of books. Philosophy, history, economics, a few volumes of poetry. Gail remembered that once Patrick had read poetry aloud to her. Open on his desk was a book by Noam Chomsky. Not poetry. There was no television. No telephone. No ashtrays or empty beer cans. No sign of a woman's presence.

A light breeze came through the jalousie windows open on three sides of the long room. Shadows of leaves moved on the screens, and birds chirped in the branches. The radio on Madame Debrosse's porch was playing a song in French.

Patrick put on a tea kettle while Gail told him what she had found out from the document examiner. She told him about her conversations with Jessica Simms and Irving Adler. She told him that the estate was bigger than he had thought, perhaps more than fifteen million dollars. And then she instructed him to keep all this to himself and not to talk about the case with anyone.

When the tea was ready he poured it into three mismatched cups. Eric sniffed his and asked for sugar, but Patrick only had raw honey. Patrick removed his heavy sandals and gracefully sank cross-legged onto the rug. Gail took off her

145

pumps, sat on one of the floor pillows, and arranged her skirt.

Eric looked at them for a moment, then awkwardly sat on the floor as well. His suit coat pulled over his shoulders, and he couldn't seem to decide where to put his feet.

Gail sipped her tea. "Coming into this neighborhood is like entering a different country. I know so little about its customs and realities."

Patrick smiled at her. "It isn't so different. We all want the same things in life. Dignity. Honest work. A safe, clean place for the children to grow up."

She reached over and squeezed his hand. "I hope you succeed here, Patrick."

Eric pulled Gail's briefcase closer. "We ought to get started. I don't want to leave my car too long."

She reluctantly put down her cup. "I suppose we should."

Patrick said, "You asked me not to talk about the case. Why?"

"Because publicity might harm our chances for a settlement," she said. "Some prominent people have done some bad things. If this hits the news, they'll fight to the death." She took a folder out of her briefcase. "What I hope to do is gather enough evidence to prove forgery before we even file the case."

"Wouldn't publicity force them to settle?"

"Very doubtful."

Patrick thought about that. "I'm not certain I agree."

"Just don't risk it, all right?"

"How much would they pay in a settlement?" he asked.

"It depends. We weigh the chances of success against the possibility of failure. We consider the time involved. If the other side drags it to the appellate court, a resolution could take two or three years. And meanwhile you're incurring costs and attorneys' fees." She held the folder in her hands for a while. "I have to consider that as well. Fees. If we lose—not that I expect to, but if it happens—I don't want your money to have been used up."

Patrick nodded at the folder. "Show me what you've got there. The fee agreement."

She opened it and withdrew two documents. "This four- page form is a contract of representation, one copy for you, one for the firm. The other is a promissory note and assignment of your bequest to Hartwell Black and Robineau." Patrick held out his hand. Gail said, "The firm won't take the case except on a contingency basis. Ten percent if we settle, fifteen for a trial, twenty after an appeal. We're going to advance the costs, twenty thousand to start."

He pushed his glasses up a little farther on his nose and slowly turned the pages. Finally he raised his eyes. "This isn't what we agreed to."

"We didn't have an agreement. And believe me, that's the best I could get for you."

He laid the papers down. "I can't sign this. It's theft."

She felt Eric looking at her, wondering what she was going to do next. She said, "Patrick, you didn't want just me. You wanted Hartwell Black. No other firm with our reputation and resources is going to do it for less. Most would charge you

147

more." When he said nothing, she added, "If we can't come to an agreement, I can't take the case."

Patrick sat impassively. "Say we settle—just suppose that we do—for ten million. Say it takes you a hundred hours. At ten percent, that's ten thousand dollars per hour in attorneys' fees. And that's not theft?"

"Who says we'll settle at all? Nobody knows. And nobody knows how many hours we'll have in this. A thousand. Five thousand. I hope for a settlement, but we could go to trial. You could get nothing."

"Let's put this on a sliding scale. Or make it an hourly rate," he said. "We're talking about money that's supposed to go to people who need it a hell of a lot more than your Flagler Street legal machine does."

Gail wasn't going to whine about her struggle to get this far. "Sorry. If you want to hire someone else, I won't argue. And no charge for what I've done so far."

He drew his hand down over his beard, then laughed. "I feel like I've been sucker-punched."

"Oh, Patrick. That was never my intention. You should know that."

He stood up, walking barefoot to the window, hands in the back pockets of his jeans. Under the sounds of traffic and birds and Madame Debrosse's radio, a shrill warble from up the block threaded its way into the room. Probably a police siren.

Patrick turned around. "You going to win this case for me?"

"I'll try to." She laughed a little. "Patrick, you don't know how hard I'm going to try to win this case."

"I don't want to go anywhere else," he said.

She felt the relief flood through her, but only nodded. "Sit down, then. We'll sign these."

Eric tilted his head and rose to his knees. "Shh-shh! What is that?" She heard the siren, still whooping. He leaped to the window, then slammed his hand on the sill. "God damn!"

"Eric, what—"

"Shit! My goddamn car! The fuckers got my Lexus!" He hurtled out the door and his footsteps thudded down the wooden stairs. He must have picked out the cry of his car alarm like a mother could hear the wail of her own child in a crowded playground.

Gail said, "He gave a guy twenty dollars to watch it."

Patrick drew a little breath through his teeth. "That could be construed as an insult."

"I feel awful. We should have taken a cab."

"They probably just got the radio." He sat down cross-legged again and signed the note and two copies of the contract, one of which he folded into neat thirds and tossed onto his desk.

When he turned around he smiled at her. "Don't feel guilty. Maybe he'll learn something. I mean, if you live for things, what have you got, right?"

She nodded. "Not a popular sentiment around my law firm, but I guess it works."

"Are you okay there? Really?"

"Sure." She took a sip of her tea. "Well, yes and no. I like being a lawyer. But it's so difficult.

Most people don't know what lawyers have to deal with. I try to do a good job."

"I know you do."

"If I could just . . . get to a certain point. Then it would be all right. I'd have more control over what I do. Make my own choices."

"Then you're where you have to be," he said. "You can't get to that unless you go through this."

She laughed. "And if I weren't at Hartwell Black, you couldn't drive me batty with your case, could you?"

He scooted over and kissed her cheek, and for a second the beard tickled her skin. "I've meant to do that. Do you mind?"

She smiled, shook her head.

"It's good to see you again, buddy."

"You too," she said.

"Hey, you're blushing," he said.

"Am not."

"Are too." He looked at her awhile. "I'm not hitting on you, Gail. Honest."

"I know."

"Bet you've got a boyfriend."

She laughed. "Boyfriend. What a word. Yes, I do, actually."

"Good. No? Not so good?"

"Very good. I think. But—it's hard. You know. After Dave. And there's Karen to consider."

He squeezed her shoulder. "Whatever is meant to happen, will."

"That was never *your* philosophy," she said. "You always told me that nothing happens in human history that is not willed into being."

Patrick laughed. "I said that? When? In my impatient youth?"

"Oh, I see. Politics is one thing, love another." Gail shook the wrinkles out of her skirt. "I should go see if Eric is all right."

Patrick picked up Eric's untouched cup of tea. Gail carried hers to the table where the kettle sat on a green and white pot holder of the sort children weave in kindergarten.

"Patrick." When he looked at her, she said. "The document examiner mentioned something that made me curious. Have the police been asking about your aunt's death? Beyond the routine questions, I mean."

He stroked his beard. "What did he say to make you wonder that?"

"Well, that it's a big estate. And she died alone. You can imagine. I looked at the death certificate. It doesn't say 'accidental.' It says 'pending.' Meaning pending further investigation."

"Yes," Patrick said.

"Yes, what?"

"Yes, the Miami Beach P.D. came around asking questions."

"When?"

"Two weeks ago. Last week. And yesterday."

"*Why?*"

Patrick sighed. "Who knows? Cops." He set his and Eric's cups on the table. "They said her neck was broken before she fell. So who did it? There weren't any signs of a break-in. She would have opened the door to me. Plus we had a big fight a week before she died."

"Oh, Patrick."

151

"They're cretins. They've got nothing better to do."

"Why didn't you tell me any of this?"

"So you could tell me you didn't want to get involved?"

They looked at each other. She said, "I wouldn't have done that."

He pointed all the cup handles in one direction. "I didn't think you'd let me get screwed on the fees either."

"Damn it, Patrick."

He smiled, not looking at her. "I guess you had to. It comes with the territory. Now you see why I got out of law school."

She crossed the room to put on her shoes. "And you talk to me about getting sucker-punched." She spun around. "Let me understand this. The Miami Beach Police suspect you of *murder?*"

"I don't know. Me, Rudy, the gardener. They ask questions. I tell them to go away. They do. Then they forget what I told them and they come back. Repeat."

Gail leaned against the table. "Did something happen to her, Patrick? Is it true?"

"I hope not. For somebody to do that—I don't want to think about it." He nodded toward his desk, where the contract lay tilted on the open book. "You want the agreement back?"

"No. I'm your attorney now, Patrick."

But how, she wondered, would she explain a murder investigation to the partners of Hartwell Black and Robineau?

chapter ten

Larry Black called Gail to his office the next afternoon. They sat on the striped satin divan under the windows. His secretary brought in a tray with coffee and miniature pastries, and placed it on an antique cherry-wood table.

He stirred his coffee. "Alan Weissman phoned me yesterday." When Gail looked at him, surprised, he said, "I suggested that you were the person to speak to, but I think he felt more at ease talking to me. We worked together on the Hurricane Andrew rebuilding committee, and he knows I was acquainted with Althea. He wants a meeting to resolve this matter before it gets out of hand, as he put it."

Gail poured cream into her cup. "He can resolve it by admitting the will was forged. What did he say?"

"We talked only in general terms," Larry said. "I did propose a time for the meeting. Next Wednesday at ten o'clock, his office on the Beach. Can you make it?"

"I'll clear my schedule. You know, if we're going to talk to Weissman, we need to get together and go over the details."

Monday or Tuesday was impossible; Larry had meetings both days. "What about this weekend?" he asked. "Come over Saturday and stay for dinner. Karen can play with Trisha." Larry's younger daughter was in Karen's class at Biscayne Academy. He added, "Dee-Dee hasn't seen you for months. She was complaining about that yesterday, in fact."

How did they do it? Gail often wondered. If Larry ever told her he and Dee-Dee were splitting up, Gail would throttle him. That, or lose all hope that marriage could work.

It had been two days since she had left a message on Anthony's machine at home. He might be busy, but not that busy. If he had anything in mind for Saturday night, it was too late now.

Gail smiled. "I'd love to come over. Thanks."

Larry uncrossed his legs and set his coffee on the table. "Oh. I have something for you." He went to his desk and lifted papers. "By the time I realized you might not have seen it, I had to go through my recycling bin at home. Althea Tillett's stepdaughter Monica is showing her work. Look." He handed her a page from the *Herald,* and his forefinger indicated the place.

It was from the weekend section, a preview of gallery openings. Gail scanned the announcement. *Eros and Metaphor, sculptures and abstracts by Monica Tillett; Tillett Gallery, 833 Lincoln Road, Miami Beach. Reception 7–9* P.M. Friday, October 4. She looked up. "What is that supposed to mean? Eros and Metaphor?"

"It's tomorrow. Go find out."

She folded the page. "I might do that. Thanks. I hope they don't slam the door in my face."

Larry sat down again, adjusting the knee of his

154

trousers. "Gail, it wasn't a criticism of you that I opposed the Norris case. I do understand about your wanting to help him, but I have the entire law firm to think about. Our long-term interests."

"I know," she said. "You're too much a friend for me to take it personally."

"Well, then. Tell me what you need. Perhaps we could assign a paralegal to the case?"

Grace in defeat. She smiled at him. "No, Miriam is enough for now. Maybe I'll ask for a raise for her, though. And how's this? Eric Ramsay volunteered to help out. I'm going to share him with corporate and tax."

"I admire your patience."

"Okay, maybe he's immature, but he's smart, and he wants to learn." Gail added, "Besides, I felt sorry for him. His dad's a factory worker back in Ohio, and he's sending his kid sister through college."

"A factory worker? His father *manages* a factory that makes engine parts. I believe that's right. Our Mr. Ramsay seems to have embellished the facts."

"Maybe he's warming up for trial law already," Gail said. Then she shrugged. "He was desperate, Larry."

He took a swallow of coffee. "Ramsay. A lawyer for the Nineties. This is what we get, hiring graduates whose main qualifications are on paper. Maybe you can turn him around."

Gail said, "He says Paul has him on probation. Is that true?"

"Yes. I heard it from Jack Warner. Paul didn't tell *me* about it."

"Larry . . . How serious is this rift between you and Paul? Is the firm in trouble?"

"Don't worry. What you witnessed the other day was only a clash of egos." He gave a suggestion of a smile. "We've lived through it before. The ship hasn't foundered yet."

Lawrence Black, the weight of five generations of lawyers on his narrow shoulders, had seemed middle-aged to Gail as long as she had known him. Not a brilliant legal mind, his great talent lay in snatching wealthy clients from firms with no snob appeal. He let his staff deal with the computers, investment managers, and pricey advertising campaigns.

Larry studied the circle of pastries before choosing a tiny cheese tart with fluted edges. "I want you to meet with the P.R. people. Would you do that?"

Like other major firms, Hartwell Black and Robineau had a public relations consultant to deal with touchy issues. He said, "We can't let anyone believe we're against widows and orphans. We're taking the case for the principle involved: exposing a forgery. I'm particularly concerned that Sanford Ehringer see it this way. Not only is he the personal representative of this will, he's chairman of the board of the Easton Trust, and they stand to lose a great deal if it's overturned. Ehringer will be doubly interested in what we're doing."

Larry turned on the divan to face Gail directly, his expression as serious as she had ever seen it. "We want to persuade Ehringer that our aim is to win justice for our client, not to make a fat fee for ourselves. That's important, Gail. Will you take my advice on this?"

After a moment, she said, "All right. God knows we don't want to tarnish the image. Larry, have you ever met Sanford Ehringer?"

"A few times. He's something of a recluse these days. He comes across as a jolly old great-uncle who likes a good glass of port and the occasional off-color joke, but he's devious and powerful. He could cause us serious trouble with many of our established clients."

She asked, "How do you know the Easton Trust's director, Howard Odell? You and he had lunch upstairs last week."

"Oh, Howard. He's always trolling for investors for his own deals. I wasn't interested."

"What do you know about him?" Gail wondered if Larry knew of Odell's connection to an alleged pornographer who operated out of the back of a dry cleaning shop.

"Nothing, really. We don't socialize."

Gail poured herself more coffee. "It's odd that I haven't heard of the Easton Trust. I was born in Miami."

Larry said, "Not so odd. They keep a very low profile—so I've heard. The board members are from old families who have known each other for years. They're picky about who they give money to, and they avoid publicity."

"Now that is odd. Most donors to charity like the applause."

Larry finished his pastry before he spoke, then wiped his fingers on a corner of his napkin. "An anonymous giver is more blessed."

157

"Uh-huh."

His lips twitched into a smile. She noticed how the light from the window made a halo of his thinning hair. Gail asked, "What do they do, Larry? Arrange no-interest loans from money donated to the trust? Take tax deductions on the repayments?"

"No, no. Nothing illegal, I should think. These are your quintessential pillars of society. They might try to influence what happens in Miami, though, and if they can use the weight of the trust to do it—Well, why not? Their opinions count as much as anybody's."

It was clear to Gail how influence might be applied. If one were a member of the Easton Trust, and wanted a certain ordinance passed, one could promise a donation to a certain city commissioner's favorite project, and he—the commissioner—could take the credit when the community center opened, or the hospital wing, or neighborhood police substation. Business as usual in local politics.

And a man like Howard Odell—whose morals were not so prissy—could be useful, arranging such favors. The pillars of society would be spared the embarrassment.

She asked, "Howard Odell manages the Trust. Who else is involved?"

"I don't know precisely," Larry said.

"Althea Tillett? With what she left to Easton—"

"That's logical." He shrugged. "I wouldn't be surprised if she'd been a member of Easton."

"There's something you ought to be aware of," Gail said. "Yesterday Patrick Norris told me that

158

the Miami Beach Police are investigating her death. They don't believe it was an accident."

His mouth opened and shut, then opened, but no sound came out.

"They think someone may have broken her neck before she went down the stairs."

"My God." He went white. "Who? Do they know? What are they basing this on?"

"The autopsy, I assume. And no signs of a break-in. They've questioned Patrick three times at his apartment."

He braced his hands on his knees and sucked in a breath.

"Larry?" Gail went to him.

"I'm fine." He smiled. Sweat shone on his forehead. "Bit of a shock, that's all. Have you told anyone else in the firm?"

"No."

"Don't. Let's decide what to do, shall we? How to handle it . . . We should have known this before the meeting. Before we decided to take this damned case."

"Larry, you can't be thinking . . . not Patrick. That's the last thing I would suspect him of."

"We should find out what the police are doing. How does one accomplish that?"

"I suppose," Gail said, "that we could begin by asking them."

She tried Anthony Quintana's office: He was in trial. She left a message for him to call. Not urgent, just some advice on a matter involving the Miami Beach police.

"Damn." For a minute or two she looked at her telephone, wondering whether to call them

159

now, and what she would say. *Hello, this is Patrick Norris's attorney. Is he a suspect in the death of Althea Tillett?*

She would think of something.

Gail looked up the number, dialed it, and asked for records. A man's voice told her that yes, police reports are public records, and she could get duplicates for a few dollars.

She checked her watch—4:15—then found Miriam typing at her keyboard, humming to herself as she worked.

"Where's *Señor* Ramsay?" Gail asked.

Miriam turned. "Oh, there you are! I've got something to tell you."

"Okay, but where's Eric?"

"Getting an insurance estimate on his car," Miriam said. She punched a button to save what she had done and the monitor chirped. "He just called and said he was on his way back."

The passenger window on his Lexus had been shattered, his cellular phone and stereo gone like teeth yanked out of a jaw.

Gail said, "I'm going over to the Beach. Tell Eric to do a final version of the Tillett petition. Plus a summons for everyone involved. Help him out. I don't think he knows a summons from a subpoena."

"But I'm only a secretary. He'd be insulted." Miriam got up from her chair, and it spun around. "Guess what. I found Carla Napolitano."

"Where?"

"I called Tallahassee, the office that keeps track of notaries." She held up a piece of paper so Gail could see it. Carla Napolitano. Home on

160

Collins Avenue. Office on Alton Road, Miami Beach. Phone numbers.

"Good girl." Gail read it. "Why don't you call that work number and see what it is."

"I did already."

"And?"

Her large brown eyes opened wide. "A man answered. He said, 'Gateway Travel,' so I said, 'Who am I speaking to, please?' And he said 'Who do you want?' Like that. So I said, 'Does Carla work here?' He said, 'Carla stepped out for a minute.' Then he asked me who I was, and what did I want? It was so weird. I didn't know what to say, so I told him my name was Patty and I was calling about the job, and never mind, I'd call back."

Miriam tugged Gail farther back into her cubicle. "Then he asked me did I mean the dancing job or what? So I say, 'Yes, dancing.' He goes, 'Do you have any experience?' And I say no. 'That's okay, we'll train you if you get hired. How old are you?' I say twenty-one. And then he says, 'Do you have implants?'"

"You're kidding."

"No! *¡Te juro!* He said that. So I said—*Ay, Diós mío*—I said, 'No, I don't need implants.' So he goes, 'Oh, you sound really cute, why don't you come over right now?'"

Miriam bounced up and down, her head bobbing at the level of Gail's shoulder. "Oh my God, *yo no lo creo que* I actually did this! *Entonces, le digo,* 'I can't get off work now.' He says, 'How about later, is seven o'clock okay?' He gives me

161

an address on North Dixie Highway, next door to Wild Cherry."

"What's that?"

"That's what I said. 'What's that?' *Y me dice,* 'It's the club where you'll be dancing, sweet cheeks.' He called me that! He goes, 'Bring a bikini and some high heels so I can take some photos.' *¡Fíjate!* He says, 'My name's Frankie, ask for me when you come.'"

Gail glanced into the empty corridor, then back at Miriam. "You're telling me that the notary on Althea Tillett's will is connected to an X-rated nightclub?"

"What else can it be, with a name like that?"

"I think you ought to go see Frankie tonight, Miriam. Supplement your income."

"*¡Alaba'o!* Danny would kill me."

Gail studied Carla Napolitano's work address again. "Look at this. The travel agency is in the same block as Alan Weissman's office. That explains where Weissman found her."

"I bet she's a stripper."

"I'd love to get that into evidence. The jury would eat it up."

"So do you want me to see what I can find out?" It was hardly a question. Miriam's face glowed with enthusiasm.

"God, yes. This is getting interesting." Gail checked her watch. "I have to go. See if you can find out who owns Gateway Travel. And give Eric the address of Wild Cherry. That should make him happy. He'll have something to do this weekend besides read IRS regulations."

★　★　★

162

Half an hour later, Gail walked into Miami Beach Police headquarters, a white-and-turquoise, terrazzo-floored lobby with a mural of fishes and the beach on the back wall. Add some tables and chairs, and put the cops into waiters' vests, and it would look like one of the trendy restaurants on Ocean Drive. The lobby was built on the quarter round, with an atrium to the ceiling and four turquoise metal railings marking the floors. The reception desk seemed suspended on lighted glass blocks.

A muscled Adonis on skates glided around Gail and darted into an alcove to take a sip at the water fountain. Tight green shorts, hair tied back in a ponytail, the rest of him tanned and shiny with sweat. He wiped his mouth, spun around, and glided out again through the automatic doors.

"He comes in here a lot," noted the girl at the desk. She was a pudgy blond in a blue Public Service Aide uniform.

"Must be nice." Gail asked the girl where records might be. She twisted around in her chair and pointed toward the muraled wall just off the lobby.

At the records counter a young man asked if she had a case number.

"No, sorry, I don't. Just the name." She wrote it down.

"Hang on." He ruffled through some papers below Gail's line of vision, then looked back at her. "I have to call upstairs on this one."

"For public records?"

"I can't let you have nothing without an okay.

Take a seat in the lobby and I'll see what I can do. What's your name?"

Gail told him, then wandered over to see the poster of Miami Beach's Ten Most Wanted. They were pathetic-looking men, most of them needing a shave.

A minute later one of two silver-doored elevators opened on the lobby and a man got out and walked in her direction. Gail stood up. He was black, heavyset, a couple of inches shorter than Gail. Graying hair was trimmed close to his head. He wore a short-sleeved shirt and a tie. His belt carried a badge and a holstered pistol.

"Detective Gary Davis," he said, keeping his hands on his hips. "Can I help you?"

"My name is Gail Connor. I'm an attorney." She gave him her card.

After he read it, he slid it into his shirt pocket. "What did you want from the records desk, Ms. Connor?"

"I asked for copies of police reports on Althea Tillett. She died last month at her home on North Bay Road."

"Mind if I ask what your interest is?"

"I represent her nephew in a civil matter."

"Her nephew being . . . ?"

"Patrick Norris. He told me your department is investigating. Is that true?"

Davis looked at her for a while, then extended an arm toward the elevators. "Do me a favor, come upstairs, we'll talk about it."

Gail glanced up into the atrium. "Detective, at this point all I want to know is what's going on."

164

"You have questions, I have questions. Please."

After a moment, Gail nodded and followed him, her heels echoing on the terrazzo. Inside the elevator Detective Davis pushed the button for the third floor. "I haven't heard anything in the news about a murder investigation," she said.

"We haven't released the pink." Davis leaned wearily against the rear wall of the elevator. "Excuse me, the press copy of the Incident Report. They're in a box down there at the desk, which is open to the news media. They sit there and go through them. Every purse-snatching, every stabbing, every shoplifting. Everything. And if they see something interesting, they ask about it. If it's not in the box, it doesn't exist."

"But Mrs. Tillett was fairly well known."

The door opened and Davis let her go out first. "Lot of well-known people on the Beach, Ms. Connor."

"Are you in charge of the case?" Gail asked.

"That's right. What's Patrick Norris doing with a lawyer?"

"I'm not a criminal lawyer," she said.

"I noticed that. Gail A. Connor, Attorney at Law, civil trial practice," Davis said, repeating what was printed on her card. "Law firm on Flagler Street."

He led her through a waiting room, then through a locked door marked INVESTIGATIONS. Inside, low partitions divided an open area of cubicles. Three men and one woman, all in plain clothes, glanced at her without interest, then returned to their conversations. On one divider

165

she spotted a mug shot of Fidel Castro with darts sticking out of it, and on the next a calendar with a back view of a girl in denim cut-offs that showed her cheeks.

Davis stopped at a glass-walled office on the south side, and Gail went in. His desk was littered with papers, forms, and folders. A green Gumby toy was bent to hang onto the in/out box. A hand-held radio sat in a battery charger, and a dispatcher's voice came through at low volume. Photos of a family looked back at her from the window ledge—a woman, two teenage boys. Beyond the window, the top of a palm tree moved silently in the breeze.

Davis still had his hand on the doorknob. "You want a cup of coffee? A cold drink?"

"No, thanks." She sat down in a chrome-legged chair.

He closed the door, then raised one forefinger. "Connor. Why does that name sound familiar?"

Gail saw no reason not to tell him. "My mother was one of the women at Althea Tillett's house playing bridge the night she died."

"Irene Connor. She's your momma? Did you know Althea Tillett also?"

"Not well, but yes, I did."

"Is that how you got involved with her nephew?"

"We met in law school."

"My. It's a small world, as they say." Gary Davis rested one hip on the edge of a metal table stacked with files, his beefy arms crossed over his stomach, one foot swinging slowly. He seemed to fill the available space in the office. He said,

"Law school? Mr. Norris didn't tell me he was a lawyer."

"He isn't. Detective, forgive me, but you still haven't told me why you were questioning him."

Davis's eyes were red-rimmed and shadowed. "You said you're representing Patrick Norris on a civil case. What would that be about?"

"It has to do with the probate of Mrs. Tillett's estate."

"Do tell."

"I prefer not to comment further on it at this time."

"Attorney-client privilege?" Davis reached into his shirt pocket and read from her card. "Civil trial practice. You do probate work too?"

"Tangentially."

"Well, there's a hundred-dollar word. You know who Alan Weissman is, right?"

"Yes. Mrs. Tillett's attorney. He represents the estate in probate court."

"Weissman says your client is going to collect two hundred and fifty grand."

"According to the will," Gail reported.

"Did Mr. Norris know about this before his aunt died?"

"I'm not prepared to comment on that."

Sighing, Davis spun her card to the desk. "Ms. Connor, I don't mean to be a pain in the ass, but you want to get yourself charged with obstruction? I'm tired. I'm working three homicides, two rapes, and a strong-arm robbery. Last night we found the body of a French tourist barbecued in a dumpster off Collins Avenue. I haven't seen my wife since Tuesday. I'm not in the mood to let a lawyer jerk me around, and I don't give a goddamn what gold-plated, Flagler Street law firm you're from."

Gail could feel her heart rate quicken. "I'm Mr. Norris's attorney. You can't arrest me for asking questions."

Davis bent forward at the waist. "You got information relevant to a homicide case? You don't represent Patrick Norris on that case? Watch what I can do."

She resisted the impulse to scoot her chair backward. "Detective Davis. I'm not going to comment on what he knew or when he knew it. So if you want to toss me in your dungeon, or wherever you put recalcitrant gold- plated Flagler Street lawyers, then go ahead. I'll call my own attorney and sue you for false imprisonment."

Gary Davis gave a short laugh, walked around behind his desk and sat down, gripping the armrests of his chair. "The only heir, and a measly quarter of a million. What did he hire you to do, Ms. Connor? Overturn her will?"

Davis may have learned this much from talking to Weissman. She would have to give him something. She nodded. "Yes. We're going to challenge the will."

"Which if you win the case, Patrick Norris collects twenty-five million dollars. I mean, hell—talk about motives, there's one right there. Wouldn't you say?"

"Twenty-five?" When Davis's eyes fixed on her, Gail retreated into silence. Twenty-five million dollars. More than she had ever imagined.

Davis reached out and grabbed the Gumby off

168

his in/out basket and straightened its green arms. "On Thursday, September 5, Althea Tillett's housekeeper called 911. Fire-Rescue arrived, saw the body, and uniformed officers sealed off the scene. It looked like an accident, which is what the *Miami Herald* reported. The housekeeper said she came in through the kitchen and turned off the alarm, like she usually does. Then she saw Mrs. Tillett lying at the foot of the stairs in the living room.

"She was coming out of rigor when I got there. I could tell she'd been laying there awhile because of the way the blood settles. Didn't look like she'd been moved from where she fell. She had on a red kimono, bra and panties underneath. White socks. Wood sandals. One of them was on her foot, the other one halfway up the stairs. Her eyes were open. She smashed her nose on the floor and broke out three teeth, and there was some blood from that. She had also evacuated her bowels, but it didn't look to me like she had done it when she landed. Might have been before."

Davis shifted his eyes up at Gail, the whites showing under the irises.

Gail clamped her teeth together, feeling a little sick.

He went on, playing with the Gumby. "I examined her hands. Her wrists weren't broken, like where she would've tried to stop her fall. I looked for where she might have grabbed at a railing on her way down the stairs. Torn fingernail, a bruise. If you're conscious, and you're falling, you grab. It's a reaction. Even people who jump off buildings grab at the last second, and you see how

169

their fingertips are scraped by trying to hang onto the bricks. The instinct to live is that strong. Not too many people try to kill themselves by diving down a flight of stairs, however. Anyway, from what I heard, Althea Tillett wasn't suicidal. So we did the usual: took statements, dusted for prints, questioned whoever saw her last, canvassed the neighborhood. Did anybody see anything odd? Hear anything? Your momma and the other ladies left at ten-fifteen. The lady next door heard them laughing and carrying on. A little while later, ten-thirty, she heard Mrs. Tillett's stereo go on. An opera. *Madame Butterfly.* It's on for a few minutes. Then it goes off. And nothing the rest of the night.

"So Mrs. Tillett got to the M.E. about two P.M., and the post was done the next morning. I was there. Anytime there's a question, I go."

Davis laid the Gumby down on a stack of folders and drew his finger down its torso. "The M.E. split her open, stem to stern. There was some decomp, but not a whole lot. He went into the neck, layer by layer. He said, Hey, Gary. I see something funny here. Some contusion that could have happened before death. I suspect foul play here, Gary. Why don't you go on back and see what you can find out?"

Gail hugged her crossed arms into her chest. "So he listed the cause of death as pending."

"Correct. But I do believe, Ms. Connor, that he filed an amended certificate this week. Homicide. You ought to get yourself a copy." He twisted the toy's head so its smiling mouth and big eyes were facing Gail. "Althea Wilma

170

Norris Tillett, age fifty-eight. Nice lady, from what I heard. Had a lot of friends to say that about her. They cried. Your own momma too."

"My mother didn't mention that you were conducting a murder investigation," Gail said. "You questioned her, didn't you? And the other women who were there that night?"

"Oh, sure, but it was pretty much routine. We didn't think we had a homicide on our hands. Anyhow, didn't seem like they could add much."

Davis bent Gumby's legs and sat him down on the edge of the desk. "Funny thing. I talk to your client about this sweet lady and all I get is the runaround. You want to know if Patrick Norris is a suspect. Yes, ma'am, he surely is. He knows how to work the alarm. He told me so. The man can't come up with an alibi. A quarter million is a hell of a motive. And frankly, Ms. Connor, his attitude sucks. We asked him to talk to us. You know what he said?"

Gail shook her head. She wanted to strangle Patrick.

"He said I should go perform an intimate act on myself. The man is rude. I get bad vibes whenever somebody doesn't want to talk to me. I ask myself, What can this person be hiding?"

Davis leaned back in his chair and tossed Gumby into the in/out box. "That answer your questions?"

"Not quite. What evidence do you have against Patrick Norris? Or is this all supposition because you don't like his attitude?"

"I'm not prepared to comment at this time." Davis smiled.

171

"Could I have a copy of the reports?"

"No."

She reached down for her purse. "Then I guess we're finished."

"For now." Gary Davis rolled his chair back. "Let me ask you something, Ms. Connor. If Patrick Norris did do it, he's out of luck, right? I mean, a killer can't inherit from his victim?" He was still smiling when he opened the door.

"I'm sure you know the answer to that, Detective."

chapter eleven

Gail arrived at her mother's at a quarter to seven the next evening with Karen's elbow in one hand and an overnight bag in the other. Irene opened the screen door and drew Karen into a big hug that knocked her Hurricanes hat to the floor of the foyer.

"Look who's here. My favorite girl in the whole world!" Irene kissed her, then glanced at Gail while Karen bent to retrieve her hat.

"I found her on the roof," Gail said.

"Oh, you scared us, honey, disappearing like that." Irene led Karen across the living room, through the dining room with its chandelier and softly ticking clock, then into the kitchen. The kitchen was big enough to eat in, with the original cabinets from the Sixties and thirty years' worth of knickknacks. Drawings of Karen's were stuck with fruit magnets to the refrigerator door. A casserole sat on the stove under an inverted plate, keeping warm. Gail could smell cheese.

Irene said, "After dinner we'll make your volcano for school. I haven't done papier-maché since your mother was a girl."

Karen hung her alligator purse over the back of a chair and petted the orange striped cat curled up on the seat. Gail gave her a look. She sighed. "Gramma?"

"What, darling?" Irene was pouring apple juice into a plastic Lion King cup.

"I am sorry for making you worry about me, and I wanted to come over here to see you. I like your house."

"Of course you do. We always have a good time, don't we?" Irene dropped Karen's hat over a knob on the chair back. "What happened to your hair?" She set the juice on the table.

"Mom cut it. I look stupid."

She laughed and squeezed Karen around the shoulders. "Why no, you don't. You're cute as a bug." She fluffed her bangs with her fingers. "There you go. The prettiest girl in Miami. Tell your mommy to take you to a real beauty salon next time." Another squeeze. "Run and wash your hands for dinner."

Karen flipped her hat back on, picked up the cat, its forelegs straight out under its chin, then went down the back hallway to the guest bathroom.

Irene took two plates from the cabinet. She wore bright yellow culottes, a tropical-print shirt,

173

and white sandals decorated with faux emeralds that glittered when she walked. She asked Gail, "Are you hungry?"

"No, I can't stay long. Anyway, we're having a dinner after the gallery," Gail said, meaning dinner on South Beach with Anthony Quintana after they went to see Monica Tillett's collection.

Irene raised an eyebrow.

"Yes, Mother, I'm spending the night with Anthony."

"Is this getting serious?"

"I don't know what it is. We enjoy each other's company. We're monogamous."

"He's certainly an attractive man." She levered a slice of macaroni out of the casserole dish and dropped it on a plate. Her nails were painted a scorching red. "What does Karen think?"

"She says he's a geek. We can't talk about it civilly, so I hardly mention his name." Gail rummaged in a drawer for the aspirin Irene kept there. "She's afraid he's going to take me away from her. She's already nervous because her father doesn't call as much as he promised. Dave says he can't—there's no phone on his sailboat. He sends her postcards."

"Well, be careful."

Gail gave her a quizzical look. "About what?"

"The charming Mr. Quintana. I'm afraid your biological urges are going to get the better of you."

"My urges are firmly in check, thank you." She closed the drawer, opened another.

"What are you looking for?"

"I have a headache."

174

Irene pointed at the brown plastic bottle on the counter, in plain sight. "What if you married him? Have you thought of that?"

"Don't worry. We haven't mentioned the M word." Gail washed the aspirin down with a sip of Karen's juice.

"I do worry. Betty Ott's daughter married a Venezuelan—a doctor, too—and within six months he was playing around. It's in their blood."

"Good lord."

"Don't believe me, then. I've read *The Mambo Kings Play Songs of Love*. It was written by a Cuban, so that should tell you something. It's bad enough, Dave leaving. I'd hate like the dickens for you to be disappointed a second time. Although freedom has its merits. Doing what you please, and no man underfoot. See if *I* ever get married again." Irene licked a smear of cheddar off her thumb. She set the plates on placemats printed with sunflowers.

"But you, darling. You're still young." She smiled up at Gail. "You can make a whole new life with someone. And I want him—whoever he is—to be right for you this time. Someone who will take good care of my girl."

Smiling, Gail pulled out a chair. "Mother, I don't need to be taken care of."

"Oh, you know very well what I mean." Irene went back across the kitchen, her sandals twinkling. "You better start asking some hard questions about what it is he wants from you."

"We aren't to that point yet," Gail said.

Irene pointed a handful of silverware at her.

175

"A woman is always at that point." She clinked the silverware down on the table, each precisely in its proper place—salad fork, dinner fork, knife, spoon. Yellow linen napkins were already poked neatly through rings made from seashells. "What does Dr. Feldman say about Karen?"

"Dr. Feldman isn't working out. Marilyn down the street from me takes her daughter to a woman therapist in Kendall who's supposed to be wonderful with preadolescent girls." Gail rubbed the back of her neck. "I'm going to call her. She works on maintaining their self-esteem by putting them in groups where they discuss mythic heroines and female archetypes."

"Good night in the morning. What next?" From behind the refrigerator door Irene said, "It doesn't help that you spend so much time away from her." Only the curly top of her auburn hair showed.

"As if I had a choice." Gail watched Irene set a ring mold of Jell-O on the table. Lime Jell-O with canned pineapple and miniature marshmallows in it. She wondered if Anthony Luis Quintana had ever eaten Jell-O salad in his life.

Coming around to where Gail sat, Irene put her arm across Gail's shoulders. "If it's the money, I could help out."

"Oh, Mom." Gail reached up and gave Irene a kiss. Her mother's cheek was dewy soft and smelled faintly of Chanel. "Thank you, but really, I'm fine."

"Well, don't be too proud." Irene ducked back into the refrigerator for carrot salad, which she scooped into a china bowl. "You never ask for help when you need it most. What are you trying to prove, I'd like to know."

Gail got up to look out the sliding glass door for Karen. The patio was growing dim now that the sun had set. Karen was sneaking up on a little gray lizard clinging to the screen. Her hand was cupped, ready to trap it. One of the older neighborhood boys had showed Karen how to tease the lizard's mouth open, how to let the lizard bite her earlobe and dangle there. It had no teeth to speak of. Karen would find two of them and make earrings. She liked to see Gail's reaction. Maybe it was lizards or other small reptiles that Karen kept in her purse. Gail wondered what the lady therapist with her female archetypes would make of that.

She turned back to the kitchen. "Let me bounce something off you about Althea Tillett's will."

Irene was laying out French bread on a cookie sheet. "All right."

Gail had already decided not to tell Irene that Althea may have been murdered. No use upsetting her now. She asked, "My initial assumption was that Rudy and Monica were behind the forgery. Look at the will. It was the same as the others, except for the addition of their bequest. But why would Jessica Simms and Irving Adler risk their reputations to help them do it? Jessica and Irving didn't even like the twins. Now I wonder if Rudy and Monica were really involved."

"Well, whether they were or not, I wouldn't know." Irene turned on the broiler and slid in the bread. "But as for why Jessica and Irving would do it? That's no mystery. They were very close to Althea. And they—like Althea—belonged to a certain group of friends in this town, going way back."

"Old money."

"Not just that." Irene drew in her chin disapprovingly. "Old Miami, let's say, because not everybody in the group has money. It's not a club. It's more a shared sense of values."

"Do you belong? The Stricklands were here before paved roads."

"Yes, many of my friends are from the old crowd," Irene said. "You could belong too, by extension—if you showed any interest, which so far you haven't."

"Like the D.A.R."

Irene gave her a look then turned to check the oven. "What I think is, Jessica and Irving saw that Althea had written her wills for years and years to benefit the organizations all her friends belonged to. So if they did help forge that will, it wasn't for Rudy and Monica. Oh, no. It was for Althea."

"Or for themselves."

"Does being a lawyer make you so suspicious? No, no. Didn't Jessica and Irving know in their hearts what she wanted? If Althie did destroy her last will, as you suspect, then what? Patrick was her only heir. Without a will, he would inherit every last dime. They must have thought, *This* isn't what Althie would have wanted! We have to *do* something."

Gail added, "The group sticks together even after death."

"I am certain that Jessica and Irving did it for the best of motives." Irene grabbed an oven mitt and pulled open the door, turning off the broiler. She fanned at the cookie sheet as she dropped it on the counter. "And you know what? If somebody had asked me to sign that fake will? I might have done it. Althea wouldn't have wanted Patrick to inherit everything."

Irene put the toast into a basket and tucked a napkin around it. "Let him collect his quarter million dollars and be happy with it." She wiped her hands on a dish towel. "What else would Karen like, I wonder?"

"That's more than enough already." Gail took a piece of toast. "What about Rudy and Monica? Are they in this group of old Miami friends?"

"Well, by blood, but I've never seen them invited to any of the better homes."

"Did you ever meet them?"

"If I did, I've forgotten."

"You may have seen them at Ransom-Everglades," Gail said. "They were two years ahead of me. I was trying to think back, and all I could remember was the time they and some other kids threw a dead raccoon into the road to see what would happen when a car ran over it."

"Oh, stop!"

"So much for their inborn values." Gail took another bite of toast. "Mother, have you ever heard of Sanford Ehringer?"

Irene halved a peach and dropped the pit into

the garbage under the sink. "Yes. Why do you ask?"

"He's the personal representative of Althea's estate. How do you know about Sanford Ehringer?"

"Well, he and my father were friends. Dad wasn't in Sanford's league financially, but they knew each other." Irene lay sections of peach in a fan on Karen's plate. "I haven't laid eyes on him in ages. He and his wife used to give lovely dinner parties around Christmas—your father and I went—but she's been dead for twenty years. He's quite elderly now. I doubt he would even remember me."

"I don't believe this. My mother knows Sanford Ehringer. What about the Easton Trust? Don't tell me you're a member."

Irene looked at her blankly. "No. I've never heard of that."

"Thank God."

"What's this about?"

"I'm going to be suing him as P.R. of the estate. And it's his charity, the Easton Trust, that could lose millions of dollars. His and a few other charities, including your own Opera Guild."

"Oh, dear." Irene lifted a hand to Gail's shoulder and straightened the neckline of her dress. "I imagine Sanford won't like your trying to give all Althie's money to her nephew."

"What's he going to do, have my mortgage called?"

"Oh, don't be silly. He's a gentleman, not likely to do anything so petty and vindictive." She

180

looked around, then crossed the kitchen and slid back the patio door.

"Karen! Dinner's ready! What are you doing? Put that creature down! They eat mosquitoes, darling. They're our friends. And don't let the cat get it." She came back inside, looked at Gail. "A strange child."

By the time Gail reached Lincoln Road Mall, walking from a lot half a block away, the street-lights were on. Seven-fifteen, but still too early to expect Anthony. She debated whether to browse in the bookstore. The doors were open, and classical music came drifting into the street, which wasn't precisely a street. It had been closed to traffic some years ago, trees planted, benches and fountains built, efforts being made at renovation. Not many people were about. An old couple with a dog. Two emaciated-looking girls in mini-dresses and platform clogs, hurrying to wherever they were going. No tourists that she could see. Tourists preferred Ocean Drive, packed with others like themselves, and models, crazies, kids, rich foreigners, gays, straights, street people, night people, or couples over from the mainland for the evening, everything rocking in a neon and pastel glow at the edge of the Atlantic.

Lincoln Road hadn't yet boomed like Ocean Drive, but it was coming along. A new boutique here, a realtor's sign there. Pages of a newspaper sliding on the soft night wind. Sleek couples speaking French going into a restaurant, but in the next doorway, the stench of urine.

Gail walked toward the middle of the next

181

block, where the Tillett Gallery would be. Under a lawn green awning, illuminated by the lights from inside the gallery, people were sipping wine from plastic stemware and chatting happily with each other. About what? Art? Gail didn't know who in Miami collected art. Art, as opposed to decoration. Certainly not her, a joint failure of imagination, time, and money. Who were these people?

Rudy and Monica Tillett would have plenty to sell if Gail lost the case. Their stepmother had collected real art as well as a boggling amount of kitsch. Gail remembered Irene's description of Althea's house: a small Degas on that wall, a collection of porcelain ballet shoes in a case below it, a Picasso upstairs. There a Manchu Dynasty screen, here a Remington bucking bronco with cowboy on a French Empire table, and there a canopic vase with mummified cat entrails sealed inside. Things— *things*—on every wall and horizontal surface.

Enough to forge a will for, maybe. But enough to murder for? Gail had considered that. How far was it, after all, from flinging a dead animal into the path of a car to tipping someone down a flight of stairs? And the payoff was so much bigger. Millions of dollars in real estate and art, not just the fleeting thrill of bones crunching and organs rupturing on the asphalt.

But it wasn't as easy as a push between the shoulder blades. First it required breaking someone's neck. Hauling her body to the stairs. And then the push. Not something a woman could do. But maybe Monica had been working out at Gold's Gym on South Beach, getting hard shoulders and some cut into those quadriceps. It was more likely to have been Rudy, although he had always seemed more sneaky than violent. Or they had done it together. One conjoined act of ultimate greed.

Gail leaned against the stanchion of an awning two doors down from the gallery, wondering what on God's sweet earth she was doing here. Anthony had asked her that. Curiosity, she had said, believing it.

She looked around for a place to wait for him, not wanting to be spotted yet by anyone she knew. Not that people she knew were part of the artsy-intellectual crowd. In the middle of the darkened street, between two trees, was a fountain, a low rectangle crusted with a mosaic of broken tiles. Water splashed in a row of arches lit from below. She walked over to it. Into the concrete edge had been stuck curlicues of buttons, a conch shell, half a radio, the head of a Barbie doll, a plastic flamingo, more bits and pieces than she could identify, all swirled together. She couldn't sit, so walked slowly back and forth, keeping an eye on the sidewalk, watching for Anthony.

The real reason she had come—obvious to her now— was to find evidence of guilt. Guilt of forgery, if not something worse. Proof that Patrick was right. The assurance of not having to tell the partners she had made an awful mistake, so sorry. She had imagined Rudy Tillett's shark-gray eyes shifting sideways, Monica reduced to nervous twitters. Sweat on their foreheads. Denials, then the truth: *Yes, we paid Alan Weissman to forge our stepmother's will!*

Just then a woman dressed in palest pink moved through the crowd to a spot beyond the awning. Her face was in shadow; blond hair curled under at her jaw. She lit a cigarette. Gail saw the flash of a gold lighter, watched it slide back into a tiny purse on a long, thin strap.

The mood Gail was in, she wished she smoked. But not unless she could do it with the elegance of this woman. How she rested her elbow in her palm. How she tilted up her chin and brought the cigarette slowly to her lips; how she pivoted it away on a turn of her wrist.

With a little laugh, Gail came around the fountain. She knew her. Half a dozen strides closed the distance between them.

"Lauren Sontag!"

The cigarette floated down to hip level. "Gail?"

"I've meant to call you so many times." The two of them lightly, quickly pressed their cheeks together.

Lauren drew back, looked intently at her, a hand still on Gail's shoulder. "How have you been? All right?"

"Much better. Thanks."

"It's awfully good to see you. I should have kept in closer touch. I'm terrible."

"We're both terrible. How's the campaign going, by the way?"

"Marvelously. We did a poll. So far I'm ahead."

"Judge Sontag has a nice sound to it."

"Oh, yes. I agree." Lauren laughed, drew on

her cigarette, and exhaled to one side. "Are you wandering around South Beach by yourself?"

"No. I'm meeting someone."

"The same man you've been dating, or . . . ?"

"The same." Gail laughed. "Did I tell you about him?"

"In glorious detail."

Lauren Sontag had been divorced a couple of years ago from a stockbroker. They had one child, a teenage daughter, who lived with him. Lauren said she and her ex were still friends. That had struck Gail as more civilized than she herself could have been. Civilized or else totally numb. Gail had decided that Lauren, then nearing forty, had become too resigned to fading away. So she had insisted Lauren make an effort, call up one of the guys, even answer some ads in the personals column. Lauren had only smiled. *I am finally myself.* Gail didn't know what that meant. It was hard to tell with Lauren.

Now she was tilting her head toward the gallery. Her hair was a shimmering cap of gold silk. "I came with Barry." Barry Fine was a friend of hers, around thirty, a professor of English lit. "He's engaged in deep debate with someone about the moral void of post-modernism. I told him I needed a smoke. You should find him and say hello—if you don't mind running into Rudy Tillett. Or Monica."

"Yes. I had thought to speak to them tonight." Gail looked toward the door, then brought her eyes back to Lauren. A silence fell between them.

Lauren finally said, "So. We seem to be on

185

opposite sides of the issue. Your office and my law partner, at any rate."

"I'll still vote for you." Gail smiled.

A soft laugh. "Thanks."

"Do you know Monica?"

"I know her work." Lauren lifted a shoulder. "It's not to everyone's taste, but I like it. I met her when I was collecting some pieces for my house."

Into the next silence Gail said, "Larry Black and I will be over to see Alan next week."

"I've heard."

Gail listened to the splash of water in the fountain. "Sorry about all this. As soon as I saw you, Althea Tillett went out of my head. I wanted us to go to lunch sometime and catch up."

"We will." Lauren raised the cigarette to her lips, then away. Her nails were perfect and diamonds winked on her fingers. "What is going on? I know you. You wouldn't take a losing case. So what is it? You can't show that Mrs. Tillett lacked the capacity to execute a will. She was as sane as you or I. Saner."

"Perhaps."

"You're going to discuss it with Alan on Wednesday. Why don't you tell me now?"

"Please don't ask me to."

"I'm hardly a stranger."

"Come on, don't."

"You come on." The words had an edge.

"Lauren—this isn't between us."

She shook her head, spoke softly. "No. I'm sorry, Gail. Forgive me." She seemed to study the gallery, where people walked among the white-painted dividers and spotlights hung in the high, black ceiling. She said, "Despite what you told Jessica Simms about Althea's competence, you think the will was forged."

When Gail made no answer, Lauren smiled. "Don't deny it. Rudy told me Patrick was throwing accusations around."

"We're investigating it," Gail said.

Lauren dropped her cigarette to the pavement, slowly pivoting the toe of her pink suede pump. "You're completely wrong about this, Gail. You're being manipulated and lied to."

"By whom?"

"Your client. He hates his cousins. I could tell you things."

"Such as?"

Lauren shook her head. "Tales of childhood. Does anyone ever escape unharmed?"

Gail asked, "What do you know about this?"

"Would you call me as a witness if I told you?"

"Lauren. My God. Whatever Alan Weissman did, it's his problem. Are you afraid you'll get splattered? You'll be safely on the bench long before the case is litigated."

"And therefore I shouldn't care about what happens to him. I do care. He brought me into this firm, he was there for me in ways you can't begin to know. No one has been as faithful to me as Alan." She smiled. "It isn't sex, if you wondered."

"You're protecting him."

Lauren seemed to consider what to say. "He may admit to you on Wednesday that he botched the signing of Althea Tillett's will. But to accuse him of forgery . . . I could laugh if it wasn't so sad."

"What happened?"

"Between you and me, all right?"

"All right," Gail said slowly. She wondered if Lauren had been drinking. Lauren had no business discussing these things with an opposing attorney. Holding her breath, Gail followed Lauren's gaze toward the people under the awning, saw a pale young man in a T-shirt and painted leather vest, his blond hair sticking straight up in two-inch dreadlocks. He spoke to a heavy woman in a long purple skirt and boots, something about having to get a tooth filled. A rather ordinary topic for this gathering, Gail thought.

Finally Lauren said, "Althea Tillett called Alan on Friday afternoon for a Saturday appointment to change her will. You have to understand. Althea would do this routinely on whatever legal matter came to mind—her will, her property, an insurance question. She would simply drop in and expect to be catered to. Naturally, Alan charged her accordingly, but he came to resent the imposition.

"He should never have allowed her to come on a Saturday because we have no staff. During the week there are people to witness a will—secretaries, the law clerk. Alan told Althea this, but she said she would bring two of her friends as witnesses. Jessica Simms didn't want to be there at all, and Irving Adler shouldn't have been. I heard you went to his house. You must have seen how fuddled he is. But Althea insisted, and they all showed up Saturday at ten o'clock."

Under the awning, the woman in the purple skirt was talking to another woman in a business suit. They sipped their wine. The second woman had a gold ring through her left nostril.

Gail looked back at Lauren. She was reaching into her purse for another cigarette, took it out of a case, lit it, snapped the bag shut again. She inhaled deeply.

"I should stop this," she said. "I'll die from it." She pushed her side-parted hair away from her face. "Where was I?"

"Althea and her friends arrived on Saturday at ten."

"Yes. Alan said he would make the changes on the word processor and call a notary. Awhile later I arrived to pick up some papers. Althea was quite annoyed. Where was Mr. Weissman? It had been nearly an hour. I found him asleep in his office. He had been drinking all night, as I found out later, and he hadn't even been home. I pulled the will off the word processor, took everyone into the library, and went back to wake Alan. By the time he came in, they had already signed the will. Alan couldn't notarize it because he isn't a notary. Neither am I. Althea and her friends wanted to leave, so Alan said he would take care of it."

Lauren inhaled smoke, let it go. "A will doesn't have to be notarized to be valid, you know, but on hers, there was a place for it. Alan couldn't leave it empty. How would it look?"

"And so he found Carla Napolitano."

The smoke drifted in the still air. "No. I found her. She's downstairs in a travel agency."

"That was . . . not smart."

"I agree. It was incredibly stupid."

Under the awning, the woman with the nose ring had hooked her arm around the neck of a man in pleated pants and a hundred-and-fifty-dollar Armani cotton shirt. Gail knew the shirt. Anthony had one.

"At the time, it seemed all right. Althea had signed so many wills. She would be back in a few months to do another."

Gail brought her gaze back around. "How did you persuade the notary to do this?"

"Fifty dollars."

"Oh, my God."

Deep blue eyes fixed on her, not wanting to plead, but pleading nonetheless. Lauren made a smile, took a drag off her cigarette. "Now what?"

"I don't know. I really wish you hadn't told me this."

"The will is valid, Gail, even if the notarization isn't. Alan's going to try to protect me, to say I wasn't involved, but I was. It was more my fault than his. He didn't know what he was doing. I was the clear-headed one." She laughed lightly. "Or maybe not." She awkwardly took Gail's hand, and her fingers were trembling. "Don't crucify him—both of us—on the way to losing this case. Please. I'm asking you as a friend."

"Lauren, I can't just drop it."

"I'm not asking for that. A settlement, before everyone in the world knows about it. Something Patrick Norris can be reasonably happy with. And

190

. . . something you can be happy with. I know things are tight for you right now—"

"Don't. I don't want to hear it. We'll talk on Wednesday, but at some point I'll have to take your deposition. Yours and Alan's."

The eyes went cold. "What I told you was between us, as friends. You agreed. I didn't think you'd attack me with it."

Off balance, Gail said, "Lauren, you committed a crime."

Lauren laughed. "A *crime?* Please. Tell me you never cut corners. What will you do, use this to force a settlement?"

Gail felt the heaviness in her chest.

The ember glowed. Lauren exhaled smoke, crushed out her cigarette. "I think I'll see if Barry's ready to go."

"What am I supposed to do, forget about this?"

"Do what you want. I'll deny it happened." She turned and made her way through the crowd, then was lost inside the gallery.

"Damn it. Damn, damn, damn." Gail spun toward the street and noticed Anthony leaning one shoulder against a tree, hands in his pockets. The street lamp cast uneven light through its branches. She walked over to him.

"How long have you been standing there?" she asked.

"A few minutes," he said. "I hate to interrupt an argument unless it comes to blows. Who was she?"

"Lauren Sontag. My friend and a candidate for judge. She just offered me a bribe."

He looked toward the gallery. "Weissman's partner. What was she doing here?"

"I don't know. Hobnobbing with a bunch of posers. She fits right in. God, you think you know someone." She hitched her purse farther up on her shoulder. "Let's go."

"Where?"

"Home. Your house. A hotel. I don't care."

"What about the gallery?"

"Screw the gallery."

"You make me curious about these people, and then you want to leave?" He took her arm and turned her toward the Beach. "We'll go to the corner and back, and then see the gallery. Tell me what happened."

She did.

They walked east, and the street was illuminated by the light shining through the windows of a drugstore, a coffeeshop, a vintage clothing store. A cop pedaled past on a bicycle, blue shorts, white shirt, a gun on his belt.

"I don't know if Lauren is lying or not. I hope she isn't." Gail leaned on Anthony's arm. "I found myself wanting to help her, and Alan too. Even to cover up for them. I mean, why be such a hard-ass? If the will is valid, why make Alan Weissman look like a drunken fool? Or cause Lauren to lose the election?"

"So you now believe the will is genuine?" he asked.

"Imagine if it is. Never mind the partnership, Mr. Robineau, I screwed up." She laughed, then was gloomily silent for a while, watching the concrete move under her feet. Anthony took her hand. They passed two other couples on the sidewalk, and he told her to slow down, they had all night. The scent of the sea began to come up on a warm breeze.

Gail looked at him. "You want to hear my mother's theory of why Jessica Simms and Irving Adler did it? Because Althea would have wanted it that way. She would have wanted the charities to get the money."

Anthony's mouth curved into a smile.

"Maybe it's true. And maybe they're right. The best of motives, as my mother said. So do I blow the whistle on them? They're nice people, respectable citizens, and all that. They just didn't want to see her dissolute nephew get it all when it could go to better causes."

"That makes more sense."

"He isn't dissolute," Gail said firmly. "He doesn't want the money for himself. It's for others. I wish my own motives were so uncluttered. Sometimes I wonder why I'm doing this. Is it because I admire Patrick's ideals or because I want a partnership?"

"But Gail. Selfish motives are mixed into everything we do. That doesn't mean we shouldn't do them." Anthony put his arm around her shoulders. They coasted to a stop in front of a dance studio. Silhouettes of dancers overlapped each other, whirling across the long, dark window.

"All right. Here is a question for you," he said. "I frequently asked myself this when I began to practice criminal law. Who is your client? Who hired you?"

"Patrick, but—"

"Patrick. Yes. And it is to Patrick that you owe your legal duty. And that is the end of the discussion."

"That's too simple. What if people are ruined by this lawsuit?"

"You're an advocate, not a judge. All right, here's another question. Was the will forged or not? If so, it's a crime, and those who did it have no right to your sympathy, and you, Gail, should not be concerned about the consequences of their actions. You have been hired by Patrick Norris. Your duty is to him. He says the will is a forgery. Your document examiner says it is a forgery. Simms and Adler are obviously lying. Lauren Sontag may be lying. Proceed accordingly."

She laughed. "Well, that cuts through the fog, doesn't it? Helps maintain an emotional distance, anyway." She slid her hands under his jacket. He was wearing a white silk shirt and a chocolate brown suit. He kissed her, lightly at first, playing, then his tongue stroked into her mouth.

After a minute, she pulled back, her face flushed. "Well. Yes. Was it a forgery or wasn't it? You know what some of my lady friends in the law would say about that approach?"

Anthony pressed against her. "What if I say I don't care?"

"I'll tell you anyway." She edged a thigh between his, pushed. "They would say it's a male system of ethics. Linear."

"Very linear," he said.

"Like a switch. On or off."

He drew in a sharp breath. "Very much on."

"See? No subtlety at all."

"Do you want subtlety?" he asked.

"No."

His hand closed around her breast. "Do you want to go back to the gallery?"

They took some time thinking about that, then Gail pulled herself out of his arms. She took her compact and lipstick from her purse. "Yes. Actually, I do. I want to see who we're dealing with. I want to see their reaction when I mention the murder investigation." She smoothed on her lipstick.

"I could remind you," Anthony said, "that your friend Patrick is the chief suspect."

"But you won't, right?" Gail smiled into her compact, powdered her nose and cheeks, then snapped it shut. "Would you like to know what Rudy and Monica Tillett used to do with dead raccoons?"

chapter twelve

Outside the Tillett Gallery the crowd had grown, spilling out past the awning. Some teenagers in tattered jeans wandered around, possibly from the School of Arts, copping the free wine. Obviously well-off young couples gathered in groups. A bearded man in running shorts and clogs spoke in French with a turbaned black woman. There weren't many Latinos. Anthony told her they preferred the galleries in Coral Gables, sticking mostly to themselves. He picked up a two-page guide from a rack at the entrance.

The gallery was long and narrow, with a concrete floor and a high ceiling. The young man with the blond dreads poured wine at a table in the corner. Above the echoing voices came the *twang-bong-click* of strange music. White dividers angled and turned like a maze.

At the door Gail stood on her toes, trying to spot Rudy or Monica. Seventeen years ago in high school their hair had been curly black. Rudy had been Gail's height, Monica several inches shorter, both of them muscular and quick, with the physiques of soccer players.

"Gail, my birthday is next month." Anthony nodded toward a pedestal supporting a machine that seemed to have been crafted from wood. Leaves and tendrils sprang from gears and sprockets. A closer look revealed the wood and leaves weren't real at all, but cleverly made of metal and painted. The machine moved, one part thrusting into another. Words slid across a small video screen: "He shew'd me lilies for my hair, and blushing roses for my brow . . ." A small white plaque announced: *Romance. Monica Tillett. $4,500.*

"Would you mind terribly if I just bought you a card?" Gail slipped her arm through his. "Although I do like this. Whatever it is."

From the other side of a divider came loud female laughter. A whoop, really. And then Gail saw a man who seemed familiar. Late forties,

196

good haircut, expensive sport jacket. He veered away from the exit and came in her direction.

He held out his hand. "Gail, how are you? We met downtown last week." He smiled. Perfect teeth, deep voice. "Howard Odell." His collar was open, and he wore a flat gold chain that gleamed sinuously against his neck.

"Of course," she said. "How do you do, Mr. Odell."

"Howard." There was no wink this time. "Tony, my friend. Haven't heard from you."

"Ah, well. Bad timing."

"Gotta get together." But his attention was back on Gail. "Wonder if I can give you a buzz at your office. Like to chat with you."

"What about?" she said pleasantly.

"Oh . . . business. A probate matter you may be involved in."

Anthony said, "Excuse me, there's someone over there I need to speak to." He drifted away, Gail looking after him.

"A probate matter, Mr. Odell?"

"Please. It's Howard." He touched his chest. "I'm not a formal kind of guy."

He handed her a card similar to the one she had seen before. His name was printed in gold, followed by the words, EXECUTIVE DIRECTOR, EASTON CHARITABLE TRUST.

She looked up.

He was smiling. "My understanding is, you've been retained by Althea Tillett's nephew to overturn her will. Gotta tell you, I'm disappointed. Althea left the residuary of her estate to the charity I'm involved with—the Easton Trust.

You know, Althea was a great gal. Her biggest joy in life, I'd say, was to help those less fortunate than herself. She wanted to start a scholarship program for inner-city youth. Week or two before she died, as a matter of fact, she called me up. Said, 'Howard, you know I've always made a provision in my will for the Easton Trust. Here's what I want you to do. You make sure that those kids—' "

Gail broke in. "Excuse me, but who told you I represent Patrick Norris?"

"Rudy Tillett, just now. We're on the Art Deco League together, so I know Rudy pretty well." Odell shook his head. "I said, 'Rudy, you're kidding. What's going on?' But I guess you're the one I should ask."

She noticed his hair—thick brown, a hint of gray at the sides. Perfect. It must have cost a fortune. "What is it, exactly, that you do as director of the Easton Trust . . . Howard?"

He laughed softly, a deep rumble. "Try to separate people from their money and then help the board decide where best to spend it, who can benefit most. So what are we going to do about Patrick Norris? Look, Gail. Your client isn't happy? Let's see what we can do to make him a little happier. Get this thing resolved *tout de suite*. You litigate, it'll be years. And from what Rudy tells me, he and Monica ain't gonna roll over. So let me take you to lunch, we'll talk."

"What you're saying is, the Easton Charitable Trust will pay Mr. Norris not to contest the will. Correct?"

He touched her arm, came in a little closer.

"What I'm suggesting—and this makes sense—the trust kicks in, the Tilletts kick in, all the major beneficiaries. Everybody sits down together, works out a reasonable compromise. I'll be glad to make the phone calls."

"No, I don't think so—not unless we're talking some serious numbers."

"How serious you want to get?"

"Do you have any idea, Howard, what the estate is worth?"

"I have a good idea. I also know you don't have much of a case." He looked at her steadily. "Rudy says you think the will was forged. How come?"

"I prefer not to get into that," Gail said.

He came closer, speaking over the noise in the gallery. She smelled breath mints and Polo. "What are you doing, Gail? Althea wanted to give her money to charity, not to taxes. Or to lawyers. She wanted to remember her best friends. And what about the ordinary folks Althea cared about? Her household help, for instance, who faithfully toiled for many years. You going to leave them with nothing?"

She dropped his card into her purse, made a smile. "It was a pleasure seeing you, Howard. Perhaps I'll give you a call sometime."

He raised a hand, pointing at her. "Be careful, Gail. The media haven't got hold of this yet. Once they do, your bargaining power's down the tubes. What have we got? A lawyer blocking disbursement of money to charity, using the system to jack up a big settlement for a man the decedent herself thought was a pain in the ass. I

199

see that Cuban station, *Canal 23,* over at his apartment, talking to the pro-Castro leftists he hangs out with. I see the *Miami Herald* uncovering his conviction for drug possession. You didn't know about that? I bet Norris has a few more surprises for you. That is not a model citizen you've picked for a client, Gail. You get the community on your back, the judge wonders about that. He has to. Human nature."

"What are you planning, a press conference?"

"It's up to you. You play nice, I'll play nice. Okay?"

Her hands trembling with anger, Gail reached back into her purse, took out his card, tore it in half, then again. The pieces fluttered to the concrete floor. She whirled around and went off to find Anthony, mumbling curses through her teeth, first cursing Howard Odell and then herself for a petty display of rage. From somewhere in the gallery came the same braying whoop she had heard before, followed by a chorus of laughter.

She found Anthony studying a miniature TV screen mounted in a rosewood box. He held his jacket over his shoulder by one finger in the neckline. Gail wanted to slip up behind him, press herself against his silk shirt, and close her eyes. She glanced at what held his attention so raptly: On scratched and grainy film a soft-fleshed woman wearing nothing but rolled stockings sank to her knees, hair flowing over her raised arms, mouth opening in a kind of ecstasy.

A slender blond man in a linen suit standing on the other side of Anthony gestured with his wine. "Incredible, what she does with the human form in her art. It's relentlessly genital. Yet there's a delicate spirituality. Do you see what I mean?"

Gail saw Anthony's head turn slowly, slowly. She could imagine the dark glitter in his eyes.

The man smiled. "Do you live on the Beach?"

"He's mine," Gail said, speaking around Anthony, taking his arm.

The man looked at her, laughed. "Well, more power to you." He withdrew a card from his shirt pocket and extended it to Anthony. "I'm with an agency. We're in the market for the Mediterranean type. There simply aren't enough good models your age. Would you be interested? If can be quite lucrative."

"No."

The man drew back his card. "Never mind, then." He went away.

Gail pinched Anthony's cheek. "Stop growling. He's right. You are pretty."

"What did Howard Odell want?"

"Oh, Howard. He was being a jerk, threatening me with exposure in the *Miami Herald* as a sorry example of why the American public despises lawyers. I'll tell you later." She laid her head on his shoulder for a second. "I have to go find Rudy and Monica. Then I want a drink."

"What did he say to you?"

"Will you beat him up for me?"

"Gail, this could be serious."

"Yes. I know that. I do know." She let out a breath. "He says Patrick was once arrested for drug possession. And please don't start on how I shouldn't have gotten involved."

"Would you like an investigator to look into this? I could have mine call you."

"It's an obvious lie. Back in law school, I never even saw Patrick smoke a joint."

"And law school has been . . . how long ago?"

"God. Poor Patrick. Such trouble. Well, Howard Odell is no saint, is he? You told me he had a friend who was a pornographer. Your client, remember?"

"Not friend, acquaintance," Anthony corrected.

"Oh. Well, forgive me, Howard." She gave Anthony's waist a quick hug. "I'll be back."

"Where are you going?"

"To find Rudy and Monica. I'm feeling reckless."

"Don't get into trouble," he said.

She smiled over her shoulder. "And don't you get picked up."

Monica Tillett—Gail knew her immediately—was in the center of a group of people. She was a sturdy, square-shouldered woman in black tights and a flowing red blouse. She had brows like blackbird wings over deep-set gray eyes. Her black hair, parted in the middle, sprang in wild curls from her head as if an electrical current had passed through it. Her hands chopped the air as she spoke about the spinelessness of the current art scene.

"We're all scared to offend somebody. Gotta be so correct, don't criticize victims of society. Victims! The victims are discriminating against everybody else! It's an excuse for a lack of talent.

202

You're discriminated against, *ergo* your art is valuable?"

Gail noticed a man taking notes. An art critic? A reporter? How much of this would appear in print?

"Like that fuckin' Whitney Biennial, those buttons they gave out. 'I can't imagine ever wanting to be white.' Hah!" And Monica laughed, a single loud peal. It was she whom Gail had heard before, over the dividers. "Oh, sure. If it doesn't have an agenda, it's not art? Adolf Hitler said that. How art has a duty to uplift. Fuck that. The minute you have an agenda, you start cranking out clichés."

A young woman asked, "But doesn't your own art contain feminist themes?"

"Excuse me? Like it's gotta fit in this little square box? With a label?" Her intense gray eyes, the brows gathering over them like storm clouds, suddenly fixed on Gail. Her words began to slow down. "Look, I don't care what it is. That's the point. It is what it is. Hey, you-all excuse me a minute, okay? I gotta talk to somebody."

Gail involuntarily took a step backward. Monica Tillett walked toward her, shorter by half a foot but moving like a heavy cat, all slit-eyed intensity. She looked up into Gail's face, then whispered, "Jesus effing Christ. I didn't think you'd show up here."

"I could leave."

"What, leave? No." Monica turned, looking for someone. "I guess we ought to talk, right? Hey! Rudy! Check out who's here."

Gail hadn't noticed him before, a brooding

man with the same wild black hair as Monica's, though his was cut a little shorter. He was staring sullenly at Gail, rocking back and forth on his heels. He wore jeans and a faded black T-shirt that clung to rippling pecs and biceps.

Monica grabbed Gail's arm. "Come on. We've got a room in the back." Gail looked over her shoulder for Anthony. Monica laughed. "What? We're going to bind and gag you?"

The dusty room, lit by a long fluorescent light, was no more than eight feet square, crammed with canvases, frames, a ladder, boxes, assorted junk. Rudy closed the door and silence fell.

Gail said, "I didn't think you'd recognize me after all these years."

"Why not? Ransom was a small school. You were student council, right? One of those girls that ran things. I remember." Monica laughed. "Cripes. You know what tonight is? My breakout. All these years of busting my buns. And get this. We had somebody from *Art in America* in here earlier. Down on vacation, sort of stumbled in by accident. He said he liked my stuff, and I don't think he was bullshitting me."

"Congratulations."

"Yeah. I'm like so high on this, then you show up."

From his place by the door Rudy crossed his arms. The muscles danced in his forearms. "What are you doing here, anyway?"

After a moment, Gail said, "Curiosity?"

"What do you want?"

Both of them, Gail noticed, had full, red lips,

and their blood seemed to be racing just below the surface of their skin.

"Rudy, honey. Chill." Monica sat heavily on a middle step of the ladder. She looked morosely up at Gail. "I know what you think we did. If Patrick told you that, he's demented. Totally out of his fuckin' mind, okay?"

By now Gail had recovered herself. "Can I ask a question?"

Monica threw up her hands. "Yes! What do you want to know? Let's get this done, over."

"Who found the will?"

"We did, in Althea's house, the day after she died. She's got a study upstairs and a desk, and we found it in a drawer."

"Why did you and Rudy go through her papers? Patrick is her nearest relative."

"So what? Althea was our stepmother for twenty-two years."

"How did you get in?"

"The housekeeper, Rosa." Monica barked a laugh. "It's our house. We grew up there!"

"What did you do with the will?"

"We took it and a bunch of other papers over to Alan Weissman's office, her attorney."

"You gave it personally to Alan Weissman?"

"No. His secretary, I forget. Whoever was at the front desk."

"Did you read it?"

"Sure. Wouldn't you? I nearly fell over. She actually did what she promised. She gave us our mother's house back. Didn't I say that, Rudy?"

"Yes, and the art." Rudy gazed coolly at Gail. "Althea said we could have it."

"When?"

"Several times. It was understood. It belonged to our parents."

"I thought you and Althea didn't get along."

"Who told you *that* lie?"

"Let's say it's a general impression I get from talking to people who knew her." Gail began to feel a little claustrophobic in the cluttered room.

"What an *asshole!*" Monica pitched over, beating her fists on her thighs, then just as quickly she straightened, glaring at Gail. "You know what's going on here, don't you? Patrick is getting his revenge. Okay, fine. We treated him like shit after Daddy let him come live with us. We were *kids.*"

"Our father, who we adored," Rudy said, "married within a few months of our mother's death a woman eighteen years younger than he. And then Patrick came into our home, and Monica and I—Well, of course we resented him." Rudy's nostrils flared, and his voice shook.

He added, "We didn't treat Althea very nicely either, to be candid with you. Nor she, us. But in later years we all put our feelings aside. A *rapprochement,* as it were."

Monica leaped up, clutching at her hair. "I cannot fucking believe this is happening."

"Monny, don't." Rudy rushed the two or three steps from the door.

"It's our home!" She buried her face in his T-shirt, and he put his arms around her and rocked her back and forth. "Mama died when we were only children, then that *witch* drove Daddy to his grave, and now Patrick wants to take our *home!*"

"Don't, don't, don't." He patted her hair. It sprang back up. His eyes were on Gail, accusing.

"Okay. Okay." Monica stiffly held out an arm, fingers splayed. She wiped her cheeks with the heel of her other hand. "How much does he want? She didn't leave him enough? Fine, Rudy, give him the Degas and the Krasner. Give him whatever the fuck he wants."

"I won't give him one pencil drawing. This is blackmail."

"Rudy, please! I can't stand it!"

His brows knotted, and the lines deepened in his forehead. He drew her back to him, holding her tightly. "It's okay, Monny," he whispered, stroking her hair. "This is the best night. The best."

"Hah!"

"It's going to be all right, I promise." He glared at Gail. "You have succeeded in ruining my sister's show. Happy?"

"Not particularly."

"Tell us what you want. Oh, do. Shall we divide the house down the middle with a chain saw? Or shall we give Patrick a shopping cart? What would please him most?"

Brushing the dust off her skirt, Gail walked the short distance to where they stood, shoulder to shoulder, both of them staring defiantly, their hair like dark penumbras around their heads. "I'll see what he has to say. I can't promise you anything. If there's a settlement, he'll have to approve it."

Monica gritted her teeth. "Tell the sanctimonious snake that there is no fucking way we're gonna give him our house."

A knock sounded on the door.

She yelled, "What? Who is it?"

It was the young man with the blond dreadlocks. He intruded only his head and one shoulder, his hand gripping the edge of the door. "I think you ought to come out here. Now."

"Why?"

"Trou-ble." He sang the syllables.

"What's going on?" Rudy asked.

The young man squinted his eyes and smiled. "Your cousin?"

"God *damn* it to hell!" Monica leaped for the door and was gone in a swirl of red, Rudy close behind.

By the time Gail caught up, Rudy and Monica were standing as if turned to stone at the edge of a small crowd gathered along the west wall of the gallery.

The tall, thin figure of Patrick Norris was at its center. The spotlights in the ceiling bounced off his wire-frame glasses, and his extended finger pointed toward an oil painting on the wall, a square of white with faint lines of gray running through it. Not one of Monica's.

"This piece, for example. What is it? Nothing. It's empty of content and meaning. But we wouldn't dare say so, not here. We'd rather pretend to see the Emperor's New Clothes. We'd rather be among the elite—" His fingers curled into quotation marks. "—than the rabble along the parade route. Those slobs from Hialeah and

208

Homestead and Kendall who can't begin to understand art and culture."

Gail groaned. "Oh, my God."

"Patrick, you son of a bitch!" Monica's voice shattered the momentary lull. Electronic music was still twanging from hidden speakers. Tears streamed down her cheeks.

He smiled at her. "Hi, Monica. Don't I recognize this from Aunt Althie's downstairs hall? If you're going to steal her paintings, you could be a little less obvious."

Gail felt a hand on her arm. Anthony. He said, "What's going on?"

"Help me get him out of here, will you?"

"*That* is Patrick Norris?"

"Afraid so."

Rudy had shouldered his way through the crowd, which seemed to waver between collective laughter and shock, everybody waiting to see what would happen.

"Get out. Get out now, before I have you thrown out into the street." They stood nearly chest to chest, Rudy half a head shorter, his hands drawn into tight fists.

Patrick smiled, his beard twitching. "Are we getting too close to the truth?" He calmly adjusted his glasses and bent to read the card affixed to the wall beside the painting. "Three thousand dollars. Goodness. This ought to pay the rent for a while. What else did you take out of her house?"

Rudy spun him around and aimed for his face. The blow glanced off and sent Patrick's glasses flying. The next caught him in the ribs and both men stumbled into a divider, Patrick with his arms crossed over his head. People screamed. Others came running to see.

"*Ay, Diós mío.*" Anthony pushed through.

Patrick stumbled and sat down hard on the concrete floor. Rudy's black lace-up boot hit him in the thigh, then again. "Get out, get out, get out!" A woman giggled nervously, her hands to her mouth. Someone yelled to call the police.

Anthony shoved Rudy aside, then bent to grab one of Patrick's arms. Gail took the other, and they pulled him toward the door, his feet bicycling along the concrete.

Around the corner from the gallery was a row of small shops with a brick planter in front. They sat on the edge of it, Gail using Anthony's handkerchief to dab at Patrick's cheekbone where the glasses had cut it. In the dim light the blood appeared dark purple. Anthony paced back and forth brushing dust off the front of his jacket.

"I went," Patrick was saying, "because I suspected this. I thought they might be looting the place already."

"You should have told me," Gail said. "I'd have handled it."

"How?" he challenged. "A restraining order? A piece of paper?"

"No, Patrick, we'd have had them assassinated. Would you please try to remember you have an attorney? Do not do anything on your own. You're in more danger than you realize."

He squinted at her. His glasses were still in the

gallery, and his face seemed empty without them. "What are you talking about?"

"The police, for one thing. I talked with a detective in the Beach Police. They believe that Althea was murdered and that you did it."

Patrick's laugh came out as a groan. "I figured that much." He glanced over at Anthony, who had reached the end of the planter, hands on his hips, and was turning back again.

Gail said, "Anthony Quintana's on our side. Besides being my friend, he's a criminal attorney. You may need him."

Anthony gave her a warning look. He would choose his own clients.

"What are the cops going on?" Patrick asked. "If they have any so-called proof, they fabricated it."

"He wouldn't tell me."

"Christ. Somebody put them up to this."

Gail heard Anthony snort, then start pacing again. She asked, "Do you know Howard Odell?"

Patrick shook his head. "No. Who's he?"

"He manages one of the charities in the will, the Easton Charitable Trust. I ran into him tonight by accident. God, what a smarmy bastard. Anyway, he threatened to kill us in the press unless you settle the case."

"Screw that."

Gail raised a hand to quiet him. "Odell says you were arrested for possession of drugs. True?"

"Yes."

She waited. "Well?"

"Heroin and narcotics implements."

"Patrick!"

"The case was dismissed. I was trying to help start a needle-exchange program in Belle Glade, and the cops didn't like it. Belle Glade, which is full of migrant workers, where the AIDS rate is higher than in San Francisco. They'd rather let everybody die from it. Get rid of your undesirables that way."

"Stop ranting, Patrick." Gail folded the handkerchief neatly and laid it on the planter. "Is there anything else you should tell me?"

"No. Nothing like that." He put his forehead on his fists. "I'm sorry. I didn't mean to get worked up. And I shouldn't have come here, you're right." He looked at her, took her hands in his. "So are you still with me, Gail? Looks like I need you more than ever."

In her peripheral vision, Gail could see Anthony stop walking.

She said, "Four people told me tonight that we're going to lose. Weissman's partner swears she saw Althea and the witnesses come into the office and sign the will. Howard Odell says the judge will rule against us on principle. And your stepcousins say that Althea promised them the house because it belonged to their parents."

Patrick said, "But the will was forged. I know it was. Our document examiner can prove it. That's what counts, isn't it?"

Gail glanced at Anthony, who smiled at her as if to say Patrick had grasped the essential point better than she had.

She sighed. "Yes, Patrick. I'm still with you."

He soundly kissed both her cheeks, then

embraced her. "I knew you wouldn't let me down."

Anthony came to a stop directly in front of Patrick, who let go of Gail and looked up at him. "Quintana. Are you Cuban?"

"Yes."

"Oh, God." He laughed, then shook his head when Anthony continued to stare at him coldly. "It's funny, that's all."

"Why?"

"It just is. Me, a socialist. You, a Miami Cuban. You have to see the humor in it."

"I stay out of politics."

"Life is politics. Everything is political. You have to pick a side. You have to choose, because in the middle there's only zeros."

Gail said, "You can't make judgments. You don't know who he is or what he believes in."

Anthony's expression darkened and his accent peppered his words. "Don't explain me to him. Don't ask me to represent him. He is an idiot. Are we finished now? I would like to go home."

Patrick looked at Gail. "Is he always this proprietary?"

"Butt out, Patrick," she said.

Under his satin comforter, Anthony explained how the machine worked. The $4,500 machine made of branches and twigs and leaves, with the gears and pulleys and screws that turned so smoothly, rolling over and over each other, *arriba y abajo y arriba,* and how the shaft was carved so precisely, so delicately, that it fit perfectly into

213

the housing, *adentro y afuera y adentro* . . . truly a work of art.

He moved his mouth from her lips to her ear. *"Te quiero."*

"Do you?"

"Do I what?"

She took his hair, lifted his head to see him. "Love me. Do you love me?"

"I just said so."

"We only say it when we're making love. It doesn't count then."

"It counts. Why not?"

"Don't pretend not to understand."

"Yes, Gail. I love you."

"You're saying that because I asked you to."

"Okay, I'll say it tomorrow while you're having your coffee."

She slid down far enough to nuzzle her face into his chest. "Patrick is right, you know. People have to make choices."

"What a pathetic excuse for a man. He only makes speeches, and those are irrational."

"You know what I mean."

Anthony rolled over to lie flat on his back. He exhaled heavily. *"Me vuelves loco."*

"Poor baby. Completely crazy." She kissed him, then propped herself on one elbow. "Talk to me," she said.

"About what?"

"I don't know." She was silent for a while. "Anything."

"Philosophy? Politics."

"Stop it, will you?" Gail sat up.

Laughing softly, he reached for her, drew her

down to him, and put his arms around her. "I know. Art."

"Be serious."

"I am." His hand cupped her breast, squeezed. Then slid between her legs. "The machine we saw tonight— did you notice the flowers?"

Gail closed her eyes and nodded. "Yes. I did notice that."

"How realistic. How the petals opened?"

"Oh, yes."

chapter thirteen

Monday morning it rained, a steady gray drizzle that brought the first real evidence that summer had finally ended. Even by noon the temperature was only eighty degrees. Gail took a cab back from a hearing at the courthouse, shook her umbrella under the awning, then went straight up to see Eric Ramsay on the sixteenth floor.

He had a small office between the computer room and personnel, with the windows of the building next door to look at. New associates would often start in the woods like this, then move closer, if they lasted. In the deserted corridor Gail could make out a low-level hum, the nerve system of Hartwell Black, its ganglia and synapses: computers whirring around the clock, printers buzzing for accounting, billing, word processing.

Eric's door was open. He wasn't there, but the light was on, and his color monitor glowed with figures. Gail hadn't been up here in weeks, and the office seemed more cluttered than ever. Besides the usual books and files and legal magazines that crammed the shelves, there were a miniature pool table on his credenza, a basketball hoop over the teak trash can, and a stack of *Wall Street Journals* beside his chair. The chair was stainless steel and black leather, and it had cost $1,200. Gail knew that because he had mentioned it to her twice. He had also complained about the measly starting salary of $55,000 for new associates. There were no family photos in his office. A fern sat in the window, unwatered, dropping tiny curls of brown on the sill.

"Hello, boss. Looking for me?" When Gail turned in the doorway, Eric moved past her with a stack of books under one arm.

"Yes. I want to tell you about my adventures with Rudy and Monica Tillett." She set her umbrella against the wall and her briefcase beside it. "I was also wondering if you finished the motions for deposition in the Norris case."

"Almost. This afternoon."

"Come on, Eric. You said you'd have it done this morning."

Eric dropped the stack of books on his desk. "Friday at six-thirty Cy Mackey dumped this shit on me. He said he had to go out of town on an emergency and he needed it by noon today." Eric motioned toward the computer screen. "I'm about done. I was here till four-thirty this

216

morning. You know what Cy's emergency was? He took his girlfriend to Cozumel for the weekend. Schoenfeld's law clerk just told me."

"That sounds familiar. I went through the same sort of thing my first two years." Gail sat down. "You must be exhausted."

He chuckled. "No."

"What are you doing, speed?"

"Me and every other clerk and junior associate who has to hump it sixteen hours a day. Don't tell me you never did."

Gail only replied, "I don't suppose you had a chance to find out about Carla Napolitano over the weekend."

"Yes, actually I did." He sat in his steel and black leather chair. "Carla Napolitano. Middle-aged brown hair, overweight. She drives a blue 1990 Toyota, lives alone, rents a unit in a beachfront condo at Fiftieth and Collins. She works at Gateway Travel, and she's a notary. That's about it." He slid a piece of paper in her direction. "The number on her license plate, which you asked for."

"How about that bar? Wild Cherry."

"A sleazy dive on West Dixie Highway next to an auto repair shop. I spent about five minutes there on my way home from the office about midnight on Saturday. I asked if they knew anybody named Carla Napolitano. They didn't. I asked about a Frankie. No to that too. Then the bouncer wanted my name, so I left. Whoever this Frankie was that Miriam talked to at Gateway Travel, I didn't find him. Maybe she got it wrong.

I don't see how we connect Napolitano to a nudie bar. Miriam's pretty scatterbrained."

"Miriam? Hardly."

"What can I tell you? I struck out." Eric clicked the point of his pen in and out several times, then made a rhythm on his tax manual.

Gail uncrossed her legs. "I see you're busy."

He gave her a crooked smile. He had a short nose and broad, ruddy cheeks. "Never that busy. I want to hear what happened at the gallery. Sit down."

She did. "Rudy and Monica denied forging the will, but I'd expected that. We were talking about settling the case, then Patrick showed up."

"No kidding."

"It was quite a scene. He accused Rudy of stealing from the estate, and Rudy attacked him. He hit him in the face. I had to get Patrick out of there fast, before it got worse."

"So did you file a police report?"

Gail waved the idea away. "Patrick's all right. Let's not stir it up. Look, I need you to draft a restraining order against Rudy and Monica. They mustn't be allowed to touch anything belonging to the estate. Can you get that done by the end of the week?"

"Sure. No problem," Eric said.

"Don't file it. Larry Black and I are talking to Alan Weissman on Wednesday. Let's see what happens with that." Gail would keep her conversation with Lauren Sontag to herself. Eric didn't need to know everything.

"I'd like to come along," Eric said. "I want to see what you do to Weissman."

"I'm not going to *do* anything to Weissman. Listen, Eric. You don't go to a conference with an attitude. The other side can sense it, then they either get hostile or they start lying, and you wind up with nothing. You have to get their trust, then pounce."

He laughed softly, playing with a rubber band. "Shuffle and jive."

Gail looked at him without smiling, then said, "I have a question about G. Howard Odell."

He tilted his head.

"In the management meeting you said you did some work for him last year."

"Right. What about him?"

Gail told Eric how she had run into Odell at the gallery, about his request for a settlement, his threats if she didn't go along.

Eric nodded. "Oh, yeah. That sounds like Howard. He can't stand not being in total control. I met him playing racquetball at the spa I go to, and he got worked up because I beat him by fifteen points. He can play, but come on."

"What kind of legal work did you do for him?"

"He was selling a house on Star Island, part of a divorce settlement, I believe. He let me review the contract." Eric was revolving the rubber band around and around his fingers. He still had the beefy hands of a college athlete.

"I thought about it later. Why would Howard let *me* review his contract? I was a new associate and he has his own attorneys at another firm. Then I remembered I'd let him win twenty bucks off me the previous two times we played." Eric stretched the rubber band from the tip of his finger to his thumb, cocking it like a pistol, squinting one eye. "So the next time I beat him twenty-one to six. That was it for the racquetball." Eric moved his thumb and the rubber band whirred toward the window and clipped some foliage off the thirsty fern.

"What did he tell you about himself?"

"Not a whole lot. He has a couple of ex-wives he pays heavy alimony to. A son at some Ivy League college. He invests. He puts deals together. He's related to Sanford Ehringer, by the way."

"I didn't know that. How?"

"His mother was Ehringer's second cousin, something like that, up in Palm Beach. The families go way back."

"Is that how Odell came to be executive director of the Trust?"

"Beats me. Why do you care about Odell?"

"Because if he's planning an attack, I want to know who I'm dealing with."

"Howard? He's full of hot air. He won't do anything to us."

"That's not the impression I get from Larry Black."

"Are they friends?"

"No. Business acquaintances."

On Saturday Gail had taken Karen over to Larry and Dee-Dee's waterfront house in Gables Estates. While Dee-Dee fixed the salad and the girls played in the pool, Larry took Gail into his study. She told him about the gallery episode, all of it, including Odell's threats. Larry had listened, then poured himself another Scotch. *I knew this*

220

would happen. Sanford Ehringer's getting into this now. We've got to settle. Twist Patrick Norris's arm if you have to. And the decanter had rattled on the rim of the glass.

Eric's laughter broke into the silence. "God *damn,* I wish I'd been there when you tore up Howard's card. I'd love to have seen his face. Do you have some nerve, or what?" Eric fixed his eyes on her. Pale green with flecks of hazel. "You're okay, Gail. I'm glad we're working together."

After a second, she nodded. "Thanks."

"I won't be much longer, then we can compare notes on Norris. Let's go to lunch. I'm buying."

She hesitated, not sure if she was reading this invitation the way it was meant. "Sorry, but I've got some things to do. Maybe later in the week."

"I'll hold you to that." Eric leaned on his forearms, the sleeves rolled up, blond hair dusting the tight muscles. "Because I'll tell you straight out. You're one hell of an attractive lady. I think we could have a good time together."

Gail looked at him in the momentary quiet, in the subsonic hum of computers and printers and electricity surging over the lines. "You know, Eric. It's not good policy to date people in the office."

He laughed softly. "Yeah? Is that your policy or office policy?"

"Mine."

He shrugged and leaned back in his chair. "By the way, did you read the *Herald* this morning?"

"No. Why?"

"Take it with you." He gestured toward a

221

section of newspaper on his desk. "My secretary brought it in. Liz Lerner's piece."

The *Business Monday* section was already turned to the right page, a column called "Legal Notes." Liz Lerner knew the dirt on every law firm in South Florida, or at least every law firm assumed she did. Leaks and gossip made the staple fare of her wickedly delicious report. Attorneys would call her up in advance to "set the record straight" on events Liz couldn't have heard about yet.

The headline queried MIAMI'S OLDEST FIRM HEADING FOR A SPLIT? Gail sat back down to read it.

Rumors are flying at Hartwell Black and Robineau, founded 1922. Paul Robineau, managing partner of the 78-lawyer firm head-quartered in Miami, did not deny he has inquired about space in the InterAmerica Tower. "A firm has to change with the times," Robineau said. "It's unfortunate that some of us are so reluctant to give up old habits." Partner Lawrence Black denied talk of a divorce. He did say, however, that he has the "utmost respect for Paul, whatever may occur."

"Makes you ask yourself," Eric said, "why you break your back for them. What's the point, if you could be out of a job tomorrow?"

She laid the paper back on his desk. "The firm has come through this sort of thing before."

Eric flipped open one of the tax manuals, then smiled up at her. "Forgive me, but I must return to Mr. Mackey's project. Let's hope he had a simply smashing time in Cozumel."

Gail unwrapped a ham and swiss sandwich and tossed the pickle slices into the trash can under Miriam's desk. Taking a bite of sandwich, she leaned over the work table to scan the finished version of the petition Eric Ramsay had prepared last week. *Patrick Norris v. Sanford V. Ehringer, as Personal Representative of the Estate of Althea Norris Tillett, Deceased.* The petition looked fine. Depending on what happened with Alan Weissman on Wednesday, it would be filed the day following. Or not.

She glanced up. Miriam had come into the cubicle with her hands full of files. Seeing Gail, she grinned as if she'd just caught one of the senior partners in the storeroom with his secretary. She was wearing flats today, her hair was down, and she could have passed for sixteen.

"You have something to tell me," Gail said.

"It's about Carla Napolitano." Miriam dropped the files on her desk and began searching for something. "This morning at the computer upstairs I got the Secretary of State's office in Tallahassee. The travel agency where Carla Napolitano works—Gateway Travel—is a fictitious name for a corporation called Seagate. Wild Cherry is owned by a company called Atlantic Enterprises."

Gail turned back her napkin far enough to take another bite of sandwich. "And then you ran those two companies through the computer?"

"Yes!" Miriam held up a long sheet of paper

223

with holes down both sides. Gail took it. Two companies were listed, one after the other. Atlantic Enterprises and Seagate, Inc. Corporate name and address, date of incorporation—1979 for Atlantic, 1981 for Seagate. Two or three names she'd never heard of were listed in each of the officer/director spaces. More addresses. Then for each corporation, an office on Brickell Avenue where you could serve a summons and complaint if you wanted to sue the corporation. All very anonymous.

"Look at the addresses for Atlantic and Seagate," Miriam said, pointing.

Gail nodded. "I am. Fourteen-seventy Drexel Avenue, Miami Beach. Both of them. Well, well . . . so this proves Gateway Travel and Wild Cherry are in bed together. But what does Carla Napolitano have to do with it? If we're going to scuttle her credibility, we'll have to do better than that."

"Maybe she's a stripper at Wild Cherry on the weekend."

"No, she is not a stripper, Miriam. Talk to Eric. The woman is way too old for stripping in public."

Miriam scowled. "Do you know what Eric wants me to call him? Mr. Ramsay. Really!"

"Don't let it bother you. Make him call you Ms. Ruiz."

"Well, I'm not going to call him Mr. Ramsay. If clients are here, then okay, but not to his face." Miriam took a sharp breath, her black-penciled eyes widening. "*¡Se me olvidó!* Your mom called, and she's on her way here with Karen."

224

"What on earth for?" It was a teacher planning day, no school, and Gail had asked Irene to baby-sit, since Phyllis couldn't come until the after-noon.

"She just said she had to talk to you."

With a sigh, Gail signed the papers in Patrick's case, then started on the other pleadings and letters and memos Miriam had laid out for her. When she finished, Miriam's slender hand, bracelets jingling, dropped a gold-embossed busi-ness card on the table. It was Howard Odell's card, which Anthony had tossed into the ashtray upstairs and Gail had retrieved and clipped into the Norris file.

"What's this for?"

"Read the address on the card." Miriam leaned against the table with her arms folded, waiting. "See where Howard Odell works?"

"One Thousand Brickell Avenue, Suite 2140." Gail looked up. "Okay. It's the same as the Easton Trust. I know that. He's the executive director."

"Yes, but look." On the computer printout Miriam pointed to the name and address of the registered agent for the companies she had found. Corporate Services, Inc. 1000 Brickell Avenue, Suite 2190, Miami FL 33131.

"Hmmmm." Gail chewed her sandwich, her eyes on the paper. "Same building as Easton. Right down the hall."

"Interesting."

The companies that operated Wild Cherry and Gateway Travel Agency were in the same building on Miami Beach. They used the same registered agent in the same building downtown as the Easton Trust.

"What now?" Miriam asked.

"Dial the registered agent's office," Gail said. When Miriam had done so, she gave the telephone to Gail, and Gail listened to the rings on the other end. Then a man's voice. "You have reached the office of Corporate Services, Inc. No one can take your call at the moment. If you leave your—"

"Dead end," she told Miriam. Gail looked down at the desk for a while, studying the computer printouts. "I'd love to know who owns Seagate and Atlantic."

Miriam shrugged. "The officers in the computer printouts?"

"Probably. But not necessarily. Someone else could own the stock. That information isn't accessible by computer, though."

"I could call Tallahassee."

"They won't know. They don't have that information. We could always contact one of these officers and ask him, but I can guess how far that would get us." Gail took the last bite of her sandwich and tossed her napkin into the trash basket. "Something is bothering me about this."

"What?"

"Carla Napolitano. She works for one of those companies. They've got a registered agent in the same building as the Easton Trust. And the will that Carla Napolitano notarized leaves money to Easton."

It didn't seem possible that Carla Napolitano

226

was linked to the Easton Trust; that pushed the bounds of believability. But still . . . .

"Let's go at this another way," she said. "Let's start with Easton."

"You don't want me to call Howard Odell, do you?" Miriam asked.

"That's the last thing I'd do. And don't bother with Tallahassee, either; a trust isn't a corporation. Look in the Dade County property index. I want to know what real estate the trust owns. What has it bought? Or sold? And to whom? That will tell us who they deal with, and we can go from there. Tell Eric to help you."

Her words were coming faster now, and she barely heard Miriam's phone buzz. "Go to the library and look in the *Miami Herald* index for Sanford Ehringer. Get me some biographical information. See if you can find out who's on the board of the Easton Charitable Trust. And another thing. Who the hell is Easton?"

Miriam nodded at the same time she put the receiver to her ear, swinging her hair to one side. "This is Miriam." She glanced at Gail, smiled. "Sure! I'll come get them." She hung up. "They're in the lobby."

Whenever Irene Connor came to Gail's office—rare indeed—she would dress for it, in due regard, she said, for Gail's position at the firm. Today she wore a dark plaid suit and black leather pumps. She sat in one of the client chairs with her sunglasses on, weeping silently.

Gail pulled the other chair a little closer and handed Irene a Kleenex. Irene raised the sunglasses far enough to dab at her eyes. "I didn't want to do this again in front of Karen. She was so sweet. She hugged me around the neck. Don't cry, Gramma. Don't cry."

"I'm so sorry," Gail took her mother's hand. "Should I have told you about Althea last week?"

"Oh, I don't want to know at all. Althea murdered. The police didn't say a *thing* to me about it when I talked to them. Oh, heaven. I wish Jessica hadn't called me."

"How did she find out?"

"Her chauffeur's son or brother—I can't remember. He's a police officer. I suppose it will be all over the news now."

"I'm afraid it might."

Through the half-open door Gail could see Karen sitting cross-legged on the floor in Miriam's cubicle, her hat in her lap, rubbing at a spot on the bill with the hem of her skirt. Her alligator purse lay on the floor beside her. Her sneakers were wet with rain.

Irene turned her head toward Gail, the gray light from the window in her sunglasses. "Jessica said the police suspect Patrick Norris. That he wanted her money—"

"They think that, but it isn't true."

"I had a dickens of a time explaining to Jessica why you agreed to be his lawyer. I had to fib in a couple of places." Irene squeezed Gail's hand. "Please don't be alone with him. Just in case?"

Gail smiled. "Don't worry about Patrick. He's a lamb."

Karen was leaning back against the metal filing cabinet now, looking idly into the corridor.

Miriam knelt to give her some markers and a legal pad, then watched while Karen drew something. Gail heard Miriam's voice, faintly. "You are such a good artist!"

Irene folded her sunglasses and put them in their case. "Do you think it would be all right if I talked to Irving Adler?"

Gail looked at her. "Why do you want to do that?"

"Well, I'd never interfere in your case, of course, but he is a friend. I want to tell him how sorry I am. He was devastated because Althea died, and then to go through it again because of *this*. I think Irving was in love with her, years ago. I could tell. He'd never have said it, though, with both of them married. He had too much respect for R.W. and for his own wife, then when Ruthie died—well, it was too late. Irving's not in good health, you know. I'm sure he regrets not telling Althie how he felt before—"

Irene's eyes filled up again.

"Oh, Mom." Gail put her arm around her shoulders. "She probably knew."

Irene blew her nose. "I don't blame him for loving her. Everybody did. Althie was so bright and funny. Oh, Gail. What a terrible, terrible thing."

Across the hall Miriam was cutting designs out of folded paper. The bill on Karen's cap rose. She smiled up at Miriam. Gail couldn't remember the last time she had sat with her daughter, drawing or doing anything at all, without also checking her watch.

"Gail. Do you mind if I speak to Irving?"

"No, of course I don't mind. It's good of you to want to. Tell him you loved her too."

Irene was silent for a moment, then asked, "Did Althea's death have anything to do with the forgery of that will?"

It had occurred to Gail that the forgery had been accomplished first, but it seemed unlikely. "I honestly don't know."

"What if he says anything to me about it?" Irene asked. "What if he wants to tell me what happened when the will was signed?"

Gail felt a small stirring of elation, as if the thorn-covered walls guarding the truth of Althea Tillett's will could be breached by a single question, one grieving friend to another. No lawsuits to grind away until the truth was revealed, but the halting words of an old man who—an old man whose story might not be credible, no matter how he told it.

"If he wants to talk, let him," she said. "But don't push him."

"Oh, yes. Kid gloves and cotton. I could just kick Jessica for telling him." Irene got up, clutching her handbag tightly with both hands. Gail walked her to the door. "Karen and I are going to a matinee—if we can find one where a dozen people don't get hacked to death or blown up in the first ten minutes."

She called to Karen. "Let's go, bunny, or we'll miss our movie."

"Bunny," muttered Karen. She put the strap of her alligator bag across her chest, then let Gail kiss her good-bye and promise they would go out somewhere special tonight, just the two of them. Karen and Irene disappeared past the turn in the corridor.

"Gail." It was Miriam. "Gwen called a minute ago. There's someone outside. A Mr. Quinn. He wants to see you."

"I don't know a Quinn. What's this about?"

"He has a message from Sanford Ehringer."

When Gail opened the door to the lobby, the receptionist nodded toward the windows. A man in a three-piece suit was waiting there, looking at the view. He held one hand behind his back, and the other rested on the carved handle of a furled black umbrella. His hair was soft and gray around a balding crown.

Gail crossed the lobby, her heels clicking on the marble floor.

He turned around, no recognition on his face. Perhaps he thought she was a secretary.

"Mr. Quinn? I'm Gail Connor."

He nodded. "How do you do. I am Thomas Quinn. Mr. Sanford Ehringer's personal secretary." His voice was richly, purely upper-class British.

She indicated the door through which she had come. "May I take you to my office?"

"Thank you, but that isn't necessary." From his breast pocket Quinn produced a small envelope. Gail's name had been written on it in flowing black. "Could I trouble you to read it now? Mr. Ehringer has instructed me to wait for a reply."

She lifted the flap and took out a crisp, folded sheet on which had been typed:

My dear Ms. Connor:

I beg the pleasure of your company at my home this evening for dinner. My car will pick you up at seven, unless some other hour is preferable. Please convey your response to Thomas Quinn, the bearer of this note. Forgive any inconvenience, and in return I promise, as amends, to make your visit most congenial.

Yours sincerely,
Sanford V. Ehringer.

The slashing black signature had been made with a fountain pen.

She looked at Thomas Quinn, whose brown eyes seemed fixed on some undefined point. "May I ask what this is in regard to?" What else but Althea Tillett?

The eyes moved to her. "I'm sorry, Ms. Connor, I couldn't say."

Or wouldn't. "This is awfully short notice."

"It is, rather. He regrets that this only just occurred to him. Unfortunately, Mr. Ehringer cannot delay until tomorrow or next week. He has business commitments." For the first time, Quinn smiled. "I can tell you that the chef is superbly talented. If you have a favorite dish, I shall request it for you."

Gail slid the note back into the envelope. "Does Mr. Ehringer require a written reply?"

"No. Simply tell me, and I'll give him the message."

"Well, then, Mr. Quinn. Tell him I accept."

chapter fourteen

At six-thirty, her hair still in hot curlers under a scarf and herself in shorts, Gail went out to the garage to check on progress there. Phyllis Farrington had arranged for two of her grandsons to come over after they finished their other jobs, and now they were busily loading a half-ton pickup truck with the things that Dave had left. The battered blue truck was backed up to the garage, out of the rain. Painted on the doors was FARRINGTON'S FAMOUS LAWN SERV., INC. The men would hitch up the boat trailer, throw a tarp over everything, and drive to a storage facility.

Phyllis was inside doing dishes from Karen's dinner, and Karen sat in the garage on an overturned recycling bin, watching. Saturday morning, Gail had spent nearly an hour on the phone with Clarinda Campbell, M.S., M.S.W., then had called Dr. Feldman to tell him Karen would not be coming any longer, to send his final bill. Clarinda—she had insisted on first names—had encouraged emptying the garage. *You and Karen must fill it with your own identities,* she had

233

said. *Let Karen choose a few things of her father's for a shelf in her room, but the rest of it must go.*

"Come inside, sweetie." Gail said, crouching down beside her. "Come talk to me while I get ready."

"It's just getting emptier and emptier," Karen said. "Daddy is going to be so mad."

"He'll understand. His things will be perfectly safe, better than here, with all the spiders and palmetto bugs." Gail watched Phyllis's grandsons load the tennis racquet stringer, wedge its legs down between some boxes and a brown tweed recliner. They were talking to each other, joking, and their voices echoed in the garage, the rain falling softly outside, the light fading.

Gail pulled up the other recycling bin and sat on that. "See that stain on the ceiling? We've got to get the roof fixed. And we ought to have the whole house painted, inside and out. We could even have a pool put in. I'm going to be a partner soon, you know, and we'll have all sorts of money."

"What if Daddy comes home and he doesn't recognize it any-more?"

Home. Dave's home was a forty-foot sloop anchored off St. Croix. Gail watched one of the grandsons lay a garment bag of coats across a stack of boxes. She said, "Your dad won't forget where you live."

Karen turned her head, frowning. She had her father's level brows, his square jaw. Her arms and legs were well formed, but she was taller and more awkward than the other girls her age, and

Gail had often seen her staring at herself in the mirror.

"Is Anthony going to move in here?"

Gail shook her head. "No. I wish you didn't dislike him. He's really very nice."

"I don't want him here all the time."

"He's hardly ever here, so don't worry about it, all right?"

The men were lowering the boat trailer onto the hitch now, and the safety chains rattled through the metal loops. Already the garage seemed different. Gail tried to picture Anthony's dark-blue, two-seater Cadillac convertible nestled snugly in next to her Buick.

"Are you going out with him tonight?"

Gail looked at her. "No. I told you, Karen. I'm going out on business. I don't lie to you."

"Right. An Englishman is going to pick you up in a Rolls-Royce limousine."

"I didn't say that."

"You said it might be a Rolls-Royce."

Gail closed her eyes. "God give me patience."

"You said we were going to Pizza Hut tonight too."

"I'm sorry."

Karen turned back around, her forearms on her knees. "Mom. I *realize* that he's your boyfriend and all." Her hair hung down on either side of her face, and she was studying something she held in her hands. "You go over to his house a lot and spend the night."

"Oh, Karen. Not a lot."

"Sometimes you do."

"Would you rather I didn't?"

235

"What I really don't like? Staying at Gramma's. I'd rather stay at Molly's. There's nothing to do at Gramma's house."

"Well, I won't be going over to Anthony's for a while."

Karen pushed her hair behind her ear. "Why?"

"Because . . . when I'm there, I always think about being here."

"He could come over. You know, like have dinner or something."

A plastic tarp settled down over the truck like a tossed bedsheet, covering the pile of boxes and bags and furniture. The grandsons passed a rope in and out of the grommets and tied the tarp all the way around.

Gail put her arm around Karen and kissed her. "Yes. We could have Anthony come over for dinner. Why don't you ask him? He'd like it if you did."

"No way." Karen snorted softly. "He hates me."

"That is absolutely not true."

"It is. He wishes I weren't around."

"Why would you think that?"

"Mom. He's only nice to me because of you, and you know it."

"Well, give him a chance. You have to admit, you don't make it easy." After a minute Gail added, "He's very special to me, and I want the two of you to be friends."

Karen said, "Fine. He can come over for dinner, but you ask him to. I'll be polite, I swear."

"Swear and promise?"

She smiled. "I'll be *so* sweet it'll make him sick.

236

I'll wear a pink dress and go like this." Karen batted her eyelashes.

"You're silly." Gail hugged her, then stood up. "I've got to go. They'll be here for me in a little while, and I'm still not ready." She saw what Karen had been holding in her hands. "What is that?"

Karen showed her: a four-inch folding knife with a curved black handle. "I found it in Daddy's tackle box."

"Well, you can't play with it," Gail said. "It's not a toy."

"*God,* Mom. I'm not five years old."

"It looks very sharp." She held out her hand. "Let me have it."

"You said I could have something of Daddy's for my room."

"Well, not a knife."

"Why?"

"Because you could get hurt. Or one of your friends could. It's dangerous."

"You think I can't do anything."

"I'm not going to argue with you, Karen. Give it to me."

Karen stood up, her body rigid. "You want to throw everything away. You don't want me to have anything of his."

"Give me that, I said." Gail reached for her arm, but Karen spun away and ran across the garage and into the rain. Phyllis's grandsons watched silently from beside the truck.

"Karen!" Gail ran into the driveway, seeing a flash of yellow shirt at the corner of the house, then nothing but sodden shrubbery and water coursing off the roof. The rain bounced on her scarf and drizzled down her cheeks. She went back inside, up the two steps to the kitchen, slamming the door.

"What happened?" Phyllis turned around from the dishwasher.

"My darling daughter just ran off with a knife. It was Dave's. I have no idea where she is. Dammit." Gail looked at the clock on the microwave. "Why does she do this? I have to leave in twenty minutes. Oh, God. Dr. Feldman was right. I shouldn't have taken Dave's things out. She thinks I'm making room for Anthony. I'm not! He wouldn't come here even if I asked him to."

Phyllis was propelling Gail gently out of the kitchen. "She'll be back. You get yourself dressed. Go on. I'll sit her down when she comes through the door. Karen's all right. But you don't look so good."

Tears stinging her eyes, Gail leaned against the living room wall. The hot curlers bumped into her head. "Ouch. Oh, damn." She laughed, pulling off her scarf.

"Go on now," Phyllis said.

From the garage came the *waum-waum-waum* of an engine cranking, then a backfire, then a steady chug. A moment later the door came rattling down.

chapter fifteen

Precisely at 7:00, Gail heard the splash of tires through the puddle at the end of the driveway. Headlights pointed toward the house, then went out. A door slammed.

"I'm leaving!" She swung her raincoat over her shoulders and picked up her purse. Phyllis was in the den with her shoes off, watching television; Karen was in her room. The knife was who-knew-where, but Phyllis had said not to worry, she would find it.

The doorbell chimed at the same instant Karen ran to the window and stuck a finger between the vertical blinds to look out. "That's not a Rolls-Royce. It's a truck!"

Gail opened the door. A mid-thirties black man in a dark suit stood on the porch with an umbrella. "Ms. Connor? Sanford Ehringer sent me. My name is Russell." He smiled, standing aside to let her by.

Karen came to the door, stared up at him, then toward the driveway. Before Karen could ask any questions, Gail turned her around. "Mind Phyllis. I'll see you when I get back."

It wasn't a truck but a boxy Range Rover with big tires. Russell helped Gail up into the front passenger seat, saying he would have brought the car, but with the streets so wet, and at night . . .

Backing out of the driveway, Russell turned to look out the rear window. Gail saw the strap of a holster under his suit coat.

A few miles later he turned off South Dixie Highway, tires humming, heading for the river. Gail tried to make conversation. Russell answered politely, saying nothing she could respond to. By now only a stripe of faintest gray remained in the west. They went up a narrow residential street, then past a boatyard, turning finally into an unmarked driveway where the banyan trees met overhead, blotting out the sky. The headlights picked up a vine-covered wall, a metal gate with only a slit to look through. Russell pressed a button on the dash and the gate slid back.

The road led briefly through a tangle of native species: buttonwood, gumbo-limbo, mahogany. Then the grounds opened up, and there were the columns, tile roof, and wide veranda of a two-story house made of coral rock. Two Dobermans at the far end of the porch lifted their heads, eyes on the Range Rover as Russell helped Gail out of it. The rain had stopped. Water dripped from the eaves onto bird-of-paradise in mildewing clay pots. The yard was not so much landscaped as tamed, with brick walkways cutting through the foliage, vanishing into the darkness. Gail stepped onto the porch with an odd sense that she had done it before, though she had no idea when.

A sudden scream came from the roof, and she jumped.

"It's only a peacock," Russell said, opening the

beveled-glass door. "Mr. Ehringer keeps them on the grounds."

She laughed a little, her heart racing.

An elderly man in a white jacket led her into the dimly lit foyer, which was floored in Spanish tile and hung with tapestries.

As she gave him her raincoat, Gail said quietly, "This house is incredible. When was it built?"

"Around 1910, I believe, miss. You'll have to ask Mr. Ehringer about that. It belonged to his father."

She followed the butler to a six-sided living room with carved wood furniture, woven rugs, and a rough, coral rock fireplace. The beamed ceiling rose to a cupola at the center, designed to pull breezes through before air conditioning. Ahead, long windows looked out onto a terrace with a jungle of plants. Her reflection came back to her in the glass. The room was familiar. She thought she had seen a photo of it.

The butler lifted an arm. "This way, miss."

Passing the staircase along one wall, Gail stepped back, startled. Someone was watching. A face had pulled away, but the hands remained, curled around the carved balusters. Now the face reappeared. It was a boy. He wore a striped pullover, and his hair was combed neatly across his forehead.

"Hi. What's your name?" The words came slowly through heavy lips.

"Gail," she said.

A wide grin nearly closed his small eyes. "I have a hamster. You want to see him?"

The old man pivoted his head to look up,

241

scolding gently. "Run along, Walter. You should be upstairs."

The boy's eyes followed Gail as she passed underneath, and his face pressed at the balusters. "Bye."

"Good-bye." She spoke to the butler, her voice low. "Who was that boy?"

He glanced at her, then said, "He lives here." At the end of a carpeted hallway, he knocked twice at a heavy door then pushed it open. "Ms. Connor, sir." He bowed stiffly and left her there.

"My dear Ms. Connor! Come in!" The man across the room, still seated, wore a bottle-green velvet jacket. A red paisley scarf was tucked into the open collar of his shirt. She saw in an instant why he had not risen: There were wheels on his chair.

"Mr. Ehringer," she said. "Good evening."

Sanford Ehringer had once been a powerful man; she could see it in the width of his shoulders, feel it when he took her hand, gripping it as eagerly as if she had been his granddaughter come to visit. "By God, aren't you lovely? And tall. A strapping young woman." He laughed. "Don't mind the familiarity. You get to be my age, you don't wait till tomorrow to say what you think."

He was completely bald. His nose and ears drooped, as old men's do, his lips were a slash, and tangled brows jutted over deeply set black eyes. And yet this face was not forbidding, but as welcoming as a fireplace in December, glowing with cheerfulness.

"We'll have dinner in here," he said. "It's cozy. What do you think? All right?"

"Certainly." Now she saw the table to one side, gleaming with china and crystal. This room must have been his library: There were bookcases, deep red leather furniture, a Persian rug on the polished wood floor. A floor lamp glowed through a shade of tasseled green silk. A bronze Art Nouveau nude crouched on a bookcase.

"Good." He wheeled over to the sofa, where an ice bucket sat in a stand, its neck wrapped in white linen. "They'll bring dinner whenever we're ready. I've got some pretty good French stuff over here. Pouilly-fuissé, I believe. Does that take your fancy?"

Gail was still looking around. "Yes, thank you." One wall was taken up with electronic equipment: television, stereo, a personal computer, a monitor, a fax machine.

"Russell get you here all right? No problems?"

"None. Your house is quite hidden. I doubt I could find my way with a map."

Ehringer chuckled. "The city just built itself around me. With that wall, sometimes I forget it's even out there."

While he poured, she studied the paintings over the sofa. The first showed a golden-haired Victorian woman by someone named Rossetti. She looked heavenward and held a lily. The other wasn't as good: a rocky landscape, bearded men in togas, people weeping.

"The Funeral of Pericles," he said. "Awful, isn't it? I got it in England when I was a boy."

"You weren't born there, were you?"

"No, I studied classics at Cambridge. No practical value at all, of course, but at the time I

243

adored it. Still do. First loves never leave you."
He wedged the bottle back into the ice. "The
original Greek is virile stuff. Don't trust the trans-
lations. You do it for yourself, that's what, then
it sticks."

He offered her a glass of wine. Tendons stood
out on his liver-spotted hands, and blue veins
roped beneath the skin.

"By God, if Hollywood could do half as well
as Homer. Desire, betrayal, revenge, honor.
Screaming horses, warriors toppling into the
dust. Think of that scene from *The Iliad:* Achilles
tying the body of Hector to his chariot by his
heels, then dragging him around the city! Bring
teenagers up on that, and they'll never want *The
Terminator.*" Ehringer raised his glass. "*Santé.*
How's the wine? Passable?"

"Excellent." She started to take another sip,
then noticed the small table by the sofa. Under
the glass were tiny boxes of varying sizes, each
containing a beetle of some unusual type.

Ehringer rolled closer. "Aren't they pretty?
There's a list in the drawer, if you want to know
the names. That green one with the horns I found
in Morocco."

Puzzled, Gail said slowly, "I've seen these."

He looked at her over his glass, smiling.

"I've been here before. Haven't I?"

"Yes!" Ehringer laughed. "I thought you had
forgotten. You were a little girl. You wanted to
play with the beetles. I let you have some rock
samples instead."

Gail turned, looking behind her at the bookcases with their rows of volumes, books with their

bindings going to dust and others on the latest topics, some in French or German, all crammed in every which way. "Who brought me here?"

"John Strickland, your grandfather. We did some business together, and he brought you along a time or two. Way back, Johnny's father Benjamin and my dad used to go bonefishing together in the Keys. Great friends, they were. Ben showed me how to tie flies. I was only a kid then. By God, I haven't thought of that in years!" He smiled up at Gail. "So. How is Irene keeping herself these days?"

"You remember her?"

"I am old, my dear, not senile. Irene Strickland. Little red-haired woman. I never knew your father though. Can't recall his name."

"Edwin Connor."

"Edwin. Sold insurance. Yes. I never thought Irene would marry a salesman. Not to say your dad wasn't a fine man, *et cetera*, but Irene—well, she was quite the debutante. My own wife was a Vanderpoole, a genuine Knickerbocker. But young people today don't care about all that, do they? I'll bet you married well, though. You have that look about you."

Gail took a sip of wine, wondering what this was leading to. "I'm divorced."

"I believe someone told me that. Irene's daughter, and so on. And you're the one they meant. You have children?"

"If you know so much about me already, Mr. Ehringer, then you must know the answer to that as well."

He smiled at her. "Yes, I made inquiries, and

why not? My poor attempt to renew our acquaintance after twenty-five years."

She set her glass on the small table. "I have to say, I didn't expect to find you so amiable, particularly after what happened with Howard Odell on Friday."

"What do you mean?" His jowls settled against the stiff shirt collar.

As she recounted the scene with Odell at the Tillett Gallery, Ehringer's gaze seemed to rest on the roseate spoonbills above the door: one with its wide bill forever dipped to the shelf, the other with pinkish wings extended, as if it would flap across the room.

"I didn't like Mr. Odell's threats," she said.

Ehringer waved a hand. "You mustn't mind Howard. He takes his duties too seriously."

"His duties are to frighten me into a settlement?"

"In no way! He does a bang-up job raising money for the trust. I suspect he considers it a personal affront if any bequest is jeopardized. Shall I speak to him for you?" He patted her arm with fierce affection. "You are a sensitive young woman of good breeding and intelligence. If he insulted you, I apologize."

"You and he are related, aren't you?"

"A second cousin once removed. I'm fond of Howard, so I hope you can forgive his abruptness. He and I don't see each other often enough for me to keep up with him. I've too much to do, Gail, a thousand and one things on my mind."

Gail said, "Mr. Ehringer. Why did you ask me

here? I assume it has to do with Althea Tillett's will."

"Oh, indulge me, Gail. We'll get to all that." He smiled at her. "For now, I would like to know you. I remember you as a child, you see. Where is this young girl, Johnny's granddaughter, who once played here on this floor? Who chased butterflies in my flower garden? The same person who is causing such a fuss among my friends?"

He supported his craggy cheekbone on his fingers, elbow on the padded armrest of his chair. "Who is this Antigone who would stand before the walls of the city and risk public censure? No. Not the public. The public doesn't give a damn. Let us say she risks her place among her peers. Why does she do it?"

Gail had to laugh. "It isn't that dramatic. I'm a lawyer, I have a client, and I believe in him."

"And that's all?"

"Yes." Then she smiled. "Of course I'm getting paid for my work."

"Handsomely too, if I know Hartwell Black and Robineau. Good for you!" Ehringer lifted his glass. "May we believe in the causes we fight for." The glass paused at his lips. "And what cause is that?"

"Pardon?"

"What is your cause? Rather, your client's cause. You said you believe in him. What is it that you believe in?" Ehringer leaned back a little in his chair, studying her. "Why do you fight for this client? Not to win, although you find pleasure in winning. Not for money—I believe you are motivated by higher interests. Not even for a job

247

well done. A dog can fetch a stick, and fetch it well. What do you believe in? We must all believe in something, or else . . . who are we?"

Gail lowered her glass. "I believe in finding out the truth, Mr. Ehringer. In trying to do what is right. How can I answer? I'm not a philosopher. I haven't been to Cambridge. I haven't lived eighty-something years thinking about these things."

"Eighty-four." He smiled. "Forgive me. I didn't mean to bully you, Gail. It's just that I so enjoy a stimulating conversation. What else can an old man do?"

She looked straight at him for a moment. "Did you know that the police believe Althea Tillett was murdered?"

Ehringer's expression became the dark side of a remote planet. "Yes. I know. If it's true, this was a barbarous act." His hand tightened to a fist which beat slowly on the arm of his chair.

"You knew her well?"

For a time Gail wondered if he had heard her. Then his face softened. "I shall always remember Althea with great fondness. If you believe passion is only for the young, you are mistaken. Love does not wither. Except among the less educated, its flame is in the heart and intellect, which grow cold only when the body is extinguished. There was one summer in 1958, on Mykonos. The Aegean was brilliant, like crystal, like . . . nothing you can imagine. The sand was hot, the sky so blue and endless it would make you weep. We stayed in a small *pension* on a cliff— by God, what a woman!"

For a moment he stroked the red silk scarf at his neck, his head sinking deep into his shoulders. Then he gripped the silver wheels of his chair and propelled himself to the linen-draped table. He pressed a button. "Dinner! Fresh salmon, with some sort of tropical sauce my chef has invented. Here, Gail. Hold my wine for a minute. I want to show you my backyard. See if you remember it."

He turned a polished knob on the French doors and pulled. The humid night air fluttered the gauzy curtains. Gail could smell flowers and hear the murmur of a fountain. She followed him down an incline to the tiled terrace, which she had seen from the living room. He flipped a switch and lights came on above. Pots of orchids, bromeliads, and miniature trees crowded shelves and hung from the beams. Ehringer's wheels glinted as he pushed himself around a bentwood rocker, going deeper into his jungle of tropical plants.

"Wasn't there a goldfish pond?" Gail asked.

"Yes! On the other end, by the fountain." He glanced over his shoulder at her. "Do you remember the spotted white carp you fed tea biscuits to? It leaped up and scared you, and you ran to your grandmother. Remember that?"

Gail laughed. "No, I'm glad to say." She ducked under an immense staghorn fern. "Your father built this house, didn't he?"

"As a botanical garden," he said. "He and Mum had the house in Palm Beach and a cottage on Brickell, but they would come out here and putter. She had the kitchen done, and pretty soon

they lived here, during the winter anyhow."
Ehringer laughed. "Country living! Ha! You can
hear the traffic now, and airplanes going over.
And gunfire! There is some excitement on a
Saturday night in these parts, Miss Gail!"

The terrace was screened, and flowering vines
twisted around the supporting rock columns. He
unlatched a door and rolled onto an open patio.
The sky was sickly brown, the anticrime lights
reflecting off the clouds. Trees blocked the view
fifty yards north, but she saw a glimmer. "The
river is through there, isn't it?" Gail asked.

"It is. When I was a boy," said Ehringer, "I
used to swim in it. The Indians had a camp near
here—a tourist trap is what it was. They'd take
you for a ride in their dugout canoes. But those
days are gone. I had to put up a fence. Not even
a fish would swim in the Miami River now. Ha.
They're too smart for that. Go somewhere else,
fishies."

"You're still here," Gail said, giving him back
his glass of wine.

"I'm not a fish!" He laughed, his mouth a dark
hole in his ancient face. He downed a swallow of
wine, then looked sharply at her.

"You wonder why I stay, don't you? Why don't
I get out, live somewhere clean and safe? A Greek
island. Hawaii. Montana! My dear young
woman! I *love* Miami! Europe is going under,
New York is filthy and cold, and one petrifies
with boredom in Palm Beach. Why *not* live here?
The medical facilities are adequate. The air is
breathable. The climate is delightful—except for

250

our vicious summers, and thank God for those, or we really would be overcrowded!"

Sanford Ehringer wheeled around. "Look up there. You won't remember that. I had it built in 1973."

It was a shaft of rock that extended up beyond the roof of the house, with windows canted outward like an airport control tower. "It's air-conditioned and bulletproof. There's a telephone. I've got a videocamera to preserve my observations. I'd spend hours up there, if I had the time."

He stared upward. "I'll tell you what I see. Miami, boiling with growth and change. Immigrants pouring in, new values. Traditions buried, others being born. I see America, fifty years from now, *fin de siècle*. Oh, yes. Upheavals of the social tectonic plates. The things I see! I feel like an astronaut in a space capsule."

Above, the city lights twinkled in the dark glass.

"You know how most people suffer," he said. "Oh, it breaks your heart. Poverty, violence, despair, perversions of every kind praised as normal! What can we *do?* We are only flecks of foam on the surging tide of evolution. And yet—"

Ehringer grasped her hand, shaking it for emphasis. His fingers were hard and dry. "There is a new world coming, Gail. Already you can sense it in small ways—people getting tired of crime and sloth and the degenerates on our streets. People wanting some values back, dammit! Let's have responsibility, chastity, integrity. We want to aim for excellence again! Each

251

of us who has the brains to think must choose: either add to the dead weight of mediocrity or reward those who can lead us out of it."

His voice deepened, trembling with emotion. "We and people like us have preserved the seed of excellence through centuries, but it isn't only for us, Gail. It's our gift to the world! Most of us are deaf and blind, but some of us—" He held her hand against the soft velvet of his coat. "Some of us can hear the music of that far-off day."

Before she could reply—if she could even have thought of an adequate reply—Ehringer turned his chair to face the black silhouettes of the trees.

"If that seed can take root here, in this city poised between good and evil, then I shall die with hope that the world will not sink back into darkness for another two thousand centuries." His head was a pale dome. "That is why I stay. I am morally required, by whatever power God has granted me, to push us toward the light."

Gail could only stare at him.

Ehringer laughed. "Inside with you. Our dinner is waiting. By God, what that chef can do with crême brulée! I am being wicked, and my doctor would scold me if he found out. Hang him, this is a special event!"

Gail held the door and let Ehringer wheel past. She shot another look at the tower, then went inside the screen.

A rustling behind some bushes stopped her cold. In her mind she saw the dripping jaws of one of Ehringer's dogs. She backed away. A round face peeked out. It was the boy she had seen before on the stairs. Walter. The branches closed, and she heard a soft laugh.

"Gail! Roll me up this ramp, will you? My wheel is stuck on a rock or some damn thing."

It was on her lips to ask Sanford Ehringer about this odd boy, but asking could get Walter into trouble.

Dinner was on the table when they returned to the study, and three tapers burned in a silver candelabrum. Ehringer dropped a CD on the player—Schumann, he said—and instructed Gail to leave the doors open: the orchids were blooming. With some effort, he swung himself from his wheelchair into the carved and embroidered mahogany chair at the table. He said a brief grace, head bowed, then shook out his napkin.

For a while they ate, commenting only on the food, which was—as Thomas Quinn had promised—superb. *Potage germiny*—cream of sorrel soup—followed by crisp romaine and watercress salad with raspberry vinaigrette. Fresh, steaming bread and sweet butter. An Asian woman in a starched apron came in as if magically summoned to clear the plates for each course and pour accompanying wine.

Sanford Ehringer's eyes twinkled over his forkful of salmon *tamarinde*. "Tell me, Gail. What do you think of my crackpot social theories?"

"Crackpot or not, I wouldn't know," she said. "It's all beyond me. These grand ideas about the tide of history and all that—"

"Beyond you? Oh, my dear. No. By blood and education, you are among the elite."

"I doubt that."

253

"But you are! Admit it! Don't be afraid others will call you elitist. Without an elite, we would still be picking berries off trees and sleeping in caves."

She paused over her julienned *haricots verts.* "I prefer to believe that societies tend to move toward equality."

"Dear God, can it be? Another victim of mush-mouth liberal hogwash. There is no equality! Don't they teach Plato in school anymore? There are people who have the capacity to advance and those who do not."

"That's rather depressing."

"The truth, my dear, is never depressing." He raised his glass. "It is only the truth."

The woman brought in a tray with dessert: custard topped with a delicate crust of carmelized sugar, lying on swirls of greengage plum sauce. She took their dinner plates and went out.

A movement at the open French door caught Gail's eye, and she turned her head. It was the boy again. He was older than she had guessed, perhaps twelve. He was half hidden by the door, smiling at her.

"What is it?" Ehringer turned around in his chair, then laughed. "Who do I see out there? You're a curious cat, aren't you, Walter? Always wanting to know what's going on."

He looked back at Gail. "My grandson, Walter."

Smiling at the floor, Walter approached with a hand behind his back. Ehringer said gruffly, "All right. What have you got? Let's see."

He brought out a brown and white hamster,

and his eyes disappeared into his grin. "She can have him. I have another one."

"Oh, I couldn't," said Gail. "He's yours." She petted the little furry head. The whiskers and pink nose quivered. "Thank you for showing me."

Ehringer shook the boy's shoulder. "Come here and give your grandpa a hug, you." The boy leaned his head on Sanford Ehringer's chest.

"Grandpa."

"Yes, Grandpa." He squeezed Walter tightly, knuckling his scalp until the boy squirmed and giggled. Softly Ehringer said to Gail, "He will never understand the world. At times, when he realizes this, he becomes sad. Luckily his attention span is short." He kissed his grandson. "What a good boy you are, Walter! Do you want a sweet? Look, a chocolate mint. Now you must promise to brush your teeth after."

"I promise to brush my teeth."

"Yes. Go on now. It's late. Where's Maggie? She'll tuck you in."

Gail smiled at him. "Goodnight, Walter."

"Bye."

When the door had closed behind him, Ehringer said, "My daughter's child. She died in the same car accident that left me in this chair."

"I'm sorry."

Ehringer nodded. "He's a dear boy. When I'm gone, I think he will miss me."

"Do you have other grandchildren?"

"No." He glanced toward the door, his eyes lingering. "I was only blessed with one. You have only one child, do you not? Karen. She must be a comfort to you."

Gail nodded. "Yes. She is."

He gestured toward her dessert plate. "How was the crème brulée? Didn't I warn you? Heavenly." He leaned to press the button. "There's coffee. A liqueur? A sip of port?"

"I'm fine, thank you."

"You won't mind if I have a toddy? Helps me sleep." Ehringer swung himself back into his wheelchair.

Gail laid her napkin by her plate and followed him across the room. "I think I know what you're doing," she said. "You want to persuade me that Althea Tillett's money shouldn't be thrown to the winds. Spending it on the poor would be useless. You'd rather it go as her will said—to the arts and education—even if the will was forged." She sat on the end of the sofa, her hands clasped at her knees. "Well?"

"By God, I must be slipping," he said. "I used to be more subtle."

The door opened. Ehringer told the Asian woman what he wanted. He wheeled himself to his humidor and selected a cigar after Gail said she didn't mind.

He clipped off the end of it. "Here's a question I'm almost afraid to hear the answer to. Have you considered what this lawsuit would do to the reputations of some very good people?"

"Yes. It has been a painful consideration."

Ehringer clicked a gold lighter and puffed on his cigar, the flame dancing in his black eyes. "Good. Such decisions should be painful, if we are honorable men and women."

"I'm a lawyer, Mr. Ehringer. Patrick Norris

came to me for help, and I intend to help him. There's honor in that."

"How much would it take to ransom my unfortunate friends?"

"Ransom?"

"A bad choice of words. I am referring to Mrs. Simms and Mr. Adler. As for the others—" He waved his cigar. "The devil take Rudy Tillett and his sister."

Gail hesitated. "Maybe I'm naive. I'll ask directly. Are you talking about a settlement of the case, or . . . a payment to me?"

"Good God! A *bribe?* I wouldn't insult you with such a suggestion. I mean a decent settlement, perhaps as much as three million dollars, payable immediately. And bear this in mind, Gail." He took a slow pull on his cigar. "Your chances of winning this case in court are very slim."

"Then why offer a settlement at all?"

"Because a trial—even if you lose—will have consequences. Our local media, with their tabloid mentality, will rush in like piranhas. Reputations will be sullied without regard for the truth. People will be hurt."

Gail asked, "Did they forge the will, Mr. Ehringer? Is that why you want to protect them?"

The pale summit of Ehringer's head seemed to float in a blue haze. "Whether they did or they didn't, I neither know nor care to know. It is irrelevant."

"Irrelevant. But it was necessary." She finished the thought. "It's what Althea Tillett would have wanted."

Gail crossed her legs, sinking farther into the

sofa, which gave off the dusky aroma of old leather. "I've learned some things about the Easton Charitable Trust," she said. "It was founded in 1937, you are the current chairman, and its members are prominent in society. They do good works, yes, but how else might they use the trust? Maybe a quiet contribution to city commissioner X's campaign fund. Or a family member on the payroll, or interest-free loans from donations. Are these the people I should worry about hurting?"

"How little you know. Sad." Ehringer sighed. "The Easton Trust was founded as an alternative to Roosevelt's leftist social programs. Its members—whom I will not name—have a point of view which is unpopular, and they prefer to keep it private. That is all."

"May I ask if you have heard of these corporations: Seagate and Atlantic Enterprises?"

"No. What are they?"

Gail said, "Seagate owns a travel agency called Gateway Travel."

He made an expansive shrug, smoke whirling into a spiral.

"And Atlantic Enterprises . . . owns a nightclub. With exotic dancers."

Ehringer pulled on his cigar, watching her over the end of it. "I do not frequent such places, my dear."

"Are either of these corporations owned by the Easton Trust?"

A laugh rumbled out of his chest. "I should say not."

There was another knock at the door. The

Asian woman brought in a tray with Ehringer's toddy on it, then went to clear the table. Ehringer smoked his cigar, turning it slowly in his mouth, the end of it wet and dark.

Gail stood up and combed through the tassel on the green silk shade. When the woman had gone, she asked, "Who is in the Easton Trust?"

"Why do you wish to know that?"

"Why must it be a secret?" she responded.

He turned to tap his ashes over a crystal ashtray. "You're worse than a government bureaucrat! Pick and probe."

"At least you can tell me who Mr. Easton was."

Ehringer brought his gaze around to settle on her. "Who was Mr. Easton?" His thin lips curved into a smile. "I'm afraid I can't tell you who he was."

"Don't be so obscure, Mr. Ehringer. And don't play with me."

He slapped the arm of his chair, laughing. "Her feathers are wet now, by God!"

Gail stood and made a polite smile. "I really must be going. It's late. Dinner was lovely." She picked up her purse from the sofa. "Perhaps you'd have Russell drive me home."

Ehringer's jowls flowed over his collar as his head sank into his shoulders. "I apologize. That was unkind of me." He went to press the button to signal his staff. "Tell me, Gail. Have you really considered what will happen if this case goes to trial?"

Cigar between his teeth, he wheeled over to where she stood. "Say by some misstep of divine judgment you win, and your client can hand out money like loaves and fishes. His parents were missionaries in El Salvador. Perhaps he is following in their footsteps. But what will become of this noble experiment? The people in the neighborhood will resent him, as well they should. Who is he? A wealthy white man telling them what to do, how to live. What presumption! A failed attorney, a veteran of trouble with the law, and now under police investigation. Yes, Gail. I know what they suspect him of."

"He didn't do it."

"Innocence, guilt. Such a thin line." Ehringer regarded the glowing end of his cigar, closing one eye against the smoke. "It would be amusing to find out how easily he could be pushed over it." He inhaled deeply, then tilted back his head.

"What do you mean?" The only answer was a circle lazily floating upward. Like a noose.

The door opened and the butler stood there in his white jacket. "Yes, sir?"

"Ms. Connor is leaving. Summon Russell, would you? Gail, one more thing before you go."

In the hall she turned around, furious.

Ehringer glided toward her, stopped. "You asked me who Mr. Easton was. Would you still like to know?"

She allowed a shrug. "Yes, if you'll tell me."

"I will give you this much. He doesn't exist. He's no one. There. Now you won't go looking for him." Sanford Ehringer reached out to close the door. He smiled. "Good night, Ms. Connor."

Gail had the phone halfway back to her bedside table when she finally heard Anthony's voice.

"It's me," she said. "Are you asleep already?"

There was a pause, a shifting of comforter and sheets. "It's . . . one-thirty. What happened?"

"That late? Oh. I've been lying here awhile. I didn't—"

"Gail. I got in at midnight. I have to meet a client at seven in the morning."

"Sorry. I went to Sanford Ehringer's house."

"Yes. You said you would. And?"

"I think he's going to set Patrick up to be framed for murder."

A tired laugh. "Only in the movies."

"I'm serious, Anthony. He could do it. He has more money and power than you can imagine. He lives in a secret compound by the river. He has a tower in his backyard where he sits with a camera and he watches—"

"*Ay, mi dios.*"

She let some seconds pass, realizing how irrational it must have sounded. "Never mind. But could you talk to the police? Find out what they're doing? And if you could talk to Patrick—"

"I don't want to talk to Patrick."

"Well, I'm sorry I woke you."

"Wait. Don't hang up." A few seconds passed. "Call me tomorrow, all right? Tomorrow afternoon." He let out his breath. "I didn't mean to be cross with you. Don't worry so much."

"Anthony. What are you doing tomorrow night? Come over for dinner. Karen suggested it."

"Karen?"

"Don't say you're busy. It'll be simple. Pizza or something." She waited. "Okay?"

261

"Okay. Six o'clock. No mushrooms."

She said, "I love you."

"Yes. I love you too. Good night."

"Anthony?" She closed her eyes, holding the phone tightly. "Do you think we love each other with our hearts and intellects?"

A few deep breaths came over the line, then: "Gail, what are you talking about?"

"It's something Sanford Ehringer said about Althea Tillett."

"Those two had an affair?"

"A passionate affair, in the summer of 1958 on an island called Mykonos, in the Aegean."

A few more seconds went by. "I don't love you with my intellect. My heart, yes. And a few more places." He yawned. "Let me go back to sleep, will you?"

chapter sixteen

Gail spent most of Tuesday buried in office work, trying to keep her mind off Sanford Ehringer. It wasn't easy. She had caught herself thinking of multinational conspiracies, the inner circles of the CIA, the Northeastern Ivy League establishment, the hidden power elite who really called the shots, while poor everyday folk trudged from home to work to home, believing their lives were their own. Sanford Ehringer and his friends were watching from their towers like Jane Goodall in

Kenya. They might lend a hand here and there, as long as it didn't upset the natural order of things.

Anthony had called. By way of a friend with the Miami Beach Police, he had found out what proof they had against Patrick Norris: *nada*. The cops didn't like him, and everyone else had an alibi. So don't worry about it, he had told her. The old toad couldn't buy off an entire police force and then corrupt a judge and jury. Anthony made a kiss into the telephone and said he would see her at six o'clock for pizza.

Three-thirty found Gail speeding eastward from downtown over the causeway to Miami Beach, passing luxury cruise ships on her right, the mansions of Palm, Hibiscus, and Star islands on her left. She swooped onto South Beach, which a consortium of financiers was snapping up like hors d'oeuvres. Then a left onto Alton Road toward Gateway Travel Agency. She wanted to see Carla Napolitano for herself.

At first Gail had assumed, because Patrick had said so, that Rudy and Monica were behind the forgery of Althea Tillett's will. Now she sensed other forces at work, chief among them the Easton Charitable Trust. Ehringer, its chairman, wanted a quiet settlement. So did its director, Howard Odell. Usually in litigation you settle if you think you can't win, not because you have something to hide. Gail wondered what she would find if she could peel back the skin of this case.

What unnerved her most was that the will might not have been forged at all. The document

263

examiner could be mistaken. Discrepancies in the witnesses' stories could be reconciled. And Lauren Sontag might have told the truth: that Althea Tillet had signed her will, but it had been improperly notarized.

These theories converged at one point: Carla Napolitano. Lauren Sontag said she had paid Carla fifty dollars to notarize the will. And Carla worked for Gateway Travel, whose registered agent was located in the same building as the Easton Trust.

Going north on Alton Road, Gail slowed past the bank building where Weissman, Woods, Merrill & Sontag, P.A., was located. Tomorrow she and Larry Black would drive back over here to meet with Alan Weissman, but for now she wanted to stay anonymous. Gateway Travel was two doors down. She parked on a side street.

Luckily she had worn a dress today. She didn't look like an attorney. As for Carla—she would be plump and middle-aged, with brown hair. A blank. Eric hadn't noticed much. The thing with Eric Ramsay was, people didn't interest him, unless they were players. But then, maybe that's what it took to get rich in the law. Stick to the facts, the numbers, the deal.

Walking slowly, Gail glanced through the plate glass windows of Gateway Travel. Discount airline tickets. Fall specials to New England. A faded cutout of a cruise ship. Possibly Carla Napolitano wasn't there at all. What about Frankie Delgado? He had answered the phone when Miriam called looking for Carla Napolitano. What kind of man was this, to offer a girl he'd never seen a job dancing naked in a nightclub?

Gail passed the door, kept going, then walked by again. There were three or four desks inside. More posters. Racks of brochures. No one inside. She stopped. Toward the back, seated at a desk, a woman. Brown hair.

She turned around and walked past the agency a third time, astonished by her own presumption. If this was Carla, what would she say to her? *Tell me: Did Lauren Sontag give you fifty dollars to notarize a phony will? Is this travel agency connected to a nude bar called Wild Cherry?*

This was crazy, Gail realized. It might even be against the Florida Bar Code of Ethics— pretending you weren't an attorney to induce a witness to give you information. Lying so you could get the truth.

Go home, Gail told herself, walking past the travel agency yet again. Her photo might have been shown to Carla Napolitano. Then what would happen when Alan Weissman confronted her with it on Wednesday?

"Miss? Are you lost?"

Gail turned to see an old man behind her with a cane, squinting through his glasses. She shook her head. "Thanks. It's right here."

A bell tinkled when she went in.

"You know, Cancun is real nice in November. And it's cheap. I could get you a weekend for two for five hundred dollars, air included."

"Well, that wasn't quite what we had in mind."

"Rio!" Carla Napolitano playfully slapped Gail on the arm. "You could do Rio. Talk about fun!"

About the only thing Eric had gotten right in describing Carla Napolitano was the brown hair. It was dark chestnut brown, or a good attempt. It was curled and teased and held up by two combs covered in fake leopard skin. She wasn't plump; she was busty. As for being middle age—Carla Napolitano would never accept that designation, whether she looked it or not. And she did. Makeup helped; her eyelashes were long and spiky, and upward slashes of powdered blush decorated her cheeks. The skin around her eyes was webbed with little lines.

"Rio?" Gail thought about it. "We don't have that much time."

"What about a package at the Doral here in town?"

"No. We don't want Miami."

"He's not married, is he? God, listen to me. None of my business."

"Well . . . yes. But he's getting a divorce."

"Mmm-hmm. You be careful, honey." Carla swung one crossed leg. She wore tight red pants and backless high heels of clear plastic with daisies on the toes.

Gail sat at one end of the desk. At the other was a computer terminal and a stack of manuals. She asked, "Did you have bad luck with a married man?"

"Oh, did I." Carla glanced past Gail, lowered her voice. "Twice, when I was young and stupid. One was a doctor. He gave me an MG convertible because he felt so guilty, then told me to give it back."

"Did you?"

"Please!" Carla laughed and turned back to the brochures on her desk. "Okay, let's see what we can find for Connie and Luis." She wore a black tank top and the soft flesh of her upper arm swayed as she moved. Her thrusting breasts hardly moved at all. Gail wondered if they were real.

She said, "I'd love to work in a travel agency."

"Ha."

"Really. How'd you get into it?"

"By accident, I guess. I'm good with people. Plus I know the manager."

"Who's that?" When Carla looked at her, Gail said, "I'd like to talk to him. You know. See if anything's available."

Carla's gold hoop earrings swung when she shook her head. "There's not. Besides, you gotta take courses for this. And let me tell you. I'm getting out of the business myself. *Adios*, Miami." She smiled at Gail. "Maybe I wouldn't if everybody was as nice as you. I mean that."

Gail smiled back. "What did you do before this?"

"Oh, God. Everything. Bookkeeping. I do books here, as a matter of fact. Let's see. I sang in a cocktail lounge. I did some modeling."

"Really? Me too," said Gail. "Where did you model?"

"New York, Jersey. Lingerie, mostly. What can I say? It pays good. But I'm too short. You got the build. You still model?"

"Not anymore, at my age."

"Tell me about it. They want you, then you're on your ass. All right, Connie, take a look at these." She fanned out the brochures so Gail could see them. "I'd recommend Ocho Rios or Club Med, unless Luis wants something more unusual."

"Unusual?" Gail looked up.

"Different. I mean, in your situation, guys sometimes like something . . . unusual. Not that *you* would, but—" She shrugged.

For a few seconds Gail studied the brightly colored pamphlets. Couples running on the beach, embracing on a balcony, dancing on a ship. "How unusual do you mean?"

"Well, I've had 'em come in here wanting to take their girlfriends to see Shakespeare plays in London, and some wanting to go on a nude boat cruise. Use your imagination."

Gail turned a page in one of the brochures. There was a back view of a woman splashing in a lagoon. Her imagination told her that this travel agency could suggest trips that dovetailed nicely with the entertainment at Wild Cherry. Casually she said, "Well, possibly Luis would like something . . . unusual." She smiled at Carla. "He's always complaining that his wife isn't much fun."

Carla swung her foot. "And he needs a little excitement in his life."

"You could say that."

"Mmm-hmm. I hope he's worth it."

"So far he's been very generous with me. He wants us to have a good time on this trip, not to worry what it costs. In fact, he said I should check with Gateway Travel. You're specialists in discreet vacations?" Gail held her breath. She might have pushed too far.

Carla didn't blink. "How come Luis isn't in here himself?"

"He's too busy. He's . . . a heart surgeon."

"Mama mia, a doctor." She directed a glance at the ceiling, then back to Gail. "Let me guess. In his forties, drives a sports car."

"A Cadillac convertible."

"Typical." Carla laughed. "I could set something up, sure. But honey, you don't seem like the type."

"What kind of vacation are we talking about?"

"I can send the both of you down to Mexico to watch girls doing it with donkeys, if that's what you want."

"Oh." She placed a hand flat on her bosom. "I don't think so."

"Sorry. You asked."

"It's okay. Does Gateway do a lot of this?"

"People are weird, what can I tell you?"

"Isn't this illegal?"

"Heck, no. We make the travel arrangements. What they do when they get there is up to them. Not everybody is kinky, now. I'm not saying that. Most people want a good time, like you and Luis. But some of them," she whispered, "I could tell you stories! Tourists come in— gay, straight, groups, whatever—they want something different. You know what I'm saying?"

"What if Luis wanted something different but closer to home?"

"It depends on what he wants."

"You mean, you could arrange . . . escorts? If he wanted an extra person on our dates? Luis mentioned it, but I think he was kidding."

"Mmm-hmm." Carla smiled indulgently.

"You don't like this very much, do you?" Gail said.

"Soon as I can get some money in the bank, and it won't be long, I'm outta here."

"Where will you go?" Gail asked.

"Paramus, New Jersey. I have family there."

Gail gestured toward the triple photo frame beside Carla's computer monitor. "The people in the pictures? Can I see?"

"Oh, those! Yes, that's my grandbaby."

"You're a *grand*mother?"

Carla laughed. "Oh, honey, everybody says I don't look old enough, but I'll claim this little fella!" She slid the triple frame across the desk. The first section showed a splotchy-faced infant with a blue blanket wrapped around him. He had chubby cheeks and crossed eyes and black hair someone had coaxed into a mohawk. A hand-written card propped on his chest said *LoRusso, Michael Roy. 9 lbs, 2 oz. 7/31*. The next photo showed the baby with his eyes uncrossed, in the arms of a pretty, dark-haired young woman. The last was a department- store portrait: Mom, Dad, smiling baby against a backdrop of out-of-focus trees.

Gail asked, "Was he just born in this first picture?"

"Fresh as an egg."

"Big boy."

"Ouch, right? They almost had to give her a cesarian."

"Were you there?"

"You bet. My son-in-law called me when Rita went into labor and I mean I was on a plane an hour later."

Gail said, "How long did you stay with her?"

"The weekend." Carla smiled at the photos. "As long as I could."

"I bet you made it back just in time for the old grind on Monday."

"You got it."

"They're a beautiful family," Gail said.

"They're my life." Carla placed the triple frame exactly where it had been, nudging it until she got it right. Her gold bracelets twinkled, ringing like little bells.

"Aren't you married?" Gail asked.

"No, me and my husband got divorced a long time ago. I don't care. He was a drunk. Rita married a great boy, a real sweetie-pie. I'm gonna help them buy a house. You have any kids?"

"A daughter. She's . . . with her grandparents . . . in Kansas City. I send money."

"Oh, my. I went through that with mine. It's hard, isn't it?" Carla Napolitano squeezed Gail's hand. "Now look here, Connie. I don't mean to preach or anything. Far be it, you know? But this kind of life. It gets old. And you get old. And then what?"

She scooped up the travel brochures and tapped them on her desk, aligning them neatly. "You forget about this asshole Luis. Excuse the language, honey, but I know whereof I speak.

You go find yourself a nice man while you're young, settle down, make a good home. Then maybe you can get your daughter back." She smiled. "We do it all for our kids, don't we? That's what matters."

Gail stood by her car with the door open for a minute, letting the heat out. She had forgotten to put the sun shield over the dash.

Across the street, over the flat-roofed white storefronts with their aluminum awnings, she could see the six-floor bank building where Lauren Sontag worked. Lauren Sontag—unless she was buzzing around collecting endorsements for her judicial candidacy—was probably up there right now. It made Gail's head spin. Lauren had lied, lied, lied.

The will was a phony, beyond question. It hadn't been signed on Saturday, August 3. The notary had been cuddling her new grandbaby in Paramus, New Jersey, making it back to Miami Beach in time for work on Monday.

Gail got in and started her car, flipping the AC to high. It worked wonderfully, now that the weather was cooling off. She took a left onto Alton Road, going back toward the causeway.

Carla Napolitano had seen some things in her life. Had done some things. She had her lapses, but she wasn't really *wicked*. Now Gail would have to betray her, and she took no pleasure in that thought. Jack Warner would have to handle Carla's deposition. Gail knew she might hesitate going for the kill, remembering how Carla had shown her the photos of that cross-eyed baby.

At the next stop light Gail checked her watch. Only 4:15. She made a U-turn. As long as she was on the Beach, on a lucky streak . . .

She stopped around the corner from 1470 Drexel Avenue, got out of her car, and ignored the meter. She would only be there long enough to take a quick look.

Moving along with the other pedestrians on the sidewalk, she could see the alley behind the two-story building. There was a pile of boxes and an old tire. A back door was open, and through the screen came the clang of pots and pans and the smell of garlic. Above, water dripped from a rattling air conditioner hanging out a window.

She turned north, passing a carry-out pizza place, then a barber shop. Old drink cups had been left among the dusty bushes in the brick planter outside. The next door was set back into an angled entranceway beside a directory listing the businesses upstairs. There were ten of them. Atlantic Enterprises was first, Seagate, Inc., near the end. Suites 203 and 205.

Gail looked through the heavy glass door, which was scratched around the metal handle. She could see an elevator.

What if, on a pretense of some kind, one could simply knock on the door? Play a part. See if they had any job openings. Pretend to be a new tenant in the building. She opened the door.

On the second floor the carpet was stained and wrinkled, and a long strand of it had frayed out of the weave as if caught by someone's shoe. Gail walked noiselessly along the corridor. At the far end a window covered in steel mesh let in a

273

yellowish light that shone on the slickly painted walls. She heard voices from somewhere, then a laugh.

Numbers 203 and 205 were painted on the same door. No names. Rock music came faintly through it. Gail started to turn the knob, but knocked instead, her heart doing a little flip before it settled.

A man's voice shouted for her to come in.

The room was about fifteen feet square with display tables along two walls. Headless torsos on a shelf wore T-shirts reading YOUR LOGO HERE. There were sales catalogs and boxes of key chains, pencils, plastic mugs, everything covered with dust.

A chunky man in his late thirties was standing in the doorway to an inner office, where the music was coming from. His black hair curled close to his head in little ringlets. He wore a loose, abstract-patterned shirt and light-green pleated pants. Behind him Gail could see a woman's bare legs, crossed, and a pair of ankle-strap silver platform shoes.

"Can I help you?" Frowning a little, curious, he walked closer to where Gail stood. He was shorter than Gail by a few inches, with a pudgy face and thick hair on his forearms. His heavy gold ID bracelet was outlined in little diamonds. She could make out the letters F-R-

"I'm looking for Frankie Delgado," she said.

He raised his eyebrows, spread his hands. "Who's looking?"

"Miriam." It was the first thing that jumped into her head. She tossed back her hair and looked down her nose at him. She thought her heart might stop. "I hear you have some openings at Wild Cherry."

He stuck a striped plastic straw in his mouth. It was bent double and already gnawed and pointed. He chewed on it for a while, looking at her. "No offense, sweetheart, but how old are you?"

"Does it matter?"

"Yeah, it matters."

The legs uncrossed and the woman they belonged to came to the door—a young woman; very slim, with a perky butt and breasts like apples. She wore a long-sleeved black top held together at the shoulders by silver circles, and her curly, white-blond hair swooped into a sparkly clip, then corkscrewed to her waist.

Frankie glanced back at her. "Hey. Turn down the radio."

Gail brought her eyes back to the man. "I wasn't aware there was an age limit." Anxiety was making her voice husky.

The radio went silent.

He said, "You don't look like a dancer."

She shrugged. "I do a lot of things."

Leaning on the door frame, the girl snorted. "She's gotta be like thirty. At least."

"Shut up." The girl folded her thin arms. Frankie chewed on his straw. "What else you do, Miriam?"

"Whatever. I have a vivid imagination."

He looked around at the girl, grinning. "Hey, maybe I should send you out for coffee, sweet cheeks."

275

She smiled at him, raising her middle finger, showing a long, iridescent purple fingernail. Her round face was absolutely without lines. She could have been fifteen.

"Miriam. Hey. Who sent you over?"

"I . . . met somebody at the travel agency."

"Somebody who?"

"A woman."

The girl laughed. "Carla's doing referrals now?"

"Hey." Frankie looked over his shoulder. "Shut up or go in the other room." She dropped into a molded plastic chair by a display table and hugged her arms around one leg. She was wearing pink underwear.

Frankie sat on a corner of the table, his trouser leg tight, his thigh big as a ham. "You go out, Miriam? You date?"

It flashed through her mind that she ought to apologize for bothering him, then twist the doorknob and flee into the hall. But she couldn't pull her eyes away—the thick arms, the gelled ringlets on his forehead. Did she *date?*

She smiled. "Yes. But I'm very particular."

He took the straw out of his mouth and bent it the other way. "You go out with businessmen? High-class–type guys?"

Gail could feel the sweat prickling her neck. "Men of intelligence appreciate my talents," she said. "Lawyers, for example."

From the chair the girl snickered.

"Shut up," he said, still looking at Gail. "You got a specialty? Something you like to do?" He slid off the table and walked toward her.

She pressed back a little, the doorknob in her spine. "Not really."

"I guess you're—what?—versatile. A lady of many talents." He turned the straw around and around in his mouth, holding it between thumb and forefinger. She could smell his heavy cologne. "Nice dress. Classy."

"Thank you. It was a gift."

"Yeah? From who? A guy?"

"We had a lovely evening."

Arms crossed, Frankie chewed on the straw. "Dinner, dessert, all that? Where'd you go?"

"Here. South Beach."

"Then what'd you do? Let him take you in the ass?"

Gail stared.

"I mean, for a dress like that." He looked into Gail's eyes without expression, then slammed his shoulder against her chest and dragged her purse off her arm too fast for her to grab it.

She coughed and sucked in a painful breath. The air had been knocked from her lungs, and the doorknob had caught her in the ribs. "Don't!"

He backed away with a hand palm up. "Hey. Hey! I'm not keeping it. Just want to see who I'm talking to, okay?" He tossed the purse to the girl, who overturned it on the table. Frankie stood in front of her and kept his eyes on Gail.

The girl swung her hair out of the way, shuffling plastic. "Her driver's license says Gail Ann Connor. Lives in South Miami. She'll be thirty-four in December. I *told* you. Account at Barnett. American Express Gold Card, Visa, Lord &

Taylor . . ." She waved one of Gail's business cards slowly back and forth.

Frankie took it. "A lawyer. No shit. Gail A. Connor. You want to tell me what the fuck you're doing here, Gail Ann?"

Her mind raced. "So what if I'm a lawyer? I do this for fun. And the extra cash."

"Yeah?" He laughed, and deep lines formed around his eyes. "An attorney who admits she's a whore. That's refreshing."

"Give me my purse back!"

"Take it easy." He poked through her things for a minute, then put her card in his shirt pocket. "I might need a lawyer, you never know. Somebody with your versatility? Could be fun. Pack up her stuff, sweet cheeks. And you. Gail Ann. Go get a paper route."

chapter seventeen

By the time she arrived home, twenty minutes late, there was a dark-blue Cadillac convertible in her driveway, next to Phyllis Farrington's old Chevy.

Gail parked on the grass. She had prayed Anthony would be late. She wanted a shower and clean clothes, wanted to wash off the scent of Frankie Delgado's cologne, which she could imagine wafting up from her dress as if a dog had lifted its leg on her.

278

The front door opened and Phyllis came out, looking a little miffed. "Is it all right if I go? I've got a neighborhood action committee meeting tonight."

"Yes. Of course." Gail stepped over a sprinkler head. "Sorry I'm late. The traffic was awful." She paused by Phyllis's car. "What are they doing in there?"

"Who?" She heaved her heavy purse through the open door. "Karen and Mr. Quintana? Why, they're in the kitchen talking to each other. What did you think?" Phyllis squeezed herself under the steering wheel and rolled down her window. "I need you to write me my check tomorrow. No, don't do it now. I got to go." She put on her brakes and stuck her head out the window. "Why're you walking like that? You hurt yourself?"

"I backed into a doorknob."

"Lord have mercy." Phyllis pulled out of the driveway.

Gail went inside, dropping her briefcase on the sofa. Anthony and Karen looked around when she appeared at the kitchen door. They were sitting at the counter on high stools. Anthony had his shirtsleeves rolled up and his tie loosened. Karen spun her seat around.

"Mom, where were you?"

"Miami Beach. It took longer than I thought, then there was an accident on the causeway." Holding herself straight, she came across the kitchen to put down her purse. She gave Karen a hug. "I am so glad to see you." She smiled at Anthony over Karen's head. "You too."

"You need a car phone," he said, frowning.

"I know. You told me." She lightly kissed his cheek. His shoulder felt warm and solid under her hand. She wanted to scratch her fingernails through his clean, dark hair. "What have you guys been doing?"

"Waiting for you," he said. "Karen fixed me some Kool- Aid. She showed me the lizards she feeds in the backyard, and I told her about a pet iguana I had when I was a kid."

Karen held up a gold-colored coin the size of a quarter. "He gave me this. It's one Cuban peso. See? It has a picture of José Mart, on the front. It says *Patria o Muerte.* That means 'fatherland or death.'" Karen took back the coin. "Can we eat now?"

Gail noticed the flat box on the table. "Who ordered the pizza?"

"I did. It just arrived," Anthony said.

"How much was it?"

"Never mind."

"No. If I invite you for dinner, I can pay for the pizza." She crossed the kitchen for her purse.

"Gail, it's okay."

"It isn't okay!" She laughed a little, pushing back her hair. "Let me do this."

Anthony and Karen looked at her steadily. He said, "I gave the delivery man twenty dollars."

"Do you guys want salad? I have some ripe plum tomatoes—" Gail took her wallet out and opened it. Wider. "Where—" She tossed it aside and rummaged through her purse, pulling out brush, notebook, makeup, and the parking ticket that had been left on her windshield. Her charge cards were in the bottom but the money was gone. "Well. I seem to be a little short of cash. I'll pay you back."

"I said forget it. Gail, what's the matter with you?"

"It appears that someone has been through my wallet."

Anthony stood up. "When did this happen? On the Beach?"

Gail crossed to the sink and turned on the hot water. "Karen, sweetie, get three plates and some forks and napkins." She pumped the liquid soap into her palm. "I went to talk to some people in that case I'm doing for Patrick Norris. Some witnesses, I guess you'd say." Her skin was turning pink under the steaming water. "When my attention was distracted, poof!"

"You need to call the police."

"Somebody stole your money?" Karen looked up at her with wide blue eyes. She held the plates in her arms.

Gail took a fresh dish towel from a drawer. There were three versions of this story. One for Karen, one for Anthony, and one she would keep to herself. She dried her hands. "I don't want to call the police. It isn't that much money."

"But you know who took it," Anthony said.

"A girl. I don't know her name."

Karen said, "When my bike got stolen you said to call the police, and we didn't even know who did it."

Gail smiled at her. "This is different, sweetie. I'll explain it later. Go set the table."

When Karen's back was turned, Gail pulled

Anthony closer and quickly kissed his mouth. "Everything's okay with you two?" she asked softly.

"Yes. Fine."

"She's been polite?"

"Perfect. How much did you have to pay her?"

"Oh, stop." She slid her hand up his shirt then tugged on his tie. "Let me go change my clothes. It won't take long. I feel grungy."

He held her by the forearms when she started to move away. "What happened to you?"

Gail glanced at Karen, who was filling turquoise plastic glasses with cherry Kool-Aid. "Have you ever wanted to take a naked sailboat cruise?"

Anthony squeezed her arms. "Gail."

"Okay, here's a preview. I found out that my friend Lauren Sontag lied to me. The will is most definitely a fake. Second, I know where we can go to arrange X-rated vacations. And third—" Gail lowered her voice still further. "I found out I'm too old to be a call girl."

"*What?*"

"I'll tell you after dinner." She laughed. "If Karen isn't in the room at the time. It's funny now, almost worth the eighty dollars I lost." She laid her hand on his cheek, and the late-afternoon stubble felt scratchy under her palm. "I wish you could stay tonight. You don't know how much I wish that."

For a moment Gail thought she could hear the sound of Karen splashing in the bathroom down the hall. Gail had always insisted that the door be left open. Lately, in deference to her daughter's growing sense of modesty, Gail had compromised: Karen could close it all the way but the last inch. There were those stories of children slipping on a bar of soap, cracking their fragile heads, drowning because their mothers hadn't heard them. But tonight, with a man around, Karen had shut it completely, then turned the lock.

Anthony stood silently in the middle of the family room with one hand on his hip and the other over his eyes as if he had a migraine.

"That was the most brainless, idiotic—"

Gail said, "I had no idea it would be like that."

He dropped his hand. "That is the point. You didn't think what you were doing."

"What difference does it make now?" she said, stung. "I got what I needed. I can prove the will is a forgery."

"No, you can't."

She laughed. "Oh, really."

"No. I would love to defend this case. I would ask the jury, What does it prove that Carla Napolitano was out of town on the third of August?"

"That the will was forged."

He shook his head slowly, his eyes fixed on Gail. "Yes, ladies and gentlemen of the jury, she was in New Jersey. But so what? Carla Napolitano could have put any date on the will. It does not mean that Althea Tillett didn't sign it."

"I can prove Carla lied! It goes to her credibility as a witness."

"All right. Let us say they admit she lied. Now

283

you have Lauren Sontag's explanation. You still must prove Althea Tillett did not sign that will." Anthony spread his hands, waiting.

"I hate it when you do this," she said, turning her back.

"Better you hear it from me than from the other side." He walked around her. "This is what I mean. In your enthusiasm to play detective, you do not think. Carla Napolitano may be related to your case, but this other! What could possibly be gained by pretending to Frankie Delgado that you were a *prostitute?*"

"I should have given you the same sanitized version I'm going to tell Karen because you obviously can't handle it."

"What do you expect? What? You tell me this man attacked you. They stole your money . . . You could have been killed. Or worse."

"A fate worse than death?"

"Yes. He could have raped you, cut you into pieces, then dumped your body, and your daughter—" Anthony raised an arm toward the hall. "—would be without a mother!"

"Enough! Okay! Thank you for your concern!"

He let out a sharp breath through his nose. "Don't ever do anything like this again."

Gail stared at him. "Don't speak to me like that. I was investigating my case. I have a responsibility to my client."

"Aha. Your client? Your friend Patrick."

"I would do the same for any client."

Anthony spun around, speaking Spanish too fast for her to grasp a word of it. He turned back to glare at her. "You were never like this. Ever.

Then you took this case—I told you not to take this case—" He pointed.

"It's my damn case, and I'll handle it as I see fit!"

"Somebody has to protect you against yourself, I think."

"How condescending! I don't need to be protected."

"No? What is that bruise you have showed me on your back?"

"If this is how you're going to react, then why should I tell you anything?"

"*Bueno. No me digas nada.*" Anthony stalked into the kitchen.

"Where are you going?"

"Home. It is impossible to talk to you." He lifted his jacket off the back of a chair. "Thank you for dinner."

"That's easy, isn't it? You get mad and you can walk out."

Calmly he slid an arm into a sleeve, hesitated with the jacket hanging on one shoulder, then took it off and threw it across the kitchen.

Together they noticed Karen sitting in one of the high stools at the counter, bouncing her bare toes off the bottom rungs. She was wrapped in one of Gail's old terry-cloth robes.

Anthony mumbled something, then went to pick up his jacket where it had landed on the floor.

"Oh, sweetie." Gail put her arm around Karen. "We weren't really fighting. We were disagreeing about a case."

He put his jacket back on, brushing his hands

down the lapels. "Yes, we were fighting. Your mother did something dangerous today, and she doesn't want—"

"Don't tell her that!"

"Why not? Is it a lie?"

"It's up to me what I tell my daughter."

For a while Anthony concentrated on getting his cuffs straight. His cheeks were blazing with color high on the cheekbones. "Yes. You are right. It is your decision." Smiling at Karen, he made a slight bow. "Good night. It was a pleasure, sharing the pizza with you and hearing about your lizards."

Karen only looked at him with big eyes.

Gail followed Anthony to the front door and leaned her forehead against the frame. "I don't know what to say to you."

"Nothing." He stared down at his hand on the doorknob. "It's all right."

"It isn't."

He let out a breath. "No. It isn't."

"Well, maybe one day we'll talk about this," she said. "This and all the other things we don't talk about."

"Perhaps." He stood there for a moment, then said, "Gail, I think maybe we should let it go for a while. A week or two."

She laughed softly, aching inside. "You're probably right."

"Yes."

She touched his sleeve, running her finger along a fold in the fabric. "And after a week or two?"

"I don't know. We'll think about it then."

She nodded. "Kiss me good night."

Anthony turned to kiss her once on the lips. And then the door was clicking shut behind him.

chapter eighteen

Gail went back to Miami Beach the next morning. She and Larry Black had an appointment with Alan Weissman to discuss settling the Tillett case. Weissman was officially the attorney for the personal representative of the estate, Sanford V. Ehringer.

However, Weissman would have more than the interests of the Tillett estate on his mind: He had to cover his own rear end from charges of forgery. Gail supposed that at some point Ehringer would force Weissman to withdraw as counsel. Weissman would then become a reluctant witness for one side or the other in this affair. But for now he was the man to talk to.

At 9:55 A.M., Larry Black's Mercedes sedan pulled into the parking lot of the bank building. Gail was waiting in the shade of the entrance overhang. Larry locked his door then leaned straight-armed on the roof, head bowed, as if he were going upstairs to hear the verdict from his oncologist. A second later he turned and came toward the building.

Gail got up from the concrete bench. When

Larry saw her she said, "I already checked in with Alan's secretary."

He nodded.

"Are you okay?" she asked. He looked tired.

"I'm fine." He gazed at the automatic doors. "Well. Are we going to make some progress this morning?"

"We'll see. By the way, I've got some news about Carla Napolitano."

"Who?"

"The notary." How could he not remember? Gail waited until a bank customer had walked by, then said, "Yesterday I went to Gateway Travel and spoke to Carla using a false name. I pretended to be interested in taking a vacation. We got to talking about this and that, and I found out she wasn't even in Florida on the date the will was supposedly notarized. She was in New Jersey visiting her new grandson."

"I'll be damned," Larry said. "You've proved it's a forgery."

"Not quite. We can show that Carla made a false notarization, but we can't prove Althea Tillett didn't sign the will on the third of August. Weissman could say that Carla notarized the will when she got back into town, and Althea Tillett's signature was already on it. All we have for sure is the document examiner's testimony and a few good guesses."

Larry was picking at the skin around his thumbnail. "What is this going to do for us with Weissman?"

"They've lost Carla Napolitano as a credible witness. It proves that Weissman is a liar. Lauren

Sontag as well, I'm sorry to say." Gail walked Larry out of the path of passersby. "There's something else, but I can't see how it ties in to the Tillett forgery. Gateway Travel and its parent company Seagate are probably fronts for some kind of illegal operation."

"What do you mean?" Larry whispered. "Illegal? How do you know this?"

"Remember I told you about Frankie Delgado? I met the man."

Quickly Gail described her visit to the shabby office on Drexel Avenue. She included the part about impersonating a prostitute.

Larry seemed stunned. "You're not going to tell Weissman."

"No, why should I? But this may come out at some point, depending on how it fits in. We can't let it slip that I spoke to Carla or Frankie. We'll call it 'confidential sources.'"

Suddenly Larry laughed, a sound nearer to a yelp. He said, "The firm took a hit with that damn column in 'Legal Notes' on Monday, telling the world we're on the verge of a split. As soon as this case is filed, people will think we're stealing from charity. Sanford Ehringer could have our client accused of murder. My God, what now? Will they say we're involved with procurers and criminals? Gail, we've got to settle it. Whatever it takes, settle it."

She shook her head slowly. "Patrick doesn't see any point in settling unless they agree to something decent. I agree, Larry. The police have nothing on Patrick. We shouldn't be afraid of what Sanford Ehringer might do."

His brows knitting, Larry asked, "What does Patrick Norris call a decent settlement?"

"Ten million dollars."

"Oh, my God."

"He'll settle for four, but don't let Weissman know that," Gail said. "I've told Patrick we don't have much of a case yet. He'd rather have four now than litigate for a year or two and possibly end up with nothing. Frankly, I'll be disappointed if we can't get them up to at least six."

Larry nibbled off a piece of cuticle, then smoothed it with the other hand. "Isn't this what Howard Odell was proposing at the gallery? A settlement?"

Gail said, "I'd rather not deal with Howard Odell. I don't trust men with toupees and capped teeth. If he and cousin Sanford want to participate in a settlement, fine, but I'm not going to delay this case for them. Unless something unexpected happens upstairs, we're filing the petition for revocation of probate tomorrow."

Larry looked desolately at the front of the building. "Well. We'd better go on upstairs, hadn't we?"

Gail grabbed his arm. "Wait. Let me take the lead on this. You're a friend of his, and that could hurt us. We have to get his attention, Larry. Weissman has to be convinced we've got a case, that we're only talking settlement as a convenience to our client, and if he won't go along, we'll slice out his heart. Larry, listen to me. Forget you ever worked with him on a civic committee. Don't smile, don't make small talk. Let me be the one to tell him what we want."

"What do I do? Sit there and growl?"

"No. What I want you to do is drag me off him the minute he gives us anything. Play the good guy. He won't like me very much, and he needs someone to go to. Can you do that?"

"My God. Trial lawyers."

Gail picked up her briefcase from the bench. "Did you get a chance to think about what Sanford Ehringer said to me about Easton?"

"That he doesn't exist?" Larry shook his head. "I have no earthly idea what he meant."

"Easton. Maybe he was a ghost. Or a character out of a Rudyard Kipling poem. You know, 'the white man's burden' and all that jolly rot."

Looking at her mournfully, Larry said, "You're awfully cheerful."

"I'm manic, are you kidding?"

They walked toward the bronze-tinted glass doors, which swung outward, the name of the bank flashing in the sun. When they got on the elevator, they were alone.

Gail said, "Larry, tell me about the Easton Trust. The last time we talked, I got the distinct impression that you knew some of the people on the board of directors. You hinted that some are clients of our firm."

"I don't believe I said that."

"You definitely said you knew some of them."

"Did I?"

Gail laughed. "Yes, Larry. You did. A couple of weeks ago you had lunch in the partners' room with Howard Odell. You know him. He's in Easton."

"We weren't discussing Easton," Larry said.

291

"Whatever. Odell is the director, Sanford Ehringer is the chairman. Who else?"

"Why do you need to know?" The sides of the elevator were mirrored in smoky glass, and his image reflected in a long curving row of heads with thinning hair and the fronts of Brooks Brothers suits.

"I don't know why I need to know," she said. "I just wonder why the registered agent for Seagate and Atlantic are in the same building as Easton. The will leaves money to the Easton Trust, and the notary works for Gateway. What's the connection?"

"Does there have to be one? You know, Gail, there are coincidences in life. Serendipitous events. Oddities placed by the God of Irony to drive us mad." He watched the numbers flashing from floor to floor.

Gail looked at him for a few seconds as the elevator rolled smoothly upward. "Who's in the Easton Trust, Larry?"

The bell sounded. "We'll talk later." The door opened and he put out a hand to let her go first.

She stuck her foot across the tracks. "Weissman can wait. I don't want to go in there to talk about this case—which involves the Easton Charitable Trust even indirectly—and get myself blindsided by a brick thrown out of nowhere."

"This is completely *irrelevant!*"

The door bucked against her foot, and Gail reached in and pulled Larry out by one arm. There was no one in the carpeted corridor, only doors in both directions and across from the

292

elevator a gilded half-table with a vase of artificial flowers.

She had her fist around the fabric of his coat sleeve. "Sanford Ehringer was positively creepy. He gave me nightmares. Then yesterday with Frankie Delgado . . . I think if I could get my fingernails under the edge of this case, and turn it over, I'd see wet, slimy things twisting into the ground."

His eyes widened. "Gail. I am sincerely worried about you. You've been under a strain lately, you know. Financial woes. Your sister's death. Divorce. The pressure of making partner—"

"Larry, please. I'm not having a breakdown." She spoke softly. "I only want to know who is on the board of the Easton Trust."

After a few seconds, he said, "I'd prefer not to discuss it."

"Why in hell not?"

"Because they have nothing to do with this. You are invading their privacy simply out of misguided curiosity."

"Curiosity? This is a twenty-five-million-dollar estate! You're supposed to be on my side. Larry, what is the big deal?"

Larry Black's usually gentle expression turned furious and hard, and his lips drew back along his teeth. "You presume too much. You show me no respect as your supervising partner. Oh, I've let you get away with it, because I tend to be too good-natured, but even I can be pushed only so far. I have championed you with the partnership committee at the firm, but I am very close to regretting that decision. Your judgment is deplorable. Speaking to Carla Napolitano on your own, and in that manner. I am shocked. Partners of major law firms are not so impetuous!"

After a moment of stunned silence, Gail took a shaky breath. "I'm sorry if I have disappointed you. I've always tried to do my best."

Larry squeezed his eyes shut for a second. "I know you have."

"Your timing's lousy."

His hand went briefly to her arm, then dropped. "I am sorry. Gail, I didn't mean what I said. It was my temper speaking."

She turned away and marched down the hall toward Weissman's office. "Let's just get this over with."

Alan R. Weissman had flown a fighter jet in Vietnam; his wings and battle ribbons hung in a glass case on a wall of his office. He had been a president of the Florida Bar, and there were photos of that. There were also photos of Weissman shaking hands with Jimmy Carter, Golda Meir, Frank Sinatra, and Arnold Palmer. There was Weissman lined up with other members of the Miami Beach Chamber of Commerce, cutting a ribbon. Alan Weissman looking tanned and fit, his suits shining like fine silk armor in the flashbulbs. He was a handsome guy with a big grin, a high forehead, and curly gray hair receding to show more of it.

He had burned up the track in his thirties and forties. He still knew people. The judges would call him by his first name in court. His clients were mostly on Miami Beach, mostly elderly. Weissman and a few other mid-fifties attorneys would congregate in a bar up on Collins Avenue in the afternoon and drink. Of his three partners, one had died last spring of a heart attack on the fifth tee at the LaGorce Country Club. The firm hadn't gotten around to changing the stationery. Another kept himself busy with real estate deals, and the last—Lauren Sontag—was a good bet for the Circuit Court bench. Weissman was her campaign manager. There were rumors they were having an affair, and rumors that this was the reason his wife had left him.

Weissman was a prominent attorney because he had been around for a long time, and because he had once been good at it. Several complaints had been made by clients who said he had neglected their cases, but the Bar had let him quietly settle with each of them. How would it look, a former Florida Bar president, disciplined for ethical violations? They made him go to a clinic in Boca Raton to dry out. His wife, Mona, had already hired a divorce lawyer. She had closed their joint accounts, and now she was going after the real estate. His younger son was in jail in New York for securities fraud, and his only daughter had converted to Catholicism.

Gail had found all this out in the last week or so by asking the right people. *Know thine enemy.*

In her car this morning, driving to the Beach, she had played out this version in her head: Alan Weissman must have wept with gratitude that Rudy and Monica Tillett showed up, asking his advice on the matter of their deceased step-mother's will. They couldn't find it. It was gone, burned, torn into pieces—God only knew. The consequences were beyond terrible: Patrick Norris, her only heir, would get their parents' house, their mother's art, everything! So perhaps Mr. Weissman would help? He would be well compensated, and surely the risk would be small.

What luck that Althea had come to see him just the month before. No problem using that date. No problem inventing a new will. After all, it would be the same as all the other wills—except for the provision giving Rudy and Monica the house and the art collection.

But then Patrick Norris showed up screaming forgery.

Alternate version: It had been Sanford Ehringer who had contacted Weissman. Dear Althea is dead; there is no will and my charity stands to lose God-knows-how-much money. Can you think of a solution? Irving and Jessica will be happy to help. And we'd better pay off Rudy and Monica to keep them quiet.

Gail had to feel a little sorry for Alan Weissman. He probably liked doing probate, except that his clientele were dying off. Not much stress to filing an estate. You fill out the right forms and have a CPA check behind you to make sure you don't screw up on the taxes. But the Tillett case! A bog, a swamp!

What didn't fit, Gail had decided, was the part Lauren Sontag had played in this little drama. Why would she risk her career for Alan Weissman? Friendship? Love?

Love. Alan Weissman was a handsome, broken man. A tragic man, in a way, and didn't Lauren possess her own streak of tragedy? There was an elegant, wistful, even a *noble* sadness to her that Gail, in the years of knowing Lauren Sontag, had never been able to fathom. So she'd had a bad marriage. Lots of women had survived that. She had a daughter, a smart and pretty girl finishing her last year of high school, planning to go on to Radcliffe College. That was cause for happiness, surely.

How fascinating that the cool and distant Lauren Sontag had lied for love. And yet she had said there was no sex between them. What, then? Truly, there were mysteries to this relationship, and the ways of love were exceedingly strange. Was there such a thing as sexless passion? Gail could not imagine it with Anthony Quintana.

And there her thoughts had broken off, and crossing the causeway to the Beach again, Gail had felt a stab of loneliness, of panic, knowing she was losing him.

She had driven the rest of the way to Alan Weissman's office with her radio turned up high, blasting into the silence.

Now Gail and Larry Black faced him across his desk. Weissman was sliding his hands along the edge of it, fingers flat, thumb underneath as if he might suddenly flip the desk over or rip it down the middle.

The desktop bore burn marks near the overflowing marble ashtray. He had put out his cigarette when they came in. The room was carpeted in brown shag and wallpapered in beige vinyl that had frayed around the light switch. Open-weave curtains hung limply on either side of metallic miniblinds, tilted shut against the morning sun.

Weissman laughed disbelievingly. "Ten million dollars? Larry, where'd you get this woman? She's out of her fucking mind."

Larry moved in his chair. "Alan, there's no need for anyone to become personal. What Gail is trying to say—"

Gail shut him up with a glance as she rose from her chair and began to walk—jacket open, hands in the pockets of her skirt. The platform pumps she had chosen for today put her just over six feet tall. "Look at the evidence, Alan. The leading document examiner in South Florida says Althea Tillett didn't sign the will. The alleged witnesses can't agree on what happened. They're going to crash and burn on the stand. You know this."

Larry said, "I'd settle it for ten, Alan."

"And you're fulla crap, both of you." He waved a hand.

Gail said, "Althea Tillett's will was forged. I believe that it was done in this office, either directly by you or with your knowledge and cooperation. If this case goes to trial, you're going to have some problems."

"*I* forged a client's will?" He poked the front of his knit shirt. "I should be so stupid?" A bit of gray hair curled from the open collar. He picked up his red appointment book. "Here's something for you to mull over, Ms. Connor. My secretary spoke to Althea. She wrote down that

Althea would come to see me on Saturday, August third, at ten A.M." He let his book drop on his desk with a thud. "And guess what. Althea showed up."

Arms folded, Gail said, "Fine. She was here on August third. Was it to sign her will? Or did you pick that date for the will because her name was already in your appointment book?"

Larry continued to gaze at Weissman without a flicker.

Gail asked, "Were you aware that the woman who notarized Althea Tillett's will was in New Jersey on the third of August?"

Alan Weissman's high forehead was flaming. He opened his arms and laughed. "Go for it. File your case. You'll get *bupkis*. Make a complaint to the Florida Bar while you're at it. I'll look like an idiot for a few months, which I admit I was. An idiot for doing Althea Tillett a favor. But you think other attorneys haven't done favors for their clients? It's done, Ms. Connor. It is done."

"Not by my firm."

"*Your* firm? You're nothing over there." Alan Weissman, gathering some steam now, stood up, hitching his trousers around his waist. "Ten million dollars! You people are nuts. We'll give him two. That's it. Patrick Norris should take it and be grateful. Althea would die all over again if she could see this."

Larry's head turned slightly toward Gail. What next?

"How much did Lauren Sontag pay the notary?" Gail asked.

Weissman lit a cigarette. "Lauren wasn't here."

"That's not what she told me," Gail said.

"I don't give a damn what she told you." He tossed the lighter to his desk, and the smoke boiled out of his lungs.

"Irving Adler also says Lauren was here," Gail said.

Weissman said to Larry, "I made you people an offer. I'd like a response."

Larry looked up at him and started to speak, but Gail broke in.

"I'm taking the notary's deposition. I want her to tell me under oath how much Lauren Sontag paid her to commit a felony."

"You're going to get sued for slander, you and the fucking partners of Hartwell Black and Robineau." Weissman glared down at Larry.

Gail spoke to him over Larry's head. "Once this case is filed, Alan, I can't keep it out of the news. What's the *Herald* going to do when it hears that a candidate for the Circuit Court is involved in a forgery?"

"Discussion's over." Weissman raised his hands. "That's it."

Larry stood up, hesitating. Gail followed Weissman to his desk, where he took another long drag on his cigarette. She played her last card.

"Lauren asked me—begged me—not to let you get hurt. She said you would try to protect her. She said you would lie for her and say she wasn't involved. But she was. She helped you. Now you're going to watch her torn to shreds by

300

the State Attorney's Office? The Judicial Qualifications Commission?"

"Get the fuck out of my office." Alan Weissman swept a hand back over his forehead.

"I'm going to find out the truth, Alan. Count on it. Are you going to lose your license for Sanford Ehringer? Are you going to ruin Lauren Sontag to save your own ass? You can do better than two. Two's an insult."

He swung on her. "Ten million is insulting, Ms. Connor."

"So give me another number."

Alan Weissman walked away, smoothing his hair back with both hands, again, again. Smoke spiraled from the cigarette between his fingers. Larry followed him to the windows. "Alan, maybe we can work something out. Nobody wants this to get nasty. We can find a way."

Gail said, "Ten's a bargain, Alan. I want an answer by tomorrow."

"I'm not talking to you!"

Larry said, "Gail. Let him have the weekend. He has to discuss it with Ehringer and the major beneficiaries. What can it hurt?"

For a while Alan Weissman stood with his back to the room, smoking his cigarette. Then Gail heard him say, "Get her out of here. I don't want her in here."

Larry looked around at Gail. She silently picked up her briefcase and left the room. She took the elevator down, leaning against the back wall, shaking. In the mirrors her reflections went away to infinity, a woman in a neat gray suit.

She stashed her briefcase in her car and waited

301

inside with the door open. Larry came out a few minutes later. Pale. Tearing at the ragged flesh on his thumb, which had begun to bleed.

By now Gail was steadier. She got out of her car. "What did he say?"

"He'll let us know Monday."

"What do you think?"

His eyes wouldn't meet hers. Larry said, "He'll try to pull something together. Patrick will probably get his four million. I guess you won."

"I don't feel like it."

"But it's quite a victory." Larry was angry, she realized, because of his part in it. "Paul Robineau will be pleased as punch."

"I wouldn't have really done it, Larry. Sacrificed them like that, I mean."

"Why not? Can't be the kind of lawyer who's all talk and no action." He took out his car keys, looked at them. "I used to enjoy my profession. Now I don't know. I don't know if it's me or the age we live in. I'll never be much good at cutting people's hearts out. Even pretending I will." He found the right key. "I'll see you back at the office."

She nodded, and a black wind ran through her, howling.

Larry gave her a final, icy look. "I want this case closed."

chapter nineteen

As Patrick and Gail walked slowly toward Biscayne Boulevard discussing a possible settlement of the case, Eric Ramsay followed close behind. He had protested the danger on these streets, but Patrick had assured him some friends were looking out for them. Now, as they passed a row of boarded-up, graffitied storefronts, Gail saw what he meant: a young man watched from the corner, his foot propped on the bumper of a car. Another kept pace on the opposite side of the street, and a third brought up the rear. All of them wore sunglasses. She wondered what they might be carrying under their loose jackets.

Just past a tavern, where a faded green sign announced that pool was played within and the thud of rap music came through the high, barred windows, Patrick stopped walking. The next lot was vacant, and broken glass glittered among the scrubby weeds. At the back of the property two palm trees leaned drunkenly together, and toward the front a pile of trash was accumulating— palm fronds, rotting lumber, an old mattress, a smashed toilet.

"This is what I wanted you to see," Patrick said to Gail. "The city took it for taxes a few years ago. They'd let it sit like this forever, but we've started cleaning it up. I want you to negotiate the purchase." He was referring to the informal group that had already come together to work on the community renewal project—all of it contingent, of course, on Patrick's winning the case, or at least getting several million in a settlement.

Gail stood on the cracked sidewalk for a minute trying to visualize rows of vegetable plants and tropical fruit trees. Two blocks beyond, on Biscayne, was the garish yellow paint of the triple-X movie theater, the Reel Stuff.

Eric Ramsay said, "I don't see how you can grow enough here to feed the neighborhood."

"Not just one garden," Patrick explained. "Dozens. One for each block, everyone helping out. Kids, old folks, parents. All it takes is organization and some cash."

"And you think people will want to do this?"

"Of course they will," Patrick said. "People want to believe in something again. They're tired of handouts and hopelessness."

He walked farther into the weeds, and the breeze fluttered the hem of his white shirt. "It isn't only a garden, it's a metaphor. It represents the possibility of creating something from nothing. Using our own hands to sustain ourselves. The real enemy here isn't violence and drugs. They're only symptoms. The real enemy is outside: mass consumer culture. It tells the people they're meaningless so often that they believe it. Nobody lacks meaning who works in his own garden, so to speak. Or when he uses his own hands to create the things he needs for himself and his family. Or her family, as the case may be. Violence isn't natural to the human animal. It's a product of despair."

Eric bit the inside of his cheek, and his eyes danced with amusement. Hands in his pockets, he swung the toe of his wing-tipped shoe at a crushed beer can. It clattered into the weeds.

Gail looked at him coolly. "Check with the city. See what they want for the property. Okay?"

"Sure."

Patrick turned around, exultant. "Gail, we're going to do it! Miami is the perfect place to start. There's so much life here, so much renewal and possibility."

He had bought a new pair of glasses, wire-rims like the pair that Rudy Tillett had smashed across his cheekbone, which still had a Band-Aid on it. The glasses were the same but the clothes were different. The khaki trousers were gone, replaced by loose cotton slacks. They added weight to his tall, thin frame. The shirt, which had neither cuffs nor collar, was embroidered around the vee neck and down the front with white-on-white Arabic designs. A grandmother up the street had made it for him. Madame DeBrosse, his landlady, was doing his laundry for him now, and a pair of sisters brought him dinner.

Gail hoped that they would not be terribly disappointed if Patrick didn't harvest a crop from his metaphorical garden. She hoped that the three young men in sunglasses would understand.

"So what do you think, Patrick? The beneficiaries are meeting as we speak. To be honest, I doubt they'll go more than three million on their first offer."

He walked back through the weeds. Thistles stuck to his pant legs and his brown leather sandals. "No good. See if you can get them up to five, and make them pay the taxes."

"Hold it. Patrick, you told me on Tuesday that you would settle for four, and you didn't say anything about *net*. You're not a charity. You have to pay taxes. That means they'll have to give you over eight million dollars for you to come out with a net of four."

"Gail, if I have to pay taxes on four, I'll end up with less than *two*. That isn't enough. I've worked it all out. It's going to take five million—net—to do a first-rate job here."

His back to the empty lot, Eric Ramsay was studying the treeless, trash-strewn apartment building across the street. "Two million is a lot of money. I'd be happy with two. But with five you could bulldoze everything north of Flagler Street."

"Eric, for God's sake."

"No, it's okay," Patrick said, smiling. "Not all the victims of society live in this neighborhood. We each despair in our own way."

Eric smiled back. "Not me. Count on it."

"The surest indicator of despair is not to know that you despair," Patrick said softly.

"Yeah? Well, you live your life, I'll live mine."

"You can't insulate yourself from the rest of the world, Eric." Patrick went on, "You grew up privileged, didn't you? Not a worry. Do you ever look around you? Most of the world isn't so lucky."

"Hey, that's not my fault, is it?" Eric's face

306

was getting pink. "You try to make people feel guilty. I'm not guilty, I was born into this world like everybody else. And I see things for what they are. This city is a cesspool. If I were you, I'd take the money and get out. Nothing you do is going to make any difference."

Patrick was still smiling. "But, Eric, this is the exact response that society creates in some of the young people here. If you were poor, you wouldn't be a lawyer, you'd be robbing tourists or looting electronics stores."

The muscles in Eric's neck tensed, and his broad face flushed.

"Would you both stop it?" Gail said. She frowned at Eric and grabbed Patrick's elbow, turning him back toward the counseling center. They walked. "Listen, Patrick. You've got to be reasonable. Going to trial is risky."

"I don't want to back down, Gail. They forged Aunt Althie's will. There are principles involved here, you know."

"So we go down slugging."

"Oh, Gail." He groaned. "Go down? I don't want to lose. I can't lose. Do you know who wants an interview with me? The *Miami Herald.*"

She stopped walking. "You weren't supposed to publicize this."

"I didn't," he said. "But how could I keep people from finding out? Everybody in the neighborhood is talking about it."

"That would explain why Liz Lerner called me this morning."

"Who's she?" Patrick asked.

"She writes a legal gossip column. I told her

I don't talk about my cases. Certainly not this one."

"If the reporter shows up, what should I say to him?"

They started walking again. Gail said, "I'm going to have our P.R. people contact you." When he laughed, she said, "It's serious as death, Patrick. The judge is going to be influenced by his opinion of you, whether he admits it or not. We can't afford any mistakes in how you are portrayed in the media."

"All right, all right."

"No speeches," she said. "Don't discuss the case. Just smile and talk in generalities. Wear a normal shirt. And get a haircut."

"Just be myself, in other words."

They walked for a while in silence. Patrick said, "Do you really think we might lose?"

Gail had told him about Carla Napolitano—the whole story, which he had found greatly amusing. She said, "Weissman and Lauren Sontag and the witnesses to the will might get their stories straight enough so that a judge could buy it, if he was looking for a reason to rule against us. We've got the document examiner, but even he says he can't swear that Althea Tillett didn't sign the will. He can only swear that three of the six signatures don't look like hers." Gail shook her head. "You want the sad truth? We could be in trouble."

Patrick said, "Rosa Portales."

"Who?"

"Rosa Portales is Aunt Althie's housekeeper. She lives on the grounds. She would know what

Aunt Althie did with her will. Why didn't I think of this before?"

"The will before the August will?"

"Yes."

"The one that gave you the fifty bucks to join the ACLU? What if it still exists?"

"It's got to be gone, torn up, burned," Patrick said. "If Aunt Althie didn't do it herself, then Rudy and Monica would have, when they went through her things and found it." Patrick made a smile in Eric Ramsay's direction. "Gail and I are going over to Miami Beach. I'll be glad to have someone drive you back downtown."

They had taken a taxi here, Eric not wanting to risk his Lexus again, but coming with Gail anyway, for her own protection, he had said. Gail checked her watch. "I don't know."

"Come on," Patrick said. "We'll find Rosa. Besides, you want to see the place, don't you? Aren't you even curious?"

They took Patrick's old brown Mazda across the Venetian Causeway, grumbling along at a steady thirty-five miles an hour. Patrick had both hands on the wheel, squinting through the cracked windshield. Gail rolled down the window; the air conditioner was broken.

"Do you think I was too hard on Eric?" Patrick asked.

"Poor Eric. He doesn't know what to do with you," Gail said. "You're not the typical client." She hung her arm out the window. She had on a tailored dress today, cooler than a suit. "Maybe he's my fate. You once said that fate sends certain people into our lives to test us."

He looked at her curiously. "I don't remember that."

"You said it. So I get a six-foot, four-inch tax jock in a pinstripe suit and a Lexus." She lifted her chin to get the breeze on her neck. "You know, Patrick, if we do win this case, it wouldn't be morally wrong of you to get the AC fixed."

Once over the causeway Patrick turned right at North Bay Road, a narrow street that curved along the western side of Miami Beach. The faded asphalt was crumbling at the edges. Banyans arched overhead. No particular architectural style unified the neighborhood, except that all of the houses were well-kept. There was a Rolls-Royce parked in one driveway, a minivan in another. The grander homes were on the bay side. Several hid behind fences or walls with security cameras at the gates.

Althea Tillett's house was set back from the street behind an arched entryway with carriage lamps on either side. It had the look of the Twenties, a rambling two-story Mediterranean with a red tile roof and blue striped awnings. Flowering vines climbed the columns along the portico. A triple garage ran east-west, forming an L-shape with the main house. The brick driveway curved through thick grass then looped around a fountain where a round-tummied, high-breasted concrete nude held a water jug on her shoulder. No water came out.

There were two cars in the driveway already, a shiny Japanese model of indeterminate make and an old vinyl-roofed green Plymouth with a bumper sticker: *Jesucristo es el señor.*

Patrick said, "Emilio's here. He's the gardener. The other car is probably Rosa's." He parked in the shade of a banyan tree. The drone of a lawnmower seemed to come from behind the house. At the front door Patrick searched through his keys, then fit one of them into the lock.

"Should we just go in like this?" Gail asked.

"Sure. This is home. I used to live here, remember?"

The air inside the dimly lit foyer was cool. Gail's eyes adjusted. A thick Oriental carpet lay on the parquet floor; gold silk shimmered on the walls. On either side of a carved mahogany screen two Chinese porcelain lions stood guard, red tongues curling past bared teeth.

Gail patted one of them between its ears.

"R.W. and Aunt Althie bought them in Hong Kong," Patrick said. "Does this look like the entrance to a Parisian brothel, or what?"

The foyer opened onto a vast living room— yellow brocade sofas, tasseled swags of floral fabric at the high windows, a pair of cubist paint-ings on one wall, modern abstracts on another. Under a chandelier, a round Art Deco table held a bronze statue: goat-footed Pan playing his pipes. Greek columns extended along one side of the room, stairs curved up the other. A replica of the headless, toga-clad *Winged Victory* stood on a pedestal beside the grand piano.

"*Maison* Tillett," Patrick said, walking slowly through the room with his hands in his pockets. "A bourgeois wet dream."

311

Gail brushed her fingertips over the back of a carved and gilded Italian chair with a red velvet cushion. "Who bought all this stuff, your aunt?"

"Most of it. R.W. would raise hell with her, but he never made her stop. I think he liked arguing about it. You ever meet R.W.?"

"Not that I remember."

Patrick laughed. "Visualize a Presbyterian minister with a black three-piece suit and a bad attitude. I mostly stayed out of his way. But he and Aunt Althie were okay together. They clicked, strange as it seems. After he died, she kept on buying things. Trying to replace him, I guess. Every time I'd come to visit, she'd have something else to show me."

He wandered around for a bit then looked at the stairs curving to the second floor. His gaze traveled up the red-carpeted steps then down to the marble at the bottom.

Gail went to stand beside him. "This is where they found her?"

After a while he nodded. "Yes. I don't know where she—where it happened. I hope it was fast. But if it wasn't . . . Well, they say you see a white light or something." He glanced at Gail, smiling a little. "Aunt Althie believed in that sort of thing."

He tapped his open palm on the end of the balustrade, then stuck his hands back into his pockets. His eyes focused on something across the room. "What the hell?" He went to peer closely at the empty space over one of the sofas. "It's gone."

"What is?"

He pointed at the pale, vacant rectangle. "Aunt

312

Althie's Gauguin. It was a Tahitian woman lying in the grass. A nude, with a fox beside her."

"A genuine Gauguin?" Gail stepped closer as if it might reappear.

"Well . . . no. It was a copy. They bought it in Amsterdam. It looked like an original, though."

Then from above them came a voice. "Excuse me, but—who are you?" Gail and Patrick turned. A woman was halfway down the stairs, a thin woman in glasses, about thirty, with a buzz cut that left a fringe of blond hair over her forehead. There was dust on the knees of her jeans.

Patrick said, "Who are *you?*"

"I asked you first," she said.

Gail walked back across the room. "This is Patrick Norris, Mrs. Tillett's nephew. I'm his attorney, Gail Connor. We're trying to locate the housekeeper. Is she upstairs with you?"

The woman hesitated as if not sure she could trust them to know she was alone in the house. "No," she said. Her eyes went back to Patrick. "How did you get in?"

He said, "I have a key. Your turn. Who are you?"

"Susan Stone. I work for Stone Art and Antiques. We're doing an appraisal for the estate."

"So the vultures are circling already. Who hired you, Alan Weissman?"

"No, Monica Tillett. Listen, she didn't tell me to let anybody in. Maybe I should call her."

Gail said, "Just tell us if you've seen Rosa Portales. She was Mrs. Tillett's housekeeper."

"This is my third day and I haven't seen any

of the help, except for the gardener." She nodded toward the backyard, visible through the wide windows. By the sea wall, a man in a straw hat was pouring grass from the mower bag into a wheelbarrow.

Patrick said, "Emilio might know where she is."

Gail said to Susan Stone, "We're going to go ask him. All right with you?"

"I suppose."

But Patrick had noticed something else, three cardboard boxes stacked by the entrance to the foyer. "What's that?" His tone sharpened. "What are you people doing in here? You have no right to take any of this. It isn't yours."

She glared back at him. "I think you'd better leave."

"My attorneys are preparing a restraining order."

Gail said, "Patrick, I'll deal with this later. Let's talk to Emilio." She smiled at Susan Stone as Patrick went to unlatch the sliding glass door. The appraiser turned and walked between two of the Greek columns, vanishing deeper into the house.

By the time Gail and Patrick had crossed the terrace, Emilio was coming across the yard with the wheelbarrow. The scent of new-mown grass filled Gail's nose.

Patrick waved. *"Oye, viejo, ¿qué pasa?"*

Squinting, the gardener put down the handles of the wheelbarrow. His face brightened. *"Señor Norris, ¿es usted?"*

"In the flesh, *amigo*. How've you been?"

"I been good."

"You're still workin' here, man?"

Emilio laughed, deep creases in a browned face. "The grass don' stop growing."

"This is my attorney, Gail Connor."

Emilio bobbed his head, then took a handkerchief out of his pants pocket and wiped the sweat off his neck. He had thick hands. The nails were cracked, the edges black with dirt. "Is a terrible thin', Mrs. Tillett. I am so sorry. She was a nice lady." He took off his hat and lowered his voice. "She give me money in the . . . ¿Cómo se dice? El testamento."

"Will," Gail said. "She left you money in her will." Ten thousand dollars, she recalled.

"Sí."

Patrick said, "Emilio, have you seen Rosa? Is she still around?"

He shook his head. "She is gone. Gone for—" He made a dismissive motion with his hand. "Oof. Long time. After Mrs. Tillett die, I don' see Rosa no more."

Gail asked, "Do you know where she went?"

Emilio shrugged. "She go to Hialeah, I think. Maybe you ask the lady inside. Or el señor Tillett." He picked up the handles of the wheelbarrow.

"Take it easy, man," Patrick said, patting him on the back.

"Que Diós te bendiga." Emilio smiled, nodded at Gail, then continued his way around the house.

"Hialeah," Gail said. "Where in Hialeah?"

Patrick was still looking after Emilio. "You remind me. If we go to trial on this case, and I win it, he gets his money."

315

"I'll remind you," she said.

He pointed toward the house. "Look at that." Gail saw the woman watching through the sliding door. Patrick cupped his hands around his mouth and yelled, "Have a nice day!"

"Let's go," Gail said.

"See those little round windows under the gables in the roof?" Patrick asked. "That's the attic. I used to sit up there and read for hours, trying to stay sane around this nuthouse."

The west side of the old house seemed to glow in the late afternoon light, in the beginning of that season when the sun slips south and the days become pastel and gold. Gail let her eyes drift along the red tile roof, the arched windows, the blue-and-white striped awnings, the expanse of green grass, flowers, and hedges, and over-hanging trees. Birds sang. The water lapped at the tiled perimeter of the long turquoise swimming pool. A lattice gazebo shaded a white metal table and chairs with bright cushions. From somewhere farther down the sea wall a motor yacht cranked up, a muffled throb.

"It's a beautiful place," Gail said. "I'd live here in a minute."

He pointed toward the second floor. "Monica's room was on the end there, with the balcony, and Rudy's was next to it. Very chummy. My room was down the hall. Six rooms upstairs, eight down, maid's quarters over the garage. God, the parties they used to have! Live music out on the terrace. Jazz, a string quartet, a salsa band, whatever. Dancing, drinking. People in gowns and tuxes. Somebody would always make a scene, or get caught with somebody else's wife in one of the bedrooms. Reminded me of those descriptions of Jay Gatsby's parties. You ever read Fitzgerald?"

"Not since I was in high school," Gail admitted.

Patrick was staring at the low outline of trees and buildings a mile across Biscayne Bay and the little islands between, dense with feathery pines. Lauren Sontag had hinted to Gail, that night they had talked, that Patrick hated his stepcousins for reasons that went beyond jealousy. *I could tell you things,* Lauren had said. Stories of a childhood from which none of them had escaped unharmed.

He said, "Look at Miami from here. What do you see?"

"I don't know. Nothing in particular."

"No. It's a mirage. You don't see the dirt or the violence or the kids on crack. You stand here and you imagine that life in America is pretty damn good, after all. What is everybody whining about?"

Suddenly Gail felt very tired of all this. "Let's go," she said again.

He looked at her for a while, frowning. "Every time I see you lately, you've got this look on your face, like you just found out the planet is run by alien beings."

"Everything is weird lately."

He draped an arm over her shoulder. "Why don't you leave that factory you're working in and do something meaningful?"

"Working on your case isn't meaningful?"

"You could come on board as our legal

317

counsel, when we get this thing up and running. We wouldn't make you work eighty hours a week, like you do for Hartwell Black and Robineau. How do you have time for a life?"

"Anthony said the same thing."

"Don't tell me. He wants you to work for him." Patrick laughed. "So he can keep an eye on you."

"No. He didn't suggest that," Gail said. "And I wouldn't, even if he asked." Then she added, "I don't expect him to ask."

The sun flashed from the terrace. One of the glass doors was sliding open.

Monica Tillett strode past the pool, hands clenched, face gathered into a scowl. The wind tossed her black hair around her face. She wore a skin-tight zebra-print jumpsuit that came to her knees and floppy white socks over black oxfords.

"What are you doing on this property, Patrick?" she yelled.

"Monica, how nice to see you."

Gail said quietly, "Don't get started, Patrick. Let's just leave."

Monica looked at Gail. "And you. You ought to know better."

"Lighten up," Gail said. "We're only looking for Rosa Portales."

"Who's that?"

Patrick said, "Don't you remember, Monica? Rosa Portales worked for Aunt Althie for the last fifteen years. Cleaned the toilets? Waxed the floors? Brought your drink on a tray, when you bothered to come visit."

Gail gave him a hard look, then said,

318

"Apparently Rosa quit after Mrs. Tillett's death. Do you know how we can reach her?"

Monica's eyes were slits. "No. I don't."

The glass door slid open again and Rudy came out on a puff of refrigerated air. Black jeans, black T-shirt, little round sunglasses with shimmery blue lenses.

"You're trespassing, Patrick. You and your attorney. I've already instructed Ms. Stone to phone 911, so you should vacate the premises immediately."

Patrick smiled. "Vacate the premises? How original."

Susan Stone was peering through the sliding door, her hands clasped nervously at her waist.

Gail said, "Rudy, do you know where Rosa Portales has gone?" The blue sunglasses swung slowly in her direction. "Rosa Portales. She worked for your stepmother as a housekeeper."

"I haven't the least idea."

"What do you want with her?" Monica asked.

Gail didn't answer. "Mrs. Tillett probably had Rosa's phone number in her address book. If it isn't a bother—"

"Check with Alan Weissman, why don't you?" Rudy said.

Gail could feel the anger building. "Just so you won't be surprised. If there's no settlement of this case by noon on Monday, then on Monday afternoon, along with the petition for revocation of probate and emergency motion for a restraining order, I'm filing a motion for appointment of a curator."

One of Rudy's eyebrows shot over the top of the lenses. "Pardon?"

"A curator. A neutral party to oversee the property of this estate until the court makes a judgment as to its disposition. Discuss it with Alan Weissman, why don't you?"

"Is it because we hired an appraiser? Is that what's making you so antsy? We have to appraise it, don't we?"

Patrick stepped around Gail. "Say, Rudy, where's that fake Gauguin that used to hang over the sofa? Did you sell it to some unsuspecting tourist from Iowa?"

Rudy turned his head toward the house, the tendons in his neck a graceful line to broad shoulders. His profile could have advertised cologne in a men's magazine. "Susan? Have the police arrived yet?"

"He didn't tell her to call," Patrick told Gail. "Rudy lies."

Gail took his arm. "Let's *go.*"

Monica stabbed a finger toward the flower-trimmed walkway leading around the house. She screamed, "Get out of here, Patrick!"

"What's in the boxes in the living room, Monica?"

"Our mother's things from the attic, not that it's any of your damn business."

Patrick strode across the terrace, but Monica ran to position herself directly in front of the glass door. She was a foot shorter than Patrick, but orange sparks seemed to fizz and pop around her. "Stay out of our house, goddammit!"

Patrick pushed her aside and flung the sliding

door so hard that the frame bounced out of the track and the glass exploded into a million crystal bits that showered like hail onto the terrace.

Gail sped through the empty frame, her shoes crunching on glass. "Patrick!"

Rudy got to him first. "You're going to pay for that door, shithead."

Patrick slammed his fist into Rudy's stomach. Rudy doubled over, gagging. His little blue sunglasses hung from one ear. Monica screamed. Patrick hit him twice in the face, then the two of them rolled across the carpet.

The replica of *Winged Victory* tipped on its pedestal, hovered, and swooped downward. Shrieking, Susan Stone leaped out of the way as it smashed through a glass table.

Springing up, Rudy sent his army boot at Patrick's head. Patrick grabbed his foot, and Rudy staggered into the Steinway, sheet music fluttering to the floor. The lid slammed shut and the strings thrummed and sang. Patrick pinned him in the curve of the piano, fingers locked around his neck. Blood covered Rudy's nose and mouth. Monica was hanging off Patrick's waist, and her screams rattled the air.

Throwing her purse aside, Gail went for Patrick's arm. "What are you doing? Stop it!"

She dimly heard a hollow banging noise, then shouts. Susan Stone sprinted for the front door. Patrick and Rudy toppled onto the coffee table, which groaned, then snapped under their weight. Patrick was on top, slamming Rudy's head against a skewed stack of *Architectural Digest*s. His black hair bounced to the rhythm of Patrick's curses.

"Fucking queer faggot son of a bitch! I'm going to kill you, shit-eating bastard! I'm going to fucking kill you!"

Rudy's eyes rolled back.

"Stop it! Patrick, stop!"

Gail felt herself being pushed roughly away, felt her backside hit the overturned piano bench, saw a blur of dark blue. A male voice yelled, "Hey! Break it up!"

Police. Two of them, one black, one white. The black cop put a baton across Patrick's throat and pulled back with both hands, biceps straining his sleeve. Patrick wheezed, legs flailing the air. Gail locked onto the officer's arm and screamed for him to stop.

Rudy came after Patrick. The officer grabbed his elbow. Rudy turned and drove a fist into the cop's ribs.

"Son of a—" He swung his baton and Rudy screamed in pain. Monica flung herself onto the officer's back and drove her fingernails into his neck like talons. "Get offa me, bitch!"

Then two more of them came through the door.

chapter twenty

The police hauled everyone outside. Curious neighbors clustered around the end of the long driveway. Emilio was watching from under a tree, turning his straw hat around and around. Susan Stone sat on the porch with her head in her hands.

They had grudgingly cut off Gail's plastic handcuffs after Susan explained that Gail had only tried to stop the fighting. Favoring her left hip, Gail walked to where Patrick was lined up by the fountain with Rudy and Monica. The officers had read everyone their rights. Now they were going through pockets, Patrick's first.

She came around him. His new glasses were gone, one eye was shut, and his jaw was swelling under his beard. "Patrick, are you okay?"

He nodded, grimacing when one of the officers moved his arms out of the way to reach into his back pocket. "I've been beaten up by the police before." The front of his shirt was streaked with blood.

"I'll follow you to the station," she said, not knowing what else to do. Perhaps call Anthony, she added to herself, but quickly dismissed that idea. "Should I call a bail bondsman?"

The cop searching Patrick said, "Back on the porch, lady."

"This is my attorney," Patrick said quietly.

"Good for you. Now shut up." He put an Ace comb, Visine, and a wallet back into Patrick's pockets, but dropped a key chain with a Swiss Army knife on it into a plastic bag the black cop was holding. Both of them wore latex gloves. The other two cops, one male, one female, stood to one side, enjoying this. The woman was resting her hand on the butt of her gun.

Gail said, "He has the right to talk to an attorney." What she knew about criminal law and procedure came more from television than from real life; her civil practice was of no help.

The officer jerked his thumb toward the porch. "I said over there. You're in the way." He looked around when Rudy moaned.

"Somebody call Fire-Rescue. Now." Rudy sounded as if he had a bad cold. Drying streaks of red ran from his nose down his chin and neck and into his chest hair. His black T-shirt was ripped open, and his lips were swollen. "I need medical attention immediately."

The cop patted Rudy's pockets, ran his hands quickly down his legs. "Shut up, asshole."

Rudy stiffened. "You can't talk to me like that. Who do you think I am? Not one of your common criminals, you can be sure. I'm injured."

"All I know is—asshole—we're takin' you in." He put an ostrich-skin wallet back into Rudy's hip pocket.

"I didn't start this, Officer. Patrick Norris attacked me."

The cop got into his face. "Shut the fuck up!"

Monica leaned over to scream at the cop. "You shut up! We're making a complaint! We know

324

the mayor, and you are in big, big trouble! What's your name?"

The cop pointed to his name tag. "Liebowitz. Be sure to spell it right." The black cop laughed.

Then Liebowitz said, "Whoo-ee, fellas." He popped open a tiny cloisonné box. "We got a little pharmaceutical store here, Mr. Tillet. What's this white powder, my man?"

Rudy glared at him. Liebowitz dropped the box into a plastic bag, then returned a tube of Chapstick to Rudy's front pocket.

Her hands cuffed behind her, Monica broke into heavy sobs. "How could you *do* this? Look at him! My brother is hurt!" Her nose was running and she wiped it on the shoulder of her zebra-print jumpsuit, which was smeared with either Rudy's or Patrick's blood— probably both. She screamed, "I'm going to have your job!"

"Hope you like it. The pay ain't that great."

The other three cops whooped with laughter, and the female officer began to search Monica's pockets.

Furious, Gail limped over to where the sergeant was doing some paperwork in the front seat of his patrol car. He had just arrived, and the blue lights were still flashing. She looked at his name tag.

"Sergeant Taylor. This is ridiculous. None of your officers was injured. This was a private matter between—"

"Ma'am? Back off." He didn't look up from his report.

"You don't have to use that tone with me, Sergeant."

He pointed his pen at her. "You got two choices. Shut up or go with them. What's it going to be?"

Gail reached into her purse and pulled out her business card, holding it in front of his face like a shield. "I'm Mr. Norris's attorney. I have a right to discuss the charges against my client, and no, I'm not going to back off."

Taylor stood up and whistled through his teeth. "Liebowitz! Put the cuffs back on this broad. Obstructing justice."

"You can't do that! I'm this man's attorney!"

The cops started laughing again. Liebowitz handed her purse to the sergeant, then jerked Gail's hands around behind her and slid another plastic handcuff around her wrists, pulling it tight. Gail winced. He pushed her toward where Patrick and the others stood by the fountain.

Patrick turned his head to look at her with his uninjured eye. "Even the privileges of class and education can't protect you now."

Gail exhaled. "Patrick. Just be quiet."

The sergeant finished what he was doing, then slid his pen back into his uniform pocket. "Okay, load 'em up." He smiled at Rudy and Patrick. "Put these two in the same car. Ought to be fun."

Last week, talking to Detective Gary Davis, Gail had seen the holding cells on the third floor of the Miami Beach Police headquarters but had paid them no attention. This time, while more paperwork was filled out, she and Monica occupied one of the cells, Rudy and Patrick the other. The gray paint was flaking off the metal door, but the cells were reasonably clean. There was a bench along one wall and a stainless steel toilet and sink in the far corner behind a chest-high screen.

The detective, whose name tag said Hanlon, let Gail out fifteen minutes later and made her sign a promise-to-appear. She was free to go.

"What about Patrick Norris?"

Hanlon looked up at her from his desk. "He's goin' downtown."

"Why? Let me call a bail bondsman."

"Not here. Nobody's bonding out on these charges. They're all goin' downtown." Hanlon was a skinny redhead with a 9-millimeter semiautomatic in his holster. "You can use the phone if you want. Here or in the lobby downstairs."

"What is my client charged with?"

"Your *client?*"

"Patrick Norris. I'm his lawyer."

Hanlon leaned back in his chair, smiling slightly. "Rudy Tillet and his sister—battery on a police officer and resisting arrest with violence. Plus Rudy's charged with possession of cocaine. Patrick Norris—criminal trespass, burglary, battery, and resisting with violence." He added, "Those are felonies, ma'am."

"*Burglary?* He didn't break in. He used a key!"

"Can we call you as a witness?" Hanlon asked. She shut up.

"Like I said, you can go."

"Not while my client is here. I'd like to use your telephone."

"Over there." He gestured toward an empty desk across the room.

As she picked up the receiver, Gail saw two uniformed officers bringing Rudy and Monica past the row of black filing cabinets that blocked her view of the holding cells. She quickly hung up, expecting Patrick to be next.

When he didn't appear, Gail picked up the phone again and dialed Anthony Quintana's office. Mirta, his secretary, said he wasn't there. Gail said never mind, then told Mirta where she was, that she had been arrested after a fight at the Tillett mansion, what should she do? *Arrested? Ay, Diós. Wait there, I'll beep him.*

Not wanting to speculate about Anthony's reaction this time, assuming he would even show up, Gail called her own office and spoke to Miriam, who was just leaving. *Where are you? I was so worried!* Gail told her quickly, then said to keep it to herself. Gail hadn't yet decided how to explain this to Larry Black.

She hung up, then pulled a dangling gold button from the front of her dress. The dress was ripped at the underarm and speckled with blood on the skirt. There were runs in both legs of her panty hose. She called her mother and asked her to pick up Karen. *Just say I'm with a client.*

In the ladies' room she cleaned up as best she could and brushed her hair. Coming out, she went around the row of filing cabinets to check on Patrick. He was on the bench of the holding cell, leaning against the wall with his eyes closed. Wet paper towels lay at his feet in soggy, rust-colored wads. He had used them to wipe the blood off his hands and face.

Gail crouched down and spoke to him through

328

the woven metal grid. "Patrick." His eyes came open. One was still puffy and red. She said softly, "I called Anthony's office. His secretary's going to try to reach him. Okay?"

"Okay."

"They're going to transport you downtown—to the county jail, I assume. I don't want you to worry. We'll get you out on bond."

"Sure." He closed his eyes.

"Patrick? Are you feeling sick?"

He shook his head.

"As soon as you're out, I'm taking you to a doctor."

"Oh, Gail." His voice was a whisper. "What I did—"

"It's going to be all right. They're charging you with a felony, but it won't stick. Once the State Attorney's Office knows what happened—"

Patrick rolled his head back and forth. "No, that isn't it. What I did to Rudy."

"If he sues you, we've got someone in our office—"

"No!" Patrick curled his fingers through the metal grid. "No. I beat him up, Gail. I called him things that I swear to you I have never called anyone. Never. I don't do that. I don't . . . *hate* like that." Patrick gulped in a breath. "But I did hate him. I wanted to kill him. If the cops hadn't pulled me off—Gail, I'd have done it. With my bare hands, I would have murdered him! I would have—"

"Shhh. Patrick, don't." He was holding the grid so tightly his fingernails were white. Gail put her hands up to his, not knowing what to say to him. "People lose their temper."

"Not like that! Oh, Christ."

Patrick broke off, looking upward. Gail turned. It was Gary Davis, whom she had last seen under better circumstances. She stood up, sucking in her breath from the pain in her hip.

"Don't let me stop you. You would have . . . say *what?*" Davis wore a crisp green shirt, and the gray in his hair glittered like metal turnings off a steel rod. He smiled down at Patrick. "I think we're gonna want to have a chat, Mr. Norris."

"He's being transported," said Gail.

"Naah, he's gonna be here with us awhile," Davis said.

Patrick staggered to the far corner of the cell, his back to them. His angular shoulders hunched up inside his loose white shirt.

Davis said, "That woman working at your aunt's house—Susan Stone?—she said you got in there with a key. Is that right?"

Gail said, "I'd prefer that you not talk to my client."

"You doing criminal law now, Ms. Connor?"

"Yes."

"Uh-huh." Davis tapped on the cell. "Mr. Norris? I had one of my officers go back over and try your keys in Mrs. Tillett's door. And you know what? One of them fit. It sure did."

"Don't say anything, Patrick." Gail's hands were shaking. She looked angrily at Davis. "He has a right not to answer any of your questions."

"Yes, ma'am." Davis's attention was still on

Patrick. "Remember a couple of weeks ago I asked you about a key? I asked if you had one. What did you tell me? You said, 'Why, no, Officer, I don't have a key.'"

Patrick turned around far enough to mutter "Fuck you."

"Skinny as you are, you don't look like you could have broke Althea Tillett's neck. But you're *strong*. You took care of Rudy Tillett. My, my."

Gail stepped closer. "Detective Davis, leave my client alone."

"Mr. Norris is gonna visit with me in the interview room. You want to stick around?" He looked at her torn, smudged, rumpled dress. "We gonna talk about Althea Tillett some more. A looo-o-ong talk."

Detective Hanlon stepped around the row of cabinets. "Gary?" He jerked his head toward the main area.

Davis smiled at Gail. "I'll be right back. Y'all don't go away."

When he was gone, Gail clutched the metal grid of the cell. "Patrick! You mustn't talk to him!"

"I know that, Gail." His voice was hollow. "I've had some experience with the police."

She dropped her head. "I'm not doing you much good, am I?"

He came back to where she stood and poked a finger through to touch her cheek. "Sure you are."

"I won't let them push you around, Patrick. I won't."

"You're my buddy."

331

She smiled, and his face grew blurry. "You bet."

Davis reappeared but stayed at the end of the cabinets. "Ms. Connor? Come out here, please."

She wiped under her eyes. "Why?"

"You've got company."

Gail followed him past two desks, then saw Anthony Quintana standing by Davis's office. His hands were in the trouser pockets of his suit—deep blue with micro-thin red lines that formed a subtle plaid. His hair was precisely combed. There was a VISITOR tag clipped to his lapel. His dark eyes took a quick inventory, but he made no move to touch her.

"Why are you limping?" he asked.

"I fell. During the fight, I tripped over the piano bench."

"Ah. What is this blood? Yours?"

"No."

"Are you all right?"

"I'll live."

"I made some phone calls from my car," he said. "They say you can go. Where is your purse?"

Gail said, "But they want to keep Patrick here."

"For what?"

"More questions about Althea Tillett. He had a key to her house and they found it on him. They want to give him the third degree, I don't know. They're charging him with burglary! He needs an attorney."

"He can find one in the yellow pages."

"I won't leave him alone in this place," she said. "I can't."

Anthony let out some air between his teeth. "Wait here."

"Where are you going?"

"To speak to the detective. Stay here." He walked to where Hanlon sat. Davis came over, and the three of them talked. Then Davis and Anthony went into Davis's glass-walled office and closed the door. She could barely hear their voices over the top of the partition, with the other conversations in the room, phones ringing, somebody telling a joke.

She detested Anthony Quintana at this moment with a force that made her want to weep with rage. She glanced toward the holding cells, which she could see from this angle. Patrick was sprawled on the metal bench again. In Davis's office, Anthony sat casually in one of the chairs, his legs crossed, not a bit of calf showing under the neatly pressed hem of his trousers.

She wondered if she ought to go in there. Then she realized who she was—the client. She had often told her own clients to stay where they were while she went down the hall to speak to the opposition. They always stayed without a murmur of protest because they knew it was her show. She knew what she was doing.

Here Anthony knew what he was doing. And like it or not, she needed him.

Awhile later the door opened and Anthony motioned for her to come in. She sat down gingerly in one of the chairs at Davis's desk.

Through his windows she could see that the sun had set.

Anthony said, "I've told Detective Davis about your case with Patrick Norris. The forgery and who you suspect did it. They'll send the paperwork through because they have to, but with a recommendation that the case not be filed. You are very fortunate."

Her hands were shaking, and she twisted them together in her lap. "Thank you."

"As for Patrick, he'll be transported immediately. I'll send a bondsman to meet him at the jail." Anthony added, "I'm representing him. For now."

She looked at him, surprised, then nodded.

"The detective would like to know what you and Patrick were doing at Althea Tillett's house. Do not discuss how you got in."

"Should I talk to him?"

"Yes. But stop immediately if I tell you to."

"We were looking for Rosa Portales." She explained that Rosa might know what Althea Tillett had done with her prior will.

Anthony said, "Gary, could we get that address from you?"

Gail wondered how he could possibly have worked into a first-name relationship with a homicide cop in ten minutes.

Davis nodded. "Don't see why not. Rosa didn't have nothing to say to me about any will, you understand. She found Mrs. Tillett's body, that's about it."

"You know where she is?" Gail asked.

"Hialeah. She's living with her sister."

Gail shifted in the chair. Her hip hurt. "Detective, have you ever heard of a man named Frankie Delgado? He has an office on Drexel Avenue. A company named Seagate. They supposedly sell promotional items, but I think he's a pimp or something."

Anthony raised a hand to cut her off, then changed his mind and dropped it to his lap. "Go on. Tell him what you did. Maybe he knows about this man."

She gave Anthony a hard look, then started her story at the door of the rundown office building on Drexel and took it upstairs. A minute later, Davis was grinning. "This Frankie Delgado sounds like one sleazy little punk. I don't have anything on him, though. There's a lot going on we don't know about. And you went in there playing like a hooker? Mmm-*mmm.*" He laughed and glanced at Anthony, who wasn't smiling.

Gail said, "It may have nothing to do with the forgery, you see, but—well, Seagate owns another company— Gateway Travel Agency. Do you know it?"

"Sure. Up Alton Road a few blocks."

"The woman who notarized the will works for Gateway. Carla Napolitano. She wasn't even in Florida on the date the will was supposedly signed. Anthony, did you tell him about Carla?"

"We didn't get to that," he said.

She asked stonily, "Well? May I?"

"Go ahead."

Gail spent a minute or two telling Gary Davis why she had gone to Gateway Travel—including the part about pretending to want an exotic

335

weekend for herself and her married cardiologist lover. Anthony's face was expressionless, but his fingers tapped a slow rhythm on his thigh.

"Hang on a second." Davis lifted his phone, punched a number. He said, "Donna? You know that case last night up on Collins and Fiftieth? Yeah. What was the lady's name? . . . Uh-huh. Thanks." He hung up and turned his brown eyes toward Gail.

"What?" Gail asked, knowing something was wrong. "What is it?"

"Carla Napolitano died last night. Fell off her balcony. Or jumped. We don't know yet. Front door was locked. Tenth floor, right onto the parking lot. Not pretty."

"Ohhh."

Anthony bent to look at her, then gently took her hands away from her face. He reached into his pocket for his handkerchief. "Gail. Take this."

Finally the shock of the fight, the humiliating arrest, and her own inability to help Patrick or herself crashed over her, sweeping her momentarily into a whirl of grief and confusion. She wanted to fall into Anthony's arms, but he remained in his chair, only his hand on the back of hers.

Davis asked, "Ms. Connor? How well did you know the woman?"

"We only met that one time. She didn't even know who I was." Gail wiped her nose. "It must have been an accident. She wouldn't have killed herself. Her daughter just had a new baby. She was going to move to New Jersey."

Davis clasped his hands on his desk. "I'd like to hear some more about this."

Anthony said, "Let me take her home, Gary. I'll talk to her first."

Gail watched them bring Patrick out of the cell. He was still depressed, but she didn't think he would hang himself. Anthony told him the bondsman would send a bill, which Gail could pay out of Patrick's cost account at Hartwell Black. Patrick thanked them both and kissed Gail's cheek before he was taken away in handcuffs.

"Will he be all right in jail, do you think?"

"For two hours? He'll be fine," Anthony said. He spoke as if he were watching something far in the distance.

"I do hate to bother you, but my car is in the parking garage at my office," Gail said sweetly. "Would you drive me there?"

"Of course."

They rode the elevator to the lobby in silence. Anthony stared at the doors. They walked outside. Gail was limping slightly. It was dark now, and men with filthy clothes and matted hair were staking out their places on the curving white concrete benches between the police station and city hall.

Just beyond the front terrace of the building, Gail whirled on him. "I suppose I should thank you for helping Patrick. All right. Thank you. Now you can go to hell!"

To her surprise, Anthony sank down on the low wall that bordered the long ramp to the street.

Light came dimly from underneath. He put his elbows on his knees and clenched his fingers in his hair.

"Ah, Gail. Why? *¿Porque me haces así?* Why do I *let* you do this to me?" He groaned. *"Estoy perdiendo mi mente."*

Losing his mind. As if she weren't. Arms crossed, she glared at him. "You were awful up there. You treated me like *shit!"*

"I know. I'm sorry."

A dozen yards away, a gray-bearded man in plaid pants and a striped pullover was watching them. He pushed the top of a paper bag down past the neck of a bottle.

She looked back at Anthony. "You wouldn't even touch me. As if I were . . . tainted. Or . . . *violated."* Her voice shook. "Which is exactly what I feel like."

He finally raised his head, then without speaking stood up and pulled her to him, locking one arm around her neck, the other around her waist. He kissed her mouth, her cheeks.

"Anthony!" She got her hands on his chest and pushed. "Let go!"

"I couldn't have touched you in Davis's office." He held her tighter. "I would have wanted to hold you like this. With them, I had to be your lawyer, nothing else. If you knew what I thought on the way here! *¡Me asustas!* Mirta told me you were in a fight, in jail, injured. I was so afraid."

"You?"

"Yes. Loving you is like watching a blind person cross a highway."

338

"Oh, thank you very much."

"My heart is going to stop." He laughed, one hand on his chest.

Wincing, Gail picked up her purse, which had fallen off her shoulder. "Are you going to drive me to my office, or not?"

A thin voice came from the plaza. "Kiss her some more!" Then a cackle. It was the old man with the paper bag. He raised it in a toast, then took a deep swallow of whatever was inside.

Anthony grabbed her hand. "Let's get out of here."

"Slow down! My hip hurts."

The sun was gone, and lights poured from the windows along Washington Avenue. His convertible waited at the next corner. He took his car keys out of his pocket. "Where is Karen?"

"With my mother. Why?"

He found the right key and unlocked the passenger side. "Let's go to a hotel." He took her purse and tossed it into the car. "We have time. Don't worry about your clothes. I'll give you my jacket. On South Beach who would notice?"

Gail stared at him.

Anthony shrugged. "Here we are. What are you going to do at home?"

"You didn't want to see me for a while, remember?"

"I was angry."

"Well, I happen to be a little pissed off myself."

"Gail—" He raised his palms to her face, but she pulled away. "I am sorry. Let me show you how sorry I am." He came closer, and this time she didn't move. "You scared me, that's all." He

339

kissed the bruise on her jaw. She felt his breath on her cheek. He laughed softly. "I think it does something to me. Gail, please. Let's find a hotel."

"You *are* out of your mind."

"Then say we're on Mykonos, in the Aegean, and it's summer." He kissed both corners of her mouth. His lips were warm and soft. "Or tell me you've been there, and I'll take you back to your office. You can get in your car and go home."

He looked straight into her eyes, and his were bottomless and the ground under her feet was giving way, and he knew it, damn him. She could already feel the white-hot sun and the surge of the sea.

chapter twenty-one

Gail sat at her desk reading the article in the local section of the *Miami Herald* for the third time. There was a short piece on Patrick Norris's case: "CHARITIES COULD LOSE IN FIGHT OVER ESTATE."

Between the lines she could see the real story: Estranged nephew hires slick downtown lawyers to contest the will. But not only is the nephew greedy, he's a nut case. He wants to buy up property in the inner city and turn it into communal farms. And a dangerous nut case: He broke into the decedent's house and beat up her stepson, Rudolph W. Tillett, Jr. and then at the end of the article came a nasty postscript: "Miami Beach

Police confirm that Althea Tillett's death has been ruled a homicide. Detective Gary Davis stated that her neck was broken by an intruder, but would not speculate as to suspects or motive."

Somebody with a sense of humor had pinned the article to the bulletin board in the coffee room with a caption: "Are you homicidal? Psychotic? Call Hartwell Black & Robineau today for free consultation!" Gail had tossed it into the garbage.

The firm got another kick in the ribs from the "Legal Notes" column in the business section: "'Unfortunately, the management committee saw an easy win and high fees with this case,' stated one source. Associate Gail A. Connor, who brought the case into the firm, refused comment."

Gail didn't know if G. Howard Odell was behind this, but he had to love it. He had arranged a meeting for two o'clock today, Monday. He would arrive in the company of Sanford Ehringer's personal attorney from Palm Beach, along with local counsel from a scorched-earth litigation firm taking over the probate from Alan Weissman. Gail could only assume that Alan Weissman was busy getting drunk.

The meeting would be held in Paul Robinea' office, with Jack Warner and Larry Black in at dance. It would be worth it, Gail thought to see the bared teeth, if she herself were danger of being set upon like a cat in a wild dogs.

At noon Gail would meet with Paul Larry. Three pairs of eyes fixed on for her to explain what she had been doing and why. She could already hear their questions: Can we force the beneficiaries to settle or not? If not, will we get our asses whipped in court?

Gail glumly dropped the newspaper into the trash can under her desk. She had not been able to recognize Patrick in the article she had read. Odd how the truth could get skewed like that. She had to keep reminding herself what it was.

Patrick had been released from jail on $2,500 bond. Anthony Quintana would appear at the arraignment in three weeks. Meanwhile, he would try to plea-bargain the charges down to misdemeanors. He would send Hartwell Black and Robineau his bill—$300 per hour.

Anthony's phone call on Saturday morning, conveying all this, had been in lieu of seeing her over the weekend. He apologized, but had a trial in federal court to prepare for. Gail said she certainly understood; she was busy too. And then there came a silence, and it continued one beat too long. They rushed to fill it with banalities, but neither of them mentioned Friday night on South Beach.

He hadn't called since, nor did Gail want to speak to him until she had decided what to say. The right words had to be sent out like strands of a spider's web. Connections between men and women were that fragile sometimes.

The hotel had been on Ocean Drive, four stories high, painted like a birthday cake, with pink neon around its name. Now Gail couldn't remember the name. She had gone inside with her head down and Anthony's jacket hiding the rip in her dress. The lobby was Art Deco, but the room was Motel 6: cheap, framed prints of palm trees over the double bed, tourist brochures on the dresser, a refrigerator that charged ten bucks for a split of domestic champagne. She found plastic glasses on a tray in the bathroom and unwrapped them while Anthony unlaced his shoes and set them beside a Danish modern chair with a cigarette burn in the cushion.

People came and went in the halls, talking in foreign languages. Mariachi music from the restaurant next door was occasionally drowned out by the bass throb of a car stereo, somebody cruising with the windows down. The champagne, too sharp to drink, went flat in the plastic glasses. Was it the place that was so off? Or their mood? By nine o'clock they were heading back across the causeway toward Miami. At one point she took Anthony's hand, but couldn't think of a damn thing to say that wouldn't ring with falsity.

She didn't want to be so ungrateful as to tell a man who had just whisked her to a hotel room, bought champagne, and kissed the bruises on her backside that she didn't have a perfectly delightful time. It would have been rude. And the truth was, she didn't know how she felt until later, when she was at home staring at the ceiling. She finally slept, but her dreams were fitful, and she awoke crying out, her nightgown twisted and soaked with sweat.

Saturday afternoon, Patrick came over to thank her and stayed to fix her roof. It cost four hundred dollars for lumber and roofing paper and white concrete tiles. He let Karen help, and they had a good time getting filthy. Gail cooked hamburgers on the grill. Patrick came back early Sunday, and Gail went up there with them, sawing and hammering and setting in the new tiles. She broke a fingernail and worked the pain out of her derriere, and wondered if it would be better to jump off the roof headfirst then, or wait till after the meeting with Paul Robineau on Monday.

Gail looked up when she heard a salsa rhythm tapped on the door. It opened and Miriam Ruiz came in, raising one shoulder, then the other. Her hair was in a ponytail, and it bounced and swung. She bumped her little fanny against the door to close it, then cha-cha'ed across the room. She carried a stack of pages from a yellow legal pad.

"You're cheerful," Gail said.

Miriam stopped, looked down at her. "Gail, are you okay?"

"I have a headache, that's all. What did you bring me?"

Smiling, she dropped the papers on Gail's desk. They were notes handwritten in four shades of ink, with doodles, cross-outs, and arrows pointing this way and that. Gail turned a few pages. Lists of property, legal descriptions, dates, addresses—

"It's my research on Easton," Miriam announced.

Gail remembered that she had wanted to know what real estate the Easton Trust owned, although now she couldn't recall why. She rubbed her forehead. "You want to just cut to the end? I'm getting ready for that meeting at noon."

Miriam plopped into a chair, her ponytail bouncing. "Okay. Here it is. I found out who owns the company Carla Napolitano worked for. And also the company that owns the nightclub. It's another company, called Biscayne Corporation. Biscayne owns both of them. And guess who's an officer in Biscayne Corporation?"

Gail shook her head.

"Take a wild guess."

"Miriam, please."

She grinned, a wide red smile. "Howard Odell."

"No."

"Yes."

"How in the world—"

"Mira." Miriam stood up and spread her notes over the desk, then ran around to see them better, standing beside Gail's chair. "Okay. I was checking the property records for the Easton Trust, like you said. I went back to the Sixties, which is as far as you can go on computers. There were fifty-six transactions. Easton acquired most of it from estates, people leaving it in their wills. Easton sold a bunch."

"Who signed the deeds, Sanford Ehringer?"

"Sure did. He was the only real person that I could find. Sanford V. Ehringer, as Trustee. And here's a list of property that they still own, for investment, I guess."

There were a shopping center, upscale apartment buildings, vacant land. All of it prime, worth

345

millions. Gail tapped one of the entries with her pen.

"Lincoln Road, numbers 801 to 839. The Tillett Gallery is in that block. The night I went to the gallery, Howard Odell was there. He said he knew Rudy from the Art Deco League, but this could be the real connection. I'll bet the Tilletts pay rent to the Easton Trust."

Miriam shuffled through her notes. "One of the properties Easton sold—here it is—1470 Drexel, Miami Beach. It's where you met Frankie Delgado."

"Easton used to own that dump?"

"Somebody died and left it to them, and the Trust sold it in 1982 to the Biscayne Corporation. So I was wondering who owns that building now, so I ran the legal description and came up with— voila!—Atlantic Enterprises."

"Which also owns Wild Cherry."

"And then I go, well, as long as I'm on the computer—" Miriam took two sheets from near the bottom"—let's see what else Atlantic owns. So I find five pieces of property, and Atlantic bought every one of them from Biscayne Corporation in 1982 and 1983. So then I start wondering about Biscayne. I found twelve more properties. Biscayne still has eight of them, but it sold four to Seagate, also in the early Eighties." On a blank sheet of paper she drew a circle, two lines coming off it, and a box at the end of each line. She labeled the circle *Biscayne* and the boxes *Atlantic* and *Seagate*. "Seventeen pieces of real estate. Biscayne sold five to Atlantic, four to Seagate, kept eight for itself."

"When were Atlantic and Seagate incorporated? Do you remember?"

"1979 and 1981."

"And Biscayne?"

"I don't know, but look what else I found. You'll like this." Miriam produced a computer printout. Between the scrawls and the phone numbers and scratch-outs, was a list of names. Two of them Gail didn't recognize. The treasurer, she did. G. Howard Odell.

Gail sat up straight in her chair. "Howard!" She read the address. 19 West Flagler Street, with a telephone number. "Did you call this?"

"It's an answering machine," Miriam said. "A woman's voice. 'You have reached the offices of the Biscayne Corporation, please leave a message, blah blah.' I called four different times and always got a recording. I could go over there and knock on the door if you want."

But her voice was trailing off. She snatched a sheet out of the stack and held it with both hands against her chest. "Ready for the juicy part? I said to myself, wow, Biscayne sold that office building on Drexel to a company that owns a nude nightclub. I wonder what the other properties are?"

She gave the page to Gail. Her rounded handwriting covered the yellow sheet and ran to the other side. "You can't tell what's on a property from the legal description, so I got the street addresses and checked with Dade County Building and Zoning."

Gail drew her finger down the page. Seagate had purchased from Biscayne three properties on Miami Beach, on which were placed three businesses: Sun Goddess Escorts, Magic City Liquors, and Gateway Travel.

"Well, well. The travel agency."

In North Miami Beach, Seagate owned a clothing store, of sorts: Naughty 'n' Nice Apparel Shoppe. Biscayne had sold five properties to Atlantic Enterprises, businesses scattered around Dade County—in Hialeah, the Aphrodite Motel. Next door to that, Carlito's Cleaners. Gail turned the page over and saw the Sans Souci Health Spa and Wild Cherry in North Miami. Then she laughed at the next one on the list. "The Reel Stuff? I don't believe it."

"What's that?"

"It's an X-rated movie theater on Biscayne Boulevard, a few blocks from where Patrick lives."

"The only thing that doesn't fit," Miriam said, pointing, "is that cleaner's. See? It's a dry cleaner's on Okeechobee Road, next door to the Aphrodite Motel."

Possibly it did fit. Anthony Quintana had once represented an acquaintance of Howard Odell's, a dry cleaner charged with selling pornography out the back of his shop. This could be the same dry cleaner.

Miriam broke into giggles. "Aphrodite Motel? Maybe they have vibrating waterbeds."

"Oh, Howard," Gail murmured. "Are these *yours?* Dare I hope?" Her heart leaping in her chest, she got up and paced across the room, back and forth, thinking of how to play this.

Miriam turned a few pages. "Speaking of

Howard Odell—In 1988 he and his wife bought a house on Star Island from Easton."

"Nice neighborhood." Then Gail remembered something and picked up her phone, dialing Eric Ramsay's extension. No answer. Another ring and his secretary answered. Gail asked her where he was.

He'd left a message; he had to deliver some papers to the federal courthouse in Fort Lauderdale.

Gail said to have him call as soon as he came in.

She hung up and looked back at Miriam. "Howard Odell sold a house last year. It was part of a divorce settlement. It could be the same house on your list. Eric might know, because Odell asked him for some legal advice concerning the sale of some real estate. If I'm upstairs with Paul Robineau when Eric comes back, tell him to call me. Interrupt if he has to. First, is it the same house, and second, how much did Odell make on the deal?"

"Why do we want to know that?"

"Because G. Howard Odell might be ripping Easton off. Sanford Ehringer may be chairman of the board, but Odell runs it. What if he bought this house for nothing, then turned around and sold it? If so, did he tell Ehringer? Odell could have a lot to hide, Miriam. And the more a man has to hide, the easier he is to maneuver."

"Into a settlement of Patrick Norris's claim."

"Precisely."

Miriam glowed. "You see? This is why I want to be a lawyer someday. Isn't this exciting?"

"Oh, Miriam." Gail sat on the arm of a chair and exhaled a long, weary breath. "Don't you know what's really going on here? We're running scared. We're afraid we can't prove forgery in court, so we're taking the easy way out. A settlement. Except it isn't that easy or that nice. We're finding dirt on someone, and we're going to threaten him with it if he doesn't go along with us. Call it exciting if you want to, or glamorous, but see it for what it is."

Miriam nodded.

Gail smiled. "You did a tremendous job, you know. I do appreciate it." She reached out to squeeze Miriam's hand, then stood up. "All right. Go find out as much as you can about the Biscayne Corporation. Who are these people listed as president and secretary? Who founded it? Cross-check the names with Seagate and Atlantic, and look up the addresses and phone numbers. Do a summary and make me a copy."

"You want this now?" Miriam asked.

"I want it before my meeting with Robineau, if possible. When Eric gets back, make him help you. And something else—" Miriam, who was just closing the door, came back in. "Did you find anything on Easton? Who the current members are?"

"Nothing. The county has no records, and I didn't see anything in the library, either." In her tight skirt, Miriam rotated one leg back and forth on the high heel of her pump. "It makes sense there's no record. I mean, Sanford Ehringer said Easton doesn't exist. Like they made him up."

"Maybe." Gail nodded slowly. "Maybe they

did. What if he wasn't a man at all. Easton. Back in '37, was there a town named Easton? East Town, East—"

"East of Nowhere," Miriam added. "Easy Town—"

"Did you see anything like that? East Something?"

"'It could be initials, like when you make a word up?'"

"An acronym. Why not? Sanford Ehringer's little puzzle. The way he said it . . . such a smug old fart. 'Easton is no one. So now you won't have to go looking for him.'"

Miriam said, "E is for Ehringer?"

"Very good. His father started Easton. Samuel Ehringer."

"So what does this do for Patrick's case?"

"Probably nothing. But it bothers me," Gail said. "Nobody will tell me who's in the Easton Trust. I don't like that."

After Miriam went out, Gail sat down with her microcassette recorder to dictate some notes. There were three other files on her desk she had to finish today.

She started on one, but couldn't concentrate. Her mind was racing over lists of real estate and corporations. The connection between Howard Odell and the Aphrodite Motel, or Sun Goddess Escorts, or even Wild Cherry, was tenuous, but Gail could see a shadow beneath the surface, moving silently as a shark.

She pushed the files aside and dialed Anthony Quintana's office number. The thrill of the hunt had made her bold. She would say to him, *Listen,*

351

I'm sorry if I acted a little strange last Friday. What a day. I was totally stressed out.

No. That sounded phony. Try again: *Anthony, I need to see you.* God, how pathetic. Maybe just *Hi. I've been thinking about you.*

His secretary told her, "I'm sorry, Ms. Connor. He's in trial."

"So he is." Gail pushed her hair behind her ear. "He said he would be, but it slipped my mind."

"Is there a message?"

"Just say . . . I'll call tonight." She nearly hung up, then said, "Mirta, wait. Did he get Rosa Portales's address and phone number from the Miami Beach Police? She was Althea Tillett's housekeeper." There was no reply. Gail said, "It's a case we have together. Patrick Norris? Surely he mentioned it to you."

"Patrick Norris. Right."

"Well? Do you have the phone number?"

"I don't think so."

"Could you check his file while I hold on?"

"I never go into his files, Ms. Connor."

"You're his secretary."

"I mean, Mr. Quintana told me not to give out that information to anybody."

"I'm not just anybody. It's my case."

"Uhhh . . ."

Gail willed herself not to scream into the phone. She smiled instead. "Mirta. Did Mr. Quintana instruct you not to give me Rosa Portales' address and phone number?"

"Of course not."

"I'll bet. Just tell him to call me, would you?"

Gail hung up, fuming. Anthony Quintana was pulling back on the reins. Why? Most likely an attempt to keep her out of trouble. *Bastard.*

She picked the phone up again, intending to ask Miriam to get Detective Davis of the Beach Police. But Davis wouldn't give out Rosa's address for free. He would want her to come in and talk to him about Carla Napolitano. About her suicide. Or accident. Or . . . murder. Gail replaced the phone and rested her forehead on her arm.

The three other files were still waiting. What she didn't get done today, she would take home with her. Karen wouldn't like that. Gail had promised to take her shopping for new jeans.

Eric Ramsay knocked at the door just after eleven o'clock carrying a folder.

"Come on in." Gail finished a time slip and stuck it in the file.

He said, "These are the motions in the Norris case you asked me to do." Standing by her desk, he flipped his hair out of his eyes. "I would have done them last week, but I had to write a brief for a tax appeal. I decided they could wait, since we aren't going to file the case until we see what happens with Odell."

Some day, Gail thought, a junior associate would drop everything to get *her* work done first. She quickly read the motions. They were packed with Eric's usual bombardment of minutiae, and ended with the demand that Rudy and Monica stay out of the decedent's mansion and that a neutral party be appointed to oversee her property.

"All right. These will do. Where are the subpoenas?" she asked.

He hesitated. "They're up in word processing."

"I see. Eric, what if we have to file these today before the courthouse closes? Or early tomorrow? We can't get motions served without subpoenas. I wanted these on Friday. If you're going to save your job at Hartwell Black—and I assume you still want to—you can't make excuses. 'Oh, I was busy with some other assignment.' Uh-uh."

He shifted his weight to the other foot. "Okay. Sorry."

"And what were you doing in Fort Lauderdale?" She knew she was getting worked up, but couldn't stop. "We have couriers for deliveries. You have a secretary."

"Look, Gail—"

"I don't want you running around South Florida on some other matter when we've got Odell and his attorneys coming in, and Miriam is absolutely buried—"

"It was for a trial, for Chrissakes! Look, I'm sorry, Gail, but I had to do some exhibits in a tax fraud case and get them to Fort Lauderdale before the client testified. We had to show why he could deduct four-point-two million dollars in accelerated depreciation."

"Okay." Gail pressed her fingertips into her forehead.

"I'd have been here if I could. You know that."

She dropped her hand to the desk.

"Hey, Gail." He leaned over and gripped her wrist. "You're coming apart." His fingers were warm. "You need something? I've got something in my office I could give you. Very mild, I promise."

"I'm fine." She sat back in her chair. "Did you find anything on Howard Odell's house on Star Island?"

"Right. It's the same house he asked me about, but I didn't do the sale. I only reviewed the contract for him. He was getting a divorce, and he wanted to save as much on taxes as possible."

"How much did he make on it?"

"Oh, gee. That was last year."

"I need the numbers. Didn't you look at the file?"

"It's in storage." He held up a hand. "But I'll ask my secretary to find it."

"And have it down here before my meeting with Paul Robineau?"

"No problem."

"Sorry, Eric. I don't mean to be so crabby. You said you wanted to be a trial lawyer? Well, this is it. Massive anxiety before you even get inside the courtroom. Most of the time you never do. You sit at your desk and make threatening phone calls and throw paper bombs at the other side. And try not to lose your breakfast."

He looked at her, his brow furrowed. "What's going to happen in this meeting with Odell?"

"Give me a crystal ball and I'll tell you."

"Let me sit in. I want to see what they say, how you handle it. Hell, it might settle by this afternoon. All the action's going to be upstairs in Robineau's office."

The phone buzzed.

"Excuse me." Gail answered it.

Her mother came on the line. "Gail, dear. It's important. Are you busy?"

"Not at all. Hang on." She put her hand over the receiver and told Eric to go help Miriam with the research on Odell. "She'll explain what she's found. Whatever else you have scheduled for anyone, including God Almighty, dump it. I need you. And Eric?"

He turned around at the door.

"About that meeting . . . not this time. Okay?"

He shrugged. "Sure."

She said into the telephone, "Mother? I'm back."

"Gail, I've just had a call from Irving."

"Irving?" She began to write a time slip for her conference with Eric Ramsay. *Conf w/ assoc atty, .2.*

"Irving *Adler*. You remember, don't you? I went to see him last week about Althea. I should have done it before. Irving isn't feeling well."

"What did he say about the will?" Gail laid down her pen. "Did he say anything about that?"

"Not when I was there last week. We had a couple of drinks and gossiped for a while. I did mention the will once, obliquely, but Irving changed the subject. Anyway, five minutes ago he called me. He said yes, Althea's will was forged, and he helped to do it."

Gail stumbled out of her chair. "But what did he say? Who was he helping? Rudy Tillett?"

"I didn't ask. He wants me to bring you to talk to him."

"Me? Why?"

"He wants to talk to you about Althea. He said, 'I don't want to die with this on my conscience.'"

"With what on his conscience? The forgery?"

"No, my impression was, he wanted to talk about Althea."

"What about her? Her death? Was that it?"

"I don't know. Oh, Gail. He was crying. Poor man, it broke my heart. We have to go see him as soon as possible. Now. Or whenever you can get away."

Gail glanced at the clock on her bookcase: 11:09. "I can't leave now. Call him back and ask if this afternoon would be all right." The meeting with Ehringer's attorneys would be over by then. "No, wait. Karen has her first session with that new psychologist at five, and I have to be there. I can't cancel it."

Irene said, "What about tomorrow morning?"

"I don't want Irving to change his mind," Gail said. "Ask if we could come tonight at seven. And, Mother, when you call, be sure to say thank you. I'll be very easy with him, I promise."

chapter twenty-two

Paul Robineau's secretary had arranged for lunch to be catered from the restaurant upstairs. There was food enough for four in his conference room, but only three sat at the table. Larry Black hadn't shown up. Gail supposed he didn't want to be closed in with Paul Robineau for two hours.

She gave Robineau and Jack Warner copies of Miriam's notes with a summary that included what Miriam and Eric had found out since this morning.

Robineau and Warner interrupted only with pertinent questions and made few notes. Warner sliced into his roast beef, smiling from time to time as if he were imagining Odell on the stand. Robineau wolfed down a ham croissant, then stood by the window, feet apart, flexing his heavy shoulders under his sleek gray jacket. His collar was as crisp and white as a folded sheet of letterhead.

Gail had worn her best suit today, a charcoal pinstripe that had cost her eight hundred dollars two years ago, on sale. Her nails and hair were perfect, and her gold jewelry glittered discreetly at her ears and throat. She had found half a Xanax rattling around in the back of her desk drawer.

For the last half hour or so, Gail had explained that G. Howard Odell, executive director of the Easton Charitable Trust, was probably knee-deep in the muck of topless bars, escort services, and adult movie houses.

She explained the connections. Atlantic and Seagate, which ran these operations, had been founded in 1979 and 1981 by the current president of Biscayne Corporation, a Leo Dolan, a former banker and sometime investment partner of Howard Odell. Odell held the position of treasurer.

Biscayne had been incorporated in 1938 by two men, Walton Nash and George Odell. Gail assumed that George was a relation of Howard, perhaps his father. In 1983 the corporation was known as Biscayne Casinos, Inc. There had been casinos in Dade County dating from the Twenties. By the Fifties, when the mob tried to push its way in, the owners closed them down voluntarily.

Biscayne, now known as the Biscayne Corporation, became a holding company. Its current operations included a rental apartment complex, two restaurants, and a company that made plastic bubble wrap. All legitimate, all clean. Atlantic and Seagate were something else. Legal? That was iffy. Clean? Depended on your definition of the word.

Who owned these corporations? As yet she had not obtained information as to which living, breathing persons actually owned stock in Biscayne or in Seagate and Atlantic, but Gail assumed they overlapped. She also assumed, without evidence, that G. Howard Odell had a stake in them.

She told Paul Robineau and Jack Warner about Irving Adler's confession: finally, to add to the document examiner's expert opinion, they had firsthand proof that the will was phony. But until Adler's testimony was safely in the form of a sworn statement, they couldn't count on it.

For now, they would demand a good settlement, playing on Howard Odell's possible connection to X-rated businesses—an adult motel in Hialeah, a porno theater on Biscayne Boulevard, an escort service on the Beach, or a travel agency that could send you on a sex tour of Bangkok.

Howard Odell's associates included a pimp, Frankie Delgado, who had an underage girlfriend. Gail couldn't prove what was going on, but something was. Threats of exposing Odell's dirty businesses could work to secure his cooperation in settling the Norris case. The members of the Easton Charitable Trust, in all their moral rectitude—whoever they were—would find it all so embarrassing that they would take away his executive directorship. The people he invested with would say he was bad for their image.

"Let me ask your opinion on something," she said. "It appears that Odell may have made a deal for himself at Easton's expense. Example: the house on Star Island. In 1987 someone donated it to the Easton Trust at a declared value of $700,000. That was probably an inflated figure for tax purposes. In any event, Odell bought the house six months later for $400,000. He sold it last year for $1.5 million. These businesses could follow that pattern. Pick up some odds and ends of Easton real estate cheaply through Biscayne, sell them to related corporations or to friends. The profits could be enormous."

Gail stood up and walked over to the cart that the restaurant had sent down. She put a few more shrimp on her plate and a dash of cocktail sauce.

"I think we ought to assume for now that Sanford Ehringer doesn't know what Odell is

360

doing. The trust is only one of dozens of activities Ehringer is involved in. If we lay it all out to his attorneys in the meeting, we might lose our advantage. I believe we should speak to Odell privately beforehand. We can't hold this over his head if Ehringer finds out about it."

Robineau nodded. "I agree. How soon can you verify his involvement in these other companies?"

Gail took a bite of shrimp. "It could take weeks, unless we hire an investigator."

"Perhaps. We'll see how it goes today."

Jack Warner patted his mouth with a cloth napkin. He had taken off his navy blue jacket and hung it over the back of a chair. She had seen him wear this suit arguing cases in the Florida Supreme Court. It would do for the meeting with Ehringer's attorneys. Jack knew the moves; he'd been a litigator for thirty years.

"Well, now," Warner said. "How much do we want for this case?"

"Patrick Norris will settle for five million," Gail said. "He wanted the beneficiaries to pay the taxes, but I told him to drop that idea. For him to net five, they'd have to pay nearly eleven million dollars, and I don't think they'd do it."

"What do we get on a settlement? Ten percent, wasn't it?"

"Yes. Plus costs."

Warner looked over at Robineau. "Five hundred K in fees. What do you think?"

"It's fifteen percent of the estate if we go to trial," Robineau said. "Assuming twenty-five million, that would be . . . three point seven-five million in fees."

"Only if we win," Gail said. She was leaning back in the softly upholstered chair with her legs crossed, one foot bouncing slowly. Brand new shoes, not a nick on them. "We don't have enough proof on our side yet to run that risk. I want to hear what Irving Adler has to say."

Robineau didn't like that response. "What are we going to tell the other side at two o'clock, Ms. Connor? Come back tomorrow?"

"No. We tell them we want ten million. They'll say either 'yes' or 'we'll get back to you.'" Gail smiled up at him, and felt the back of her neck getting moist with nervous sweat.

He paced to the windows, rolling his shoulders. "That son-of-a-bitch Ted Mercer is taking over the probate, now that Weissman's out. He's going to ask if we're here to play or jerk off."

Looking at him, Jack Warner chuckled. "Oh, it makes you itchy, doesn't it, Paul? You want to say, 'Why, hell, a jury of blind men could see that the will was forged. Let's just go to trial.'"

"Is that your advice?" Robineau asked. "Go for it?"

"Not on what we've got. Gail's right." Finishing off his iced tea, Warner glanced at his watch. "Where the hell is Larry?"

"He must have better things to do." Robineau walked over to stand by Gail's chair. He asked, "Why hasn't this case been filed already?"

She said, "Until the *Miami Herald* printed the story this morning, everybody had a stake in keeping it quiet."

"It doesn't matter, Paul. This is one we need to finesse." Warner stood up and put on his jacket. "But let's get the case in court. Get it filed. Are you ready to move on that, Gail?"

"I can do it tomorrow," she said. "The pleadings are ready, along with an emergency motion for deposition. I want Irving Adler before a court reporter as soon as possible." Gail raised a warning hand. "Please do not mention Irving Adler in the meeting this afternoon. We don't want to let them know what we've got until we've got it."

Warner said, "I'm tempted to tell them to go to hell." He smiled at her. "But as you say, not yet. Not yet."

Gail asked, "Who's going to talk to Howard Odell before the meeting?"

Robineau's eyes went to Warner, who made an almost imperceptible shrug. Robineau said to Gail, "It's your case. You feel like taking him on?"

She took her time answering. If she and Odell went into a private room to talk about this, would he listen to her? Or would he only grin and give her one of his patronizing winks? Jack Warner might do better with him. Or Paul Robineau, who could snap Odell's spine over his knee. One of them should do it. What, after all, did she have to prove? The goal was to obtain the best settlement for her client.

And yet . . . Paul Robineau, managing partner of Hartwell Black, had asked her if she could handle it. It wasn't a question. It was a challenge.

Gail nodded and took the leap. "Give me fifteen minutes with Odell before the meeting starts. You can keep Ehringer's attorneys busy for that long."

She chose the main conference room, empty now except for the two of them, and quiet, only the *whoosh* of cool air coming through the vents. The walls were richly paneled, the floor carpeted in green with a pattern of gold and red.

It took her ten minutes to tell Howard Odell what she had learned and what she wanted in a settlement. Now he was watching something through the window. He had a deep tan, but he was not as young as she had thought at the gallery. There were no sporty clothes today; he wore a business suit and white-on-white shirt.

"Nice view," he said after a while, in his rich bass voice. "Sunshine, blue sky. Makes me want to crank up my boat and take off for the islands. Do some fishing."

"I'd like an answer," she said.

"Ms. Connor, you're a bitch. Not that I can't appreciate that in a woman. I married two of them." He walked farther along the windows, lightly rapping his knuckles on the marble sill. "You know, it's not my decision how much Easton or the other beneficiaries will give up."

"Sanford Ehringer lets you run the trust," she said. "The others will follow your lead."

"Not as far as ten million dollars. No way."

"It isn't coming out of your pocket," she said.

He laughed, the lines in his cheeks making slashes. "Lawyers. Jesus. No, it's not my money, Ms. Connor. It's only numbers. A few million here, a few million there."

"If I wanted to squeeze this case, I'd do it. The will was forged. We can prove it. My client wants it now, not two or three years from now. You're getting a break. You and the other beneficiaries come out with over half."

"Blah blah blah." Laughing again, he turned toward her. "I don't give a damn. I don't. You believe that? It's true. You know, Gail—Gail? You mind? People today, they're in a cage. On a wheel. You, for instance. Same thing, maybe you don't see it. Most people don't. I'm fifty-four years old next month. I'm getting off my wheel. So settle the case, I don't care. Like you said—it's not my money."

She looked at him for a minute. "What are you going to tell Ehringer's lawyers?"

"What do you want me to tell them?" Odell spread his arms. "I'm not telling them ten."

"Any less than eight, we go to trial," she said.

"Six sounds better. They might go with six."

"Eight. Payable within three months."

"That's up to the beneficiaries' committee, isn't it? I don't write the checks." His eyes were fixed on the eastern horizon again. "We'll give you a call next week. Ted Mercer will. He's got the probate now, let him earn his fees."

"The case will be filed tomorrow, but it won't affect our negotiations," Gail said. She added, "As long as you don't impede them, you can count on my discretion."

Howard Odell's smile worked into a low chuckle. "You and my ex-wives ought to form a club, you really should."

Gail leaned casually against the windowsill; her

knees had gone weak. She swallowed to clear her throat. "I'm curious about something. Who are the current members of the Easton Trust?"

He turned around, quizzical. "Why?"

"I'd like to know, that's all."

"Sanford said you asked him that. If he wouldn't discuss it, then don't ask me."

"Is the name an acronym?"

"I don't know, is it?"

"Try this. Samuel Ehringer and five of his politically conservative friends in 1937. E for Ehringer?"

He grinned at her, perfect teeth, almost too white in his deeply tanned face. "My grandpa George used to play poker with Sanford's dad. There. You get one for free."

O for Odell, Gail thought.

"One other question. How well did you know the woman who notarized the will? Carla Napolitano. She worked at Gateway Travel."

A puff of air escaped his pursed lips. "I know who she is, that's about it. Why are you asking?"

"She died last Thursday night."

"Yes, I heard. Fell off her balcony. Too bad."

"You don't seem sorry. She was a nice woman."

"I hardly knew her. Look, Gail. Carla was not a nice woman. She used to be a heroin addict and a prostitute. This is true. The manager at Gateway was giving her a chance. But, you know, people like that, they don't change." When Gail said nothing more, Howard Odell smiled sadly and lifted his shoulders.

She checked her watch. "You'll want a few

366

minutes with Mr. Ehringer's attorneys. You may use this conference room if you like."

"Tell them to come in, would you, Gail?" He winked at her. "Thanks."

She looked at him for a moment, then turned and left him standing by the windows.

Last night she had dreamed of Carla Napolitano. Carla was dancing along the railing of her balcony in her high, clear plastic shoes with the daisies on the toes. Bracelets jingled on her wrists. Then Carla was airborne, slowly flapping her arms toward New Jersey. The sky was startlingly blue, with puffy white clouds. Below, little Greek fishing boats sailed on clear turquoise water. Then the sea turned gray and flat, with yellow lines marking the parking places, and it came rushing toward her like a fist. She tumbled down and down to the bottom of the stairs, and a crimson pool began to spread on the cold white marble.

chapter twenty-three

It was 7:35 before Gail got to Irene's, 7:45 when they crested the Venetian Causeway bridge, heading for Irving Adler's house on Miami Beach. Karen sat in the backseat with a box of Chicken McNuggets and a large order of fries.

Irene said, "Gail, please. You drive like someone is chasing us. I told him we'd be late."

367

"I'm only five miles an hour over the speed limit."

"Well, it's dark, and you know driving in Miami at night makes me jittery."

Gail let her foot off the gas a little, then turned on the dome light and adjusted the rearview mirror. "Hold that Coke between your knees so it doesn't fall over," Gail said to Karen's reflection. "And don't get anything on your clothes." She left the light on.

A pair of blue eyes stared back at her for a moment, then Karen scooted over to sit directly behind the driver's seat. She was still mad because Gail couldn't take her shopping. Usually Karen didn't give a damn about clothes. Now suddenly she did. It had taken a screaming match and five dollars' advance on her allowance to get Karen to come along. Phyllis couldn't stay over, there was no answer at Karen's friend Molly's house, and Gail refused to leave her by herself.

She said quietly to Irene, "You're positive Irving won't mind? I think Karen feels out of place."

"Mind? No, he has five grandchildren." Irene smiled at Karen and reached between the seats to pat her knee. "He has the cutest dog you ever saw. A tiny little white poodle."

Gail heard Karen mutter, "Oh, yay." Yay, indeed. Mitzi. Ill-tempered little bitch. Suited Gail's mood exactly. She took another sip of her soda, then wedged it back into the holder on the dashboard. "Maybe we can sit in the kitchen and Karen can watch the TV in the living room. Could you suggest that to him? People feel more

368

at ease in kitchens," Gail said. "I brought my tape recorder. It's in my purse."

Irene gave her a look. "Irving is my friend. He is not a witness to be cross-examined."

"Mother, I won't do that. Watch. I'll be an angel."

Karen snickered from the backseat. Gail turned her head to speak to her. "If you're finished, put everything in a bag. On the floor, please, not on the seat." She turned the dome light off.

They had gone to see Clarinda Campbell at five o'clock. Two hundred bucks for the first session, one hundred thereafter. The first time was for the whole family, but a third of the family, Gail had explained by telephone last week, was now sailing from St. Croix to Curaçao. Clarinda had said Dave could come when he was in town, but it was the family here that she must work with. The two of them, mother and daughter. Then Clarinda had gently asked whether she should speak with Anthony Quintana. I don't think so, Gail had replied. Not yet. *Maybe not ever,* she had added to herself.

Clarinda Campbell was an elfin woman with protruding eyes, arching eyebrows, and light-brown hair that was brushed straight up, so that she looked constantly delighted. She wore soft clothes that she had designed and stitched together from old shirts and dresses. Green plants in Navajo pottery decorated the knotty pine bookcase, and in one corner of her consulting room was a drum made of elk hide, which she

369

and a group of other women had made and painted with berry juice.

She told Karen that she herself had kept a secret box when she was a girl, full of things that no one else could know about. Then she complimented Karen on the alligator purse. Beautiful. Much better than her own gray metal box, because the purse was alive, and it had come from her own grandmother, besides.

Her voice was like soft, steady rain.

At ten years old, Clarinda explained, Karen was constructing her identity. During their time together she would take the threads of her life and weave them into her womanhood. And meanwhile, Mother should supervise the television, not allow Karen to watch violence or mindless comedies. Best to view it together, talking afterward about what it meant. They would study myths together. It would take time, but all precious things take time.

By then Gail's watch said 6:20. Clarinda gave them a list of special foods they could prepare together in the evenings, for the spirit as well as the body. No heavy meats, no grease, low sugar, plenty of fruit and whole grains.

As they left, Clarinda reached up to squeeze the back of Gail's neck. The small fingers were cool and strong. *So tense! Have you tried hatha yoga?* Gail smiled and wrote a check. By then it was 6:30. Too late for cooking. They would go by McDonald's on the way to Irene's. Brown rice and veggies tomorrow.

Gail turned north onto Alton Road, the headlights sweeping around curves in the darkness.

She said, "Mom, here's a puzzle for you from Sanford Ehringer. It's an acronym." She told Irene her theory about the letters in Easton. They represented names. Most likely, last names of men with money and influence who had been business and political intimates of Sanford Ehringer's father, Samuel. "I have two of them, Ehringer and Odell. You know people. Who do you think the other four are?"

Irene looked at her. "From 1937? How old do you think I am?"

"What about my grandfather, John B. Strickland?" Gail asked. "He was a friend of Ehringer's. He could be the S."

"I never heard anything about that," Irene said. "It might have been my second cousin Eugene Spencer. He knew the Ehringers. Gene started the Bank of Miami, if I remember my history."

"There's still a Spencer at the bank, Leland. He's a cousin?" Gail stopped for a traffic light. "You know what? He's a client of Hartwell Black."

"Is that important?"

"Larry told me that some of the current members of the Easton Trust are clients. He wouldn't say who they are." She would ask him about that tomorrow. She had wanted to talk to him this afternoon, to tell him what had happened with Howard Odell, but Larry had still been out of the office. The light turned green and she stepped on the gas.

Now she could guess why Ehringer had not told her the names of the founders. The current members had the same names. The originals had been a tight group of friends. As they died off, wouldn't they have passed their membership along? Grandfather to son to grandson.

"Slow down!" Irene said.

Gail put on her brakes. "Okay, we've got E, O, and maybe S. Who else?"

"Adler," Irene announced. "Irving's uncle—I can't remember his name—was the Ehringers' attorney in New York. What was his . . . Jacob. Jacob Adler." She clapped her hands together. "This is fun. Jacob Adler spent the winters here. I remember seeing him play the cello at a party at the Ehringers' home. My goodness, that must have been thirty years ago. He played the cello and Sanford played the violin."

"A is for Adler, then. Karen, stop kicking the back of my seat. Is Irving on the current board of the Easton Trust?"

"I have no idea," Irene said.

"I'll ask him. What about T for Tillett? Larry suggested Althea was a member."

"Althea wasn't a Tillett. She was a Norris."

"The letter N is in Easton too. Was her family prominent in the Thirties, before she was born?"

"Oh my, no. Althea got where she was on her own efforts. Her father was an engineer on the Seaboard Railroad and her mother died young. Althea worked very hard in the hotel business and spent every dime she earned on herself. Beautiful clothes, a nice car, going to the right society events. She met R.W. Tillett at the opera. He often went alone because the first Mrs. Tillett was so ill. I think Althea had an affair with him before his wife finally died. They were married just a few months after that."

"A woman who knew what she wanted. She went to Greece with Sanford Ehringer in 1958. He told me so."

"Yes." Irene sighed. "I wish I'd have had the nerve."

Gail looked at her. "What do you mean?"

"Nothing." Headlights swept into the car, passing over Irene's face.

"Mother . . ."

Glancing toward the backseat, she whispered, "He asked me to go with him to Italy. I chickened out. My father would have disowned me."

"You're making that up!"

Irene's mouth turned down. "I was considered very pretty when I was young."

"You're still pretty. It's never too late," Gail said. "He's a bachelor now."

"The man is in his eighties." She pointed. "Take the next left up here." Gail put on her blinker. Irene said, "Don't mention this, but Irving and Althea . . . before she married R.W. He told me when I was there last week."

"No. I thought Irving was married."

"He was." Irene made a sigh. "Some people stumble into these things like falling through a trapdoor. He says he was ready to leave his wife, but Althea called it off. It was for the best. He never forgot her, though. Then to learn she was murdered. Such a blow."

Karen's head appeared between the seats. "Who got murdered?"

"No one you know, sweetie," Gail said.

Irene turned around and took Karen's hand. "One of my dearest friends. Her name was Althea Tillett. Someone broke her neck and threw her down the stairs in her own house."

"Mother, please!"

"Good lord, they see thousands of murders on television by the time they're her age."

"Those aren't real!" Gail reached over to cup Karen's cheek. "Someone came into her house, but they won't come into ours."

"I think we ought to buy a gun. Molly's dad has an Uzi."

"Ryan Perlmutter does not have an Uzi."

"She said he does."

"That's a fib. Sit down. We're almost there." Gail turned at the next corner. "Is this affair what Irving has on his conscience?"

"I doubt it," Irene said. "I'm sure he treasures that memory. Neither of them were kids, but Althea had such . . . *fire*. You could never accuse Althea of being shy. She didn't wait for life to come to her; she went out and took it. Not like me. I was too timid. Someday my prince will come, all that sort of nonsense. I tell you, Gail, it ruins you for real men. You expect them all to be heroes, and they aren't, bless their hearts."

"Very true," Gail said.

"I never raised you girls to believe in fantasy, I hope."

"No, Mother. I think it's in the air. We can't help ourselves."

Gail slowed down. The street looked different at night. Quiet. Pulling itself in like a black drawstring bag. There was a wind, a cold front moving

374

through, and the light from the street lamps shifted and danced in the branches of the trees.

Irving Adler's living room curtains were drawn, but the lights were on, glowing through the folds in the fabric. Gail pulled the car into his driveway and turned off the engine.

"Karen, I want you to be very polite with Mr. Adler. You hear me?"

She nodded, looking at the house.

"He's an elderly gentleman, and he's very sad about his friend dying. We must be very respectful. Okay?"

"Okay."

Irene closed her door. "This yard is so dark. He should have put the porch light on. Watch where you're stepping, girls."

Shifting Karen's alligator purse to one side, Gail brushed some crumbs off her Miami Hurricanes sweatshirt. She had refused to let Karen wear the hat. Gail still had her suit on, not a minute to change to anything else.

They walked up the three steps to the front porch and Irene rang the bell. Gail waited for Adler's poodle to throw herself against the inner door, yapping and snarling.

The storm door rattled slightly in a gust of wind, and their dark images trembled in the glass.

Irene pressed the button again, and the same long tones sounded from inside the house. She opened the storm door and rapped loudly with her knuckles on the little fan-shaped window level with the top of her head. "Irving? It's me, Irene." She moved aside and said, "What can you see through here?"

Gail stood on tiptoes. "Nothing. His entrance hall." Irene reached past her and tried the door. Locked. "Should we go around back?" Gail asked.

"No." Irene's chest rose and fell and she laid her hands on Karen's shoulders. "Stay here with your mama. I'm going next door to use the telephone."

A patrol car arrived first, and the officers tried knocking again, then calling out, before they broke a pane of glass in the kitchen door and reached through to turn the deadbolt.

The rescue van came, lights circling around the yard, flashing across the house. The paramedics went through the front door with their equipment. Gail had made Karen sit in the car. Now Irene appeared in the open doorway. She leaned on the white wrought-iron railing to come down off the porch.

Gail knew the answer before she went to put her arms around her. "Oh, Mom. He's gone?"

"Yes. His heart, they think."

"Oh, my God. If we had come—"

"He's been dead for a while." She took a tissue from her purse. Her voice trembled. "They tried to find a pulse and they said he was cold. I saw his face. It didn't look like Irving. It didn't."

Gail hugged her.

A neighbor woman called out from the next yard, "What happened? Is Irving all right?" Someone else called from across the street. Irene wiped her eyes, then went to tell them.

Gail looked around. "Karen, stay in the car. I'll be back."

"Mom, is he dead?"

"His heart gave out, sweetie. He was a very old man, and I'm sure he went peacefully. You know this happens."

"Can I see?"

"No. Stay with your gramma."

Gail went inside the house. The kitchen was noisy and crowded with men in uniforms. One officer was on his two-way radio; the other was watching the paramedics pack up. A chair was overturned, and Irving Adler lay beside it as if he had fallen asleep there, his legs pointed toward the dining room. She could see the spotless soles of his running shoes, his thin ankles, the pressed creases in his trousers, and one upturned hand. It was a neat kitchen, and the floor was shiny blue. A pot was on the stove. The table was set. Saltines formed a white wreath around a bowl of noodle soup.

Gail went to the open door to breathe some air. The swimming pool shimmered in the light from the kitchen. She could faintly hear a television playing in the house next door. The yard was dark, circled by a wood fence.

One of the officers came over and asked what she wanted. She told him who she was. Her mother, Mr. Adler's friend, might know how to reach his family.

The officer nodded. "We'll ask her." He lifted an arm toward the dining room, a suggestion that she should leave.

Gail said, "Did he die of a heart attack?"

"Apparently. Can I get you to wait outside?"

"Tonight Mr. Adler was going to tell me who forged a will. It's an estate worth several million dollars. Althea Tillett. Do you know the name?"

The cop looked at her awhile. He was young, with large brown eyes and a straight part in his black hair. He turned his head toward the other officer and said to call investigations back and tell them to hurry up.

Detective Gary Davis arrived ten minutes later. He went into the kitchen while Gail waited in the living room with Irene and Karen. Karen wanted to see the body, but Gail said no. She nearly told Irene to go on home and take Karen with her, but Irene didn't look as if she was in any condition to drive. Awhile later an ambulance arrived—no lights or siren—and took Irving away. Irene had called several of their friends, and Irving's son was on his way over.

Davis asked the younger man to check all the windows and sent the blond officer outside with a flashlight. Karen asked if she could watch. Gail said no, but Davis said it was okay with him, as long as she didn't get in the way.

He sat on the edge of Irving Adler's chintz-covered armchair. He said, "Here's what I think, Ms. Connor. You tell me the man had a triple bypass last year. I don't see any marks on him, no signs of struggle. Doors were locked. It looks like a plain ol' heart attack to me."

"I just thought . . ." Gail's words trailed off with a motion of her hand.

"No, it's good to ask. Tough luck about your case, though, him being a witness and all."

"Oh, well." Gail touched Irene's arm and spoke quietly. "Mother, are you ready to go home?" Irene nodded, red-eyed and subdued. Gail stood up, then asked, "Detective, do you know anything more about Carla Napolitano? Did she fall? Or what?"

"Far as I know, it was an accident. There was a half-empty bottle of Southern Comfort on the patio, and the M.E. says she had a blood alcohol level of one point six. It would help if you could tell me anything you know."

Gail felt utterly drained. "Let me call tomorrow. There isn't much more to tell you."

"Tell me now, then."

Irene sat back down. Gail told him what Howard Odell had said about Carla. She asked, "Was she ever on drugs? Did the autopsy show anything?"

"The M.E. didn't find evidence of current drug use," Davis said. "I don't know her history. According to her neighbors, she led a pretty quiet life."

"Carla told me she kept books, as well as making travel arrangements."

"Right. The manager confirmed that. Frankie Delgado."

Gail glanced at her mother, then looked back at Davis. She hadn't told her about impersonating a hooker. "I believe I may have mentioned Mr. Delgado to you before."

"I believe you did."

"Did you ask him where he was last Thursday

night, by any chance? When Ms. Napolitano had her accident?"

"Sure did. A private party at Tony Roma's, which I confirmed with the maître d'." Davis smiled. "You practicing to be an investigator?"

"I'm not doing any worse than your department. You still suspect Patrick Norris." Gail picked up her purse from the coffee table. "If you're going back to headquarters tonight, could I call you? I need the address and phone number of Mrs. Tillett's housekeeper."

He scratched the side of his face. "I gave it to Quintana already."

"Yes, but he's in trial and I can't reach him."

"What are you gonna do?"

"Talk to her."

"No. Uh-uh. In fact, you tell Quintana I said nobody talks to Rosa Portales. I want to interview her again myself, in light of what you told me about the will. Maybe I missed something."

"Detective Davis, she may be important to my case."

"Mine too. And I'm talking about a homicide."

"You can't forbid me to interview witnesses on a civil case. I'm certainly not going out of mere curiosity—"

He held a finger in her face. "I don't want to hear you've been to see Rosa Portales until you clear it with me. I might want to reinstitute some paperwork from an incident over at Mrs. Tillett's house. You understand what I'm saying?"

A long, piercing wail, as of a child in pain, came from deeper in the house. Gail gasped, then dropped her purse and raced across the dining

380

room, colliding with Karen at the doorway to the kitchen.

"Mommeeeee!" There was a smear of blood on her sweatshirt.

"What is it?" Gail grabbed her by the arms. "Karen! Oh, my God! Are you all right?"

"Noooooo! Please!"

"What's going on?" Davis shouted.

"The dog! It's hurt! Mom, it's bleeding! You have to take it to a vet!"

Irene came around Detective Davis. "Do you mean Mitzi? Gail, I haven't seen that dog since we got here."

"She was in the trash! I heard a noise and I lifted the lid and she was crying!" Karen squeezed her eye shut and drummed her feet, quick little steps in her torn canvas sneakers. "I dropped her. I didn't mean to!"

"Where is she, Karen?" Irene asked.

Karen spun around and ran for the door. The floodlights were on in the backyard now, a spotlight pointing in each direction from the corner of the roof, and the yard was a contrast of white and deep shadow. The young officer with the black hair pointed to the grass beside a garbage can filled nearly to the top with plastic bags. "It's a puppy or something."

Davis went over to see. "Oh, I hate this. God damn."

Gail pulled Karen back. Davis looked at Gail and shook his head.

The blond officer bent over the grass. "Yipes. It's flat in the back. Gross."

The young cop said, "What'd the old bastard do, throw it out?"

Karen buried her face in Gail's stomach and clung to her waist, screaming. "Mommy! Take her to a doctor. Pleeeese!"

Gail hugged her tightly. "All right. The policemen will take it to a vet. Won't you?" She looked at them. "Won't you?"

"A vet?" The young cop looked down at Karen. "That's right. We'll take good care of her."

"Now! Take her now!" Karen sobbed, and Gail pulled her toward the house. She glanced back. The blond cop toed the dog gently with his shoe and it yelped. Karen put her hands over her ears. "Don't!" She screamed. "Mommeeeee!"

Irene pushed past him and fell to her knees on the ground. Mitzi was whimpering, a high, staccato cry, as if her jaws were trembling. Irene looked around at the young cop and yelled at him, "Go get me a hand towel out of the kitchen! Move!"

Davis jerked his head in that direction and he took off. Irene pushed her sweater sleeves to her elbows. When he returned with a blue checked towel, Irene told him to spread it on the ground. She picked up the small shape, laid it on the towel, and wrapped it tightly. The cries were muffled now. She got up, walked quickly to the edge of the swimming pool, knelt, and plunged the bundle into the water, holding it there. The water darkened, blood spreading.

"Oh, shit." The young officer turned and looked up at the sky.

Karen stared.

Gail dragged her to the house. "Come inside."

"Leave her here!" Irene's arm was still straight down into the water. "Karen. You listen to me. Stop crying. This dog was too badly hurt to live, and she was suffering. She wouldn't have made it to the vet. Do you understand?"

Karen wailed.

"Answer me!"

"Yes, ma'am."

"Good. Now you and your mother go inside and find me another towel. A pretty one. Bring a spoon and we'll make a place to lay Mitzi to rest. It's all right now. It's all right. Go on."

They found an embroidered hand towel in Irving Adler's linen closet. Gail went into the bathroom and wet a washcloth and cleaned off Karen's face. Karen was weeping silently, taking big gulps of air.

Gail said, "I'm so sorry, sweetie. I'm so sorry." Her throat hurt too much to talk, not from grieving over the life of Adler's poodle, or from the horror of watching it die, but from shame. When she was a child she had seen Irene drown a kitten in a bucket that way, after a dog got it. Gail and her sister Renee had said prayers and sung songs over the little mound of dirt in the backyard.

This time she should have been the one to do it.

chapter twenty-four

At the federal courthouse, Gail looked inside the courtroom on the twelfth floor. Empty. Only the flags, the empty judge's bench, and a few rows of seats upholstered in mauve. Anthony's trial would restart at nine o'clock, according to the court clerk. Gail had detoured a few blocks north on the way to her office, hoping to find him here by now, half an hour early.

She took the elevator back downstairs to the lobby. Through two-story plate glass, light poured in from outside, a glare on the brown marble floor. She felt clumsy and disconnected; she had not been able to sleep last night.

People came and went, voices echoing. She scanned the faces, then glanced toward the street. He was just coming along the sidewalk, carrying his briefcase. Three people were with him, a younger associate from Ferrer & Quintana on his left, and a man and a woman on his right. The man would be the client—Latin, mid- forties. He was a co-defendant in an embezzlement case, and he held the woman's hand. Anthony spoke to the client, touching his shoulder for emphasis. He wore a conservative gray suit today, which said this must be a jury trial. He had told Gail that jurors prefer such suits, having seen them on lawyers in the movies or on television.

From an insider's vantage point she had watched him in trial. He was measured and calm, or could explode with enough raw emotion to make a jury gasp. His timing was superb, his gestures so assured they seemed completely without artifice—the eyes up to heaven, the little shrug, the ruffling through papers as if he had just recalled a vital point. But he had done his homework; he knew his lines. Once when he had finished mangling a government witness, he stalked back across the courtroom, blood still on his claws, and his eyes had caught Gail's, and the desire that had shot between them in that instant had nearly made her faint.

At the top of the steps the associate held the glass door. Anthony let the client and his wife go first, then followed them inside. He noticed Gail and said something to the others.

He crossed the lobby, curious, smiling. "This is a surprise."

Gail said, "I wouldn't bother you during a trial, but I need a favor."

"Why are you so pale? What's wrong?"

"I didn't get much sleep. Irving Adler died last night."

"Died? How?"

"A heart attack. He had called my mother, wanting her to bring me over to talk to him. He was going to confess the will was forged. When we got there, he was dead. Karen was with me. She found the dog with its back broken and thrown in the trash. She had nightmares all night."

Anthony took Gail's hand.

She said, "I thought of calling you, but it was so late."

"No, no. You should have called." With an arm around her shoulders, Anthony steered Gail out of the way of people walking past. There was a deserted spot along one wall, and he set his briefcase down. "Where is Karen now?"

"With my mother. She's all right. Anthony, what I need from you is Rosa Portales's address and phone number. My case just took a hit. Irving would have told me the truth. Now he's gone. I want to talk to Rosa Portales today."

"Why? Is there a rush?"

"Yes. We're in settlement. I told them I could prove the forgery. Now I'm not sure I can," Gail said. "Do I have to explain it all now? I want to talk to her."

"When this trial is over next week I'll go with you," he said.

"I don't need you to go with me," she said sharply, then dropped her voice when a woman glanced at her. "You told your secretary not to give me Rosa's number. Why?"

He took a moment, then without looking at her spoke as if she were a law clerk asking an obvious question. "Because this involves the criminal prosecution of my client, and I prefer to speak to the witness first, before her memories have been altered by questions on other matters."

Gail laughed a little. "Excuse me? Your client?"

"Yes. Patrick Norris."

She felt the blood pounding in her head. "You didn't even want him as a client."

"But now I have him, no?"

"You don't care about Patrick. You want to control what I do, and I don't like it."

He looked down his fine, narrow nose. "Where a client is involved, what anyone else does or does not like is of minor importance."

The room seemed to tilt. "Well, where was that noble sentiment when I was telling you the same thing? You were screaming at me because I wanted to handle my case in my way. True? Yes?"

"It isn't the same."

"Yes. It is. Call Mirta. I believe you have a phone in your briefcase?" She made a polite little smile.

"I have a client waiting for me, Gail." Face completely neutral, he moved closer, not to let anyone hear them. "I'll call you tonight. We'll discuss it then."

"Forget it." Rage leaped up her throat and for an instant the corridor vanished into a blur. "Forget calling, forget everything."

"What do you mean?"

"I made a reasonable request. You're being a jerk. It's what you always do. I've had it. I can't take this from you anymore."

Anthony picked up his briefcase with one hand and clamped the other on her elbow. He looked around, smiled across the lobby at his associate, then headed for the doors.. He spoke through his teeth. "I'll give you the damn phone number, but first we're going to talk."

She nearly tripped going down the steps. He

took her around the corner. The sun was glaring over the buildings across the street.

He said, "Now tell me what is the matter with you."

As if she should explain her surly attitude. The talons of her rage sank deeper. "My mother always told me, Try to end a bad relationship with a man before it goes completely sour, so you can remain friends. Am I too late? What do you think?"

Anthony looked at her, stunned. She closed her eyes and said, "Oh, Christ. Just go back to your clients. I don't want to talk about this now. I don't, don't, don't."

He set his briefcase down as though it might contain a bomb. "What are you saying to me? We're through? What have I done?"

"It isn't you." She pushed back her hair, laughing a little. "I always wanted to go to Mykonos, now I've been there. I want to go home."

"What has happened?" The sun was on his face, making him squint. "I know. It started Friday, at the hotel on South Beach. All right. It was a bad idea. I shouldn't have suggested it. You were too upset about the police—"

"Anthony—no. What happened at the hotel— it was going to happen sooner or later. I've felt it for weeks."

He continued to look at her. "Why didn't you tell me this? If you felt this way, you should have told me."

"I know that. Oh, God, I know." She leaned heavily against the wall. "Anthony, what are we doing with each other? Do you ever really think about it? We play at being in love. It's loads of fun, but it isn't *real*. I play with you and neglect my daughter. Last night—last night I saw what I've been doing to her. She needs me. I'm all she has. My marriage died because I neglected it. Now my daughter is without her father. There's only so much of me—"

"Ah, this is it. You feel guilty. You blame yourself for her problems. Gail, he never writes her. You said so. A postcard. A phone call if he thinks of it." Anthony's voice was rising. "He abandoned you. He is living on a boat in the Caribbean with another woman. You told me this!"

"Well, good for Dave. Let him do what he wants. I can't be so free."

Two men in suits came nearer. One of them raised a hand to Anthony. He nodded. Gail studied the sidewalk, a pattern of a leaf that had dried there long ago.

The men were gone. Anthony said, "You complained that I didn't know what I wanted from this relationship. Are you asking me to make a decision?"

She shook her head. "I couldn't tell you what to do, even if I wanted to." Gail wasn't angry anymore. She regretted the way she had spoken to him. She smiled, touching the front of his jacket. "You had the most placid life until I came along, didn't you? You'd always say 'Oh, Gail, you make me crazy.' I know you never meant it, but it's true. If we spent a lot of time together, I really would drive you crazy. I know you. You'd

389

feel trapped. I can't ask you to be anything but what you are. It wouldn't be fair."

"A lovely speech. And you said *I* was condescending."

Her smile faded. "I'm trying—really trying—to be honest with you."

"Unbelievable." He moved away from her, paced, looked at his watch, then came back. "You arrive at the federal courthouse just as I am about to go into a trial and you deliver me a package. I unwrap it, and it's a notice that we are through. I didn't ask for it. I wasn't consulted."

"Listen to you," she said. "That's what I mean. Have you ever noticed that you've got to have everything exactly the way you want it, when you want it?"

He laughed. "*¿Y tú?*" You don't? I think you want me to beg you change your mind, no? Is that what you want?"

She flared again. "I don't want you to do a damn thing. You like not making choices. Look at you. You float between Miami and Havana and your whole life is like that. You believe in nothing unless it affects *you.*"

"Aha. *Ahora tenemos la verdad.* This is it. Now I know what you really think of me. Finally the truth."

She felt a sudden, unreasoning urge to weep, but only crossed her arms tightly over her chest. "You were right. I should never have taken this case for Patrick. It made me open my eyes."

"This man is a self-deluded—*¡Este mongólico retardado! ¡Este hombre estáfundido!*"

"You want more honesty?" Her voice was

shaking. "You thought we must have been lovers because I wanted to help him. I denied it. Well, you were right about that too. I did have an affair with Patrick. Me, a married woman at the time. I didn't tell you because I knew it would only have pissed you off."

Anthony said nothing, but a muscle in his jaw bunched into a knot.

She smiled a little. "See?"

"No. I don't give a *damn* what you did with Patrick Norris in law school. What you do now is worse. This is not our affair, it is yours. Gail—poor, suffering Gail—must decide what will happen because Anthony's emotions can't be trusted. Your conceit is beyond belief!"

Suddenly he laughed and let his hands fall to his sides. "*Bueno.* Maybe you're right, you know? We should end it. Yes, I agree. You're not so easy to put up with either."

Gail saw heads turn in their direction. She said quietly, "Well. We've had our talk. Are you going to give me Rosa Portales's address or not?"

For a long moment Anthony looked at her, eyes blazing. Then he sat on his heels to click open his briefcase. He pulled out his portable telephone, hit some numbers with a stiff forefinger, crossed his arms, and walked away a few paces, his back to her.

"*Mirta. Es Quintana. Llama a la secretaria de la Señora Connor con la dirección y numero de teléfono de Rosa Portales.*" In another burst of Spanish he said no, he didn't want his messages; he would be back at six.

Anthony rammed the little antenna back into

the phone, threw it into his briefcase, and slammed the lid. "All right?" He grabbed it up and tucked his tie into the front of his jacket, not looking at Gail. "Mirta will call your secretary. Is there anything else? I have a trial, which now I do not know if I can get through without shooting someone."

There was that feeling again. The same calm a person must feel when the airplane is plunging toward the ground, and there is nothing, nothing you can do.

She said, "I'm so sorry. Please try to understand."

"Understand? You want me to *understand?* What do you think I am?" He took a few steps, then came back, one hand clutching his briefcase, the other frozen in midair.

"You know, the crazy thing—" He took a breath. "The crazy thing is, I have loved you with all my heart. And now what? I am to let it die? Don't tell me to understand what you are doing. I can't. It is too much to ask."

chapter twenty-five

Gail found Eric Ramsay in the library at one of the computers, the screen reflecting in his eyes. He noticed Gail and looked up. "Hey, boss."

She let herself down in the adjacent chair. "Miriam says you filed the Norris case this morning."

"Yeah. First in line at the clerk's office. I got the summonses and subpoenas issued, ready to be served whenever you say. They're in the file." Eric hit some buttons on the keyboard, and the screen went blank. He swung around in his chair. "Miriam told me about Irving Adler. I guess we can toss out his subpoena for deposition."

Gail nodded. Her head felt heavy, off-balance.

"And you found him," Eric said. "That must've been a shock. I don't think his death is going to hurt us, though. We've got a settlement going. Why should Odell back out now?"

"Odell wouldn't, necessarily, but Sanford Ehringer's attorneys might." She propped her cheekbone on her hand. "If Irving can't testify that the will was forged, what have we got?"

"Now what?"

"I'm going to go see Mrs. Tillett's house-keeper," Gail said. She closed her eyes. They felt hot and dry, as if someone were pushing them back into the sockets. "We've got her address. I called her. Eric, would you drive?"

"Sure. You look beat."

"I didn't get much sleep."

"Oh, hey." He put his hand on her back. "You ought to go on home, get some rest. We can talk to Mrs. Portales later."

She could have fallen against him and for a moment let him gently squeeze her shoulder. He had large, warm hands. "No, let's go now." She pulled away. "Eric—" She glanced into the room. A law clerk was at the far end of a corridor of ceiling-high shelves, turning slowly through a book.

"What?" Eric asked.

"I'm not going to make it till five o'clock. Do you have anything?"

"Sure," he said quietly. His hand went to her back again. "I've got something you could take. It's not too strong."

"I hate to ask," she said. "I don't do this, usually."

"Don't worry about it." He turned off the computer. "When do you want to go to Rosa's?"

"In a little while. I have to make a phone call."

Gail stood up. Irene had come over early in the morning to be with Karen, who wouldn't go to school. Gail wanted to see if Karen was still sleeping.

"Come up to my office first." Eric was gathering his notes. He was wearing navy-blue suspenders with little leather straps that buttoned inside the waist of his trousers. He stuck a thick enameled pen into his shirt pocket.

Gail said, "On the way to Rosa's I'd like to make a couple of side trips, if you don't mind."

"No, I don't mind. Where to?"

"I'm curious. I want to see what Wild Cherry looks like."

Half an hour later the two of them were ten miles or so north of downtown, heading up West Dixie Highway past an Italian pizza place, a discount store, a used car lot.

Eric slowed down. "It's up ahead on the right."

Wild Cherry didn't look as dangerous as he had described it two weeks ago. In fact, the place had neatly clipped hedges and a gold-trimmed sign. There was a red awning at the entrance, like a downtown hotel. The tree-lined parking lot was a quarter full at ten-thirty in the morning. A security guard sat on a stool outside. But still, you couldn't mistake what it was: MIAMI'S HOTTEST EXOTIC DANCERS. LADIES NO COVER CHARGE, DRINK HALF PRICE. LET YOUR FANTASIES RUN WILD.

Gail craned her neck as they drove past. "This doesn't seem too bad. How much money do they make here, do you think?"

"How much do they make, or how much do they report? These establishments can be money machines," Eric said. "Particularly one that's geared to tourists and businessmen. I had to pay ten dollars for a mixed drink, six if I'd wanted a beer. Plus a ten-dollar cover."

She looked sideways at him. "I thought you only stayed five minutes."

He grinned at her. "Can I put it on my expense account?"

"No, you probably enjoyed it too much."

"You ever been to a nude bar?"

"No."

"We can turn around. They let women in." Eric was wearing his sunglasses with the gold frames and leather trim. He playfully tapped the brake.

"I'll pass." Gail asked, "When you were talking to Howard Odell last year, did he mention Wild Cherry?"

"Not at all. He said he invested, but I didn't know it was in this kind of thing."

"Howard Odell is a hypocritical S.O.B.," Gail

said. "Collecting money for the poor at the same time he's involved in companies that own nude bars and porno movie houses, and using Easton as his own slush fund, no doubt."

Gail had wanted to see what Larry Black thought, but he had not come in yet. His secretary said he hadn't even gone home last night and his wife, Dee-Dee, was frantic. Gail told Eric to take a left at Northwest 167th Street, a six-lane road of shopping centers, kosher delis, Chinese takeout, small storefronts. Naughty 'n' Nice Apparel Shoppe would be among them.

Eric asked, "Tell me what happened last night. What did the police say?"

Gail described how Irene had knocked at Irving Adler's door. The paramedics arriving. Adler dead on the kitchen floor.

"They say it was of a heart attack. No sign that anyone broke in. The doors were locked. Just like with Carla Napolitano and Althea Tillett, if you think about it. Except there was a mangled dog in the garbage."

Eric took his eyes off the road to look at her. "Three dead people, three locked doors? Is that supposed to be a pattern?"

"And all three people were somehow involved in this case." She made a laugh. "Next, the body of Jessica Simms, the other witness, will be found stuffed into a kettle drum."

"It's possible." Eric said, "I think you ought to call that detective with the Beach police. See what he thinks."

"He'd think I was demented," Gail said.

396

"What bothers me is Mitzi. Why would Irving Adler throw his pet poodle into a garbage can?"

Eric shrugged. "Maybe a car hit it, and he thought it was dead."

"No, he'd have buried her. Besides, a car would have flattened Mitzi into a little fur rug."

"Maybe Adler accidentally stepped on her," Eric said. "Then he became so distraught that he had a heart attack and died."

Gail remembered the neat kitchen, the carefully placed crackers on his plate. "I don't think so." She pointed through the windshield. "Slow down. It's up ahead on the left."

Eric turned into the parking lot of the strip shopping center, then cruised along the storefronts. Gail looked past him at the shop. Naughty 'n' Nice looked like just another boutique, except for the black silhouettes of a man and woman on the sign, framed in a red heart. Mannequins in frothy nighties stared blankly back from the windows. A poster read FIFTY PERCENT OFF ALL TOYS AND NOVELTIES.

"Let's go," Gail said. "I've seen enough."

Eric braked at the sidewalk, then guided the Lexus into the flow of traffic. "You know, I used to think you were cold, uptight . . . by the book. It was wild, you going to see Frankie Delgado that way, telling him that story about being a call girl. I'd never have expected it from Gail Connor. Now here we are, looking at a sex shop."

Her head on the headrest, Gail shifted her eyes toward Eric. "Better than tax law, right?"

They made their way to Okeechobee Road, which as U.S. 27 would eventually bisect the flat

397

sugarcane fields fifty miles to the northwest. In Hialeah, the road ran past shops and gas stations on the right, with signs in Spanish. A drainage canal bordered the south side of the street, where tall pines shed needles on the rocky ground.

Finally Gail spotted the Aphrodite Motel. A mildewing goddess of poured concrete stood outside the flat-roofed, U-shaped building. There was a wood fence around it. High hedges divided the parking spaces for privacy, and there were a few enclosed garages. A guest could pay and get the key at a drive-up window while his secretary or neighbor's wife ducked down in the seat. ABIERTO 24 HORAS. Special hourly rates for business meetings. Visa and MasterCard accepted. A block beyond, there was another motel. Cupid's Arrow. ADULT VIDEOS AND WATERBEDS. It was, Gail decided, totally depressing.

The Lexus idled in the parking lot of the convenience store next door, air conditioner blowing through the vents.

"Hey."

Gail looked around. Eric was facing her in his seat, smiling through his sunglasses. "We're not in that big a rush. Let's go in."

She laughed. "Are you serious?"

"Sure. Come on."

"No." She let out a breath. "Jesus, Eric."

His smile faded. He turned around, put the car into gear, and gunned it out of the parking lot.

"I didn't mean to laugh," she said. "Really."

"Yeah." He gestured toward her file. "Give me Rosa's address."

She found it in her notes and told him to turn north on West Twelfth Avenue. She looked at him for a minute. His face was expressionless. Shaking her head, she watched the traffic. After a while, she said, "There were some files I didn't get to last night. I could use some help this afternoon, if you're not busy."

Eric adjusted the AC vent. "I'm not busy. Pretty soon I won't be busy at all. Paul Robineau gave me my notice yesterday. Take as long as I need to finish up, then get out."

"What? How can he do that?"

"He does what he wants, he runs the firm."

Gail said, "No. He should have told me. He knows you're working with me."

Eric pushed his sunglasses farther up the bridge of his nose. "No big loss. And I'm sick of it. Nobody likes lawyers, not even other lawyers. You're a high-class prostitute. They love you when they need you, then it's over."

"Then why did you go to law school?"

"It made as much sense as anything else. The pay's good." He laughed. "The hours are a bitch."

"Don't quit," Gail said. "This job is like anything else. You do the best you can, and you don't throw it away when it gets tough. Your clients come to you in trouble, and you help them. That's worth a lot."

Gail could see her own face in the lenses of his glasses. The mouth under them smiled, and the cheeks made ruddy circles. "I'm gonna miss you," he said. "Our little talks. Your pointers about life and the law."

"Forget it, then," she said, aware of how vacuous she must have sounded. Quotes from a self-help book. "Go north on West Twelfth."

He put on the brakes and turned the corner.

This part of Hialeah was light industry, small restaurants with a window at the front to serve *café*, and off-brand gas stations. A mile or so farther on, Eric turned east into a residential area of boxy houses with flat roofs and chain-link fences dividing the yards. They parked on the sparse grass outside the house where Rosa Portales was living with her sister. There was a shrine to the Virgin Mary under a palm tree.

Inside, Rosa Portales sat them down on the sofa. Tile gleamed on the floor and pleated curtains hung at the open windows. On the chrome-and-glass etagere were a statue of San Lázaro, a vase of artificial flowers made of feathers, and a silver-framed photo of a young man and woman in tux and wedding gown, their gazes fixed rapturously on each other. Rock music played faintly from one of the back rooms. Her nephew's day off, Rosa explained.

She sat on the matching love seat to their right with her legs crossed at the ankle, stockings shining on her plump knees. She wore a belted green dress and loose jacket. She had an exquisite manicure, with long red nails. Her short blond hair was fluffed and sprayed into place, with big earrings peeping out. Her lips were traced with brown lip liner. She was not what Gail had expected.

Rosa offered *café*; they declined. There was some small talk. Yes, living in Hialeah was quite a change from North Bay Road. No, Rosa didn't plan to be here long. How terrible about Mrs. Tillett. Yes, Rosa had met Irene Connor. In fact, Rosa would probably not have talked to Gail otherwise.

She had been born in New York. Her husband, a Puerto Rican, had been transferred to the air force base down in Homestead, and they had stayed. When he died, there were no children, and a friend recommended Rosa to Mrs. Tillett. For sixteen years, she had mopped, scrubbed, and polished Althea Tillett's house as though it were her own.

"Did they find who killed her?" Rosa frowned. There was a permanent crease between her eyebrows.

Gail said, "No. Not yet."

"I always spent Wednesday nights with my sister, or I would have been there." She made a little shudder. "Do they think Patrick was the one? It sounded like it, in the paper. He beat up Rudy, did you see that part?"

"Yes, I read that. Did you know them when they were kids?"

"No, the twins were in college already, and Patrick was finishing high school. I don't want to say anything bad, but he was strange. He would stay up in the attic with his books for hours. I don't think he could have killed her, though."

"What happened after Mrs. Tillett died? I believe Rudy and Monica came looking for a will?"

Rosa said, "Did you know I found Mrs. Tillett dead on the floor? Yes. I cried like you would not believe. The police asked me questions. They said I could clean up the floor the next day when they were finished." Rosa looked into her lap, her hands smoothing her skirt. "It was my place to do it for her, you know? I didn't want anyone else to. But it was real hard. That afternoon Rudy and Monica came over. I found them upstairs going through her papers. I said, 'What are you looking for?' And they said it was none of my business. And I told them if they were looking for a will, she didn't have one. But I guess I was wrong about that."

Gail looked at Eric, then said, "Why did you think there wasn't a will? Did Mrs. Tillett destroy it?"

"I thought she might have. She was out back about a month before she died, with a can of lighter fluid burning some papers on the seawall. She did the same thing about six months ago, and I asked her then and she said it was her will. She threw the ashes into the water."

Eric asked, "The papers she burned a month go—did she say it was her will?"

"No, I just thought it was. One time she tore a will into pieces and flushed it down the toilet. I know because it clogged up and I had to clean it out. I thought maybe she burned her last will, so I told Rudy and Monica." Rosa's brown eyes showed she was insulted. "They told me I could go. My services were no longer required. They said that. They took my keys and sent me a check for five hundred dollars. But I guess they had the right. They're her family."

"Did you call Patrick?"

"No. I didn't know where he was. Rudy said he would tell him."

"I understand Mrs. Tillett left you some money in the will," Gail said.

"Yes. The lawyer wrote me a letter. Twenty thousand dollars. I want to put a down payment on a condo. I have a job as a receptionist in the afternoons. That's why I'm dressed up."

Gail smiled at her. Here was another person Patrick would want to pay in full if he won his case. "Did you ever meet Irving Adler? He was one of Mrs. Tillett's friends."

"Oh, yes. I know Mr. Adler." Rosa laughed. "The man with the little dog. If that dog was bigger, someone would have to shoot it, it's so mean."

"Mitzi," Gail said.

"Mitzi, right. He would bring gourmet dog food for her to Mrs. Tillett's house in case she got hungry. In the winter, he put a sweater on her that his wife had knitted." Rosa lifted her eyes.

"Mr. Adler died last night of a heart attack."

"He did? Oh. I am sorry."

Gail said, "Before he died, he wanted to talk to me about Mrs. Tillett. Something weighing on his conscience. Do you know what he could have felt guilty about? What he could have meant?"

Her head was moving back and forth, her face blank.

"Did Mrs. Tillett say anything about that?"

Rosa's gaze focused past the security bars on the front window. The panes in the windows were

403

cranked open, and a pickup truck went by, mufflers throbbing, then fading away. Rosa said, "He came to see her. It was Monday, the week she died. I got back from grocery shopping—I shop on Mondays—and he was there. He didn't come very often. They were outside on the terrace."

"Did you hear what they said?"

"I don't eavesdrop."

"Of course not," said Gail. "But did you hear anything accidentally?"

She thought about it. "When I went out to take them some drinks they were arguing. Mrs. Tillett sounded mad."

"Mad? About what?"

Rosa closed her eyes. "Oh, what did she . . . something like, she was fed up, she was going to put a stop to it, I don't know. And Mr. Adler was saying 'No, no, no. Don't do it, I won't let you do it.' Then they saw me and they didn't say anything else."

Gail exchanged a look with Eric. His face was pink with excitement, and he was sitting on the edge of the sofa, hands clasped between his knees. He said to Rosa, "What about other people who came to the house that week? She must have had visitors."

The crease deepened between her brows. "It was the usual thing, like Mrs. Simms came over for lunch on Tuesday. That's Jessica Simms, a friend of hers. All I heard them talk about was gossip. Oh, and Rudy came over—no, that was the week before."

"Rudy Tillett?" Eric asked. "Was Monica with him?"

"No, just Rudy."

"What did they talk about?"

"I don't eavesdrop," Rosa said firmly.

Gail asked, "Did she seem happy when she talked to him? Angry?"

"They were on their way up the stairs, so I didn't hear anything. She didn't sound angry. I'd say she was regular."

"How long was he there?"

"About an hour, I guess," Rosa said. "Then Mrs. Tillett said to me, 'Rosa, how would you like to work for Rudy and Monica?' So I said 'No, Mrs. Tillett, I want to work for *you.*' I started to cry, like she was going to send me away." Rosa smiled, embarrassed at herself. "But no, she said Rudy and Monica were going to have the house after she died." Gail gasped, but Rosa went on. "So I said, 'Mrs. Tillett, I guess this means you have to write another will.'"

"And did she?" Eric asked.

"She called up her attorney about it."

"Alan Weissman," Gail said, her hopes plummeting.

Rosa nodded. "She made an appointment for that Friday, but she canceled it, I guess because she had so much to do, getting ready for her vacation. She had the airline tickets and everything, but she never got to go."

Gail asked, "Did you hear Mrs. Tillett mention Rudy when Irving Adler came to visit on Monday?"

"No."

"How about phone calls? Did Mrs. Tillett call anyone that week?"

"Of course, but she always does. I mean, she used to."

"Did she go out to meet anyone?"

Rosa's eyes searched the ceiling. "She did see an attorney."

"Who? Alan Weissman?"

"No." She leaned forward to pick up Gail's business card, which she had earlier put down on the glass-topped coffee table. She looked at it. "Black."

"Lawrence Black?" Gail and Eric said in unison.

"Mrs. Tillett left a card like this one in the kitchen after she used the phone, but it had his name on it. I asked her if she wanted it or should I throw it away. She called him Larry."

"When was this?" Eric asked.

"Wednesday morning. Right after she hung up she told me what to make for the bridge party that night, that's how I remember." Rosa smiled at Gail. "Your mother was at the party."

Eric asked, "Did she talk to Larry Black about her will?"

"I don't know."

"You must remember something about the conversation."

"She said she had to see him, I remember that. She finished her breakfast, she went upstairs to get dressed, then she left."

"How did she sound?" Gail asked. "What was her tone of voice when she was talking to Larry Black?"

"Like she was going to have her way. Mrs. Tillett usually sounded like that, though. She said, 'We're going to talk about this *now.*'"

"So she went to his office?"

"No. They were going to meet for coffee, I don't know where."

Gail asked, "When she got back, what kind of mood was she in? Did she say anything?"

"I wasn't there. I left at noon, like I usually do on Wednesdays. Like I did. That was the last time I ever saw her. Except the next day. When she was dead." The last word came out as a whisper.

Gail reached over and took her hand. "Is there anything else you can tell us?" Rosa shook her head.

"All right." Gail exchanged a look with Eric, then collected her purse. "You've been very helpful, Mrs. Portales." Eric stood up and moved a little toward the door, expecting Gail to follow. But she continued to sit there on the sofa. She asked, "You said Mrs. Tillett was going on vacation?"

"Yes."

Irene had mentioned something about that. How Althea Tillett would take vacations by herself. How adventurous, how brave, Irene had said, admiring her friend.

Gail asked, "Where was she going?"

"Greece. Well, first she was going to fly to Athens, then go to Mykonos. I think. Yes."

"Did Mrs. Tillett travel frequently?"

"Oh, sure. She'd go somewhere every year, just about. Rome, Nice, London. Last year she went to Ibiza. That's an island near Spain. She went to Amsterdam once, but didn't like it. She said it was too dirty. She liked Greece best. The islands."

"And she went alone?"

Rosa's cheeks colored a little, and her eyes cut over to Eric, who was still standing by the door, jingling some change in his trousers pocket. She whispered, "She would meet people there. You know. Men. Not old ones either."

"Really."

"Oh, yes. She would come back looking so happy. She always brought me something. A blouse or sandals or some wine." Rosa smiled. "A woman her age."

Gail said, "Do you know who her travel agent was?"

"For *you?*"

"No. I was just wondering. Did she use Gateway Travel?"

"Well . . . I remember a picture of a gate on the folder the tickets came in."

Gail nodded slowly. "Who did she speak to over there? Anyone in particular? Carla?"

Rosa Portales went blank again. "I don't know."

At the door, Gail said, "Mrs. Portales, if Miami Beach Detective Gary Davis comes by, I'd appreciate your not telling him I was here."

"All right."

"One more thing. A lawyer named Anthony Quintana will call you."

"And you weren't here."

"No. He knows I came. He's Patrick's other

attorney. He's also a friend of mine, and a good man. You can talk to him."

"All right." Rosa smiled. "I'm glad I got to meet you. Your mother said she had a daughter who's an attorney. She's very proud."

The elevator rose toward the fourteenth floor of the Hartwell Building. Gail impatiently watched the numbers counting up, and punched the "close door" button every time someone got off. It was lunchtime, and the elevator stopped at nearly every floor.

Eric stepped back a little to let a delivery boy get on with his cardboard box of sandwiches and drinks, a bill from the deli downstairs clipped to one of the bags.

He whispered to Gail, "I think Adler was sorry he'd talked Althea out of whatever it was she wanted to do. He probably blamed himself when she died. Maybe he even thought her murder was his fault."

The delivery boy looked around. Gail made a quick shake of her head in Eric's direction.

Between the tenth and eleventh floors they were alone. Gail said, "You've been speculating all the way from Hialeah. You don't have to. I'm going to see Larry Black."

Larry could be at lunch. Usually he had lunch at the Hartwell Club. She would track him down, wherever he was, take him into a room. *Larry, you nearly passed out when I told you Althea had been murdered. Now I know why. She was involved in something, Larry. What was it? Easton? You're going to answer me this time.*

Eric said, "Gail—" When the elevator stopped again, three women got on, laughing about getting stuck on the Metromover. He shifted closer. "Let me go with you."

"I'll handle it."

He leaned down to whisper in her ear. "Come on. You're always cutting me out. I thought we were partners on this . . . . What if he gets violent?"

She looked up at him. "Larry?"

"Yeah. He won't take me on." A fierceness hardened his boyish features, and Gail imagined for a moment what Eric had been like in cleats and shoulder pads and a helmet.

When the women got off she said, "You can't think Larry Black murdered Althea Tillett."

"But if they argued—"

"No. Larry must have known what she and Irving talked about, that's all."

At fourteen the elevator door opened and they got off, Gail's heels tapping quickly toward the lobby.

Eric held open the door to the inner offices. He said, "Adler and Mrs. Tillett were talking about the Easton Trust. They had to be. That's why Larry wouldn't tell you who was in it. And remember who came to see her the week before. Rudy Tillett. T is for Tillett, Gail. The acronym?"

"I thought of that."

"Maybe Rudy did it. Killed her, then forged the will."

"I thought of that, too."

They made a turn, and Gail was suddenly

410

aware, like thunder catching up with a lightning flash, of what she had sensed from the moment they had entered the lobby. The place was quiet as a tomb. No clacking keyboards, no buzzing conversations. At the end of the hall, three attorneys and a group of secretaries had gathered.

"What's going on?" Eric asked.

Miriam spotted Gail and ran to her.

"Miriam! What is it? What happened?"

Her words came out in a breathless rush. "Larry Black. They found him. He's been at Jackson Memorial for a whole day, and they didn't know who he was."

Gail grabbed her shoulders. "Is he all right?"

Miriam shook her head and burst into tears.

chapter twenty-six

Three teenagers truant from school had found Larry Black on Monday, shortly after noon, in a vacant lot west of the airport, left behind a pile of trash dumped weeks or months ago. He had been struck more than a dozen times with something heavy and metallic that had broken an arm and some ribs, cracked his skull, and made his face unrecognizable. His wallet, watch, and wedding ring were gone. At the hospital Larry was one more unidentified male crime victim, but his expensive clothing said that someone would be looking for him. Dee-Dee Black

411

reported him missing early Tuesday morning, and they quickly made the connection.

Gail got to the lobby of Jackson Memorial at one-thirty and met Paul Robineau coming out. He had insisted on speaking to Larry's doctor, who had nothing new to say. Internal bleeding, possible brain damage. He had not been optimistic.

Outside intensive care Gail said hello to some of Larry's friends and family. No one was allowed in, except for Dee-Dee. Gail heard a man and woman whisper about Larry in the past tense.

Using a pay phone, she dialed Clarinda Campbell's number for some advice on what to tell Karen. It had to be handled just right. Karen hadn't known Irving Adler, but she knew Larry. Clarinda's answering machine came on. Gail left a message then called home and told Phyllis what had happened, and please not to let Karen watch the news on TV. Phyllis said she would say a prayer for Mr. Black.

After she hung up, Gail kept her hand on the telephone, wishing she could speak to Anthony. Wishing this morning at the courthouse had not happened.

There was nothing to do but go back to the office. The pill Eric had given her earlier was wearing off. Now she was going on nerves. If she went home and pulled the blinds and lay in bed, sleep would still not come.

Down the corridor Gail noticed a thin, auburn-haired woman walking an elderly man to the elevator. In a minute she would come this way, and the people in the waiting area would cluster around her. Gail left the pay phone and hurried toward the elevator, where the doors were just closing.

Dee-Dee's hair was tied back, and her eyes were swollen, her face splotched. Gail came up beside her and gently took her arm. "Dee-Dee, I'm so sorry. Please, is there anything I can do?"

A wan smile. "Nothing but wait. Our boy is doing better, though. He opened his eyes for a few seconds—the one that isn't bandaged. I think he even knew me. God, he looks like hell."

"How are Trisha and Mandy?"

"A mess. They're with my sister. I don't want them to see him this way, but if—if something happens to him before . . ."

Gail hugged her.

They clung for a moment, then Dee-Dee looked over Gail's shoulder toward the people gathered at the end of the hall. "I should go say hello. They're so dear, waiting like this."

They walked slowly together. Gail asked if the police had found out what had happened.

Dee-Dee said, "Larry left the house about a quarter to eight. His secretary called about eleven to ask if he was coming in. I didn't know what to tell her, maybe he'd gone to see clients. I ran some errands in the afternoon. Larry never came home. I waited till nearly midnight, then called the police. They wouldn't even take a report until this morning." She spoke as if she had recited these events a dozen times already. "Those boys found him just in time. Somebody robbed him and left him there to die."

She stopped walking and ducked behind a

head-high laundry cart, out of the visitors' line of sight. "Gail, they found things in his pockets." Her eyes were shiny with tears. "Cocaine in a little plastic bag. And a pack of condoms. One was gone."

"I don't believe that. Not Larry."

"You can imagine what they think. Where he had been, what he was doing!" Her voice was tight.

"Don't. Don't even think about that now." Gail leaned against the wall beside her, their shoulders pressed together. "Dee-Dee, you know the case I'm doing on Althea Tillett's estate?" When she nodded, Gail said, "The housekeeper told me this morning that Althea went to see Larry the day she died. Did he tell you about this?"

Dee-Dee shook her head. "Oh, Gail. I can't think."

"I wouldn't ask you now, but it might be important."

"How? Does it relate to what happened to Larry?" Her eyes shifted back and forth, meeting Gail's.

"It might. I don't know yet."

Dee-Dee reached around the edge of the laundry cart and stole a washcloth to blow her nose on. She laughed. "What was the question?"

"What Althea and Larry talked about."

"I didn't even know he saw her. He didn't mention it to me."

A nurse walked by, her shoes squeaking on the polished floor. "Something's been going on with

414

him lately," Gail said. "Ever since the firm took the Norris case, he's been jumpy as hell."

"I've noticed. It isn't like him."

"Has Larry ever talked to you about the Easton Charitable Trust?"

"Not particularly. Larry's into so many clubs and organizations."

"He's a member of the Easton Trust? He said he wasn't."

Dee-Dee smiled tiredly. "They're so silly. He says they don't like people begging them for handouts, so they keep it quiet."

"Althea Tillett was a member, wasn't she?"

"Yes. Maybe that's what they talked about," said Dee- Dee. "I don't know what else it could have been. Not church business. Althea rarely attended. And she wasn't a client of his."

Gail asked, "Who else is in it? Do you know?"

"Some of them. Howard Odell runs it. And Sanford Ehringer—have you ever met him?"

"I've met him. He's the chairman."

"Isn't he a character? Who else? Judge Joe Herran. And Kevin McCarr with the Downtown Development Council. He's one of Larry's clients. And Leland Spencer with First Miami Bank. And that fat woman with the opera. God, what's her name?"

"Jessica Simms," Gail said. "What about Irving Adler?"

"Yes, him too," Dee-Dee said.

"How did Larry become a member?"

"My dad got him interested. Dad died a few years ago."

"What was his name?"

"Herbert Nash."

"And your grandfather?" When Dee-Dee looked at her curiously, Gail said, "Was he one of the original founders in 1937?"

Dee-Dee said, "I never heard that, but . . . My grandfather, Walton Nash, was a friend of Samuel Ehringer's, Sanford's father." She pushed a stray lock of hair behind one ear. "Althea Tillett's husband R.W. was in it, and his father Wade Tillett before him. R.W. was related by marriage to Judge Herran. They all seem to know each other."

"How many are there?"

"Now? The board has about a dozen members, I think, but they rotate. Maybe twenty in all. I don't know. Larry and I haven't talked much about it. He never goes to meetings. In fact, there aren't many meetings anymore. I thought that Easton was just about extinct." Dee-Dee wiped her nose, then took a heavy breath as if she had just climbed a flight of stairs. "The Easton Trust used to be a power in Miami, years ago. I think some of them pretend it still is. Hardly anybody donates big money anymore, only the diehards."

"Like Althea."

"Yes. Like Althea." Her voice was dull with exhaustion. "Gail, what is this about?"

Gail shook her head. "Nothing. Come on, you've got some people who want to see you." She said she would get in touch in a day or so, when Larry was out of danger. They walked the rest of the way down the hall, then Dee-Dee was surrounded by friends waiting there to hear good news.

Going back toward the elevator Gail passed the wide door to intensive care and let her fingers trail across it. If only she had made Larry tell her what was going on. She had seen his anxiety and had let it go, minding her manners. She should have shaken him by the lapels. *Damn it, what is the matter with you? I'm your friend. Tell me.*

Her stomach floated as the elevator dropped to the ground floor. He had not told her about his visit to Althea Tillett. He had lied to her about the Easton Trust. When she had told him Althea had been murdered, he'd been more than upset; he'd been panicked.

Gail's mind began to churn, a whirl of confusing connections and odd facts. The simple truth could be that Larry had taken a wrong turn in his Mercedes, then had been dragged off by some of Miami's ubiquitous street scum. But the cocaine and the condoms in his pocket? Perhaps Larry's life at home was not the warm ideal she had imagined. He was a philandering coke addict, and Dee-Dee was a sweet, credulous fool.

When the automatic doors flung themselves open outside the lobby, the sun was lost among the mottled clouds, which seemed ready to drop from the sky like stones. At the curb Gail looked automatically to her left, then stopped dead in her tracks.

A white Lincoln limousine had pulled up in a no-parking zone across the street, and a uniformed chauffeur stood by the open back door. Gail saw a voluminous bosom, a tiny black shoe, an ankle in white hose. A plump arm extended a vase of flowers and the chauffeur took

417

it, then closed the door and walked toward the hospital.

Gail went over and tapped on the window. Jessica Simms slowly appeared as the tinted glass slid down. She wore a black straw hat, a polka-dotted dress, and a string of pearls.

Her mouth in its nest of chins and cheeks made a smile. "Gail. How nice to see you."

"I'm sure. Are the flowers for Larry Black, by any chance?"

"Why, yes. Have you been to see him?"

"He's still in intensive care." Gail planted her hands on the window opening and leaned closer. The engine was running and the air conditioner was on. "I suppose you've heard about Irving Adler, too."

"Yes. I'm just on my way to visit the family." There was another flower arrangement on the seat beside her. "You know, it was a blessing he went so quickly and didn't suffer. My husband took weeks."

Gail spoke in measured tones. "Mrs. Simms, listen carefully to what I'm going to say. Before he died, Irving Adler confessed that you and he helped forge Althea Tillett's will."

The mouth sagged open. "He never—"

"You did it. If you lie to me, I'll fry you on the witness stand. I'll have you thrown in jail for commission of a felony."

"But it isn't true! I wouldn't—"

"Shut up! If you had told the truth when I asked you before, Larry might not be up there dying," Gail said.

"Larry was beaten by thugs! How could you dare to say I was responsible!"

Gail continued to look at her for a moment. "How did you get into the Easton Trust, through your late husband?"

"Yes, what of it?" Jessica Simms was breathing heavily; her dimpled hand, heavy with diamonds, twisted the strand of pearls.

"Who in the family was a member before him?"

"His elder cousin Fauntroy Simms. Why?"

"Anyone before Fauntroy?"

Jessica shook her head. Tears were making two shiny trails down her cheeks. "Why are you asking me these things?"

"How about Rudy and Monica Tillett? They're in Easton too, aren't they? Answer me, Mrs. Simms."

"Yes. Now leave me alone."

"Who asked you to sign the will? Rudy Tillett? Howard Odell?"

She fumbled for the window button. "Please leave."

"Why did you do it? For Althea? Or for the money in the trust?" The dark glass began to rise, and Gail had to move her hands.

Jessica Simms's voice quavered. "Go away, go away."

After half an hour of dead ends and doublebacks, Gail finally found the narrow driveway leading to Sanford Ehringer's house. It was not far from the hospital, only across the river and up a bit. She drove through the trees until she could see the metal gate. Gray light leaked in

419

through the canopy of leaves, revealing silvery razor wire looped along the top of the wall on either side. There was a camera on one of the columns, and under the camera, an intercom. She got out, walked to the gate, and pressed a button by the speaker. No answer. She leaned on it, not letting up.

Finally a male voice came through. "Who is it? What do you want?" There was a slight African-American intonation.

She stepped back and stared up into the camera. "Russell, is that you? This is Gail Connor. I want to talk to Sanford Ehringer."

"Mr. Ehringer's not available, Ms. Connor."

Gail paused, then said, "Tell him I know who Easton is. I've solved the acronym."

"The what?"

She exhaled. "Acronym. A-c-r-o-"

"I can spell it." There was a silence. "I'll see if he's in."

Fifteen minutes later, on the point of trying the buzzer again, Gail heard the growl of an engine. It died. A car door slammed. Then the gate slid into the wall on oiled tracks. Ehringer's driver Russell stood on the other side, dressed in his black suit. He walked over to glance inside her car, then told her to follow the Range Rover to the house.

The same elderly butler led Gail through the six-sided living room, then past the stairs with their dark, carved balusters. Floor lamps beside the long sofas pressed their yellowish light into the corners of the room. The scent of orchids drifted through the open windows.

The old man knocked lightly at the door of Sanford Ehringer's study, let her in, then closed it behind her. Ehringer's wheelchair was drawn up to his desk, and his secretary, Thomas Quinn, stood beside him, notebook in hand. The two men glanced at Gail, then Ehringer finished dictating a letter about elections in Singapore, Quinn writing in shorthand. Ehringer's computer screen was forming geometric shapes of purple and red that would collapse upon themselves, then spin into new configurations. Ehringer wore glasses today, a turtleneck sweater, and a pair of soft red leather slippers.

Thomas Quinn bowed slightly to Gail on his way out. "Good afternoon, Ms. Connor. Delightful to see you again."

Ehringer laid his glasses on the desk. "Sit down, Gail. Russell says you wish to see me. You have found our mysterious Mr. Easton. I must say, I am surprised at your tenacity."

She was pacing. "Have you heard about Larry Black?"

Ehringer swung his chair around. "Yes. Damn shame."

"More than a shame, I should think," Gail said stiffly. "He may not survive."

Ehringer followed her with his eyes, nearly lost under his heavy black brows. "I suspected you had other reasons for coming than to offer a solution to my puzzle."

"I have a puzzle for you," she said. "Two days before Althea Tillett's death, Irving Adler comes to see her. They argue. The morning before she dies, she meets Larry Black. All three of them

421

belong to the Easton Charitable Trust. Then Althea is found dead—murdered. Her will leaves the residuary of her estate—millions of dollars— to Easton. Then the woman who notarized the fake will dies too, supposedly in an accidental fall from her balcony. Then Irving dies of a heart attack. And now someone tries to kill Larry Black. So I ask you, Mr. Ehringer, are these random events? Or is there a pattern?"

"This could be a religious inquiry, could it not? A matter of teleology: Is there a pattern to the universe, or are we only subject to its whims—"

"Mr. Ehringer, answer the question."

His yellow teeth showed behind thin lips. "You assume that *I* have special knowledge of these events?"

"I assume one of them—Larry, Althea, or Irving—must have spoken to you. Or that you know what it was they talked about. I wager that very little goes on at Easton that you don't know about."

"How flattering," he said.

Gail studied him. His black eyes, set in heavy pouches, gave up nothing. The loose skin of his jowls seemed as pale and cool as the throat flap of a lizard. She said, "What is going on?"

Noiselessly his chair glided across the room to where she stood by the bookcase with its heavy volumes. He smiled at her. "What's the acronym? Tell me that first."

She took a breath, then began, "The Easton Charitable Trust. The name represents the six founding members. Your father Samuel was the E. His attorney Jacob Adler, the A. S is for

422

Fauntroy Simms. T is for your father's business associate Wade Tillett. Howard Odell's grandfather George was the O. The N is for Samuel's friend Walton Nash, Dee-Dee Black's grandfather. Those six died off, but others—family and friends—have taken their place. I can't name them all, but they're a secretive, closely knit group from the remnants of old Miami society."

"By God, that's impressive!" Ehringer said, hitting the arms of his wheelchair with his open hands. "You've got it almost right."

She clamped her teeth on a retort, then said, "I believe there is more to Easton than that. I believe that certain members of this group have used the trust for their own purposes, diverting money for investment or to influence local politicians. But donations have dried up lately, and there isn't much Easton real estate left to sell. So they planned to murder Althea Tillett and loot her estate. And they would have, if Patrick Norris hadn't seen the will for what it was—a forgery."

Ehringer was tapping his tented fingers slowly on his chin. "A murderer among us? How very gothic! Have you any evidence?"

A tremor danced its way across her chest, as if she were walking into a cellar with only a sputtering candle. She said, "I prefer not to share that information." Which was, she had to admit, half guesswork. She would keep Ehringer guessing as well.

He seemed amused, vastly so. His eyes gleamed. "If I didn't know you for a young woman of intelligence, I would think you had gone around the bend. Who are these conspirators? Tell me that. Irving Adler and Jessica Simms?"

"I think they were lied to. They helped forge the will because they were persuaded that it was what Althea would have wanted. As for others involved . . ." She took a moment. "I'm not sure. However, my mind keeps going to Howard Odell, Rudy Tillett, and Alan Weissman. There may be others. I believe Rudy Tillett knew that Althea had destroyed her will, because he spoke to her a week before she died. Without a will, his step-cousin Patrick would inherit everything. Perhaps he mentioned this to Howard Odell, and they found someone who could be paid to . . . carry out their intentions. Then after it was done—or perhaps before, I don't know—they persuaded Alan Weissman to help them. Weissman and Odell are acquainted, and Weissman needed the money. They found a notary—"

Gail stopped speaking. It had not been Weissman who had found the notary, but Lauren Sontag. Or so Lauren had said.

She turned to Ehringer. "You have to help me. I want you to tell me about these people, what they were doing. Give me something to go on. Larry Black must have found out about it, based on what Althea told him that day she died. What was it? You're a part of Easton. You have to help me find out what happened. If Larry dies—"

"He won't!" Ehringer held up a hand. "My own doctor has spoken to the chief of staff at Jackson Memorial. Larry's chances are excellent."

"Why don't I feel comforted by that?" Gail

said tightly. "Didn't Althea talk to you before she died? She would have, if she was worried enough to call Larry Black. Did you speak to her?"

Now both Ehringer's hands were raised. "Good God, woman! Conspiracies among the members of the Easton Trust? Howard Odell plotting murder? *Howard?* I've known the man since he was born. I know his family. It is completely impossible. I do not misjudge character, I assure you."

"Did Althea call you?" Gail insisted.

Ehringer frowned at her. "I was in New York."

"She tried to call you, didn't she? But you returned too late." Ehringer abruptly grabbed his wheels and turned them in opposite directions, whirling himself around. Gail followed. "Or maybe you didn't care to return her call."

He shook a trembling finger at her. "If Althea had needed me, and I had been in the Kalahari Desert, I would have come to her. Yes, she called me. She left a message, but there was no urgency to it. Do not try to make me feel guilty. I am already . . . so torn—" He hid his eyes with a hand for a moment, then scowled thunderously up at her. "What are you doing here, Ms. Connor? What is your game?"

"None. This is no game."

"Throwing accusations of murder with no proof—"

"I think I know what Althea wanted to tell you. She argued with Irving Adler over whether Easton should get out of the dirty businesses it's been investing in. You told me last time you'd

425

never heard of Seagate or Atlantic Enterprises. That was a lie, wasn't it?"

Gail put both hands on the arms of his wheel-chair and leaned into Sanford Ehringer's stony face. "You know what I'm talking about, don't you?"

"Get to the point," he said.

"I believe that beginning in 1938, when Walton Nash and George Odell formed Biscayne Casinos, the Easton Charitable Trust has derived a portion of its income from such activities as gambling or nightclubs. These businesses pro-duced an excellent return. They were intended to be high class and exclusive, very genteel. But tastes aren't genteel anymore. Now, using one company to shield another, Easton owns adult motels, sex shops, nude bars, and a travel agency where you can arrange vacations of the most exotic sort. As long as the money comes in, nobody wants to admit what's really going on. Their reputations would be ruined! Imagine little Timmy telling the other kids at the country club, 'My daddy owns an XXX movie theater.' So they close their eyes and let Howard Odell handle it."

Through the open French doors, and at the far edge of Ehringer's property, cars on the expressway across the river flashed in the spaces between the tall trees. Rush hour had started, people going home. There was a faint *whoosh* of traffic.

Gail looked back at Ehringer. She said, "Larry Black didn't want our firm to take this case. You tried to pressure me into dropping it, appealing to my ties to your so- called elite. At first I thought you didn't know what was going on, but now I'm convinced you do. I threatened Howard Odell by telling him I would reveal everything to you, and he didn't care."

Sanford Ehringer's shoulders began to shake with silent laughter. "Of course Howard didn't care. I *did* know about these businesses. But you are wrong if you think that the Easton Charitable Trust is involved. It absolutely is not. Most of our members may own shares in certain . . . companies, but Easton owns none of them. Oh, what a thought!"

"This is hardly funny," she said.

"But my dear, to find a young person today who believes such activities are shocking! I am not shocked, far from it. If people wish to be amused, leave them alone. You can't stop them, you can only observe. This darker side of our human natures is bred into the bone. We haven't evolved from it yet, and I doubt we ever shall. Read Freud. Read erotic literature in the original Latin, if you want your eyes opened. Peruse the Marquis de Sade."

Ehringer's chuckles faded into a long sigh. "No, Althea did not suddenly find out about these dirty businesses, as you put it, and fly into a rage. She'd known for years."

Now his face was as serene as a Buddha. "My advice to you, Gail, is that you look in simpler places for the answers to your puzzles. Yesterday my secretary, Mr. Quinn, spoke personally to the Dade County Medical Examiner, at my request. Irving Adler died of a heart attack, not poison or voodoo. And as for Larry Black—" His heavy head moved slowly back and forth. "Under the sunshine and frolic, my dear, this is dangerous city."

"What about Althea?" Gail asked sharply. "Give me another easy answer. What happened to her?"

The light from the desk lamp behind him formed a crescent on his hairless head. "Haven't you forgotten someone on your list of suspects? Your client? The man with a hidden streak of violence, the man with a key to Althea's house? Yes, I keep my eye on that case. The police will establish the truth sooner or later. If Althea told Rudy she had destroyed her will, why not tell her nephew? He didn't kill her for a quarter of a million dollars, but for twenty-five!"

Ehringer rolled across his study to the door. "Forgive me if we cut this meeting short. I have heard enough nonsense for a month. You have been duped. Patrick Norris! Damn his perfidious soul."

"He didn't kill her," Gail said.

The chair stopped so quickly the wheels skidded on the floor. He turned it around. "How can you be sure? You haven't seen the man since you were students together."

Gail was frozen for a moment by his icy stare. "It doesn't matter. I know what he's like." When Ehringer continued to look at her, she said. "I know him. That's all."

"You're such a clever woman. You know him." Sanford Ehringer smiled. "Before you go, Gail, let me enlighten you. The S in Easton. It wasn't Fauntroy Simms. He came in later, after the

Second World War. The S was Strickland—your great-grandfather Benjamin."

"I don't believe that," Gail said. "My mother would have told me."

He gave an expansive shrug. "Would she? In the short history of this city, the Stricklands walk among the gods. Why, they're right up there with Henry Flagler and Julia Tuttle. How painful to think that one's ancestors belched and farted, like everybody else. Benjamin Strickland was kicked off the board of the Easton Trust in 1942 for indiscretions with the mayor's wife. His son John—your grandpa and my friend—gambled on more than real estate. Rich one day, poor the next. In and out of scrapes with some Italian gentlemen from New York. A dusky mistress in Overtown—well, never mind that."

Gazing across the study at the leather armchair, Ehringer said, "He sat right there, begging me for help. Goodness, this is déjà-vu. You came with him, a little girl, and you played on my carpet while your granddaddy signed a personal note. I lent Johnny half a million dollars. He died of a stroke a month thereafter. I tore up the paper. What could I do? Have your grandma thrown out into the snow?"

Still smiling, Ehringer rolled toward the heavy wooden door. "So, Gail. Meet Mr. Easton. You are not as far removed from him as you may think. Good afternoon."

chapter twenty-seven

After Lauren Sontag's divorce two years ago, she had bought a top-floor condo with a view of Coconut Grove. Gail had been there a few times, so she had no difficulty finding the building. She gave her name to the security guard downstairs, and he phoned up.

Lauren Sontag was in a white satin robe, barefoot. She held on to the door for a second, then smiled. "Well. Look who's here."

"I called your office. They said you were working at home today."

Lauren's blond hair hung straight around her face, and her skin was gray without makeup. "Come in and sit down. Or something."

"You're not feeling well?" Gail asked.

"I'm on a little vacation. Look. Still in my jammies. Can I fix you a drink?" She held up a short, heavy glass, clinking with ice cubes in pale amber liquid.

"No, thanks."

The apartment wrapped around a corner of the building, a curve of terrace outside with a view south and west. The color scheme was ivory and pastel, with a good collection of minimalist paintings on the walls and lots of windows. Now the curtains were closed, and the air was still and heavy, as if the oxygen were running out.

Lauren's high-arched feet sank into the carpet, and the hem of her robe fluttered behind her. "Let me guess. You came to talk about Althea Tillett's will."

"Yes, I did."

"I thought you would, sooner or later." She veered into the tiled kitchen. Dishes were stacked in the sink.

Gail stood by the door. "I don't know if you heard or not, but Larry Black is in the hospital."

The ice dispenser dropped some cubes into Lauren's glass. "Hospital?"

"He was beaten nearly to death yesterday, and robbed. They don't know who did it. It's bad. He'll live . . . at least they say he will."

"Oh, God. Don't tell me that. It's too depressing." A sliver of ice hit the floor. Lauren poured more scotch. "Did I ever meet Larry?"

"At the cocktail party at Hartwell Black last Christmas—"

"I remember. Larry's a nice guy. A little prissy, but he's all right. You and Larry paid a visit to Alan last week. I should have been there to join the fray." She tasted her drink. "He didn't want me there. Alan didn't, I mean."

Lauren snapped off the kitchen light and Gail followed her through the dining area. There was a divider that marked the living room. On the end of it, lit by a tiny spotlight in the ceiling, was the upturned face of a young woman, lifelike in its details. Realistic red roses tumbled from her wild black curls. Her eyes were closed as if in pain or passion, and the lips were slightly parted. The skin seemed to glow.

Lauren gestured with her scotch. "Monica did that."

"Yes. I thought I recognized the style," Gail said. There were words along her cheek, as if the swirling black letters were wayward strands of hair: *I made a garland for her head, and bracelets too, and fragrant zone; She look'd at me as she did love, And made sweet moan.*

"It's very good," Gail said.

"You want it?" Lauren patted the top of the sculpture's head. "It doesn't fit my decor." She crossed the living room and picked up her cigarettes from the coffee table, then reached into a pocket of her robe for her gold lighter. She wore no bra, and her breasts moved under the white satin. "What about the will?" The lighter flamed, then clicked shut.

Gail dropped her purse on the sectional sofa. Beside it lay three pairs of shoes, as if Lauren had stepped out of them on three successive days. "One of the witnesses passed away last night. Irving Adler."

"Alan called me. He said it was on the news this morning."

"I was there," Gail said. "Not when it happened, but just after. My mother and I went to his house. Irving had called her earlier in the day. He told her the will was forged."

Lauren drew in smoke. "What else did he tell her?"

"No details. I saw Jessica Simms a little while ago. She'll break before this gets to trial. And the notary was in New Jersey on August the third, the date you said you got her to sign the will.

432

Lauren, it's all going to come out. I wanted you to know this. You should decide what to do. You and Alan."

Lauren sat on a white leather ottoman and crossed her legs, pulling her robe closed. "Are you feeling sorry, Gail?"

"What?"

"Sorry for what you did in Alan's office. You used me to get to him."

"I am sorry. Truly."

One arm resting languidly across her knee, Lauren smoked her cigarette.

Gail said, "I know how you feel about Alan, but you shouldn't sacrifice yourself for him."

Lauren turned her eyes toward Gail.

Gail said, "Tell him to go to the probate judge before it's too late. Alan knows the judge. They're friends. This can be handled without publicity."

A long moment passed, then Lauren slowly smiled. "You think we're lovers."

"I know he's in love with you."

"Poor Alan."

"And you care for him," Gail said.

"So I should tell him to go to the judge. What a neat way to win your case."

"No. I'm trying to help you. You didn't do anything except find the notary."

Lauren leaned to tap ashes into a coffee cup. "Alan told me she fell off her balcony last week."

"Yes. They say it was an accident. I'm not sure."

"Well, I didn't push her."

"I know that, Lauren. Look. Tell Alan to take responsibility for what he did. He doesn't have to bring you into it. Whoever else was involved—" Gail waited, then said, "It's going to blow up, Lauren. I'm not sure how yet, but it will. Get out if you can."

A long moment passed. Lauren drew on her cigarette. "Is it true, about Irving and Jessica, what they said? Maybe it's a lie. Maybe you're lying to me."

"Oh, God."

"Or maybe you're a real pal after all. Maybe. Trying to save me from"—she circled a hand in the air— "something. Don't worry about the election. I withdrew my name yesterday. I'm off the ballot."

"You didn't have to do that."

"Doesn't matter."

"I'm sorry. I hate this. What do you want, Lauren? I can't drop the case. I was working on a settlement, but I don't see the point of settling anymore. Not when I can prove the will was forged."

A haze of smoke drifted around Lauren's head.

"Can I open a window?" Gail asked. "It's warm in here."

"I'll do it." At the sliding door Lauren fumbled with the lock. A wind came through and lifted the hair at her cheek and pressed the satin robe against her thighs. She stood motionless for a moment, holding back the curtain. "Look, the sun's finally out." She laughed. "Is it nearly sundown already? Or is the sun on the wrong side of the sky?"

Gail pressed her fingertips into her forehead. "Fine. Forget going to the judge. When it comes up for trial, I won't put you on the stand. After I finish with Alan, I won't need you."

Lauren let the curtain fall and the room dimmed. Laughing softly, she walked back to where Gail sat and hugged her around the neck with one arm. "You're sweet. You are."

"And you're drunk, Lauren. I shouldn't be discussing this with you at all."

Lauren rested her cheek for a moment on the top of Gail's head. "I can't do what you want. I can't."

"Don't lie for him!"

She laughed, sinking onto the ottoman again. "You don't see it, do you? Sweet dunce. It wasn't Alan. It was me."

"You."

"He's bleeding already. He's bleeding and he doesn't know I did it to him."

Gail took a long breath. "What did you do?"

"I was very bad." She smiled, pushing a hand back through her hair. "Alan says he remembers Althea coming to the office on August third. She did come in, but for something else. I was there. Alan was asleep with a hangover, as I told you. That was true. I had to wake him up. But there was no will. He thinks he did her will, but he doesn't remember. He thinks he screwed it up because he was drunk. He thinks I've been trying to cover for him."

Gail waited, knowing what was coming next.

"After Althea died—five days after—I rewrote her will on our word processor and Rudy signed Althea's name. Then I took it to Jessica's house.

Irving was there. They signed as witnesses. That's what I did."

"And the notary?"

"Rudy knew Carla Napolitano from some business or other. He paid her five thousand dollars. That was awfully generous of him." Lauren rested her face in her hand, and the cigarette smoke curled upward.

"What are you going to do?" Gail asked.

"I do not fucking know."

"You have to tell Alan."

She nodded.

After a minute, Gail said, "Can I help?"

"No."

They sat without speaking for a while. "How did Jessica and Irving get into this?"

"Rudy talked to them. They knew each other."

"Knew them how?"

"He just knew them. I don't know." Lauren leaned over to crush out her cigarette. "I am sure Patrick Norris is a wonderful guy, if you have him for a client, Gail, but really. To give him all that money. And the Tillett house too. Althea said she would leave it to Rudy and Monica. Rudy told me they talked about it before she died."

Gail said, "Did she tell him she had destroyed her will?"

"No. I wish she had. He and Monica went looking for it, and it wasn't there. God, they were frantic! Then the housekeeper said Althea had burned it. So they had to turn around and tell her 'No, no, we found it, it's here.' She believed them."

Lauren laughed, then picked up her glass and stared down into it. The ice cubes slid. "Rudy told me Althea asked him to make a list of their mother's things. She said he and Monica could take them, then she would change her will and leave them the house. But she never made a new will. Althea." Lauren laughed again. "God save us from clients like Althea."

"And so Rudy did the will for her. With your help."

Lauren leaned forward on crossed arms as though she ached. "It was the right thing, wasn't it? I told myself that. I'm a lawyer. I could make something happen that *should* have happened. Make it come out right. Don't throw stones. You would have lied to save my sorry ass."

Gail asked, "Why did you do it?"

Lauren looked toward the sliver of light that fell in through the curtains at the open door.

"Lauren?"

"Stupidest reason in the world. I was in love."

The ways of love. Very strange. Rudy Tillett was not what he had seemed either. Then Gail said, "Do you think it's possible that Rudy could have killed Althea when he found out she had changed her mind?"

Lauren's eyes fell closed, the short blond lashes and fragile, fatigue-pink lids. "I have considered that. He first mentioned forgery a month before she died. He wanted to know whether she kept her wills in our office, and I said no. And he said what if. What if. It would be so easy. And then— she tripped and fell down her stairs. I didn't think about it, until the police said someone had pushed her." Lauren pressed her forehead into her hands and softly moaned. "I didn't want to ask him. I didn't want to know."

"You were too much in love with him."

The slender hands came down from her face. "Rudy?"

"You said—"

A soft laugh. "No. Not Rudy."

It took Gail a moment. Then she understood.

Still smiling, Lauren leaned to brush a bit of carpet fuzz off her foot. "Oh, you didn't suspect I was one of *those*, did you?"

Gail let out a breath. "No, but—I don't care."

"What a surprise. Even to me. Perfectly normal life—husband, a child, a career. Friends. But it's so empty. It feels so . . . flat. As if you're walking around dead, or in a dream, pretending. And then suddenly, suddenly—you're alive. Everything you touch or taste or hear, it's alive and real and so are you. And you know it could kill you, but you can't stop. Your husband suspected an affair, but never *this*, and he's oh-so-nice about it, and you part so amicably. Then he tells your daughter you are sick, twisted, and she can't bear to be around you anymore.

"My short, happy life." Lauren lifted her eyes. "Have you ever loved so deeply that if that person walked out of your life, you would want to die? Have you?"

Gail said, "I don't know."

"You would know. You would know that, if it happened."

Lauren's lips trembled, and she bit them fiercely. "Monica isn't the type to sneak around,

438

but she did, for me. For a while. Then she got tired of it. Last year we were together again, and it was lovely for a few weeks. Then we split up, then back together. I have never been so wretched. She asked me to do this for her. I did it."

"She used you."

"Maybe. I don't want to think that. Rudy talked her into it. She does whatever he tells her. In the end, I couldn't compete. Not that it matters. So. That's that." She shook another cigarette out of the pack.

"Is it over?" Gail asked.

"It? Is it over?" Lauren smiled. "I am forty-two years old and I am walking around with a gaping, bleeding hole in my chest."

Gail took her hand and held it tightly. "Lauren. People go through these things."

"Yes. It's a fad, in fact. Everybody's doing it now. It's in, it's cool." She pulled her hand away.

"That's not what I meant," Gail said. "People have tragic love affairs. They survive them."

Lauren only looked at her.

"Talk to your daughter. She's old enough to understand. You aren't alone. There are groups, people you could—"

"Gail, why don't you just go?"

After a few seconds Gail stood up, her head ringing with confusion. "Tell me you won't do anything stupid."

"What, kill myself? No. I've already done that."

★   ★   ★

439

Gail stood by her car for a while in the parking lot watching the sun turn into an orange flare in the tangled branches of a black olive tree. She drove a few blocks and parked on the street across from the Mayfair Hotel and went inside and got some quarters at the cashier's desk.

The pay phone was in a quiet, paneled nook off the lobby, with an upholstered chair. Classical music was playing. She called Phyllis and said she would be home soon.

For a minute or so she sat with her eyes closed. She lifted a quarter to the slot and dropped it in, then dialed.

After four rings, Anthony's answering machine came on.

She started to hang up, but didn't, and said, "This is Gail. I'd like to talk to you, so . . . please call me."

She hung up.

Then dialed again, waiting through the same message.

"Anthony, it's me. Gail. I guess you know that. Anyway. This morning . . . I'm sure you are monumentally angry. Which I don't blame you for. You probably don't want to talk to me at all. If you were home—I'm glad you're not, in a way, because you can't hang up, can you?"

She took a ragged breath. "I think . . . I was so afraid of losing you that I pushed you away, so it wouldn't hurt as bad when you finally decided to leave anyway. Does that makes sense? I never thought you would stay. But at the same time, I wanted you to. I was waiting for you to

440

rescue me . . . and you didn't. I mean, what about happily-ever-afters?"

Gail laughed a little, turning aside to wipe her fingers under her nose. "It is funny. I never wanted to be weak that way. To be rescued. All that romantic shit. It's the worst sort of lie."

The silver edge of the pay phone was cool under her forehead. "I've been thinking about ~~what~~ what you said this morning, that you—that you love me . . . with all your heart—"

She laughed again, her voice thick. "You know, that was pretty romantic. It was lovely. I've never said anything like that to you, have I? Not really. Not like that." She closed her eyes. "This can't be all. Things don't . . . end like this."

There was a beep, then silence, then a dial tone.

chapter twenty-eight

Paul Robineau invited Gail to the partners' dining room for lunch the next day. He wanted to know what was up with the Norris case, now that Irving Adler, a witness to the will, had died of a heart attack.

There were a dozen or so Hartwell Black lawyers there, plus their guests, doing the bump and grind of schmoozing and deal-making. Forrest Putney, filling his pipe, presided over a table for eight by the windows. Maxine Canady,

441

tax genius, resplendent in a cherry red suit, was listening to Cy Mackey tell a joke to a director of First Union Bank. The egos in the room gave off a kind of erotic perfume, like musk in a locker room at halftime, the players bleeding a little but ready to go out and slam somebody into the ground at the whistle.

At a table in one of the far corners, Gail talked and Robineau ate his veal chop and looked at the comings and goings with a neutral stare. He could be pleased or pissed, it would be hard to say from a distance. Up close, Gail thought he might swoon over what she was telling him—Lauren Sontag printing out the fake will at Weissman's office, Rudy signing Althea's name, Jessica and Irving adding theirs as witnesses, five grand paid to the notary.

Gail thought Robineau must already have computed the attorneys' fees: ten percent on twenty-eight million dollars, plus costs . . . .

He picked up his iced tea glass without looking at it. "You're certain Alan Weissman had nothing to do with the forgery?"

"Only in trying to protect Lauren Sontag."

He tipped back his glass and took a swallow, then wiped a napkin across his mouth. "I still don't understand her motivation."

"She wasn't specific," Gail said carefully. "I was lucky to get what I did."

"Will she be prosecuted?"

"I doubt it. If the State Attorney's Office doesn't ask, I won't tell them. Lauren dropped out of the judge's race. That's enough damage."

"Unreal," he said.

442

"I'm going to let it sit over the weekend to see what Lauren might do on her own. Then we'll decide what the next step is."

Robineau gave her a quizzical glance. "What do you mean, next step? Contact Ted Mercer. He's got the probate now. Tell him it's over. No discount-rate settlement, no trial. He hears this, he's going to shit in his drawers. He's ours."

Gail shook her head. "Let's take it slow, Paul. Lauren Sontag hasn't given a statement. As far as I know, I'm the only one she's told. She could change her mind."

"Is it likely?"

She took some time answering. "Probably not."

"Okay, then. You handle it, but for God's sake, don't let her backslide." Robineau rattled the ice in his glass, took a swallow, then asked, "What's the deal in probate? When the will is tossed out, is Ehringer out as personal representative?"

"Right. The judge would have to appoint somebody else."

"Patrick Norris. He's the only heir." Robineau smiled, no doubt joyous about the prospect of snatching the probate out of Ted Mercer's office. Mercer had been a real bastard in the settlement conference two days ago with Howard Odell and Ehringer's Palm Beach counsel.

Gail said, "The judge won't let Patrick do an estate this size. He'd appoint one of his friends first. His campaign manager does probate."

Robineau snorted, a soundless laugh. "What about Patrick beating up Rudy Tillett? Will it affect us?"

"I doubt it. He has a criminal lawyer who's taking care of that. Anthony Quintana."

"That's your friend Quintana, correct?"

Gail nodded. "I imagine Anthony will speak to Rudy's attorney, whoever that is, and tell him that if Rudy declines to prosecute, we won't mention the forgery to the police."

"From what you've told me, Rudy Tillett might have done more than forge Althea's will."

"Possibly."

"Who else could have killed her? Any theories?"

Gail had a few. Maybe Howard Odell and Rudy had conspired, and Lauren knew nothing about it. Or Frankie Delgado had to keep Althea from telling that the businesses had crossed the line from naughty to illegal. Or Sanford Ehringer had sent Russell over. The old man had said he loved Althea, but maybe he was crazier than he appeared.

What worried Gail was Larry Black's part in this. He knew the people involved. Now, lying semiconscious in a hospital, he didn't need anyone speculating about his connection to a murder.

Gail shrugged her shoulders and said to Robineau, "Your guess is as good as mine, who killed Althea Tillett."

The waiter came with a dessert tray. Robineau didn't want any, but said Gail should try the kiwi-and-strawberry tart. The waiter set it down on a doilied plate, a shimmering jewel with a sprig of mint alongside. It was one of Paul Robineau's talents to make you feel like a friend, although the day before he might have smacked you around. Nothing personal. Just part of his job.

She tried the tart. Like cardboard, but nothing had tasted right today. She had gone to bed at nine o'clock last night, awakened long enough to send Karen off on the school bus, then had slept like a stone until nearly ten this morning. Anthony still had not called.

Robineau flexed his shoulders, then asked, "How's your schedule? Busy?"

He was going to give her a case, she could feel it coming. "Yes, but I'm always busy. What do you need?"

"Jack Warner's going up to West Palm Beach next week to talk to Pan-Atlantic Airways. It's a new charter service. He thinks we can get their business. Are you interested?"

"One question. Have you given any thought to my partnership? If I'm a partner, I might want the case. If I'm going to work under someone else, then . . . I don't know."

Robineau cracked a smile. "Given that we haven't put the Norris case to bed, I can't make any assurances. But I don't think there's going to be a problem, do you?"

She shook her head, wishing she were so sure.

"Good. Then let's say Pan-Atlantic is your welcome-aboard present."

"Thank you, Paul."

Partnership. Percentage of the profits, bonuses, car allowance, membership at her choice of country clubs and downtown luncheon clubs, privileges at the firm's condos in Colorado and Key West. It would happen as soon as

Patrick's case was on safe ground. And yet she felt no triumph. She was almost there, and she felt not much of anything.

Robineau's iced tea glass was pushed to one side now and his arms were on the table, heavy fingers interlaced. He wore a steel-gray suit, and his hair was perfectly styled. He spoke softly. "You know, Larry's going to be out for weeks. Months, who knows?"

They had heard this morning that Larry Black would make it. The neurologist wouldn't say much more than that. The police were ready to take a statement, whenever Larry was able. But before that, Gail wanted to speak to him herself. Larry had to see a criminal attorney before the police came in. She would recommend Anthony Quintana. Anthony might not do it as a favor to her, but he would do it for Larry.

"I want you to help reassign his files," Robineau said. "We can't let the clients feel like they've fallen through the cracks. Those who don't already know should be contacted."

"All right." It had to be done.

"Use one of the law clerks. Whatever you need." He shook his head. "Jesus. I thought we were going to attend a funeral. It would have been a loss, Gail, a great loss to this firm. Oh, sure, Larry and I have disagreed now and again, but I'll tell you, something like this . . . it makes you appreciate the man."

His voice was hushed and reverent. He meant it. Gail wouldn't wager on how long he would mean it once Larry came back.

446

She said, "Paul, there's a matter I have to bring up. Eric Ramsay. He says you let him go."

"That's correct."

"He was working with me on the Norris case," Gail said. "I'd have appreciated your asking me about it. I could still use him, especially if I'm going to be picking up some of Larry's cases."

Robineau looked out over the dining room, smiling, not believing he was hearing this. "Here's a point of protocol, Ms. Connor. Don't act like a partner until you are one."

"You should have talked to me and you know it."

"Ramsay's work at this firm was substandard. He has no place here. What's wrong, are you feeling sorry for him?"

"Come on, Paul. At least until he finds another job."

Paul Robineau gave her a neutral stare.

She waited. "Well?"

In her office, Gail checked her desk for phone messages Miriam might have left before going to lunch. Nothing. For an instant she felt a nudge of anger. After pouring her heart out on Anthony's answering machine, it was rude of him not to reply.

She sat down and began to review some documents, making a few corrections on drafts. She paused with her forehead on her fist. Maybe he had arrived home too late to call her back, or hadn't checked his messages. Or he'd been shot dead by a client.

She crossed the hall to look on Miriam's desk

and found three pink slips, messages from opposing attorneys on matters Gail should have attended to last week.

Possibly he was so distraught from their fight that he'd gotten drunk on Havana Club and didn't hear the telephone. Or he was glad their affair had ended and would never call.

Gail tapped out a message on Miriam's computer. *Send flowers to Larry Black's house for the girls. Something cheerful, with balloons. With love from Gail and Karen.*

She added a postscript. *Have gone upstairs to Eric's office.*

Eric Ramsay was dropping things into a cardboard box on his desk—a calculator, a Rolodex, papers with their edges every which way. He turned around to toss his miniature pool table into the trash can. The little cue and balls rattled to the bottom.

He noticed Gail. "Hello there, boss."

"Eric, what are you doing?"

"I am preparing for my imminent departure."

She came in and closed the door. "I spoke to Paul Robineau at lunch. He says you can stay." Eric tossed a stack of *Forbes* into his trash basket. "You'll be working full-time for me. I'm going to get my partnership, barring disaster on Patrick's case."

"Congratulations. I'm sure you'll be very happy here."

"And where are you going?" she asked.

He looked through some folders, putting them one by one into a banker's box on the floor. "Oh . . . I've always wanted to see Wyoming. I could become a forest ranger. Or a ski bum—got to learn to ski first, I guess." He laughed.

"This is a joke, right? Go to Wyoming in late October, without a job—"

"Want to come along?" Eric grinned at her. "Yeah, you do. Think of it. *Good-bye, all you suckers, have a happy heart attack!* I'm going to live in a cabin, go fishing, get drunk, work when I feel like it—"

"Eric. You can't just walk out."

"Why, did they lock the doors?" He sat on his heels to go through a bottom drawer of the credenza. His expensive dress shirt strained across his shoulders.

"You've got projects you're working on. You have clients." She gestured toward the case files in the box. "What about these?"

"Let Robineau handle them. Did you ever notice how clean that man's desk is?"

Gail shoved the credenza drawer shut with her foot. "And never mind the sister you're sending to college back home," she said. "Or was that a lie?"

Eric looked up at her, pale green eyes. "No, I have a sister." Then he slumped a little. "I wanted to find out if I could be a trial attorney. I can't. I'm no good at litigation and I hate tax."

"So you're running away to Wyoming," Gail said.

"No. You're missing the point," he said, standing up. His collar was open, his tie askew. "I'm not running away. I'm running to. You want to bust your buns for these people? Go for it." He carried the box to the door and set it down.

Gail watched him come back and toss more folders into another box. "I used to think it was important to bust my buns for Paul Robineau or Jack Warner or the others," she said. "Bill the hours. Come in early, leave late, show my face on Saturdays. But you're right. They don't matter. What matters to me is my clients. Doing my job. Look, I don't usually ask for help, but I'm asking you. I need some help with Patrick's case."

"Why? It's going to settle, isn't it?"

"Maybe. Last night Lauren Sontag admitted she helped Rudy Tillett forge the will."

Eric glanced at her. "No shit. What about Weissman?"

"He was drunk and didn't know what was going on. She took advantage of him to help Rudy and Monica. As we thought, Jessica Simms and Irving Adler went along with it for Althea's sake."

"Damn. Why'd Lauren do it? Money?"

"Something like that," Gail said.

He dropped the second box by the door. "So what's the problem? You've won."

"Maybe not," Gail said. "The judge will know that Patrick is under investigation for Althea Tillett's murder. Is he likely to throw out the will? No. He says to himself, 'If I do that, and Patrick Norris is guilty, then the State of Florida gets the money, everybody will be mad at me, and I won't get reelected.' But say he does declare the will invalid. He still won't release the money, not as long as Patrick is a murder suspect, because a murderer can't inherit from his victim. We could be tied up for a long time. You think the beneficiaries won't figure this out? This is millions of dollars. Sanford Ehringer won't give up easily. He believes Patrick is guilty and he's going to turn on the pressure."

Eric leaned on the edge of his desk, arms crossed. He shoved a box aside with one foot. "What would he do? Pay witnesses to say they saw Patrick hanging around outside Althea Tillett's house?"

"Maybe not go that far, but he could stir up the police and the State Attorney's Office to make an arrest. Or use the media to create bad publicity. I don't want Patrick to go through that. We might have to pay the beneficiaries so they'll leave us alone."

She flicked some dead leaves off the dry fern in the window. "I saw Sanford Ehringer yesterday. He's taking it personally that I haven't dropped the case."

"Why? Because he was buddies with your grandfather?"

"No loyalty to my class," said Gail. "I'm a traitor."

"He could mess you up."

"I don't think he will." She smiled tiredly. "I'm Johnny Strickland's granddaughter. But he'll nail Patrick if he can. What I want to do is give the police someone else to think about besides Patrick."

"Such as who?"

Gail said. "I don't know exactly. I have some theories."

Eric played with the end of his tie, then asked. "What do you want me to do?"

"Be my bodyguard?" She gestured toward the

boxes he had stacked. "Along with finishing out your cases, or at least turning them over to someone in a more orderly—"

"Wait, wait." He held up a hand. "What do you mean, bodyguard?"

"I didn't tell you this before, but when I was in Frankie Delgado's office, he slammed me into a door. I still have the bruise."

"Shit," Eric muttered, and pushed his sandy hair off his forehead. "I don't think we ought to get into a confrontation—"

"No." She laughed a little. "Just . . . be there. If I want to talk to Rudy Tillett, for instance. Or ask Frankie some more questions."

After a few seconds, Eric went over and picked up the boxes he had stacked, then dropped them on his desk. He looked around at Gail. "One thing. Keep Robineau off my back." Then he gave her a wry smile. "I'm still going to Wyoming after we wrap this case up."

chapter twenty-nine

Gail dropped her purse and briefcase on the kitchen table and pushed open the back door. Phyllis Farrington was spraying off the patio with the garden hose, and a rainbow of mist hung in the air. The sun slanted across the backyard, saturating the treetops with gold. She saw Gail and nodded.

"Did anyone call?"

"The plumber." Phyllis flipped the hose over a lawn chair. "Said you got a leak in that back bathroom, might have to tear out the wall to get to it."

"Wonderful."

Gail started to go inside, then said, "How's Karen?"

"Bus dropped her off and she went straight to her room." Phyllis aimed the nozzle out of the way so she could pick up a big yellow leaf that had fallen from the umbrella tree. "I tried to talk to her. She's got it in her mind to lie on her bed with the lights out, feeling sorry for herself."

"Phyllis, really. It was awful for her, what happened at Mr. Adler's house, then to hear about Larry Black."

"Well. You go take a look at her, then." Phyllis turned off the spigot and looped the hose into circles as easily as a cowboy with a rope. The red-and-green striped crotons bordering the patio dripped into the wet earth.

Gail hesitated at the door. "If anyone calls, please say I'm busy for a minute, but to call back."

Phyllis eyed her from the other end of the patio. "All right."

"Sweetie?" Gail knocked lightly at Karen's door, then pushed it open. She took a minute to look around. The curtains were drawn, and the dinosaur quilt was tied to the rod with shoelaces. A navy blue pillowcase was draped over the desk lamp.

Karen lay with her arms at her sides. Her eyes opened and moved toward Gail, who came in and sat on the edge of the bed. Sheets torn off a roll of pink toilet paper were neatly stacked on the nightstand.

"Hi, honey." Gail straightened Karen's bangs. "Larry's a little better today. The doctors say he'll pull through."

"That's good," Karen said softly. Her eyes were fixed on Gail. "You promised to be home early today."

"I am—well, earlier than usual." Gail tugged on her elbow. "Come on. I'll fix you some dinner."

"I'm not hungry." Karen closed her eyes.

"There's some pizza."

"No, thank you. Go work on your files. I'll be all right."

Gail held her hand. Karen's fingernails had rims of gray underneath. "Karen. How long do you plan to lie here, sweetie?"

"I don't know," she mumbled.

"Do you want me to call Clarinda again?" Clarinda Campbell had spent half an hour on the phone with Karen last night, telling her the Lakota Sioux story of the wolf who climbed to heaven, leaving stars wherever he stepped. Gail wasn't sure what it meant, but Karen had seemed comforted.

"Clarinda was nice." Karen's smile was as fleeting as a shadow. "But I don't feel like talking to anyone."

"Not even me?"

She took a long, slow breath. "Mommy?"

"Yes, baby."

"I love you."

"Oh, sweetie. I love you too." Gail leaned over and kissed her cheek. "Can't I bring you anything?"

"No, it's all right." She closed her eyes.

"Some hot chocolate with a marshmallow?"

She sighed. "If you want to. Three marshmallows, please."

When Gail went back into the kitchen, Phyllis was at the counter folding her apron. She turned around. "Well? She going to live?"

"My daughter has decided to have a nervous breakdown at age ten. Fine. Saves me from having one." Gail reached into the cabinet for a mug. "Hot chocolate. Three marshmallows, please." Phyllis chuckled and pulled the bag down from the top shelf of the pantry, untwisting the tie at the top. Gail poured the milk.

The phone rang and Gail's arm jerked. A splash of milk hit the counter.

"Connor residence." Phyllis listened, one eye on Gail. "No, the lady of the house is out and we don't want any, thank you." She hung up. "Brooms for the blind or some such thing."

Gail wiped up the spill. "I need to write you a check before you leave, don't I?"

"Uh-huh. Who you expecting on the phone?"

She made a vague motion with her hand, then tossed the wet paper towel into the trash can under the sink. The mug of milk went into the microwave. Gail pressed the buttons, then crossed the kitchen to get her checkbook. She bumped the table, and her briefcase tipped over. A stack of papers slid out and hit the floor.

Gail pulled her checkbook and a pen out of her purse, sat down, and began to write. "I thought perhaps Anthony might call."

"You-all have a fight?"

"Not really. A disagreement." Gail wrote slowly, carefully. "Actually, Phyllis, we had a fight. You are quite correct. I told him—in effect—that I never wanted to see him again." She laughed and pushed her hair off her forehead. "And then . . . he said the same to me. And I haven't heard from him since. There."

"Why don't you call him?"

Gail capped her pen. "I did. I left a message yesterday on his answering machine at home. He hasn't returned my call, so I assume . . ." She made another vague motion of her hand. The microwave buzzer sounded and she got up to see about the mug of milk.

Phyllis folded the check and tucked it into the front pocket of her blue uniform dress, over her wide, rounded bosom. "Must have been some fight. How you doing?"

A long stream of chocolate syrup went into the milk. "It's sweet of you to be concerned, but at the moment there are other things more pressing. My daughter is seeing a therapist. Larry Black might be incapacitated for life, if he doesn't die first. A friend of mine is being investigated for a murder he didn't commit. Another may be suicidal, and there is nothing I can do for any of them. I have a hearing tomorrow I haven't begun to prepare for. And now the plumber says I have

456

to tear out my bathroom wall. Believe me, Phyllis, I have enough on my mind."

Phyllis nodded. "Seems like if you got trouble with your man, nothing goes right."

Gail glanced at her, then stirred the chocolate in with a spoon.

"He was always nice to me," Phyllis said.

"Anthony can be very charming when he decides to be."

"I guess you can't tell about men from their outsides."

"No, you can't." She dropped three marshmallows into the steaming mug, then a fourth.

Phyllis stood with her purse hanging from her arm. Her old button-front sweater was draped through the handles. "If it was me, I'd call him again."

Gail turned her head to look at her.

Phyllis nodded gravely.

"I've already called him once."

"Now it's his turn?"

"Yes. If he wants to resume our relationship, he can damn well make some effort in that direction. Why should it be solely up to me?" Gail grabbed a small plate and put a napkin on it, then opened a box of oatmeal cookies.

Phyllis was still standing there. "I can stay with Karen for a while if you want to go see him."

Gail laughed. "See him? He's not interested in calling me. He certainly doesn't want me showing up on his doorstep." She dropped the cookies on the plate.

"That's right. Soon as I laid eyes on him, I could tell he was a spirited man."

457

"He's impossible." Gail picked up the mug and plate. "At this point in my life, I don't have the energy to fight with him any more."

"You scared he's gonna turn you away?"

Gail looked at her. "Not at all. I—it's—"

Phyllis waited.

"What would I say to Karen? Sorry, sweetheart, Mommy just got home to take care of you, but now she has to run off to Anthony's house, so please have your breakdown with Phyllis."

Phyllis's brown eyes rolled upward for an instant, a quick flash of white. "Sweet Jesus in the manger." Then she fixed on Gail. "I got to be home by nine o'clock."

By the time she reached the Rickenbacker Causeway to Key Biscayne, paying her dollar toll, it was dark, the days getting measurably shorter now.

Karen had not been understanding. She had rolled over with the pillow on top of her head. Gail pulled up a corner of it to say she had to leave now, before it was too late. Karen told her to go away. Gail promised they would talk about it with Clarinda. She had showered, changed into slacks and a silk blouse, and put a dab of perfume on her wrists. Leaving, she had paused at the telephone, wondering if she should call first. But if he answered, what would she say?

As she drove she thought about what she would say to him. The words had to be clever enough to get his attention before he slammed the door. Regretful, but not abject. Dignified, not aloof.

When she reached the end of the waterfront

458

cul-de-sac where he lived, his townhouse was dark except for the low lamps along the walkway leading to the front patio. The door was six feet beyond a security gate. She sat in her car for a while, breathing deeply. She finally got out and pressed the buzzer on the wall next to the gate. Nothing. At the end of the street was the bay. The white mast light of a sailboat slid by a hundred yards out. The sails were down, motor faintly purring. The cool breeze made her shiver. Gail walked back and forth, hugging her arms across her chest.

What to say? What combination of words? It was possible that Anthony—because he was, after all, Latin—would respond to passion, but she doubted that she could work herself up into screaming and weeping. For a while she imagined the two of them playing a scene from *Carmen,* and she hummed the music under her breath.

Headlights played along the cul-de-sac, then turned into another driveway. She watched for a while, expecting to see his dark-blue Cadillac at any moment. Lights were on in the other town-houses—people doing the dishes, yelling at each other, putting the kids to bed, watching television, each a little universe of love and disappointment and hope.

It was after eight o'clock now. Anthony's house was quiet, only the fronds of a palm tree whispering at his upstairs window. Gail couldn't imagine living alone, no one there when she got home. She had never asked Anthony how he managed. She had never thought of asking till now. She stood in front of his gate, looking through. There were no clever words to say to him, only true ones.

On the floor of her car she found a sheet of notebook paper—Karen's math homework, already handed in and graded, a 65. She turned it over and wrote a note. She slipped it underneath the gate, where it lay folded on the reddish tile leading to his door.

At the street she waited against traffic to take a left turn, headlights in her eyes. She would go home and read a story to Karen. The hearing tomorrow at the courthouse could take care of itself. She had done enough of them to wing it.

She waited for another car to go by. Its turn signal went on. The car cornered, its headlights sweeping over her. Behind her she heard the screech of tires and glanced in her rearview mirror. The car—dark color, low profile—sat there motionless, red brake lights flaring.

Gail took a breath. The backup lights went on. When the Cadillac came even with her car, the driver's tinted window slid down. She reached for her window crank.

Anthony looked at her across the three-foot divide between them. He seemed to be debating what to say.

"I want to talk to you," Gail said.

He unlocked the gate and Gail followed. Before she could reach the note, he picked it up as if it might have been blown there by the wind. He dropped it, crumpled, into his jacket pocket. Inside the living room he flipped a switch and lamps came on. Not looking at her, he dropped

460

his briefcase on the long table behind the L-shaped sofa. The table was stacked with mail and magazines.

Gail stood unmoving. "Did you get my message? I need to know."

He nodded, eyes shadowed with fatigue. He waited, then said, "What do you want to talk about, Gail?"

"Why didn't you call me?"

He loosened his tie. "You want to sit down? I'm going to fix a drink." He went into his kitchen, squinting for a second when he turned on the light. He took a heavy glass out of the cabinet over the sink.

From the open entrance she asked, "How's the trial going?"

"All right. I have to review some testimony tonight."

She watched him drop ice cubes into his glass, then pour bourbon. Out of breath, she studied the tiles on the floor. "Maybe I shouldn't have come."

Anthony put the bottle back in the cabinet. "I didn't ask you to leave."

She crossed the kitchen, took down another glass, and held it out. "Just a Coke or something. I'm not staying long, and I have to drive home."

He opened his refrigerator. "I heard what happened to Larry. Damn criminals in this city. He should carry a gun." Anthony put in some ice cubes and unscrewed the top off a plastic bottle of Coke. It fizzed. The front of his white shirt seemed to blaze in the bright kitchen, and his hair was dark against the collar. "How is he?"

Gail took the glass. "Thank you." She took a sip. "They say he'll be all right. They say, but . . . I don't know. I went to see him, but they won't let anyone in but family. I spoke to his wife."

"Dee-Dee? Is that her name?" Anthony drank, looking at Gail over the glass.

"Yes. Dee-Dee says . . . he looks awful. And she doesn't want their girls to see him like that but if he—if he doesn't . . ." Gail put down her glass on the counter next to the stove and turned away, weeping.

Anthony's hand was on her arm. "Gail, don't."

She pressed her face into his shoulder. His arms went around her. "Anthony. I don't know what to say. I'm no good at this."

He pressed his lips against her temple. "I should have called you. I was going to."

She laughed and reached for a napkin. "Did you want to make me suffer?"

"No." He pulled her back to him, holding her tightly. "No, not to suffer. Maybe to be sure. Please. Don't do this again. I can't . . . I'm not so good at this either. Maybe I wouldn't have called you. I don't know."

"I'm here."

He nodded. "I am very glad. Yes." He let out a heavy sigh.

Gail felt his jacket pocket for the note she had written and he opened his eyes.

"What is this?" He unfolded it and read. "You love me? Well. This is . . . I like this. And if I don't call you, you'll be back." He cleared his throat. "Yes, I like this very much." He turned the page over. "Arithmetic? I see. Karen's. Only a sixty-five? But she's such a smart girl. You should think about a tutor for her."

Gail reached for the note. He held it away. "No. I'll keep this to show you, if you change your mind."

"I won't."

"I'll keep it anyway." He put it back into his pocket, then locked his arms around her waist. "And where is Karen? With your mother?"

"No. She's home with Phyllis." Gail glanced at the clock on the stove. "I can't stay. I promised Phyllis I'd be back by a quarter to nine."

He made a little sigh of disappointment. "Not much time." He kissed her gently, then again, deeper.

"Wait. I have something to say to you." The stubble around his mouth scratched the tender place at the base of her neck. She lifted her shoulder. "Anthony. Listen to me. Please?"

He rested his forehead on hers.

She held his face, smoothed the lines at his eyes with her thumbs. "I don't want an easy time of it with you—an affair that's going to fit into our schedules. I don't want to think fondly of you when I'm old, as a man I used to know who made exquisite love to me. It has to be difficult and painful."

"*Ay*, Gail." He laughed. "Yes, I think we have that already."

"I want us to love each other so much that if it ended, we'd want to die. If you hadn't let me in—" These last words came out on a whisper, and her eyes filled.

He held her. "How could I not have let you in?"

"Anthony? I would like to get married someday. You don't have to decide now, but I need to know that you wouldn't rule it out entirely."

"No, I wouldn't rule it out. I've never ruled it out."

"Good. And something else," she said. "Stay with me occasionally. You're too alone, and I can't come here as often as I'd like. My bedroom has been redecorated. Everything is new. You haven't even seen it."

"Someday I will," he said.

"Should I find a *santero* to exorcise the evil spirits?"

"Gail, it's not that. What about Karen? If I stayed overnight at your house—" He shook his head. "Not yet."

"Maybe you're right."

"I am right." He drew back far enough to focus on her. "Gail. We're more to each other than what we do in bed."

"We are. Yes. A lot more." She turned to kiss the palm that cupped her cheek, then laughed. "But I still wish you had come home earlier."

"So do I."

They stood in the brightly lit kitchen, embracing, until it was time for her to leave.

chapter thirty

When Gail turned into the parking lot at the Sea Towers Condominium on Collins Avenue, Eric was already there, leaning against his Lexus. The sky was boiling with clouds, and wind ruffled the surface of the puddles.

She closed her door, walked over to him. "What do you think?"

His hair lifted off his forehead, then settled. "I walked around before you got here. There's no doorman or security desk. Front, rear, and garage entrances lock automatically. I'd say whoever shoved Carla off her balcony had a key. Or she let him in."

The building had fifteen floors, each with a row of terraces and white metal railings. Gail counted up ten floors. Plants hung in baskets from many of the balconies. Had Carla grabbed for them, for anything, in that last hideous moment? She let her gaze fall to the parking lot with its slanting yellow lines.

"They probably hosed it down," Eric said. The reflection of clouds swept across his sunglasses.

Gail let out a breath and looked away. At the rear of the building, beyond a low wall, the tops of folded umbrellas rattled in the wind. She could smell the ocean and hear the breakers on the beach.

She headed toward the front of the building, and Eric followed. The pastel-painted lobby had a terrazzo floor, potted palms, and ceiling fans.

Eric said, "You see a connection between this and whoever did Althea Tillett. Correct?"

She nodded.

"Because both Carla and Althea knew about the X-rated businesses Easton owned—"

"Not Easton's," Gail said. "Some Easton members owned shares in Biscayne, which owned the companies that ran the businesses. Biscayne is a front. Charging ten dollars for a drink in a nude bar is legal. Running a call-girl service using teenagers isn't. They were probably into gambling, sports betting, pornography . . . - Carla knew. I think she told Althea when she handled her travel arrangements, and Althea argued with Irving Adler about it. He didn't want her to expose the truth, because it would have ruined too many of their friends' reputations." Gail added wryly, "A lot of supposing."

"But it makes sense," Eric said.

"Add Larry Black to the equation," Gail said, "then ask, Who had a reason to want them all dead? My first choice is Howard Odell."

"Obviously. He had a lot to lose." Above his sunglasses, Eric's forehead creased. "However . . . beating Larry Black like that? I don't think he's capable. And why go after Larry? Did Howard think he was a threat?"

"I saw them together at lunch in the Hartwell Club a few weeks ago," Gail said. "Larry told me they were discussing investments, but I doubt it." She hesitated, then said, "Larry was a

466

member of the Easton Trust. His wife Dee-Dee told me."

Eric nodded as though the news were no surprise.

"What you haven't heard about Larry—and you're not hearing it now—was that the police found cocaine in his pocket. Larry doesn't do coke. I think it was planted there to make the crimes look unrelated. When you knew Howard, was he using it?"

"No." Eric shrugged, then smiled a little. "I would have known. But Gail, in Miami cocaine is common as dirt. Rudy Tillett had it on him when he was arrested. That doesn't mean he went after Larry. I can get him for the other two, though. Althea, for her estate. And Carla, because she may have demanded more than the five thousand he paid her, after she found out how much the estate was worth."

"I can get Howard Odell for all three," Gail said. "All of them knew about his dirty businesses and any one of them could have shut him down."

"True." Eric swung around to study the lobby again. The wind lifted his tie over his shoulder. "Question. Would Carla have let Howard Odell into her apartment? Did they know each other?"

"He said they did." Gail remembered Odell's claim that he hadn't known Carla well. But he had also said she had once been a heroin addict and prostitute. He had known her well enough. For a moment Gail could see Howard Odell standing by the window in the conference room at Hartwell Black. Seeming older than he had at the gallery. Wanting to give it all up, go fishing.

467

Eric said, "Carla would have let Frankie Delgado in. He manages the travel agency. He had as much to lose as Howard Odell. And consider what he did to you. That shows a capacity for violence."

Frankie Delgado's muscular arm had snaked out to grab her purse before he shoved her against his office door. The blond-haired girl looking on, smirking—

"He could have been working for Howard," Gail said.

"Could have been."

They walked back to the parking lot.

"You know, Gail, instead of beating our heads against a brick wall, we could wait till Larry wakes up and ask him."

"When will that be? He's barely conscious, and they don't know if he'll remember anything. The neurologist doesn't want to push him."

Leaning on the fender of Gail's car, Eric said, "You haven't mentioned Irving Adler in this scenario."

"I talked to one of his sons. Irving died of a heart attack. His doctor found nothing suspicious. I'm going to his funeral this afternoon with my mother. She was a friend of his."

"Did they ever find out what happened to Adler's poodle?"

"No," Gail said.

There was a high wooden fence around Adler's backyard, she recalled. Someone could have come into his house unobserved, even in broad daylight. And then what? Viciously kicked the dog? Adler saw this and dropped dead? She had thought of Mitzi a few times, followed by the image of Rudy and Monica Tillett throwing raccoons under the wheels of oncoming cars.

"Where to now?"

"Are you up for talking to Howard Odell?" When Eric gave her a surprised glance, she said, "You've got a car phone, let's see if we can find out where he is." She reached into her purse for the business card she had saved, still creased.

Eric stood there with his keys in his hand. "Seriously?"

"It's a place to start. Look what I found out when I asked Carla a few questions."

"Yeah, look what happened when you met Frankie Delgado."

"You're bigger than Howard." She got in when Eric unlocked the doors.

He turned on the engine. "What are you going to say?"

She punched the number for the Easton Charitable Trust printed on Howard Odell's business card. "I'll probably make it up as I go."

He laughed. "Jesus Christ. And what am I supposed to do, hang him out a window by his ankles?"

When a woman's voice answered, Gail motioned for him to be quiet, then announced herself as a Ms. Miriam Ruiz with First Florida Bank, was Mr. Odell in? No, he wasn't. How could he be reached, as the matter was quite urgent. There was a little pause, then the woman replied that she wasn't certain. Perhaps Ms. Ruiz could leave a number?

Gail said she would call back.

"Now what?"

"Back to the office." She got out and spoke to Eric through the open door. "Miriam is getting some information on the other officers of the Biscayne Corporation. I want to check them out. We're also going to dig into some bank records, see how all these businesses overlap. Biscayne and Atlantic and Seagate. Find out who owns what."

Eric's expression was disbelieving. "How do you do that?"

"Contacts."

He smiled. "Not exactly legal."

"There's a lot to be said for a big law firm when you need something done. You ought to think again before you throw it all away."

"Wait a minute." He looked up at her through the window. "You know, something doesn't fit here. What about Althea Tillett's will? The forgery? What does that have to do with Easton?"

After a moment, Gail said, "I'm not sure."

"Another question. How did he—whoever it was—get into Althea Tillett's house?"

Gail followed Eric to North Bay Road, pulling in behind him alongside the wall that ran around Althea Tillett's property. A lone bicyclist passed, splashing through a puddle. Gail locked her car, leaving her purse under the seat.

The gate was set between columns covered in flowering pink bougainvillaea. Standing beside Eric she could see the colonnaded portico, the overhanging trees, the circular drive where the

470

police had taken her and Patrick and the Tilletts into custody.

"If you were Althea Tillett," he said, "would you let a stranger into your house in the middle of the night?"

"Howard Odell wasn't a stranger."

He slid a hand down one of the metal bars, then took off his sunglasses and put them inside his jacket. Backing up a little, he glanced both ways along the street, then toward the house on the other side, hidden behind hedges and Bahama shutters. He stripped off his jacket and tossed it at Gail. "Hold this."

"What are you—"

He jumped, grabbed the top of the wall with both hands, and pulled himself up, supported finally on straight arms. His suspenders made an X on his white shirt. He brought up his knees, crouched, and disappeared. Gail heard a thud and looked through the gate. Eric came from behind a tree, dusting off his trousers.

"Are you crazy?"

He spotted something on the latch and smiled. The gate swung inward with a metallic creak. "It wasn't locked, Gail."

"Get out of there!"

He grabbed her wrist and pulled her through, then closed the gate. "No one saw us." He took his jacket from her and put it on. He started down the curving brick driveway, empty of cars.

Gail glanced toward the street. The day was cool, but she had broken into a nervous sweat. Overhead, leaves rustled in the banyan tree. A blackbird screeched, loudly clattering its wings.

Eric went onto the front patio and cupped his hands, looking through the window.

"Don't touch the glass," Gail warned. "There's an alarm system."

"I remember. Rosa Portales turned it off when she came in that morning." He moved to the next window, looked in. "I can see stairs. Is that where they found the body?" He walked along the colonnade. The front entrance was a double wooden door, painted white, with a heavy brass handle and two locks.

Gail said, "She was wearing a red silk kimono and her underwear, that's it." Eric looked around. "I wouldn't entertain unexpected guests like that. Maybe you're right. Whoever came in had a key. Or she knew him very well indeed."

Eric stepped off the patio. "How well did she know Howard Odell? They had the Easton Trust in common. She might have let him in." He motioned toward the walkway that led around the side of the house. "Let's go around back."

Gail remembered that trees shielded the view along the edges of the property. No one was likely to see them, unless from the bay. She said, "We might as well."

The house seemed huge from this angle, sand-colored stucco going up and up to the red barrel tile at the roof. Now she could see the rear terrace, the striped awnings, the gazebo. The surface of the pool wobbled, and occasional drops of rain made circles that expanded slowly to the Italian-tiled edges. At the edge of the sea-wall, the long, heavy fronds of the royal palms hung motionless, as though the wind was holding its breath.

Inside the house, the long sofas, laden tables, and cluttered walls showed dimly through the expanse of glass. One sliding door had been replaced by a sheet of plywood.

"Is this the one Patrick broke?" Eric laughed. "I wish I'd seen that." He opened his hands on the wood. "Glass doors can be lifted off the tracks, you know."

"What about the alarm?"

"Maybe it wasn't on. People forget. Didn't the detective say the women had been drinking? Althea forgets to reset the alarm, she goes upstairs to bed . . ."

Eric stretched out his arms, easily spanning the door. He grasped either side of the frame. "Our intruder lifts—which I won't do—and pulls outward from the bottom, like so. He moves the door away like this . . . ." Eric continued his pantomime. "He sets it down. It takes him—what?—ten seconds. He goes upstairs, kills her, pushes her body down the stairs. On his way out he replaces the door and sets the alarm. No one will suspect her fall was anything but an accident. Otherwise, the police will start asking too many questions."

Gail shaded the glass to see across the living room, where the stairs curved to the second floor. "She went upstairs to change her clothes, then she came down again. My mother told me that Althea was wearing slacks and a blouse at the party." She walked farther along the terrace. The lid of the grand piano was still down, where it had crashed when Patrick was attacking Rudy.

"Althea put on some music. Her neighbor heard it. What was it?"

"Music? Yes." Eric's hand was moving as if to grasp the title. "An opera. You wrote it in the file. *Madama Butterfly*. Yeah, that explains the kimono. The intruder lifts the door while she's upstairs. No, forget that. Too risky. What if the alarm was on? This murder was planned better than that."

Eric blinked away a raindrop. "This isn't getting us anywhere, Gail. You can devise any theory you want to about how Althea's killer got in here: Howard Odell rang the doorbell. Rudy had a key. Frankie walked in through the sliding glass door, which was wide open."

"I want to hear that one." Laughing, Gail stepped under one of the blue and white striped awnings. Drops of rain were making silvery crowns in the swimming pool.

Eric backed up, looking at the house. "All right. The open door theory. Between this house and the closest neighbor—about fifty yards away—there's an eight-foot concrete wall and a jungle of trees. Althea died on September sixth. Summer. Windows are shut and the AC is running. But the neighbor hears *Madame Butterfly*. Not for the entire opera, but only for five or ten minutes. How is this possible?" He nodded toward the sliding glass door. "The door was open. And if the door was open, our intruder could have come in without a key."

She had to smile. "Or perhaps, Eric, this was when our intruder was lifting the sliding glass

474

door off the tracks, and Althea was upstairs changing into her kimono."

"No, we have to ditch that theory. What about the alarm? The intruder must have had a key. There was no forced entry. The alarm didn't go off. And he didn't simply walk through an open door. So who had a key? Rosa Portales." He laughed, then suddenly his smile faded. "Gail, do you remember, when we were at Rosa's, what she said? Rudy and Monica were upstairs going through their stepmother's papers. Did Rosa say she found them there, or did she let them in?"

Over the bay hung a long, low cloud, and rain fell in the distance like a swirl of gray chiffon. Gail watched it for a minute, knowing that soon it would be overhead. Already fat drops were dotting the terrace.

She said, "Rosa found them upstairs."

"Maybe Rosa left the front door unlocked."

"Maybe."

"You sure it wasn't Patrick? He had a key."

"Ha-ha. Yes, I'm sure."

"What about Sanford Ehringer? He could have sent his bodyguard over."

"No. Ehringer told me he and Althea used to be lovers. He wouldn't have let anything happen to her."

"Yeah? You two must be pretty tight."

"He isn't the ogre I once thought, no."

Eric walked back along the perimeter of the pool, joining her under the canvas awning. His hair was darker blond on top, dampened by the rain. He said, "Where was Rudy Tillett on Monday morning, when Larry was attacked?"

Gail shook her head.

"We could find out easily enough," Eric said.

The rain began to patter on the canvas awning. The bay was empty, only a sportfisher half a mile out. A pelican on the seawall lifted its wings then flapped away.

"Let's go," she said.

Running, they went back around the corner of the house. Rain whispered in the trees, drizzling through in places.

Eric said, "It's too late to get anything else done this morning. What are you doing later?"

"Later when?"

"After work. We could go over to the Beach. Rudy Tillett runs his catering and party business out of a building on Fifth Street." The rain was falling harder now, and Eric swung his jacket over their heads.

As they hurried along the driveway more questions formed in Gail's mind. Larry hadn't wanted the firm to take the forgery case. He had said they shouldn't alienate prominent members of society. Who was he really afraid of, and why?

Eric pushed open the gate, holding his jacket over Gail while she took her car keys out of her pocket and unlocked the door. She got in.

"I can't do anything tonight," she said. "I have a deposition in the morning to prepare for."

He leaned closer, the jacket over his head, rain making a racket on the roof. "You want me to talk to Rudy? He doesn't know me." His hair was stuck to his forehead. "I could get friendly with his secretary, if he has one." He grinned. "Unless his secretary's a guy, then I don't know."

"No. Don't do anything yet," Gail said. "Tomorrow. We'll talk about it then."

She closed her door, waving through the window.

The graveside services for Irving Adler were held at 2:00 P.M. at Menorah Gardens, a cemetery at the western edge of development one county to the north. The family sat under a green canopy whose scalloped edges flapped in the wind. Past the trees, four lanes of U.S. 27, and a drainage canal, the Everglades extended for miles to the west. Clouds were moving like a lid being slowly pulled across the earth, but for now the rain had stopped.

Irene and Gail stood among the crowd of fifty or so, holding hands. When it was over, Irene went to speak to Adler's family. Gail had noticed Jessica Simms earlier, but the woman had only looked icily through her big round sunglasses, pretending not to see her. Now Irene was picking her way across the grass. Her red hair stood out in the background of dull gray suits and dark dresses.

"Are you okay?" Gail asked.

"Oh, yes. We all knew Irving wouldn't be with us much longer. This isn't like Althea's funeral. No. I cried buckets over Althea."

They made their way toward where the cars were parked. The tops of the trees swayed and rustled.

"Mother, I think Anthony and I may get married."

Irene blinked. "When?"

"I don't know when," Gail said. "I mentioned it to him, and he said he wouldn't rule it out."

"Only a lawyer would give that kind of answer," Irene said. "Do you love him? No, that's a dumb question. Obviously you're ga-ga over this man. I'm not going to offer any advice."

"I don't want advice, Mother," Gail said. "I'm just letting you know. And be nice to him."

"Nice? When have I not been nice?" Irene tilted her head up to look directly at Gail. Her blue eyeshadow was the same shade as her dress. "He'd better take good care of you, that's all I have to say about it." She hugged Gail's arm. "Or else. What does Karen think?"

"We'll have to work up to that. There are a lot of things we still have to resolve."

"Well. If he makes you happy."

"Happy? Yes. And miserable." Gail laughed. "But I'd be more so without him."

"Now, listen," Irene said. "Don't mention marriage to him again. If he's serious about you, he'll bring it up. Men are another species, darling. Their minds don't work the same as ours. It might ruffle his pride if you ask him directly."

"I'll certainly keep that in mind, Mother."

They came out on a narrow asphalt road bordered with low hedges. Already mourners were getting into their cars, doors slamming, moving slowly toward the gated exit.

Gail said, "I spoke to Sanford Ehringer on Tuesday about the case I have for Patrick. I went to his house by the river. I'd been there before, as a kid. Do you remember taking me?"

"It's been years! Were you with me?"

"I know that my grandfather brought me. Ehringer says John Strickland was a friend of his. He also told me that your grandfather Benjamin was one of the founders of the Easton Charitable Trust. Is that true?"

"Grandpa Benny? I didn't know that."

"Really you didn't?" A gust of wind blew Gail's hair across her face, and she shook it back.

"No. I would have told you, Gail. Is Sanford certain? Well, I guess he'd know." Irene's skirt fluttered. "Now, why on earth didn't anybody in the family mention that Grandpa was a founder of Easton? Maybe they did, and I forgot."

It was more likely, Gail decided, that the family hadn't wanted Irene Strickland Connor to know about Grandpa Benny's ignominious departure from the board of the Easton Trust after getting caught with the mayor's wife.

"What do you remember about him?" Gail asked.

Irene smiled. "He was a wonderful man, very kind and funny. He used to take all his grandchildren rowing on Biscayne Bay, and we'd play like we were pirates. I swear, he could catch a fish on a safety pin. He passed away when I was just a girl."

Gail took her mother's arm and they began to walk. "I didn't know I'd missed so much. Mother, could you tell me about my grandfather John sometime? I want to hear the real story. Never mind the version I could read at the Historical Museum. Sanford Ehringer says he was a gambler."

"Oh, he drove Momma batty. Card parties,

479

coming home at all hours. He loved the casinos, till they went out of business, then he'd fly down to Havana for the weekend. Momma hated it, but she went along to keep Daddy out of trouble. These days she would have divorced him, but fifty years ago husbands and wives didn't do that."

Fingers pressed to her face, Irene laughed. "Oh, I remember one time this loo-o-ong black Chrysler brought him home just before dawn. I was about Karen's age, and I saw it through my bedroom window. Daddy got out, drunk as a skunk, and they had to help him to the door. He couldn't find his keys so I sneaked downstairs and let him in. There were men in tuxedos inside the car, and a black-haired woman in a sparkly dress. I just knew they were gangsters! But Daddy said no. I still wonder. He had to bring Momma three dozen red roses before she would let him back in their bedroom."

"You never told me this story."

"I did, too. I must have. You didn't pay attention."

Gail unlocked the passenger side door and opened it. "It's forty minutes back to Miami. Come on. I want to hear more of this."

It didn't occur to Gail until later, after she had dropped her mother off at home, that she had forgotten to mention that soon she would be voted in as a partner of Hartwell Black and Robineau.

chapter thirty-one

"Hang on a second." Gail put her palm over the phone and said, "Go back to bed, sweetie. It's late."

Karen frowned from the door of the kitchen. "You said you would tuck me in half an hour ago." Her hair was tangled and she squinted in the light.

"It was ten minutes ago, and I'm still on the phone."

"With *him*."

Gail gave her a hard look. "Yes. I am speaking with Anthony about Larry Black. This is very important. I will be there in a minute." When Karen had gone, Gail said, "Did you hear any of that? Mom is being mean."

"You should go. I'll see you tomorrow." Anthony would go with her to speak to Dee-Dee Black. "And Gail—" His voice became more emphatic. "Don't talk to Rudy Tillett, not by phone, not in person. Not you and not Eric Ramsay."

"Of course not."

"Gail, I mean it. Your physical safety is one of my concerns, but now I have to think about Larry Black as well, his possible involvement, even unwittingly, in criminal activities—"

"Anthony, I won't."

481

She heard him exhale. "I worry about you."

"And I love you for worrying." She kissed him good-bye over the phone and hung up. She had not mentioned that she had actually gone onto Althea Tillett's property—Anthony would not have understood—but she had relayed what she and Eric had talked about.

The latest news in the office was that Larry had come out of his coma. Still groggy from pain medication, but conscious. Anthony had called Dee-Dee; they would meet with her before the police could question Larry about the attack.

Gail took one more sip of coffee, looked for a moment at the stack of papers on her kitchen table, then went to say good night to Karen. She pushed open the door. Karen was sprawled across the bed with her mouth open, snoring softly.

Returning to the living room, she heard a light knock on the front door. She looked through the blinds. Eric Ramsay stood there, dressed in jeans, T-shirt, denim jacket, and running shoes with reflective stripes. She unlocked the door. "Eric?"

His face was alive with excitement. "I talked to Rudy."

"You what?"

He glanced past her into the house. "It's kind of late. Is Karen asleep?"

"Yes. Come in." She closed the door. "Eric, what have you done?"

Standing in the middle of the living room, Eric unsnapped the top pocket of his denim jacket and took out a small, leather-covered notebook. "Come here, look at this. It's Rudy's address book. I stole it from his office."

She walked over. His green eyes were on her face. They seemed hollow. The strangeness of this came to her a split second before she saw the blur of his arm. Then she dropped in a black, gagging spin.

Slowly she became aware of a man's voice. Carpet under her cheek. A knee in her back. She couldn't breathe. The voice came closer, whispering. "Shhh. Gail, I'm sorry I had to do that. Can you hear me? Hey."

She saw the ivory-colored upholstery of the sofa, a flexed running shoe. Now Eric's face was over her, blond hair hanging around his forehead. He spoke. "Be quiet and listen—"

She jerked, but his hand was over her mouth. Her muffled scream tore at her throat.

"Listen to me." He looked toward the bedrooms, then back. "We're going to go somewhere, the three of us. Do what I tell you, and everything will be okay. Tell Karen we have to go to a client's house, and his kids have video games she can play."

Gail's chest was burning, heaving, air not coming fast enough. Her eyes watered.

Eric leaned closer. "Gail. I won't hurt you unless you make me. Okay? Speak to me."

She let out a long, low moan.

"All right. We're going to get up. Be quiet or I'll hit you again. Gail?" When she nodded, he slowly lifted his hand. "I'm going to borrow you for a few hours, then you can go." She sobbed. "I mean it. Shut up. If you give me any trouble, I'll hurt you, but I'll hurt Karen first." He pulled her up.

Her heart fluttered like a trapped bird. She whispered, "Oh, God. Eric, don't. Why are you doing this? What do you want? Tell me—"

He hit her again, holding her up when she collapsed. "Don't you listen? Jesus. Nothing's going to happen. Are you going to make me do this again?" He jerked her head up by her hair. "Gail?"

"No." Her voice was raspy.

"Good. Calm down. And don't scare Karen." He straightened her hair and gave her a little shove toward the hall.

Eric told Gail to drive her own car. His Lexus was not in her driveway. She hadn't noticed that before. Eric sat in the backseat with Karen and did tricks with quarters, making them disappear, then reappear behind his ear. He dropped one into Karen's alligator bag before she could move it away.

Karen wanted to sit up front and Eric said, "Gail, you better tell her to stay put. She could get hurt moving around in a car." Gail spoke to her sharply. In the rearview mirror Karen's eyes met hers from under the brim of her Hurricanes hat. It was not the defiant expression she usually put on when yelled at. She shrank into the seat and said nothing more.

The windshield wipers hissed across the glass, clearing away red and white dots of light. Gail thought of swerving into a tree. She searched traffic for a police car. Tears ran down her face, and she wiped them off with her hand. She heard Eric explain to Karen that the client was a good friend of her mother's, and he was sick, and Gail was worried. A short visit, Eric said, then they could go home.

Gail's mind churned. Eric was in this with Rudy. With Howard Odell. Frankie. Nothing made sense.

He told her to take the causeway toward Miami Beach, then turn left at Palm Island. At the gated entrance he aimed a black box and the striped mechanical gate went up. They passed a dark playground behind a chain link fence. On narrow lots, the houses hid behind walls or high shrubbery, and across the bay the buildings of downtown Miami were lost in cloudy mist.

"Pull into that next driveway and park past the fence." The one-story house had a roof with turned-up corners. In the yard was a dry fountain with a small stone pagoda. There were no lights on in the house.

Eric told Gail to latch the gate, then follow him and Karen around back. For an instant she stood at the narrowing gap between gate and fence and thought of screaming for help, then turned and saw Karen's small, white face, and Eric's hand on her shoulder.

Behind the house a single floodlight illuminated the wooden deck. There were a few seagrape trees and a hammock, then a dock, and a big Hatteras sportfisher. Light shone dimly from inside the boat, through the curtains in the salon.

Howard Odell was loading something aboard. He saw them and stepped onto the dock. He wore a windbreaker and a billed khaki hat.

He looked at Karen, then said, "Why'd you bring the girl?"

"She was there. Two for one."

Odell scowled at him. "Dammit, Eric."

Gail hugged Karen closer. "Howard, what are you doing? What do you want?"

His face was grim as he untied the ropes on the dock. "Get on the boat. We're making a stop in Bimini. We'll let you out there." When Gail only stared at the sportfisher, horrified, he said to Eric, "Help them on board."

Karen clung to her, and for a moment Gail thought of flinging her into the dark water, screaming for her to swim, go to the next house, hurry hurry, but Eric already had his hand around Karen's arm. He said quietly to Gail, "Would you stop worrying? Nothing's going to happen."

"Eric. I get seasick. I hate boats—"

"Tough."

The boat had a short rear deck with a fishing chair bolted to the floor. There was a long prow, a swept-back bridge above, and higher still, a tower. Radio antennas and long fishing poles—outriggers—extended past that. Howard Odell turned off the porch light, taking a last look around. He climbed the ladder to the bridge. The engines whined, then steadied to a deep, throbbing rumble.

The salon was done in blue with teakwood trim, a nautical motif. A fake brass porthole with a mirror in it hung on one wall. There were a color TV, a stereo, and a little sink with liquor bottles in a cabinet above. Cardboard boxes and suitcases were stacked along the bulkheads, a garment bag thrown across them. A golf bag leaned into the corner.

Gail and Karen clung to each other on the upholstered sofa. Eric sat opposite, long legs stretched out, ankles crossed. Through a crack in the curtains she could see Palm Island slipping past, then the bridge that arched over to Miami Beach. The water slapped on the hull. Eric stood up, the top of his head brushing the paneled ceiling. He went below. Stairs led down to an area Gail knew would contain a galley, head, and forward cabin. Dave had rented space to sportfishers at the marina, when they had owned the marina.

A boat like this could cost a million dollars, new. Gail wondered who it belonged to. The Easton Trust? The Biscayne Corporation? Or was it Howard Odell's own toy? The money must have attracted Eric Ramsay, the first time he had played racquetball with Odell. But Eric had kept this relationship a secret, and so had Odell.

Eric came up with two canned Cokes and a bottled beer. Gail shook her head, and Karen only glared at him through narrowed eyes, her arms around Gail's waist.

"Suit yourself." He tossed the Cokes into an empty armchair and twisted the cap off his beer. He and Gail looked at each other across the salon.

She said, "Did you go to see Rudy?"

He tipped back his beer. "No."

"What about the address book?"

"It was mine."

"Where are we going?"

"Bimini. You heard Howard. You and Karen

are going to Bimini, we're going somewhere else."

"Why?"

He put his fingers to his temples. "Gail . . . shut up. Please? We won't be in this boat long, so let's try to enjoy it. If that's not possible, then at least try not to be a pain in the ass." He leaned over, elbow across his knees. "Hey, kid. Some adventure. You ever been on a boat like this?"

Karen was sitting straight up now, her arms crossed over her chest, her hat low on her head.

Gail said, "Can she go get me some water?"

"You've got a Coke over there."

"I don't like soft drinks. I need some water." When Eric gestured toward the stairs, Gail shoved Karen off her lap.

"You know where the kitchen is?" he asked.

Karen turned around. "Galley. On a boat, it's a galley."

"Galley. Jesus. Hurry up, and don't mess around with anything."

When Karen had vanished down the companionway, Gail said, "Don't touch her. Don't even try. You'll have to kill me to get me off of you."

"Take it easy, Gail."

"Whose idea was this? Howard's?" When he didn't answer, she asked, "Are you both in it with Rudy?"

"What? You mean—no, you've got the wrong idea here. Howard and I had nothing to do with Althea Tillett. It was Rudy."

"Why are we here? What are you going to do?"

"Don't worry about it."

She sat there for a minute trying to breathe

normally. "You're getting out of the country, aren't you? Both of you. That's what all the boxes and suitcases are for. What are we, your security?"

Still looking at her, he finished a swallow of beer, then wiped his mouth on a knuckle. "Yes. That should be reassuring. We have to take good care of the security."

Now she could see. "Howard has been stealing from the Easton Trust. No. Not Easton, because Sanford Ehringer would know. He stole from the Biscayne Corporation, is that it?"

Rolling his beer bottle between his hands Eric finally said, "Not all of Biscayne, only the adult businesses. Wild Cherry, Sun Goddess Escorts and the rest. They ran on cash and Howard's been skimming. I can tell you this because, shit, everybody's going to know about it when they find out he's gone."

"What are *you* doing here?"

"Helping out."

"Like this? Beating me up?"

"I said I was sorry."

"And that makes it all right?"

His face went flat and empty, then he shrugged. "Howard taught me a lot. I owe him. We traded tips on investments and tax, and one thing led to another. He's a player, but he had some bad breaks. He got screwed on his divorce. The IRS came after him. He lost his house. Then Seagate and Atlantic started getting out of hand." Eric took another drink. "Like Frankie Delgado. Frankie knows some very bad people, and they wanted in. Frankie suspected what Howard was

489

doing. Between Frankie and all this shit coming out about the estate, we decided to leave before everything went kaflooey."

"What's the matter, Eric, you weren't satisfied with a Lexus?"

"I left the Lexus in Coconut Grove with the keys in it. Too bad. A fine ride, that car. Oh, well." He swallowed some beer. "No, I wasn't satisfied, not with a salary. The lawyers at the top—Hartwell Black, any big firm— they're not in it for the paychecks. Three, four hundred thousand a year? No, they want the contacts. Cy Mackey, for instance. He goes out to dinner with bankers or real estate investors four or five nights a week. You know, Gail—" Eric grinned. "Some of those upstanding lawyers you work with have offshore accounts. I could give names. The problem is, it takes so damn long to get into that position. Look at you. Eight years trying to make it on your salary. Which is what? Seventy, eighty grand?"

He leaned forward, looking down the companionway stairs. "What's she doing?"

Gail shivered, not from cold but from nerves. Her jaw was so tight her teeth hurt. She asked, "If Howard's got an offshore account, why do you need Karen and me?"

"Well, we didn't expect to, but Sanford Ehringer had the accounts frozen. He must have known something. It's not Ehringer's damn money, or Easton's, but he's got the contacts. The old man is sneaky."

Eric raised his bottle in a salute, then smiled at Gail. "Bringing you was my idea, sort of a last-minute inspiration. You said Ehringer likes you. Howard will call him in the morning and tell him you and Karen are our guests—he won't say where, naturally—and he'll ask that the funds be freed up. If they are, we can all go our separate ways."

The boat gathered speed, moving into the channel leading to the Atlantic. Karen came up the stairs carrying a mug painted with nautical flags, walking in her sneakers as easily as a circus rider on a bareback horse, her alligator purse across her chest. She gave Gail the mug and a small yellow pill.

"That's Dramamine," she said. "I found it in the head."

"Bathroom," Eric said.

Karen sat back down on the sofa, her hands between her knees.

Gail sipped the water. She said to Eric, "How much money are you talking about?"

"Enough." He made a laugh of pure delight. "Almost two million on board, cash. Six million at the other end. Enough to find a congenial island, let us say, with white beaches and clear blue water. You don't waste your money living high. You get to know people, make some solid investment decisions. You live comfortably the rest of your life. It's what everybody wants."

"Not everyone."

"Bullshit. Given the choice, wouldn't you? You're trapped where you are, so you convince yourself you like it."

"What about Wyoming?"

"Wyoming?" He laughed.

491

"You also lied about wanting to be a trial attorney. What were you doing, spying? You wanted to be on the case to find out how close I was getting."

"You know what, Gail? I lied about wanting to fuck you too."

She glanced at Karen, then said, "Does Howard mind if we know? What would he do?"

"Nothing. What are you going to say when you get back to Miami? That he's an embezzler? So? Who would testify against him? The high-society, opera-going hypocrites who own stock in these companies? They're not going to show their sweet white asses. The companies will go under, and so will Frankie Delgado and his crowd. You can't object to that, can you?"

"No, I object to this."

Eric acknowledged her complaint with a shrug. "We'll leave you with enough cash to make up for my bad manners, and you charter a plane home." He said to Karen, "You get to skip school tomorrow."

Karen only looked at him.

He stood up, opened the salon door, and sent his beer bottle sailing into the darkness. He reached around, did three pull-ups on the door frame, then cupped a hand at his mouth. "Howard! Hey! What's that reggae station, mon? I'm in the mood for de island music." He nodded, then came back in and turned on the stereo. Static, then the steady thud of guitars and drums, a song without melody.

"Can we go outside?" Gail asked.

492

"Yeah." He turned around, smiling. "Don't fall overboard."

The wind wasn't cold, but it was steady from the southeast, and the boat was running at an angle over the swells, churning through the water. Karen wore jeans and a sweatshirt. Gail had on a pullover sweater. Her hair whipped around her face. The lights from Miami north to Fort Lauderdale were a sparkling line ten miles off the stern.

If she could find two life vests, one for Karen, another for herself, and then if on a signal they could both jump into the water . . . they could last the night if they held on to each other, keeping warm. There were dozens of boats in these waters. If they had a flashlight as a signal—

Howard Odell was above, leaning against the captain's stool, feet apart. The lights from the dash glowed amber. He took off his hat for a second to scratch his head. He wasn't wearing his toupee. He put his hat back on and picked up a lit cigarette from an ashtray. A diamond ring sparkled on his pinky.

Karen climbed into the fighting chair, facing the horizon, which was slowly slipping away. "Mom. They kidnapped us, didn't they?"

Gail put an arm around her. "We're going to Bimini. You've been to Bimini before, remember? You and your dad and I went on the sailboat. We slept out on deck that night . . . ."

Karen looked at her.

Gail took Karen's face in her hands. "We'll be all right. I promise. I won't let anything happen to you."

493

The stars overhead were blazing now, but less bright in the west, where the skyline glowed. Gail knew it was fifty miles from Miami to Bimini. The sportfisher was moving at a good, steady pace. It was midnight now. They might make it by three o'clock, depending on the wind. They would call Sanford Ehringer. Everything would be all right.

The music became louder. Eric had opened the salon door, fresh beer in his hand. Dancing with the beat, he did a little two-step over to where Gail stood by the fighting chair.

The boat wallowed into a wave, and Gail braced herself. Karen's hair twirled around her Hurricanes hat. "Mom. Can I go below and lie down?" She slid out of the chair.

Eric said, "No, stay up here." He held on to the ladder.

"I feel sick."

"No." He finished his beer and tossed it over the side.

"You shouldn't litter," Karen said.

"You're right. I shouldn't. You're your mother's daughter, aren't you?" He sat down on the padded bench along the side. "Hey. What's in the purse?"

"Leave her alone, Eric." Gail pulled her away, but he grabbed the strap.

"No! It's mine!"

"Karen, can you swim?" He peered under her hat brim. "Hey. Are you a good swimmer?"

"Yes."

"Good. That's good. You might need to know that someday." He smiled at Gail.

Gail said stiffly, "Let him have it, Karen."

Eric clicked the gold clasp at the top and looked inside. "Ooooh, what have we here?" He pulled out a quartz crystal and held it up to the light, then dropped it back. Then a black rock shaped like an egg. A thin gold chain, then a Polaroid of Dave and Gail and Karen together, everyone smiling.

Karen turned her face into Gail's shoulder. Gail hugged her, watching Eric take out pink lipstick and a compact. Gail had thrown them away, nearly empty. He pulled out a carved stick that Karen had made in Clarinda Campbell's office. Then the one-peso coin that Anthony had given her.

He slowly drew out Dave's silver knife. He unfolded it and tested the blade on his thumb. "What kind of kid have you got here, Gail?"

"It's my daddy's!"

"Well, I'm just going to hang onto this for you, kiddo." He slid it, folded, into the pocket of his jacket.

"I hate you!" Karen screamed.

From the wheel came a shout. Howard Odell said, "What's going on?"

Gail said, "Karen wants to lie down. She's not feeling well."

"Eric, take them below."

"I get claustrophobic. She can lie on the sofa."

Odell said, "Karen! Go below if you want to, but don't touch anything."

"I'm coming too," Gail said.

"Stay here," Eric said. "I don't want to go in

495

yet." His arms were stretched along the gunwales.

If she shoved him, hard, Gail thought, he would fall backward and vanish. Or get sucked into the propellers. "Go on, sweetie. I'll be right here." When Karen had gone, Gail turned fiercely to Eric. "Bastard. You fucking bastard."

"Gail. Shut up." She started to leave, and he grabbed her arm, pulling her down on the seat. His thigh pressed against hers. The water was rushing past the hull, a white froth in the darkness.

He glanced toward the bridge, then said, "You asked me who killed Althea Tillett. It was Rudy. He and Monica planned it. They killed her, then they forged her will. Monica told Howard all about it." Eric smiled, came close, the wind ruffling his hair. "Howard was having an affair with her."

"Howard and Monica?"

"Wild, huh?" Eric glanced upward again. "Don't mention it to him. He doesn't know I told you about it. I want you and Karen to get to Bimini okay."

"Why did you let me make an idiot of myself at Althea Tillett's house this morning, if you already knew who did it?"

"Because you'd have wondered how I knew Rudy did it. What would I have told you?" He shook his head. "Howard and I were making plans to leave. I couldn't jeopardize that."

Gail knew she should go inside. Leave it alone. But she looked up at Howard Odell, then at Eric. "What about Larry Black?"

"Larry? Rudy didn't do it, according to Howard. Larry was going to sue Frankie Delgado—stupid move—and one of Frankie's thugs tried to kill him. It had nothing to do with the forgery." Eric propped his ankle on his knee, bounced his foot. "Planting the cocaine and condoms was their way of making a joke, I guess."

"I don't see the humor," Gail said.

"Sure. It is kind of funny," Eric said, "and I can only say this because Larry's going to pull through, thank God. How's he going to explain it to his wife? He's such an uptight little nerd." Eric patted her knee. "You get back to Miami, talk to Detective Davis. I'd like to see him nail Frankie for this."

Gail watched the opposite side of the boat rising, falling. The lights of the city were dimmer now, and she could feel the engine vibrations under her feet, and the swells of deeper water. Even in the cool wind, her neck was wet with perspiration.

"Let me go check on Karen," she said, steadying herself on the gunwale, standing up.

"I'll go with you. I need another beer anyway." He looked up. "Hey! Howard! I'm going to grab a beer? You want one?"

"Coffee! It's cold up here."

Eric stepped toward the salon door. The light from inside shone on his face. Then his eyes widened. He dived. A blaze of sparks flew past him, then slammed into the back of the boat, bouncing and fizzing and boiling in a cloud of orange smoke.

"You little bitch!" Eric jumped to his feet and vanished into the salon.

chapter thirty-two

Gail scrambled for the door, nearly colliding with Howard Odell, who had leaped off the ladder from the bridge with a fire extinguisher.

Eric was vaulting down the companionway stairs. "Come here, you brat!"

"Stop it!" Gail screamed. "She was playing! She didn't mean to."

Eric hauled Karen back along the corridor by her sweatshirt. "Playing, my ass!" Eric pushed Gail off him. Karen was a flailing, screeching windmill of arms and legs. "She fucking tried to kill me!" He pulled back his fist.

Gail grabbed Eric's arm. "Don't! Don't hurt her!"

"What in God's holy hell is going on in here?" Howard Odell shouted from the top of the stairs. "Stop it! Now!" He still held the fire extinguisher.

Karen slid under the table, sobbing. Gail crawled over to her. "Oh, baby. Mommy's here. Are you all right?"

"Is *she* all right?" Eric straightened his jacket. "Fucking bitch tried to shoot me with the flare gun." He whirled around, finding it on the galley floor. "You little shit, I hope you can swim, I ought to throw you overboard and let the sharks eat you." He slid open a window and tossed out the flare gun.

"Hey!" Howard Odell jerked his thumb toward the bridge. "Get up there and take the wheel. *Now.* I'll handle this."

When Eric was gone, feet thudding across the salon, Howard Odell looked down at Gail and Karen, still on the floor under the table. A little gold anchor was embroidered on the front of his billed hat. Scowling, he unzipped his windbreaker. "Come sit up here where I can watch you." They slid into the bench seat, Karen next to the window.

He had a Thermos of coffee and drank it from a mug while Gail wiped Karen's face with a paper towel. There was a purpling bruise over one eyebrow. The reggae music was still playing in the salon, and the boat thundered through the choppy water. Odell went to turn off the music, then came back. He sat with his knees toward the galley, holding his mug. "I hate reggae." Karen's head was in Gail's lap now, her eyes closed.

Gail whispered, "Howard, you have to let us off in Bimini. If you don't, Sanford Ehringer will hunt you down. He'll have you killed."

He held up a hand. "Gail. Nothing's going to happen to you. We're stopping in Bimini, I promise. Look, Eric got a little excited there. We've been under some pressure with this trip."

"He beat me up!"

Odell's eyes traveled over her face. "Where?"

"How the hell do you think he got me here? He hit me in the stomach, twice, and knocked

499

me out. He threatened to kill my daughter if I didn't do what he said!"

"Gail . . . I'm sorry. He wasn't supposed to bring Karen, just you. Don't worry about it. You'll be okay." He turned back to the galley. "Won't help to bitch about it now."

"You swear we're going to Bimini."

"Yes, but don't expect me to fill you in on my itinerary." He took another swallow of coffee. "Keep quiet, all right?"

"One question. Please?"

He let out his breath and glanced over his shoulder. "What?"

"Did Althea Tillett know about Frankie Delgado and his crowd moving in on Seagate and Atlantic? Please. I want to know."

"Who?"

"Dammit, Howard. You know who Frankie Delgado is. Tell me."

"Althea knew. So what?"

"And she found out from Carla Napolitano?"

"You said one question."

Gail reached across the table. "Howard, please. If I have to get beat up, and my daughter nearly got killed two minutes ago, the least you can do is tell me the truth!"

"Christ! Okay, yes. Althea found out from Carla—who later tried to blackmail me, by the way, before she jumped off her balcony. I told you she was a damn loser. Anyhow, Althea went on the warpath. By then things were getting out of control. I tried to stop it. Ain't easy. Like turning a cruise liner around. We were making good money."

"And the shareholders in the parent company didn't care, as long as they were getting their dividends."

"Right. Some cared, most didn't." He added, "Well, the truth is, most of them didn't know exactly what was going on."

"Did Larry Black know?"

"Larry said shut it down, to hell with the money."

"He found out from Althea, didn't he? And that's what you talked to him about over lunch, the day I met you."

"The whole thing was coming down," Odell said. "Once you let that element in, it goes to hell."

"So you cleaned out the accounts and packed your bags." When Howard glared at her, Gail quickly said, "Eric told me. He said it wouldn't matter if I knew. That people would find out anyway."

"Yeah, I guess it doesn't matter." He made a laugh. "Frankie Delgado ain't gonna be happy. Let him come get me."

"Howard—"

He gave her a pained look. "Don't talk. You'll wake the girl. She's already caused too much trouble." He mumbled into his coffee, "Stupid move, bringing a kid along."

Gail gripped his forearm. "Who . . . killed Althea Tillett?"

"What are you asking me that for?" Odell demanded. "Pretending like you don't know. Eric's kept me up to date on you, sweetheart, so cut the B.S."

"What did he tell you? Please, Howard."

"Rudy Tillett."

Her voice came out on a croak. She cleared her throat. "Can I ask you a personal question?"

"No."

"Did you—were you . . . dating Monica Tillett?"

"Who? Monica?" He smiled, swirling his mug. "I'm not Monica's type." He drank.

The cabin seemed suddenly stifling, and a massive wave of panic swept over her. She said, "Howard—" He exhaled. "Eric told me Rudy Tillett murdered Althea. And that Monica told you this."

Odell didn't answer for a minute. "Don't play your little games with me, Gail."

"No, Howard—"

"You pulled my chain pretty good in that meeting on Monday at your law firm. Not here, baby."

"Listen to me! Eric told me he was in court in Fort Lauderdale last Monday morning, filing exhibits for testimony in a trial that day. I should have caught it! That's totally incorrect procedure! You don't file exhibits the day of trial."

"Yeah, yeah." Odell stood up, finishing his coffee.

"Don't you *see?* On Monday morning someone beat Larry senseless and left him for dead! Eric lied about where he was!" She reached for his arm, whispering urgently. "Larry was found with cocaine and condoms in his pockets. Only the police and his wife knew about it. She told me. I mentioned cocaine to Eric, but not condoms.

Not that. I'm sure of it. How does he know? *How?*"

"I can't listen to this." Odell jerked his arm away.

"You have to!"

Karen stirred and moaned, and Gail glanced down.

Odell put his mug in the sink. "I'm going to trade off with Eric. He'll probably steer us to Haiti by mistake."

Gail caught her breath. The pitch of the engines had dropped, and the boat slowed, the weight shifting forward. Eric had taken it out of gear.

"Don't go up!" She grabbed the sleeve of Odell's windbreaker and held on. "He won't let us go, Howard. He can't. Rudy didn't kill Althea, Eric did."

"You're crazy. He had no reason."

"Oh my God, why didn't I see this? The forgery had nothing to do with Althea's death! Rudy and Monica Tillett took advantage of her accident, but it wasn't an accident. Eric broke her neck. He couldn't risk losing what he had with you."

"That's enough." Odell pointed at her.

"You were cleaning out the accounts. Eric was helping, wasn't he? He knew where to find the offshore contacts, how to evade the IRS. You promised him a share. But Althea started causing trouble. And Carla. She was blackmailing you. Eric had to shut her up."

"Carla? She jumped."

"Impossible. She was moving north to be with

her new grandchild, as soon as she had the money. Money from where? Blackmail?"

Now Odell was staring at Gail, breathing hard.

"Eric and Carla—did they ever meet? Tell me! Would she have let him into her apartment?"

Odell passed his hand over his face. "He took her the money a couple of times."

"Oh, God."

"He couldn't . . . come on, this is crazy talk." Odell cleared his throat. "I know the kid."

"How much were you going to give him, Howard? He told me you've got two million on board. If he gets the rest wherever you're going, fine. But he doesn't need it. He doesn't need you!"

There was a thud, as from someone heavy jumping off the ladder to the bridge.

She clutched his forearm, whispering, "Do you have a gun on board?"

His upper lip gleamed with sweat. "No."

She heard the salon door open.

"I've got . . . a bang stick."

Gail knew what it was. A rod with a hollow chamber at the front. Drop in a 12-gauge shell. It worked on contact. Good for sharks. One tap and the shell would blow like a shotgun.

"Where is it? Howard!"

"Oh, Jesus." His face going gray, he nodded toward the bow. "Closet by the head, with the other fishing equipment."

Eric swung into the galley, brushing his fingers through his tousled hair. His cheeks were pink from the cool wind. Gail and Howard Odell

504

looked at him silently, and Eric stared back at them. His head nearly touched the cabin ceiling. "Chilly outside." He smiled. "Howard, how about some coffee?" He shook the Thermos. "Guess I'd better make us some more."

Groggily Karen sat up, frowning. She noticed Eric and stiffened. Gail put her arms around her.

Eric looked from Odell to Gail, back again. "What's going on?"

Odell said, "Go on up. I'll make your coffee."

"No. You go up. I think Gail and I need to talk."

"Okay." Odell didn't move. "Eric, you know what might be a good idea? We're almost to Bimini. I don't want to take any chances losing these two. They might do something stupid. Jump overboard. What do you think?"

Eric didn't answer, only stood looming over the table.

Gail backed up, pressing Karen behind her. "Howard! Don't!"

"Shut up!" Odell slammed his hand on the table, then said, "I've got some duct tape. I want them tied, hands and feet. We're going to avoid another flare gun incident." He passed beside Eric. "I'll be back. Keep an eye on them."

Eric was watching Odell. Gail breathed into Karen's ear, "Run on deck. Now." She shoved her, and Karen scrambled over the table.

Eric whirled around, grabbed, missed. He started up the stairs, then stopped. "You bitch." He came for Gail, reaching into the corner of the bench seat, taking the front of her sweater in his fist.

"Let her go!" Odell shouted. He held a metal rod, pointing it at Eric's chest. His face was slick with sweat. An eighteen-inch wooden fish bat was stuck into the front pocket of his khaki trousers.

"What the fuck? Howard—" Still holding Gail's sweater, Eric stared at him. "What are you doing, man? What's she been telling you? This woman is tricky. You ought to see her in a jury trial—"

"Shut up!" Odell jabbed the bang stick closer. "Turn around and put your palms flat on the ceiling."

"No. Come on, Howard."

"Did you kill Althea Tillett?"

Eric laughed. *"Me?"* He kept his eyes on the end of the steel rod. "Did she tell you that? It's a lie, I swear to God. She's fucking with you."

Odell gasped for breath. "I said turn around, palms on the ceiling."

Gail dug her fingers into Eric's closed fist. "Oh God, oh God, let go!"

Eric was staring at the end of the rod. "Howard . . . I think you forgot to load it, man."

"I keep it loaded, asshole. Bet on it."

Eric smiled. "Come on, then. Do it. Blow my guts through the wall."

"Let go!" Gail screamed.

Odell lunged. The bang stick landed on a brass snap on Eric's denim jacket, making a soft clink. Eric twisted it out of Odell's hands.

"Fucker, I told you it was empty." He threw it down, clanging against the stove. But Odell was running forward, pulling the fish bat out of his pocket. The blow hit Eric's upraised arm, and

506

he tripped on the bang stick, crashing to the galley floor.

Gail was on the table. Eric had fallen against the stairs, cutting off escape. Odell smashed the bat into Eric's knee. He screamed, caught the second blow with his hand, then grabbed the bat. He rammed upward and Odell staggered into the table. His hat fell off, revealing his pale head and fringe of brown hair.

Eric came for him as Gail leaped off the table. Eric raised the fish bat, then brought it down, thudding into flesh. Up the companionway stairs she could hear a sickening crack, then silence.

Gail screamed for Karen. The deck was empty. She whirled around.

Eric was in the salon doorway, a silhouette, hopping on one leg. She backed up. There were dark smears on his jacket.

"Fuck!" He inhaled deeply, catching his breath, hands on his hips. "Dammit, Gail. If you'd kept your mouth shut!"

"Let Karen go. She's only a baby. Eric, please!" She moved behind the fighting chair, then noticed a movement above the bridge. Karen was climbing the tuna tower. The sea rolled, and the outriggers swung and clattered.

"I don't want to hurt you, Gail. Believe me, I don't. But if you stay on board, I'll have to. So jump. Make it easy." The black water curled into frothy wavelets that smacked against the hull.

He braced both hands on the chair to steady himself.

"You killed Althea Tillett, didn't you?" She

had to keep him talking to give herself time to think.

He lowered his head to the level of his arms. "Yes, Gail. She was going to call the police about Howard's embezzling. I made it look like an accident. I came in through her sliding glass door when she went out on the terrace, just like I told you this morning. I would have come in another way if I'd had to, but I got lucky."

"Oh, God. And Carla."

"And Carla." Eric raised his head, then swung around the chair. Gail went one way, he countered, and she went back the other, trapped.

"Karen! Jump! Find the life ring and jump!"

"You too, Gail." Eric said. "I want both of you off this fucking boat."

She grabbed a beer bottle out of a holder on the transom and threw it at him. It missed, bouncing off the salon windows.

"Work on that forward pass," Eric said. "I am sorry about Larry, but he'll make it, so all is not lost."

"Bastard. I hope you die!"

Eric laughed. "I'll tell you something funny, the way it happened. Irving Adler. I told him I was from Alan Weissman's office. He let me right in. The back door, no less. That dog of his bit my ankle, and I stepped on it. I didn't even mean to." Eric clutched at his chest and rolled his eyes. "Adler just . . . went down." His smile vanished. "Well. I guess you had to be there."

The engines rumbled and the water bubbled at the stern. Gail glanced up. Karen had reached the tuna tower. The boat pitched. Karen slipped sideways, then grabbed the ladder and held on.

"You're pissing me off, Gail." Eric fumbled into his jacket pocket and came out with Dave's fishing knife, quickly snapping it open. Gail leaped back as the blade slashed through her sweater sleeve. She fell backward past the transom onto the latticed wood deck that extended over the stern, rolling toward the water. She could smell the diesel exhaust. A wave splashed up through the wood. Gail clawed, scrambling back into the boat, dropping into the starboard corner. Eric had gone to port. He was looking for something—the knife.

"Shit." He hopped once, then grabbed the flying gaff, hooked over the ladder to the bridge. He let the gaff slide down through his hands. The gaff was topped with a hook six inches across. The other end was tied to the ladder by a dozen feet of polyester line that would easily reach to the starboard corner where Gail now cowered.

"Jump, Gail. Jump off the fucking boat right now, and tell your daughter to jump, too. You want to watch me slit her open?"

"Give her a life vest. For God's sake! Give her a life vest and I'll jump without one, I swear."

In the darkness above, Karen's fingers were curled over the edge of the tuna tower, and her eyes were huge in her pale face. The boat shuddered into a trough and the outriggers clattered over her head, thin white lines in the darkness.

Eric cupped his hands around his mouth. "Hey! Karen! You can swim, can't you? Don't make me come up there."

On her feet, Gail ran for the open salon door. She would find the fish bat, anything. Eric swung around, the light glittering for an instant on the hook of the gaff before it smashed across the entrance and shattered the window on the other side.

He came after her. The hook caught in the hem of her sweater. He pulled and she fell to the deck, drawn closer before the yarn shredded. Gail scooted backward. The hook swept inches from her face.

She rolled between transom and chair, coming out on the port side. She ran for the bridge, up the ladder. A life preserver was there, hanging by the engine controls. Eric grabbed her ankle. She kicked, screaming, connecting with his face.

"Goddamn bitch!" His nose was bloody. He was pulling himself up with his one good leg and one hand, the other still around the gaff. The boat rolled and he hung on, then climbed another rung.

Gail grabbed the life preserver, a hard white ring with rope around the edge. She would throw it, jump, scream for Karen to jump as well.

"Karen!" She flung the life preserver starboard. It caught on the back of the tall captain's chair and bounced back to the lower deck.

Eric was at the top of the ladder. Gail rushed forward and kicked him squarely in the chest.

Then for a long moment, during which Gail watched as if this were all happening somewhere else, and Eric Ramsay was a man she did not even know, he stood balanced on one foot, arms outflung, holding the flying gaff, the line making a long, lazy S against the empty black sky.

He dropped. The line snagged around an outrigger stanchion and went taut. The gaff slipped through Eric's fingers. Then he screamed, thudding against the side of the boat at water level.

Gail gripped the railing of the bridge, staring over the side. Eric was dangling there, and the salon lights danced crazily on the water. He grabbed the rope with his free hand. Supporting his weight, he worked the hook out of his palm. It came free and clanked on the hull. He began to pull himself up the gaff line, hand over hand, eyes fixed on Gail.

She heard a high-pitched cry. "Mom!" She looked up. Karen was on the roof, pointing to the deck. "Dad's knife!"

Gail slid down the ladder, clutching at the slippery metal. She looked over the side. Eric was struggling to catch hold of the metal railing along the gunwale. Gail grabbed the knife, stood on the second rung of the ladder, and sawed at the gaff line.

Eric stretched his bloody hand for the railing. The rope frayed, then snapped. The end still tied to the ladder danced. The ocean slapped against the hull, and the wave crests gurgled and frothed, white in the starlight.

Suddenly there was a rush of noise and motion, and Gail rolled backward, hitting the transom. Karen was on the bridge, throttle forward. The engines screamed. The boat turned, turned, coming back, its long prow aiming for the spot where Eric had fallen.

Gail was not certain that the boat ran over his body, but there seemed to be a thud. When she looked over the stern, she saw nothing but empty ocean.

A few hundred yards later, the engines finally slowed, went silent.

Gail sank to the deck, then heard the quick scurry of Karen's feet.

"Mom, are you okay?"

She opened her eyes and pulled Karen into her arms.

"We need to radio for help."

"I don't know how," Gail said.

"I do." Karen stood up, her slight figure moving easily on the rolling surface. "We should do it like really quick."

Gail struggled up. "Let's just start the engines and go back. Don't worry. We'll find our way. See that glow on the horizon?"

"I don't think we have time."

"What do you mean, sweetie?"

"You know when I was below by myself?"

"Yes."

"I shot the bang stick. I wrapped a pillow around the end of it to make it not as loud, and I hit it on the deck in the vee berth. It didn't make a really big hole, but . . . we ought to look for the life vests."

chapter thirty-three

At midmorning in the autumn, the light could pour through the upper-floor windows of the Hartwell Building with such blue intensity that Gail could imagine stepping out and soaring on the updrafts. The islands and the Beach seemed to float on swirls of turquoise, and the clouds were like the full, white spinnakers on sailboats.

She stood by the windows in Larry Black's office; he sat on the divan, a cane propped beside him. Larry had dropped in only to attend the management committee meeting; he was still too weak to come back even part-time. His face was bandaged and one arm was in a sling.

He was shaking his head. "But how could you do this? We're about to vote on your partnership, Gail."

"I've made up my mind, Larry. I spoke to Paul Robineau yesterday about it, and he told the others."

"Are you sure? Maybe you only need some time off. Gail, you've been through a lot lately."

"Oh, it isn't my nerves." Laughing, she sat down beside him. "I'll tell you what it is. Larry, I saw a man clubbed to death. I thought I was going to die. Worse than that—much worse—I was going to watch my daughter die. Then our boat sank under us. Coming that close to the

513

ultimate reality has to change your priorities." She smiled at him. "Doesn't it?"

Larry let out a long breath. "Yes. Perhaps it does." He looked at her. One of his eyes was still heavily bruised. "What will you do?"

In the two weeks since the Coast Guard cutter had rescued her and Karen from an inflatable life raft sixty miles off Daytona Beach, swept north on the Gulf Stream for a day and a half, she had been thinking about what to do.

She took his uninjured hand in both of hers. "I may ask a certain friend to open a new law firm with me. What do you think?"

Larry smiled. "Yes. I've heard many couples practice together. It's not easy, but Anthony seems—"

"Larry! I meant you."

"Me?" He looked at her as if she had lost her mind.

"Yes. I couldn't share an office with Anthony. My God. There has to be some distance between a man and a woman, otherwise they get tired of each other." Gail whispered, "Larry. I know you've considered leaving. Take the plunge. You can do it."

"Leave Hartwell Black? My father practiced here. My grandfather."

"So?"

"I don't know. After the stories in the news about those despicable corporations, in which I had the lunacy to own shares . . . No, it would appear that I'm turning tail because I can't take the heat."

"Appear to whom? Your other friends who

were doing the same thing? Larry, you shouldn't care what people think. You're humane and honest, the very thing a lawyer needs to be. Clients can see that. And if nobody else can, then to hell with 'em."

He laughed, then winced, touching his side.

The door opened and Larry's secretary stuck her head in. "Ms. Connor? There's a Mr. Ehringer on the phone for you. I told him you were busy, but he insisted."

"Ehringer?" She got up. "I'll take it. Excuse me, Larry." She picked up the phone on his desk.

He wanted to speak to her; he was downstairs in his car on his way to the airport. Perhaps she had a moment? Gail said she did, then hung up, curious.

She went over to the divan for her purse, then stood there for a moment. "Larry, would you think about what I asked you? If you tell me no, I'll only harass you until you change your mind."

He smiled up at her. "Well. All right, I'll think about it."

"Remember Althea," she said. "Live fearlessly."

"Althea Tillett?"

Gail laughed. "If you knew!"

Pushing her way through the revolving door on Flagler Street, Gail saw a sweep of glittering black and deepest red. He had arrived in a Rolls-Royce limousine, not a new one, but stately and square, with a long hood, immense grill, and the winged lady about to soar off the silvery point of

515

it. Russell stood by the rear passenger door. He saw Gail, nodded, and reached for the handle.

Gail walked over and peered inside. Sanford Ehringer sat on the backseat, Walter beside him. Ehringer was in white, with two-tone shoes; Walter wore a suit of navy blue, perfectly tailored. There were some picture books beside him.

Ehringer asked if she had time for a spin around the block; he had a matter to briefly discuss with her. Gail replied that she was about to find a taxi anyway, so perhaps he could drop her off near 62nd Street? Unless it would make him late for his flight? No, they had chartered a jet; it could wait.

Walter smiled at her and scooted over. The gray upholstery was soft as velvet. As the Rolls pulled away from the curb, she looked around. A telephone, computer, and fax machine were built into a burled walnut cabinet. Little vases with pink rosebuds hung at the curtained windows. The sounds of the street had disappeared, replaced by Vivaldi.

Ehringer chuckled. "Never been in one of these, eh? This is a 1954 Phantom V, as solid as the day she was born. I got a deal on it second-hand. It used to belong to the Queen Mother."

"I am . . . hideously jealous."

Walter said, "We're going to Japan."

"Are you really? How lucky!"

"That's right, we're going to take care of some business and see the sights. Have some fun, eh, Walter?"

Walter gave Gail an open-mouthed grin. "Do you want to go?"

"I'd love it, but I have to stay and take care of my daughter. Will you send me a postcard?"

"I'll send you a big postcard."

Ehringer said, "You must come to our house for dinner after we return. Say yes. I must meet the intrepid Karen."

"All right. Yes."

"What a drama! Lost at sea—"

"Really, we were all right, once we got off the boat," Gail said. "We managed to load enough food and water, and a tarp to cover ourselves." She added, "I am so sorry about Howard Odell."

"I misjudged the man."

"He tried to save us," Gail said, "just before—"

"Did he? Good. He salvaged some scrap of manhood, then."

Russell, visible through a glass panel, looked both ways then rounded the corner at Biscayne Boulevard, heading north. Gail could barely feel the motion of the car. There was a gray-haired woman in the front seat—a nurse, perhaps, or Walter's governess.

When Gail glanced back at Sanford Ehringer, he was gazing through the side window.

He said, "I wish I'd known what was going on. I paid no attention to those companies. I had no stake in them. But the shareholders! You'd think that men and women of intelligence would not allow themselves to become complacent. Oh, the love of money! Many reputations went down on that boat, Gail. Some mighty highfalutin folks are scrambling to explain themselves."

Ehringer's eyes suddenly sparkled. "What a thing to watch! As Cervantes said, 'A private sin is not so prejudicial in this world as a public indecency.' ''

He reached over to pat her hand. "And so you have won. A battle well fought, I grant you that much, even if—" He drew his head down onto his shoulders, heavy jowls spreading over his starched collar. "Even if Patrick Norris will inherit twenty-nine point six million dollars. Egad! I would sooner let Walter drive this car."

Walter looked around from the window where he stood on his knees. He grinned, and Gail smiled back.

Gail said, "It may please you to know, Mr. Ehringer, that Patrick will make sure that all of Althea's friends receive what she wanted them to have."

"That's something," he said grudgingly.

"I never wanted to bring anyone down," Gail said. "The embezzlement was completely unrelated to the forgery. All I ever wanted was to do a good job for my client."

"Oh, yes. What was it you told me? You believe in truth and in doing what is right. Noble of you, really. Yes, Gail, I admire that in a young person. You and I may disagree on some things at present, but experience in life should bring you around."

Gail had to laugh a little at that. "You would never bring Patrick Norris around."

"I'm certain! He's too committed to his causes. His project won't make much difference in the long run, but it keeps them happy, doesn't it?"

"In the very long run, Mr. Ehringer, we will all be dust."

He sobered. "Yes. I sooner than you."

Russell's voice came over the speaker. "Ms. Connor? Is this the place?"

She looked out the window, then nodded, and Ehringer pressed a button. "Stop here, Russell."

Gail picked up her purse from the seat. "Thank you for the ride, you and Walter."

Ehringer held out his hand. "We will see you when we return from Japan. May I bring you a present?"

"No, you mustn't—"

"Matching kimonos for you and your daughter. Allow an old man this small pleasure."

"All right." She smiled at Walter. "Her name is Karen. She'd love to see your hamsters."

"Okay." Walter grinned. "She can have some."

"Well . . ."

Gail turned to get out of the car. Through the wide door she could see passersby staring.

"Before you go!" Ehringer motioned to her. "Close the door for a minute, Russell." When Gail sat back down, Ehringer was looking at her from under his tangled black eyebrows. A smile danced on his thin lips.

"It was lucky you had time to load food and water on board your life raft before the ship went down. But what about the other?"

"Other?"

"My friends at the bank report that Howard withdrew a rather large amount of cash from the Seagate and Atlantic accounts two days before his departure. He wouldn't have left it behind."

Ehringer smiled wolfishly. "Did it . . . sink to the bottom?"

Gail hesitated, then said, "No. It didn't."

He put a veiny hand to his heart. "My dear! Surely you plan to return the money to its rightful owners."

"No."

"But what of truth and honor?"

"The truth is," said Gail, "I have no desire to return it to people like Frankie Delgado so he and his pals can purchase more X-rated movies and vibrating waterbeds."

"But is this not desire cloaked in morality? As Nietzsche pointed out—"

"Call it my hazardous duty pay."

Ehringer began to chuckle. "We make our own rules, don't we, Gail?"

"We?"

"We who have the capacity to make the rules." Grinning, Ehringer tapped on the window and the door opened. He touched his forehead with extended fingers, a salute. *"Au revoir,* my dear."

She could still hear him chuckling as Russell closed the door.

Gail and Patrick stood on the weedy sidewalk across the street from the vacant lot and watched an orange front-end loader scrape together a pile of junk, leaves, and rusty auto parts. Black smoke belched from the stack. A group of kids were watching, some sitting sideways on bicycles, others venturing to climb on the pile, until their mothers yelled at them to come away from there.

"How can you start on this already?" Gail asked.

"It's all donated," Patrick said. "One of the men in the neighborhood works for a construction company, and he talked them into letting him use the heavy equipment for the day."

"Do you have zoning clearance? A permit?"

"No," Patrick said. "We tried, but it would take weeks. I say go ahead and do it. What can happen?"

"If someone gets hurt, they could sue you for—"

He laughed. "Gail, stop! You lawyers." He pointed toward Biscayne Boulevard, where the Reel Stuff squatted on the corner. "That's next on my list," he said. "I want to buy it and convert it to a community theater."

Gail held back her smile. "I've heard they're about to go out of business. You could probably get it cheap. Want me to check it out for you?"

"Thanks, that'd be great." Patrick put his arm over her shoulders. "Say, Gail, now that you're going to have your own office, you want to be our attorney?"

"Sure. Why not?"

"Pro bono?"

She laughed. "Patrick—"

"It can be your good deed for the decade." He squeezed her shoulders. "How about it?"

"Fine. But you can pay the overhead." She began to tick off for him a list of things he had to do—see a tax attorney, incorporate, get some investment advice—

"Stop! Stop!"

They stood and watched the front-end loader for a while. Above its rattle and clank, Gail said, "As slow as probate is, you'll have to wait six months or so to collect. I'm going to advance you enough to get started."

Patrick waved a hand. "No, Gail, you don't—"

"I know I don't have to. But I've just come into some cash rather unexpectedly, so don't worry about it."

"All right. Thanks." Patrick said, "I want you to know. I'm going to take your suggestion and let Rudy and Monica have the house and the art collection. In fact, I called Rudy about it last night. He sounded as snotty as ever over the phone, but that's Rudy." He idly played with the end of his beard. "I never wanted Rudy and Monica not to have the house. If they had asked me, I would have given it to them."

The front-end loader made another run at the trash, and the pile rolled. The children ran out of the way. Gail said half to herself, "I hope this does some good, in the long run."

"Do some good? Just look around you, Gail. Of course it will do some good. We have to start somewhere."

He took her arm and they continued along the sidewalk. "Over there is where we'll put the Althea Norris Tillett Community Center. What about that name?" He laughed. "If Aunt Althie could see this, she would want to strangle me."

With a final blast of smoke, the loader picked up the last mound of trash. The scoop lifted, extending over the rusty bed of the dump truck, then tilted. The debris fell in with a crash, rocking the truck on its wheels, and a cloud of dust rose over the vacant lot on 62nd Street.

epilogue

The raucous chirping outside made Anthony come suddenly awake. He had drifted off to sleep again. The windows were already gray with light, and he could see the bed and dresser and his clothes laid neatly across a chair. He got up and dressed quickly, not bothering to tuck in his shirt or put on his shoes. He felt for his car keys and slid them quietly into his pocket.

Sitting on the edge of the bed, he pulled the blanket away from Gail's face and bent down close to her ear. "Gail. Wake up for a minute, *amor*, I'm leaving."

"Hmmm?"

"I have to go. It's dawn."

This was the fifth—no, sixth—time he had been in her bed. The first had been a month ago, a rainy afternoon when they had found themselves alone in the house. Gail had coaxed him into her bedroom, which was the color of ripe peaches. A cool breeze had come through the windows, but his body had been on fire.

Last night was the first time with Karen in the house. They had talked until midnight in the kitchen, then suddenly it had been past one o'clock, and so much easier for him to walk fifty feet than to drive fifteen miles. Karen never came into Gail's room at night, she assured him. It had been strange, making love so quietly.

Anthony lowered his head to Gail's pillow, her breath gently touching his cheek. Perhaps he could lie with her a few more minutes. But to see Karen's face at the door in broad daylight—

"Gail. Wake up."

Her eyelids fluttered, then she held out her arms.

He kissed her, wanting more than that. He could feel her breasts against him. "Gail."

Now her eyes were opening. Blue-gray, like the sky at dawn. The color the sky would soon be if he didn't leave this minute. He stood.

"Sneaking out on me, are you?" She smiled. "Call me later."

"Te quiero." He blew her a kiss at the door, then closed it with barely a click, his shoes in his other hand. With the night light in the bathroom to show the way, he slipped quietly past Karen's room. He would go out the back door, the farthest exit, first turning off the burglar alarm. Gail had fought him over the alarm system, but he had insisted. She was far too trusting. A brilliant woman, but lacking common sense about the world. To let that man Ramsay into her house! It still made Anthony shake with anger, thinking of what had nearly happened. He had dreamed of parachuting onto the deck of the boat, screaming for Gail and Karen to get down, then emptying his pistol into that *hijo de puta.*

A shoe dropped from his hand and clunked against the wall. He froze. But there was no sound from behind Karen's door. He silently crossed the living room, then bent down to put on his shoes and tie the laces, feeling foolish. One could not carry on this sort of thing forever, of course, but the situation with her daughter was delicate. He unzipped his fly and tucked in his shirt, zipped it back again, and walked into the kitchen buckling his belt.

Karen stood by the refrigerator watching him. The light was on over the stove.

"*¡Ay! Diós mío.*" He smoothed his hair and came in. "Good morning."

She had a carton of orange juice in one hand and a glass in the other. She was wearing a long gray T-shirt with an ibis, the Hurricanes mascot, its teeth bared. From the family room he heard the sound of a cartoon show on low volume.

"I must have fallen asleep." He smiled at her. "You're up early."

Her lips were pressed tightly together. She went over to pour herself some juice at the counter. Her hair was halfway down her back, tangled from sleep. "I know you were in her room last night."

Anthony let his hands fall at his sides. "Yes. I was."

Karen picked up her glass and drank, watching him over the rim with her intensely blue eyes.

"We—when men and women are in love— as your mother and I are—they want to . . . be together."

He stared at the counter for a while, at three bottles of nail polish, a cracked mug stuffed with grocery coupons, a loaf of raisin bread, the Indian blanket Karen had been weaving with that strange woman counselor . . .

Pulling out a stool, he sat down beside her. "Karen. Listen. It isn't good for your mother to be alone. Well, she has you, so she isn't alone, but—she should be married. I haven't asked her yet. No, it's true. I haven't. We've talked about it, of course, but I haven't said to her Let's do this. You see, at our age, it's a big step. We have many things to work out between us."

He leaned an elbow on the counter, arranging his thoughts. "For me particularly. A big step. And there is you to consider too. I would never try to replace your father, or to come between you and Gail. She wouldn't be happy if you weren't happy, I know this. And yet I think she needs me as well. So." He nodded. "There are some things to think about." He brought his eyes up to Karen's. "I love her very much. Before I ask her to marry me, I would like to have your permission."

Karen put down her glass. "Mine?"

"Yes. I want to know how you feel about it, if we were together, all of us. What do you think?"

Karen looked at him for a while longer, then said, "I think it might be okay."

He felt a rush of relief so great he wanted to put his head down on his arms. He nodded.

"Do you want some orange juice?" Karen asked.

"Sure. Why not?"

She crossed the kitchen for another glass, then poured, not spilling any. She sat down again and brushed her hair back over her shoulder. Her toes curled around the rungs of the stool.

"Thank you." He took a sip, then leaned back to reach into his pocket. "I forgot this last night. It's another *peso* to replace the one you lost."

"Oh, great." She held it in her palm.

"It's too bad about your alligator purse. Maybe we can find you another one like it."

"No." Karen laid down the coin and sipped her orange juice. "I really am getting too old for that. Thank you anyway."

He nodded and drank some of his juice.

"I'm learning Spanish in school," she said.

"Your mother told me that, yes."

Karen untwisted the tie on the raisin bread. "*¿Quiere usted tostada, señor?*"

"*Sí me gustaría mucho. Gracias.*"

She dropped two slices into the toaster and watched the coils turn red. "You have to be careful with my mother," Karen said. "She doesn't pay attention, and somebody has to watch her."

"I know what you mean," he said.

"Last week she put garlic bread in here and it caught on fire."

"No." He widened his eyes.

"It's true. She did."

IF YOU HAVE ENJOYED READING THIS
LARGE PRINT BOOK AND YOU
WOULD LIKE MORE INFORMATION
ON HOW TO ORDER A WHEELER
LARGE PRINT BOOK, PLEASE WRITE
TO:

WHEELER PUBLISHING, INC.
P.O. BOX 531
ACCORD, MA 02018-0531